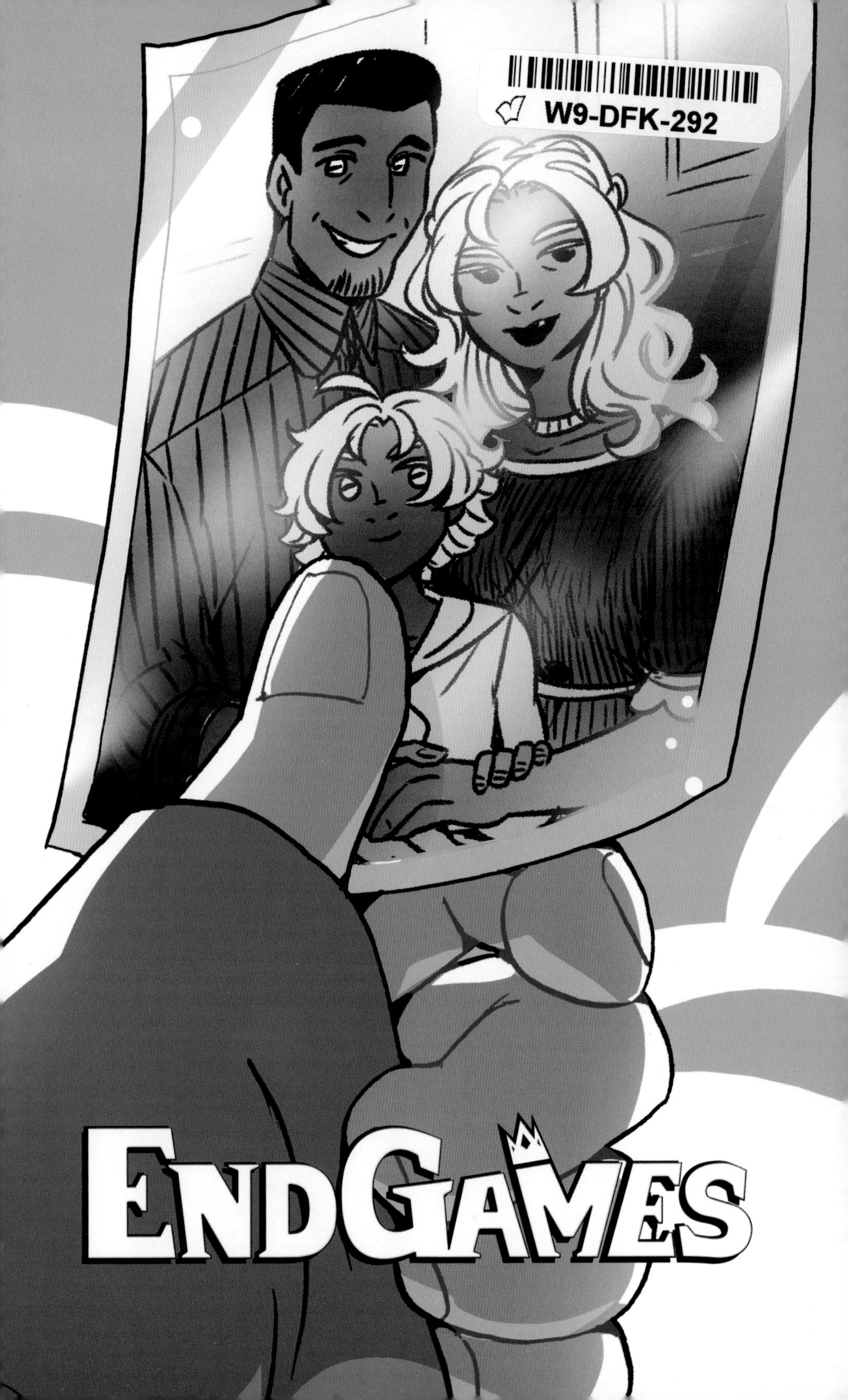
EndGames

For the people we could
have been, had we not chosen
to be who we are.

All rights reserved. Published by Graphix, an imprint of Scholastic Inc., *Publishers since 1920*. SCHOLASTIC, GRAPHIX, and associated logos are trademarks and/or registered trademarks of Scholastic Inc.

The publisher does not have any control over and does not assume any responsibility for author or third-party websites or their content.

Library of Congress Control Number: 2017962945

ISBN 978-0-545-80316-8 (hardcover)
ISBN 978-0-545-80317-5 (paperback)

10 9 8 7 6 5 4 3 2 1   19 20 21 22 23
Printed in China   62
First edition, February 2019
Edited by Cassandra Pelham Fulton
Author photo by Casey Gardner
Book design by Ru Xu and Phil Falco
Creative Director: David Saylor

EndGames

Ru Xu

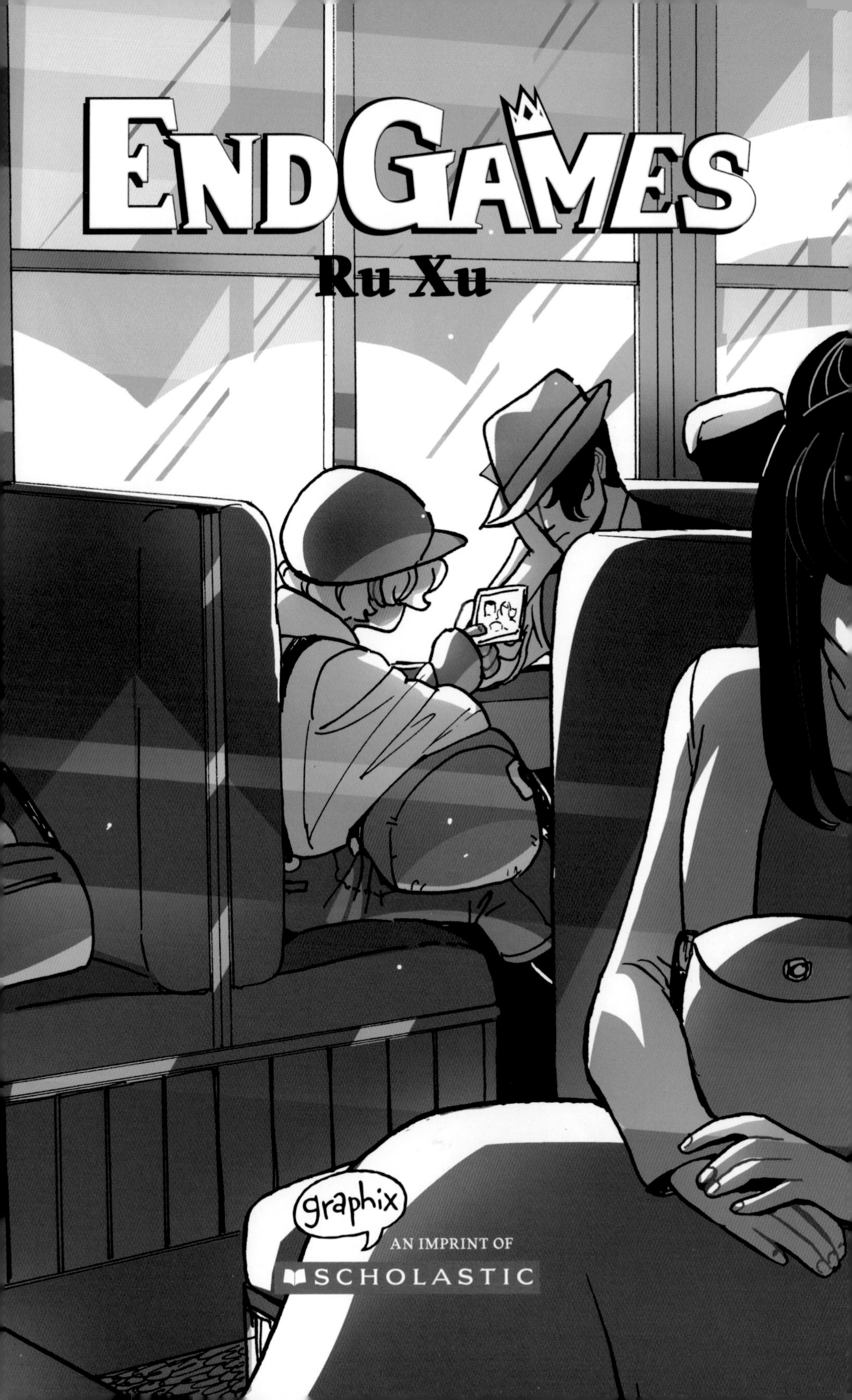

graphix
AN IMPRINT OF
SCHOLASTIC

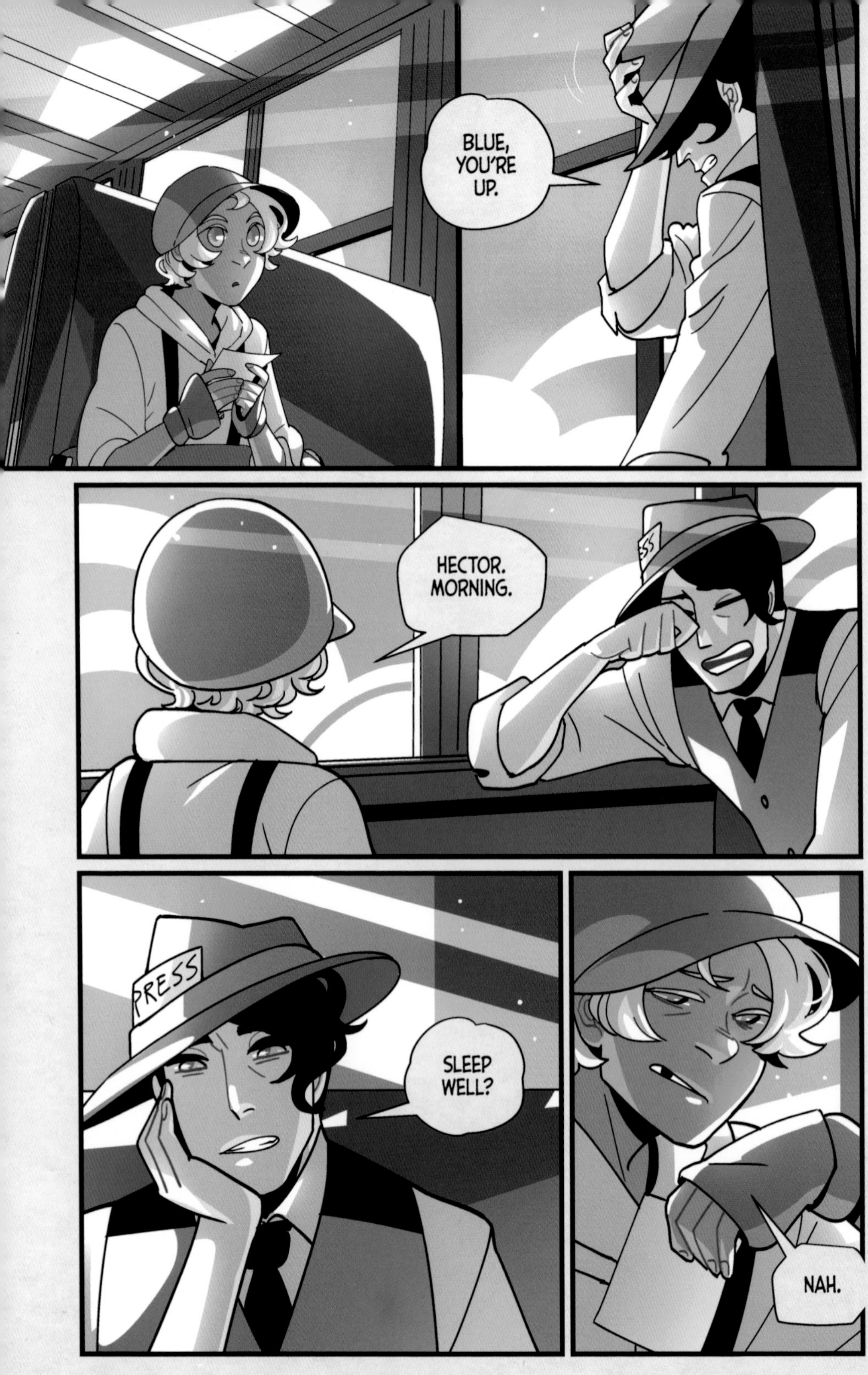
BLUE, YOU'RE UP.
HECTOR. MORNING.
SLEEP WELL?
NAH.

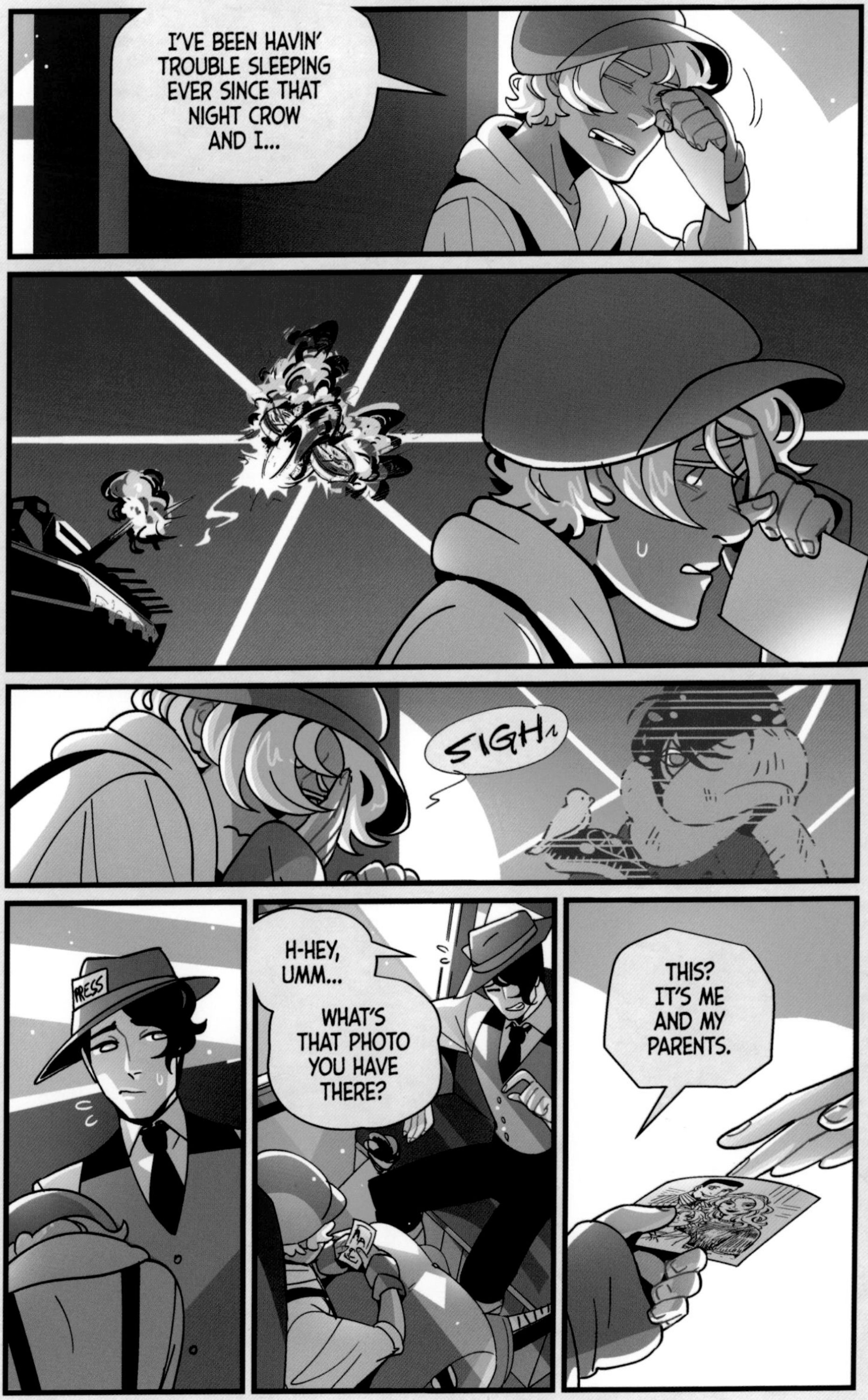

I'VE BEEN HAVIN' TROUBLE SLEEPING EVER SINCE THAT NIGHT CROW AND I...
SIGH
PRESS
H-HEY, UMM...
WHAT'S THAT PHOTO YOU HAVE THERE?
THIS? IT'S ME AND MY PARENTS.

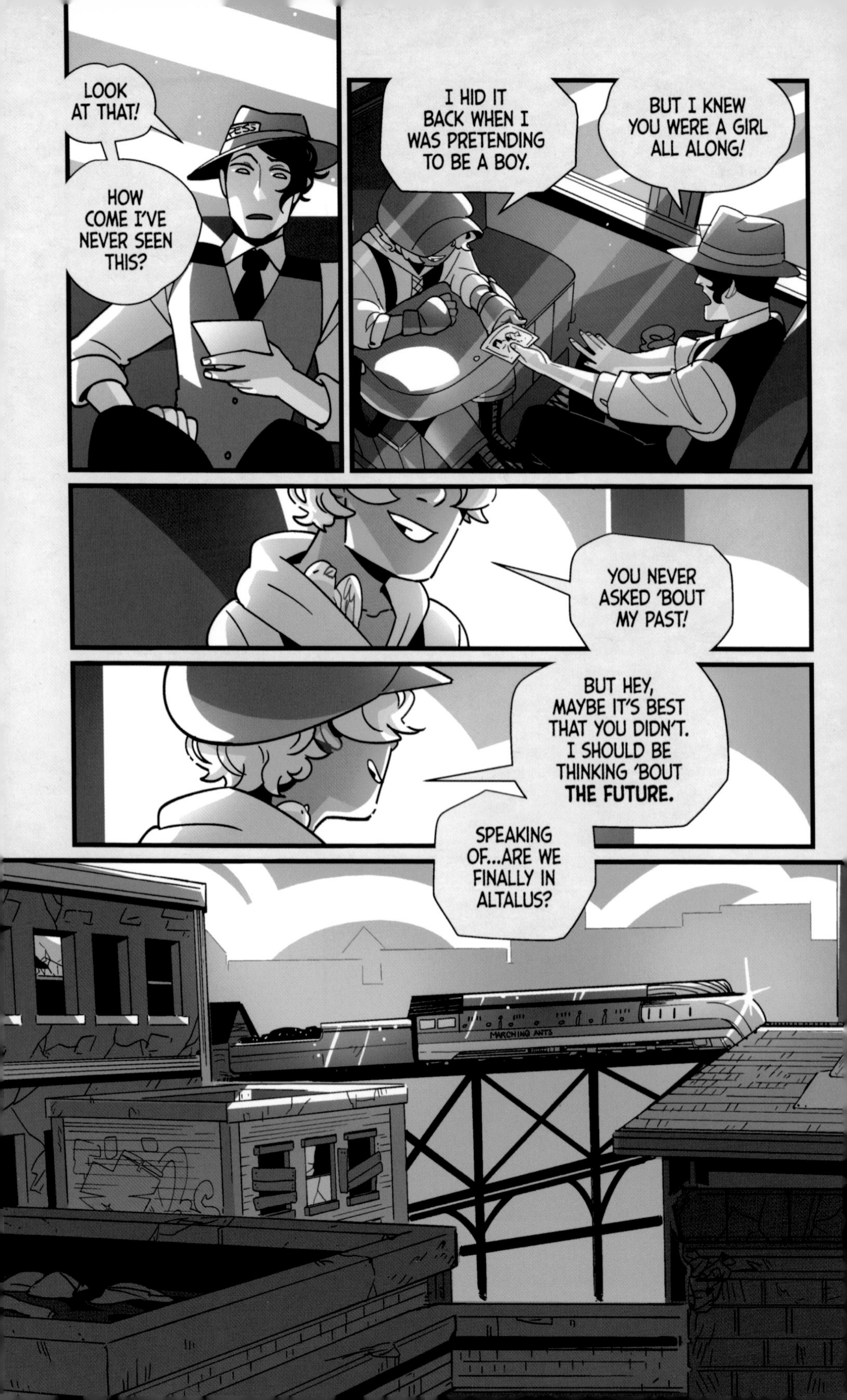
LOOK AT THAT!
HOW COME I'VE NEVER SEEN THIS?
I HID IT BACK WHEN I WAS PRETENDING TO BE A BOY.
BUT I KNEW YOU WERE A GIRL ALL ALONG!
YOU NEVER ASKED 'BOUT MY PAST!
BUT HEY, MAYBE IT'S BEST THAT YOU DIDN'T. I SHOULD BE THINKING 'BOUT **THE FUTURE.**
SPEAKING OF...ARE WE FINALLY IN ALTALUS?
MARCHING ANTS

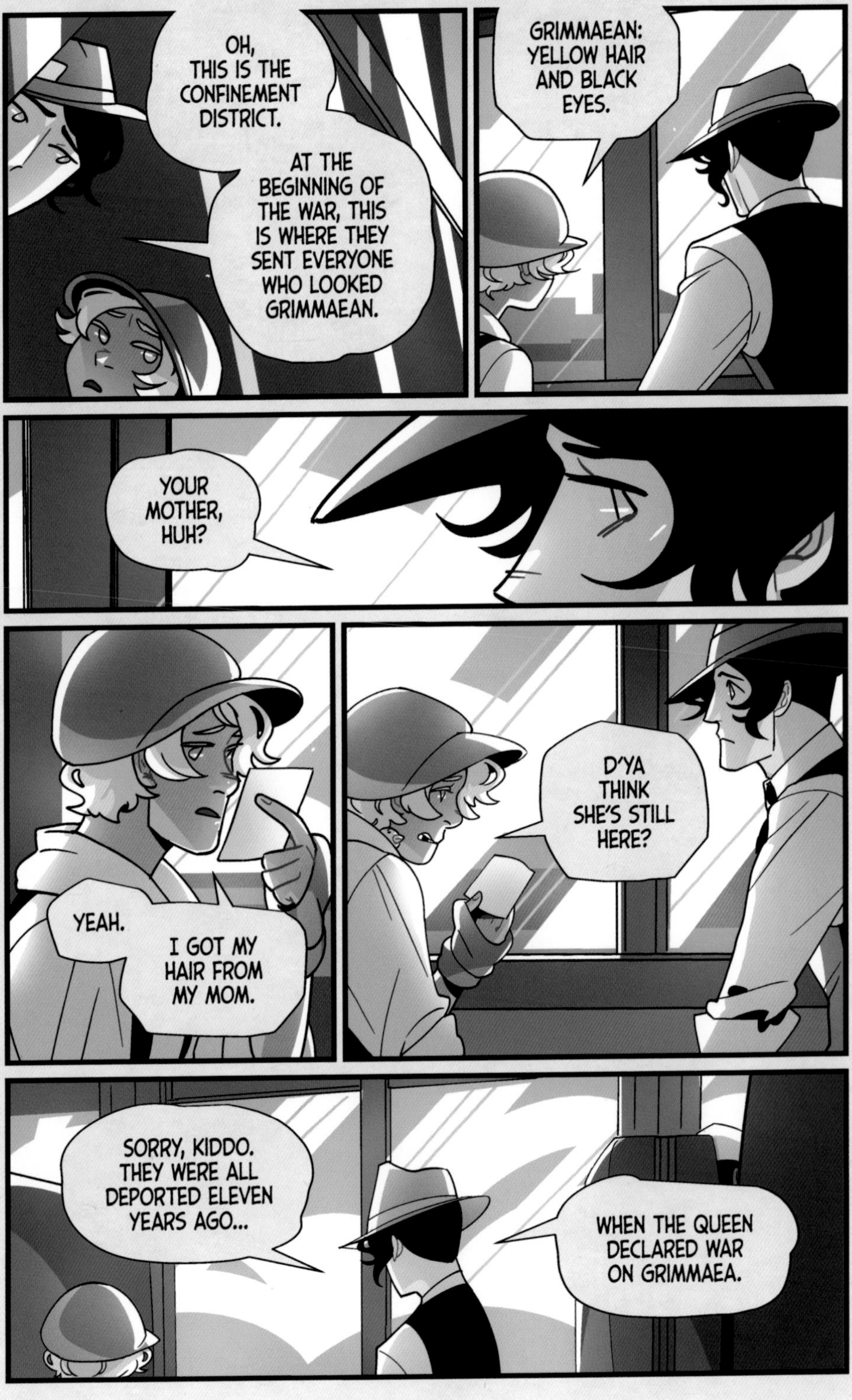
OH, THIS IS THE CONFINEMENT DISTRICT.
AT THE BEGINNING OF THE WAR, THIS IS WHERE THEY SENT EVERYONE WHO LOOKED GRIMMAEAN.
GRIMMAEAN: YELLOW HAIR AND BLACK EYES.
YOUR MOTHER, HUH?
YEAH.
I GOT MY HAIR FROM MY MOM.
D'YA THINK SHE'S STILL HERE?
SORRY, KIDDO. THEY WERE ALL DEPORTED ELEVEN YEARS AGO...
WHEN THE QUEEN DECLARED WAR ON GRIMMAEA.

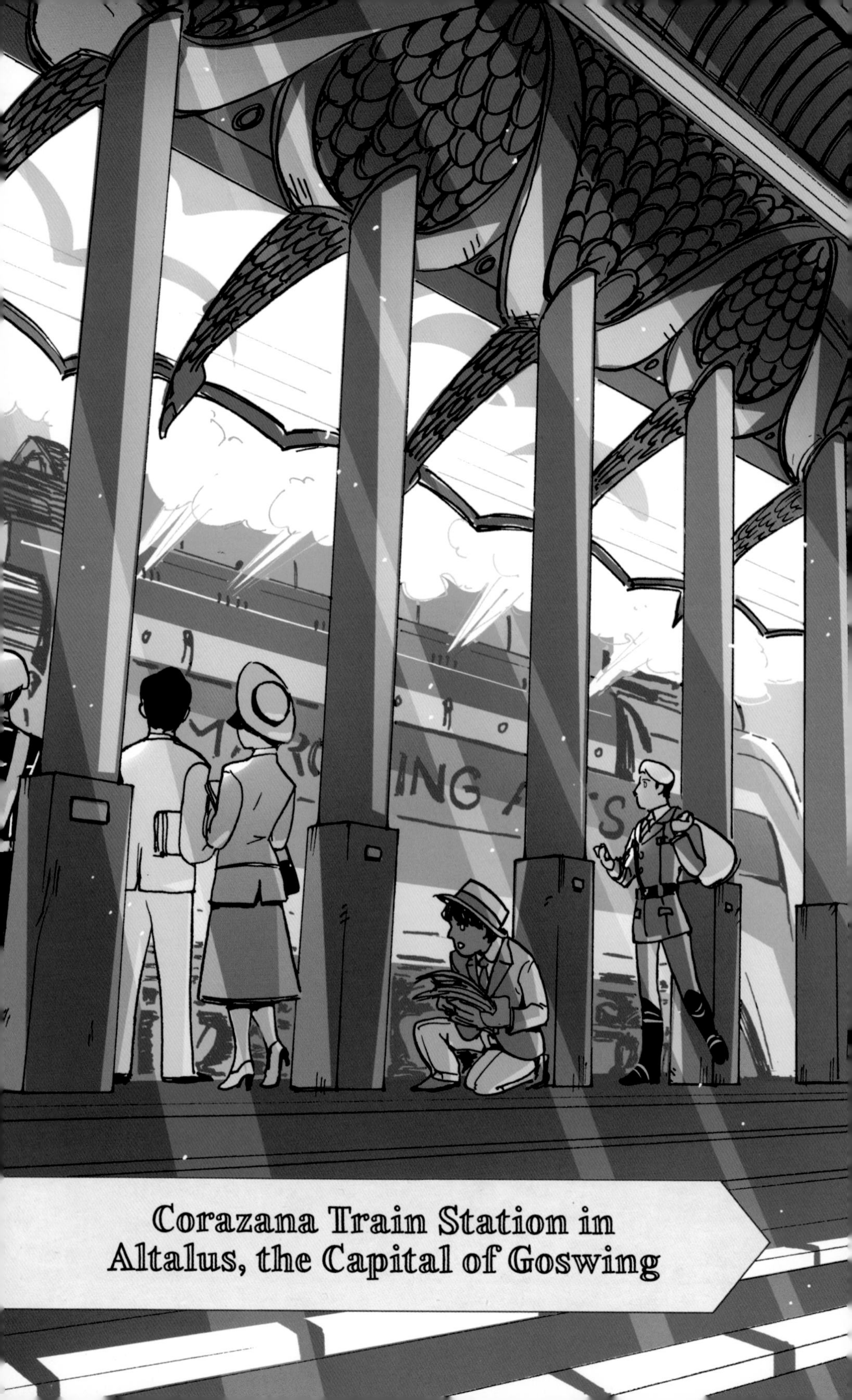
Corazana Train Station in Altalus, the Capital of Goswing

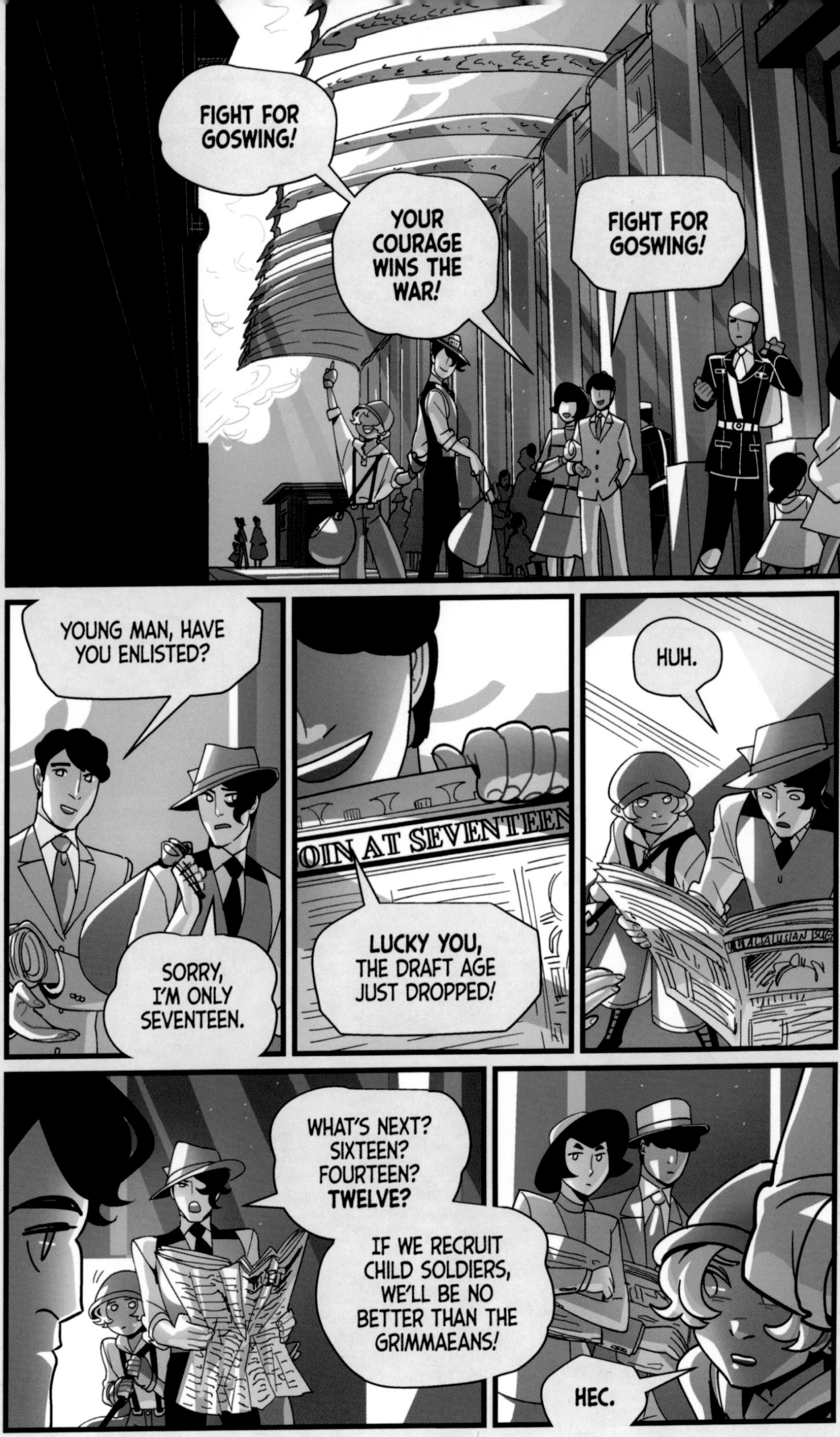
FIGHT FOR GOSWING!
YOUR COURAGE WINS THE WAR!
FIGHT FOR GOSWING!
YOUNG MAN, HAVE YOU ENLISTED?
SORRY, I'M ONLY SEVENTEEN.
OIN AT SEVENTEEN
LUCKY YOU, THE DRAFT AGE JUST DROPPED!
HUH.
WHAT'S NEXT? SIXTEEN? FOURTEEN? TWELVE?
IF WE RECRUIT CHILD SOLDIERS, WE'LL BE NO BETTER THAN THE GRIMMAEANS!
HEC.

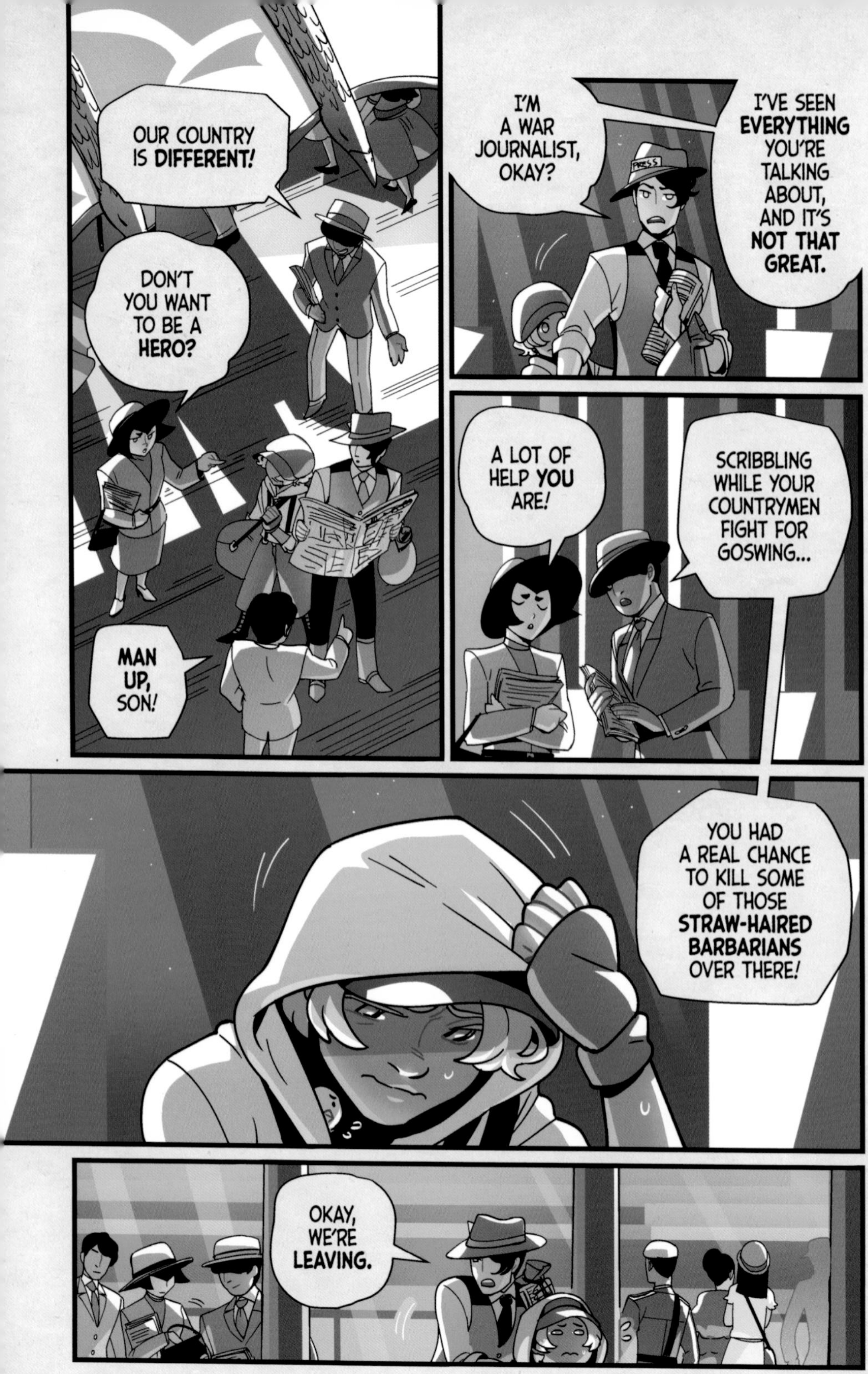
OUR COUNTRY IS DIFFERENT!
DON'T YOU WANT TO BE A HERO?
MAN UP, SON!
I'M A WAR JOURNALIST, OKAY?
I'VE SEEN EVERYTHING YOU'RE TALKING ABOUT, AND IT'S NOT THAT GREAT.
PRESS
A LOT OF HELP YOU ARE!
SCRIBBLING WHILE YOUR COUNTRYMEN FIGHT FOR GOSWING...
YOU HAD A REAL CHANCE TO KILL SOME OF THOSE STRAW-HAIRED BARBARIANS OVER THERE!
OKAY, WE'RE LEAVING.

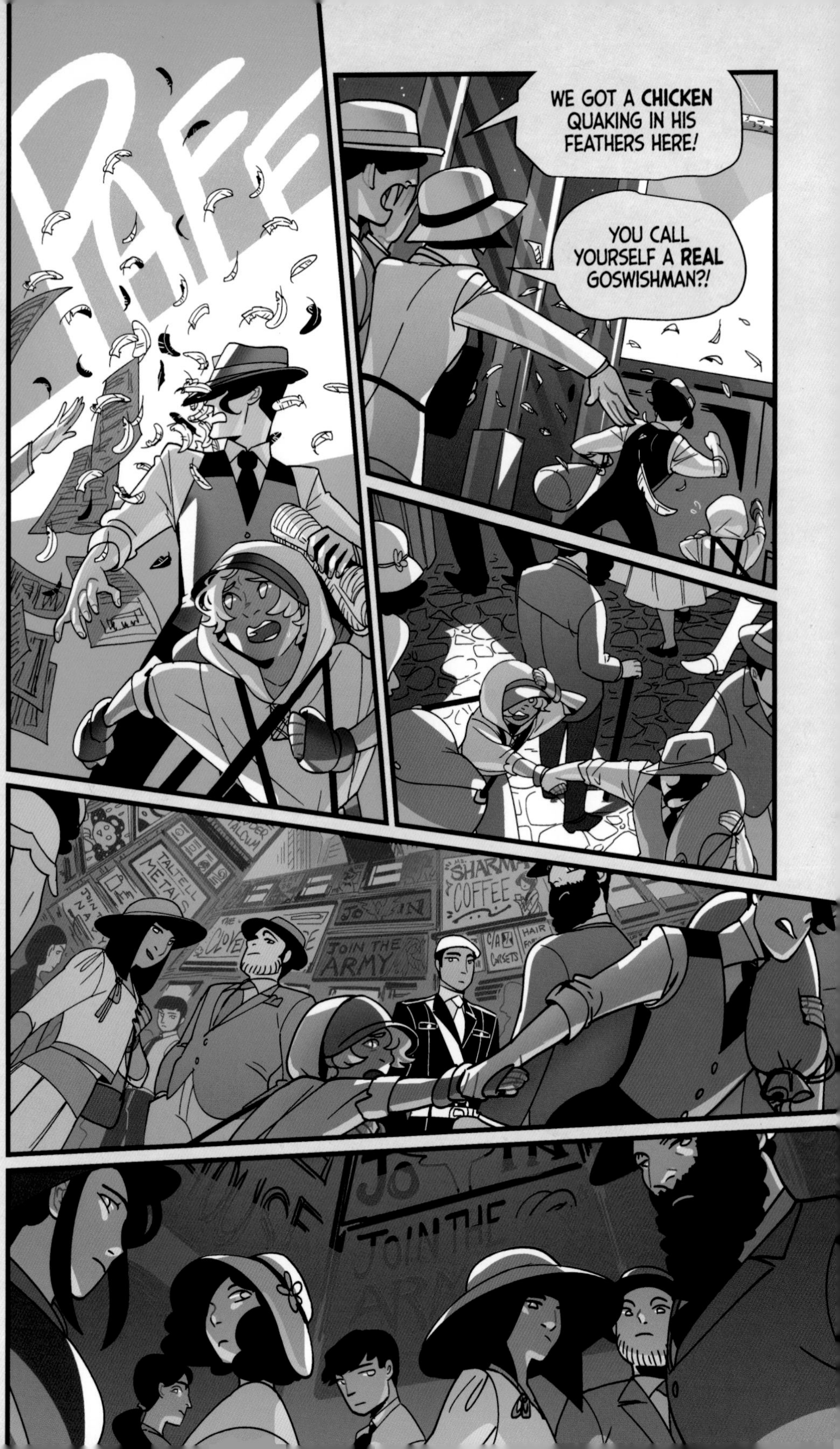
PAFF
WE GOT A **CHICKEN** QUAKING IN HIS FEATHERS HERE!
YOU CALL YOURSELF A **REAL** GOSWISHMAN?!
TALTELL METALS
JOIN THE ARMY
COFFEE
CORSETS
HAIR

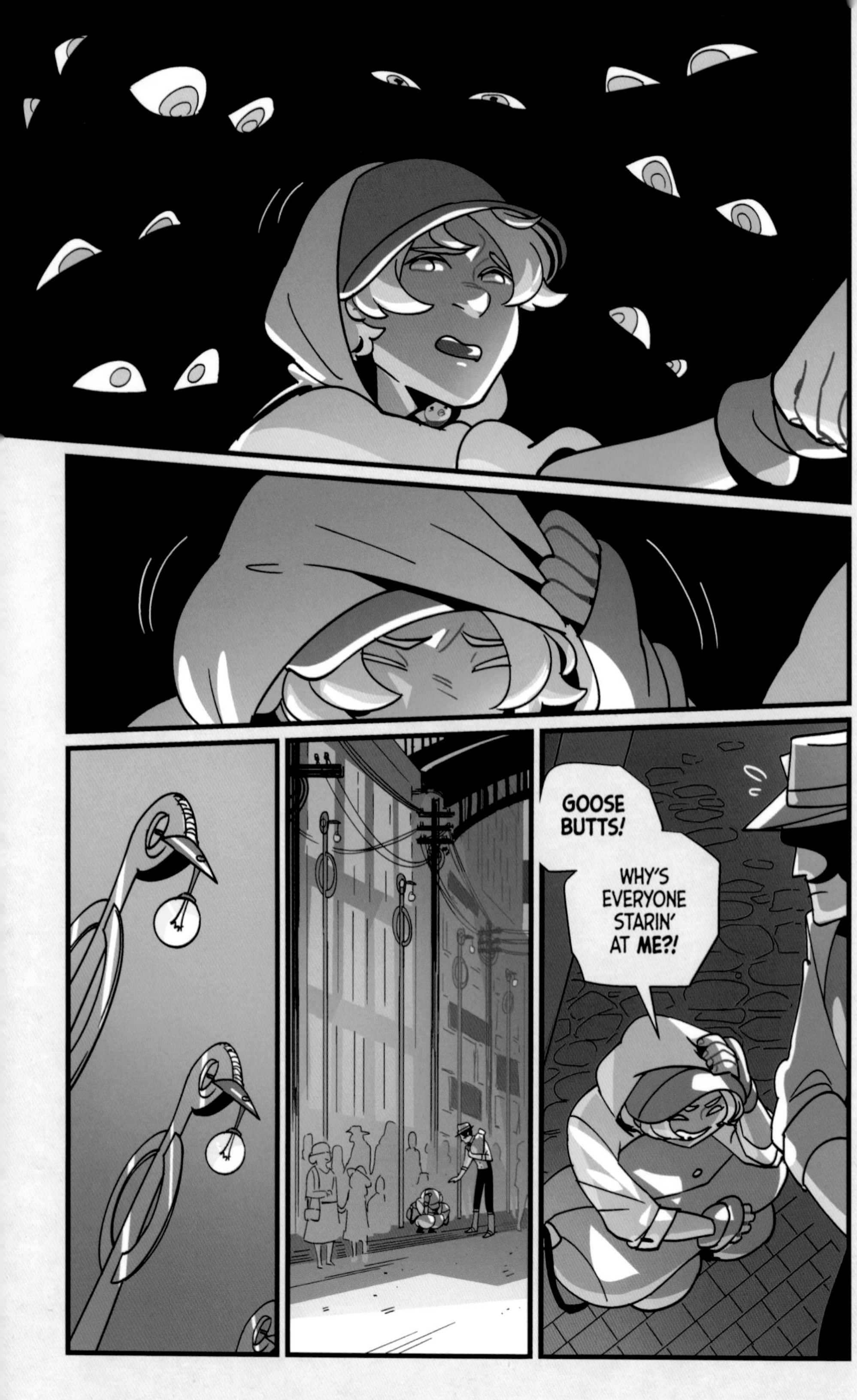
GOOSE BUTTS!
WHY'S EVERYONE STARIN' AT ME?!

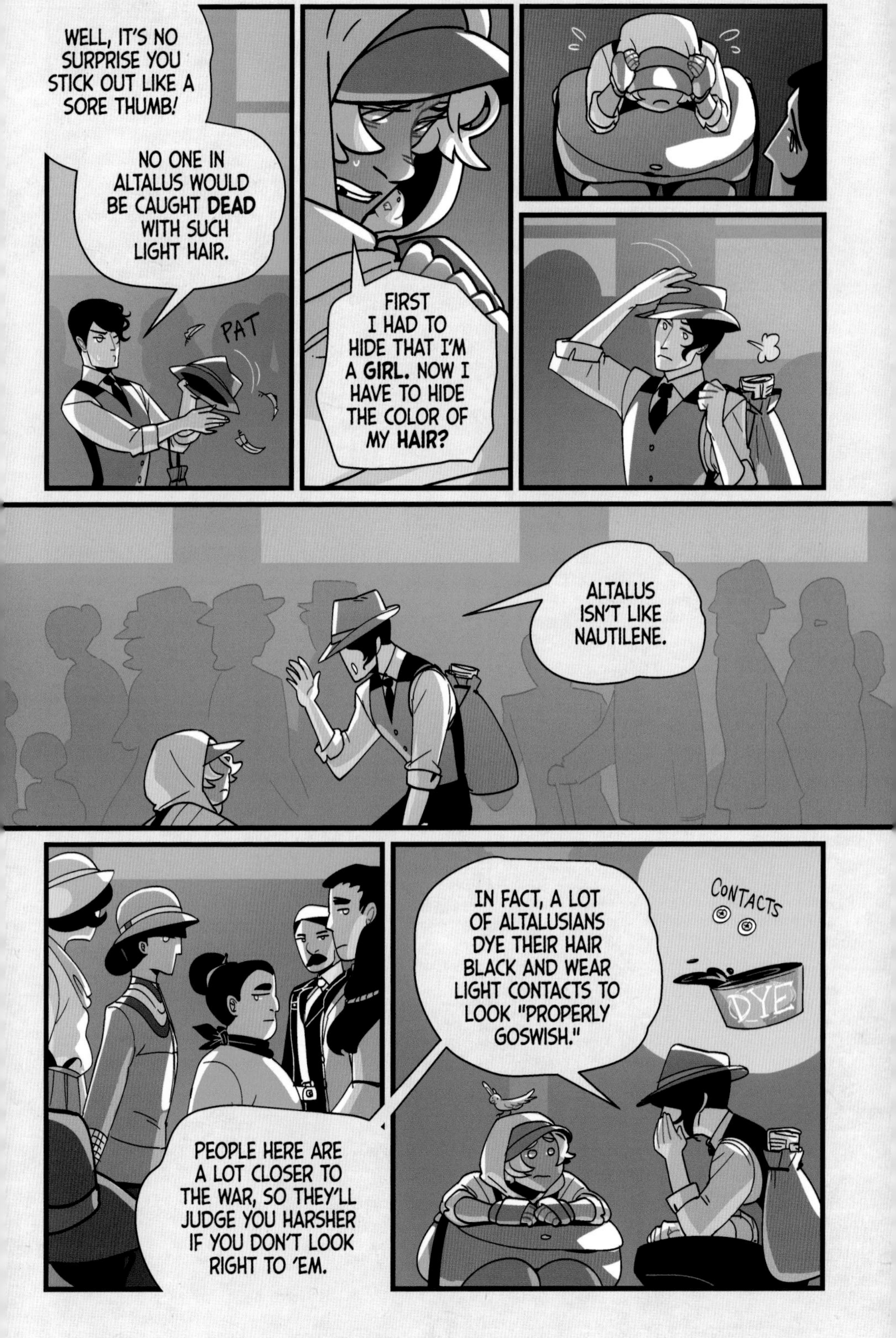
WELL, IT'S NO SURPRISE YOU STICK OUT LIKE A SORE THUMB!
NO ONE IN ALTALUS WOULD BE CAUGHT **DEAD** WITH SUCH LIGHT HAIR.
PAT
FIRST I HAD TO HIDE THAT I'M A **GIRL.** NOW I HAVE TO HIDE THE COLOR OF MY **HAIR?**
ALTALUS ISN'T LIKE NAUTILENE.
PEOPLE HERE ARE A LOT CLOSER TO THE WAR, SO THEY'LL JUDGE YOU HARSHER IF YOU DON'T LOOK RIGHT TO 'EM.
IN FACT, A LOT OF ALTALUSIANS DYE THEIR HAIR BLACK AND WEAR LIGHT CONTACTS TO LOOK "PROPERLY GOSWISH."
CONTACTS
DYE

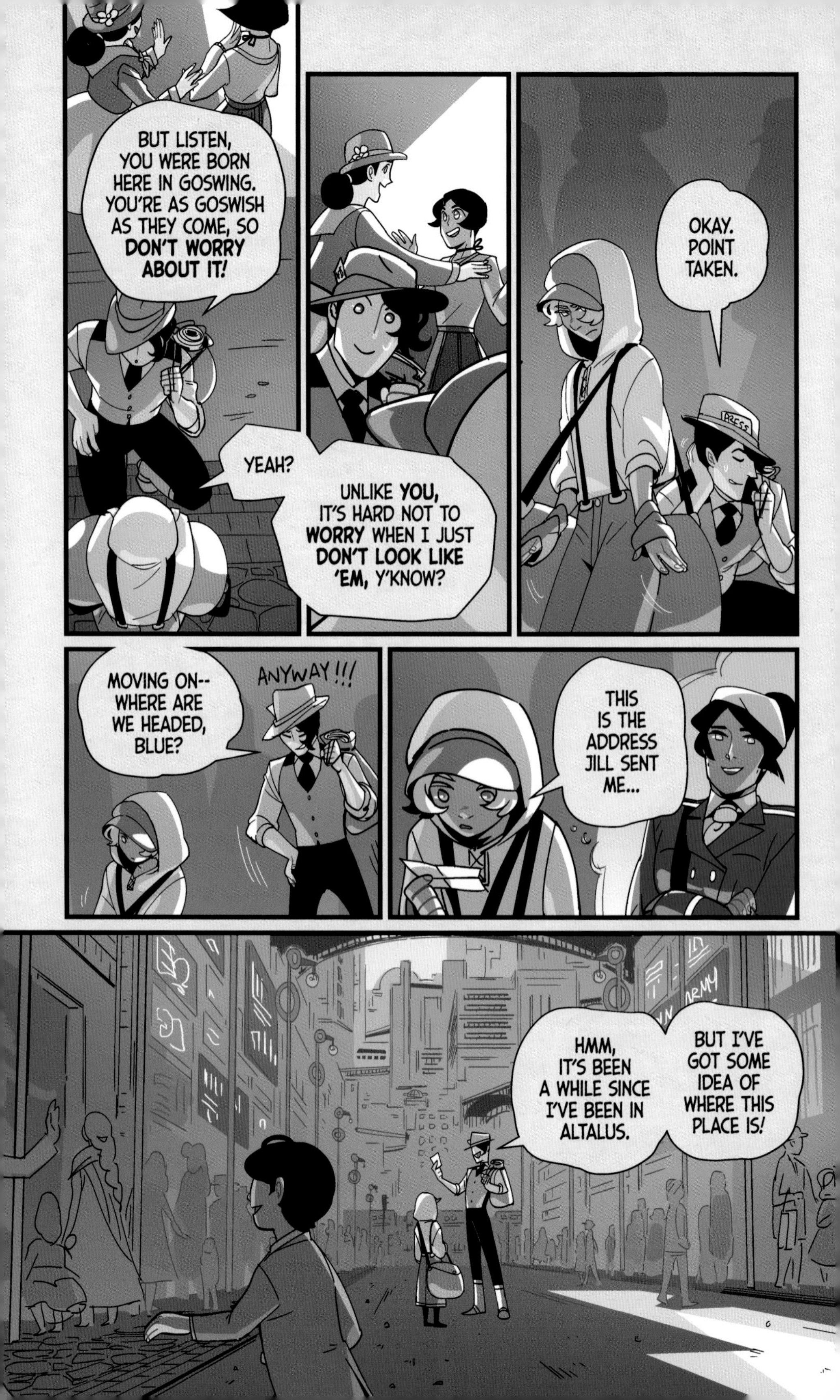

BUT LISTEN, YOU WERE BORN HERE IN GOSWING. YOU'RE AS GOSWISH AS THEY COME, SO **DON'T WORRY** ABOUT IT!
YEAH?
UNLIKE **YOU**, IT'S HARD NOT TO **WORRY** WHEN I JUST **DON'T LOOK LIKE 'EM**, Y'KNOW?
OKAY. POINT TAKEN.
PRESS
MOVING ON-- WHERE ARE WE HEADED, BLUE?
ANYWAY!!!
THIS IS THE ADDRESS JILL SENT ME...
HMM, IT'S BEEN A WHILE SINCE I'VE BEEN IN ALTALUS.
BUT I'VE GOT SOME IDEA OF WHERE THIS PLACE IS!

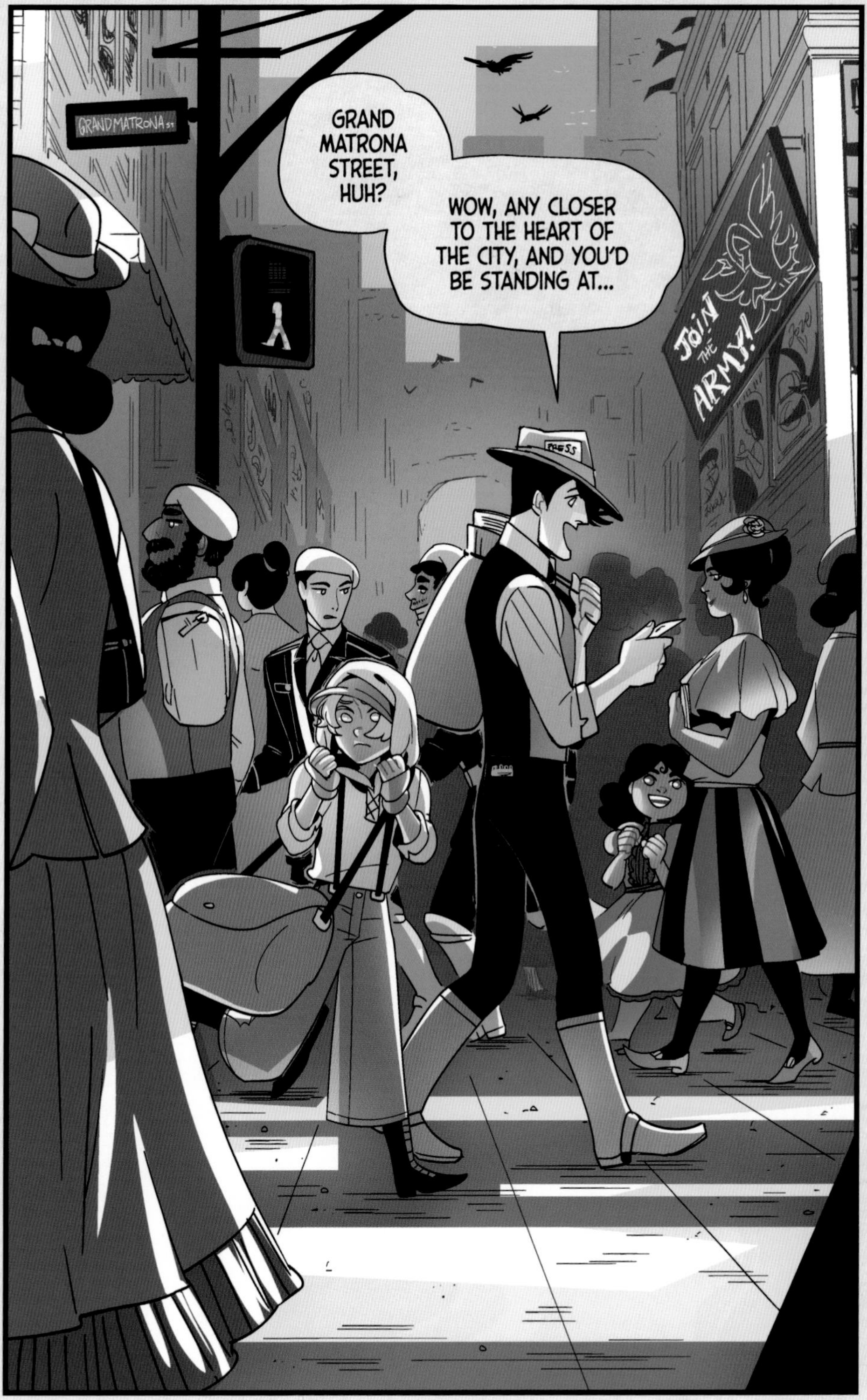
GRANDMATRONA ST
GRAND MATRONA STREET, HUH?
WOW, ANY CLOSER TO THE HEART OF THE CITY, AND YOU'D BE STANDING AT...
JOIN THE ARMY!
PRESS

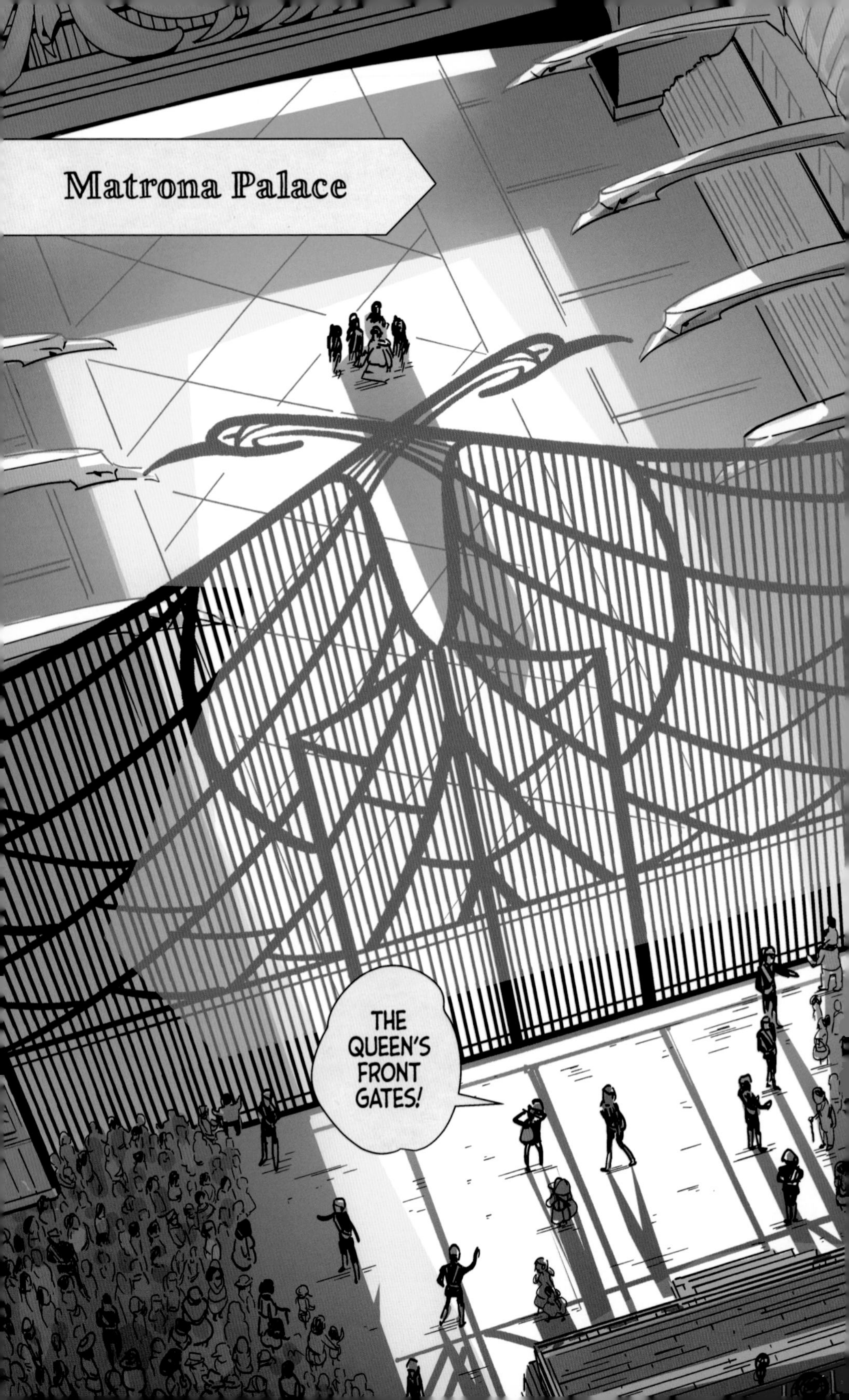
Matrona Palace
THE QUEEN'S FRONT GATES!

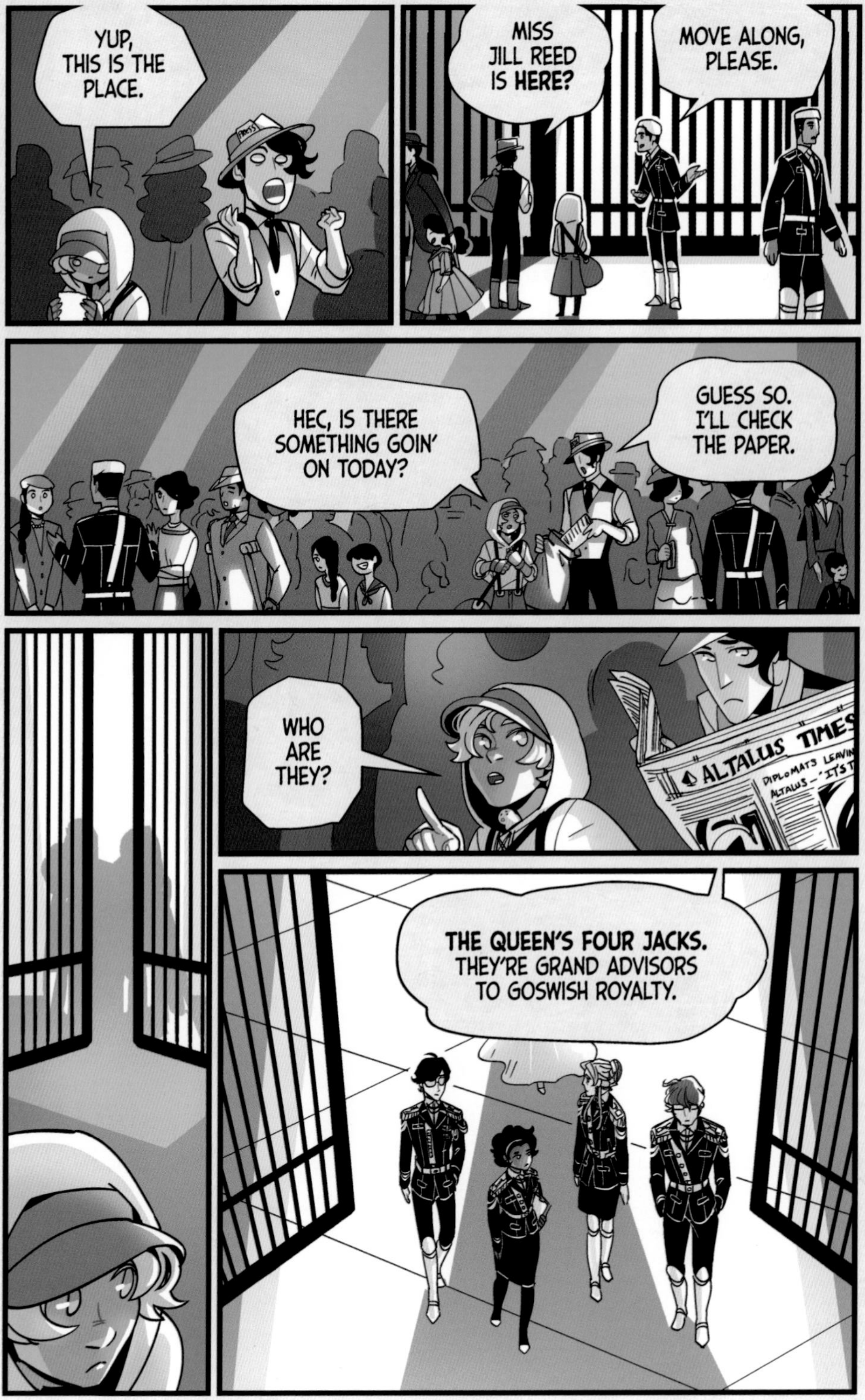
YUP, THIS IS THE PLACE.
MISS JILL REED IS HERE?
MOVE ALONG, PLEASE.
HEC, IS THERE SOMETHING GOIN' ON TODAY?
GUESS SO. I'LL CHECK THE PAPER.
WHO ARE THEY?
ALTALUS TIMES
THE QUEEN'S FOUR JACKS. THEY'RE GRAND ADVISORS TO GOSWISH ROYALTY.

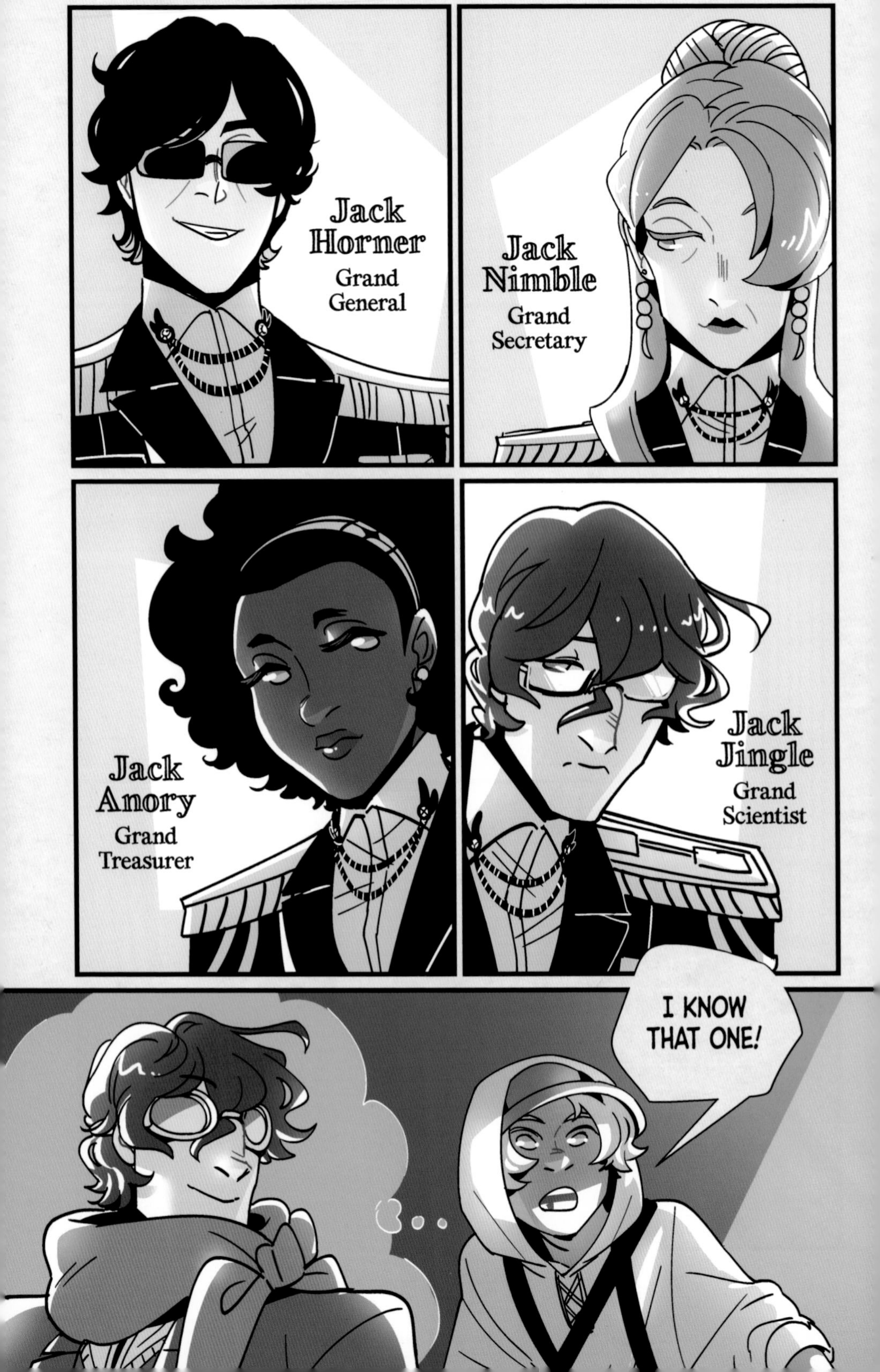
Jack Horner
Grand General
Jack Nimble
Grand Secretary
Jack Anory
Grand Treasurer
Jack Jingle
Grand Scientist
I KNOW THAT ONE!

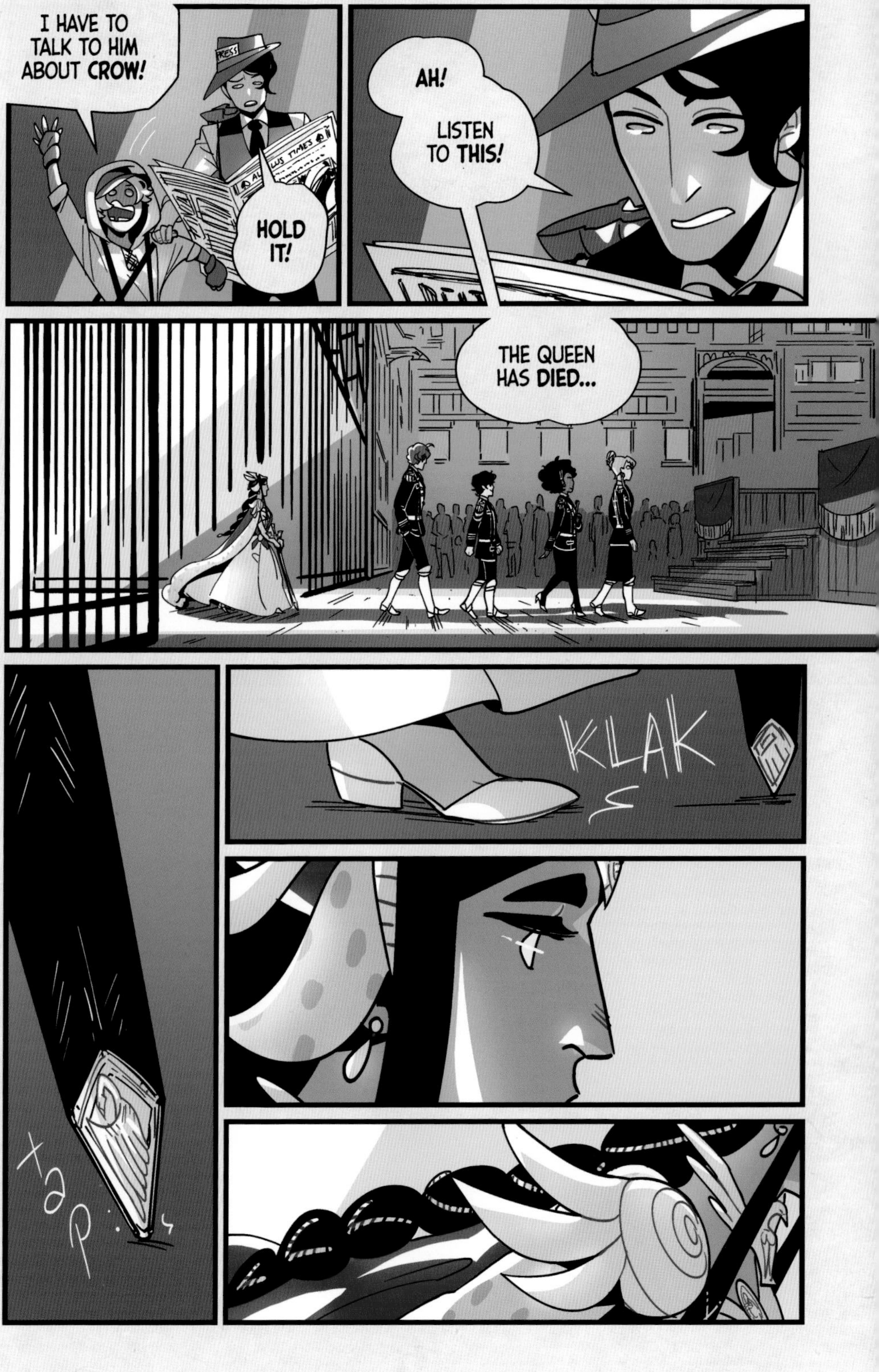
I HAVE TO TALK TO HIM ABOUT CROW!
PRESS
HOLD IT!
AH!
LISTEN TO THIS!
THE QUEEN HAS DIED...
KLAK
tap

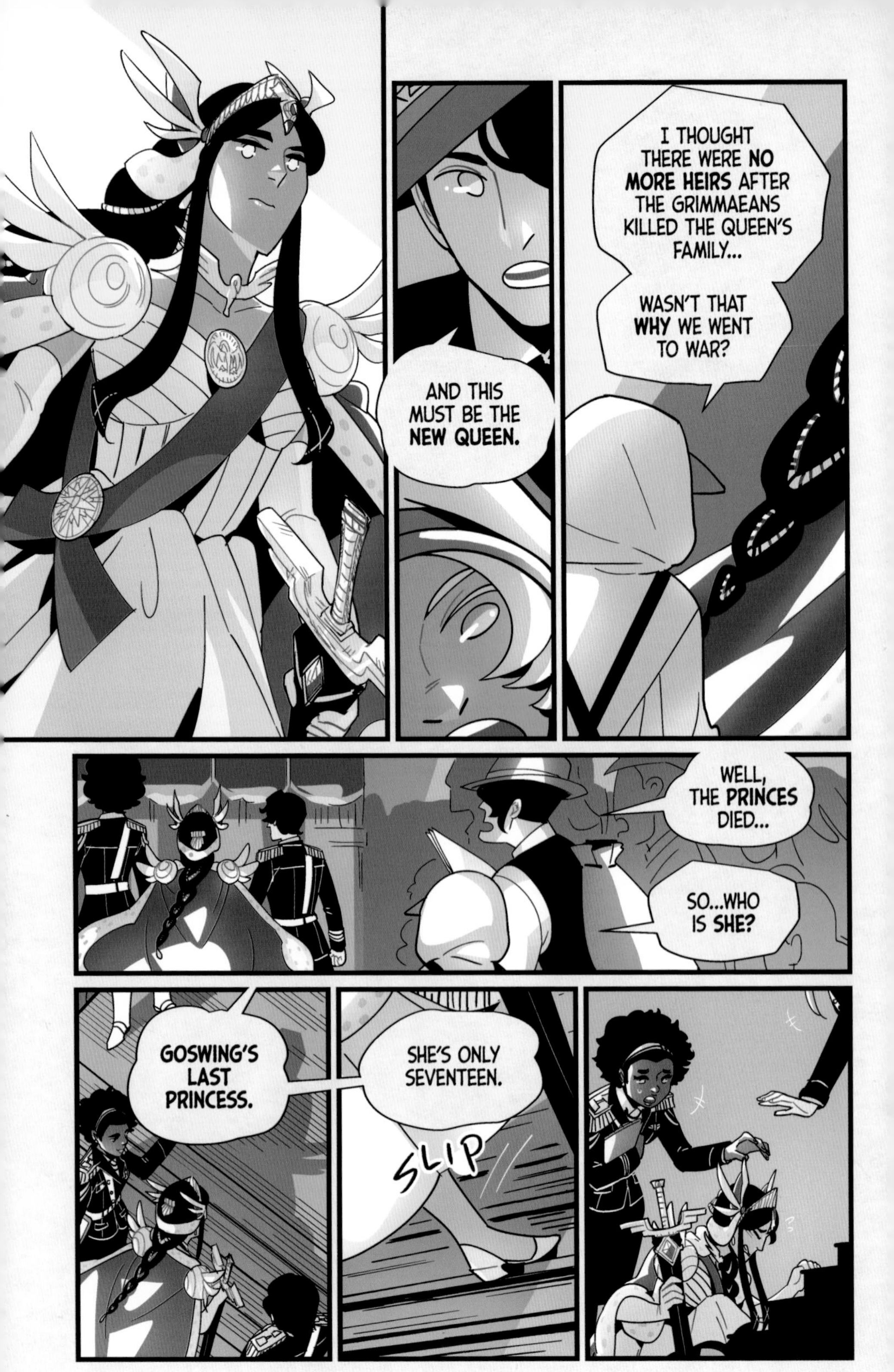

AND THIS MUST BE THE NEW QUEEN.
I THOUGHT THERE WERE NO MORE HEIRS AFTER THE GRIMMAEANS KILLED THE QUEEN'S FAMILY...
WASN'T THAT WHY WE WENT TO WAR?
WELL, THE PRINCES DIED...
SO...WHO IS SHE?
GOSWING'S LAST PRINCESS.
SHE'S ONLY SEVENTEEN.
SLIP

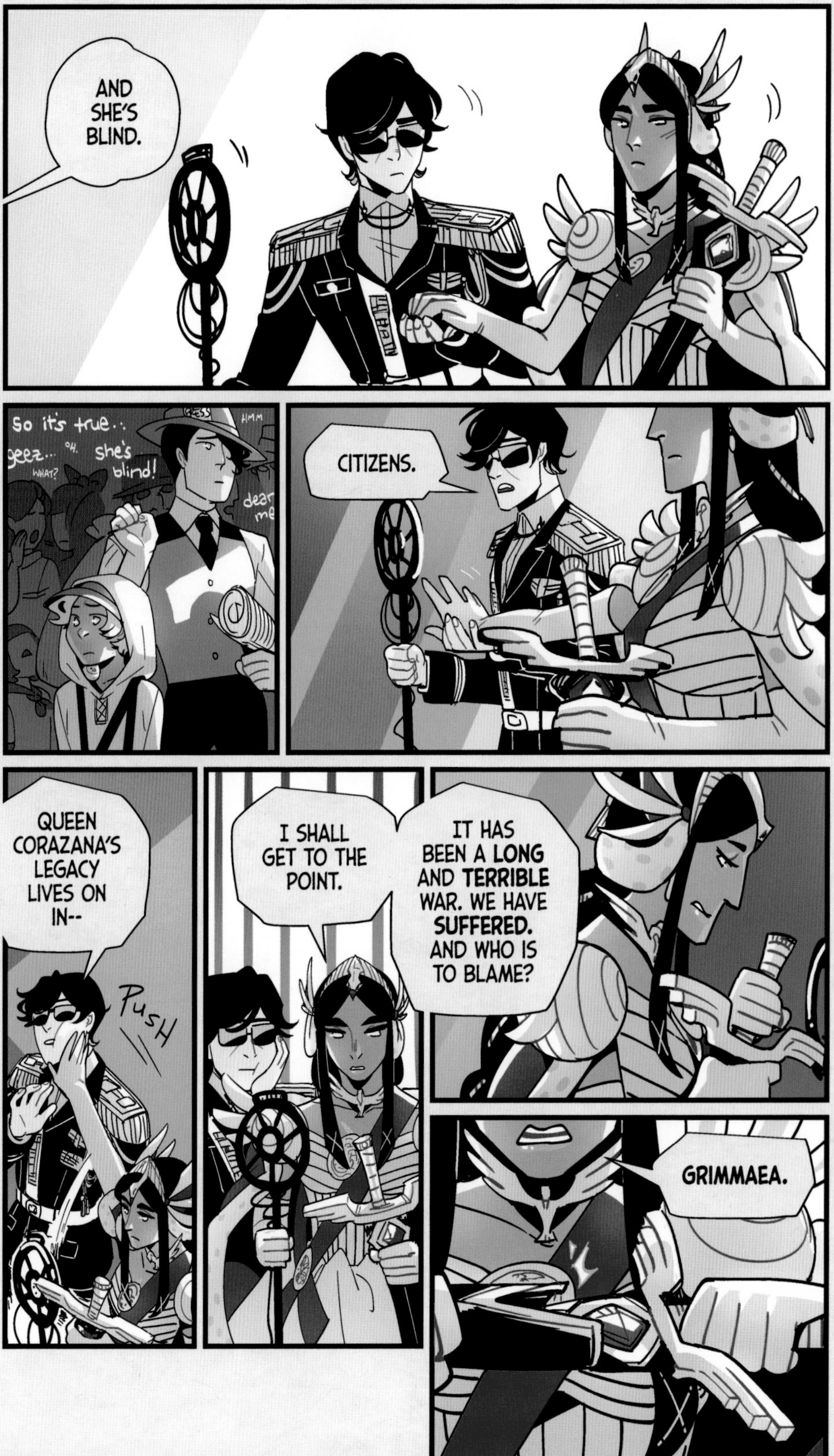
AND SHE'S BLIND.
so it's true..
geez...
OH.
she's blind!
WHAT?
HMM
dear me
CITIZENS.
QUEEN CORAZANA'S LEGACY LIVES ON IN--
PUSH
I SHALL GET TO THE POINT.
IT HAS BEEN A **LONG** AND **TERRIBLE** WAR. WE HAVE **SUFFERED**. AND WHO IS TO BLAME?
GRIMMAEA.

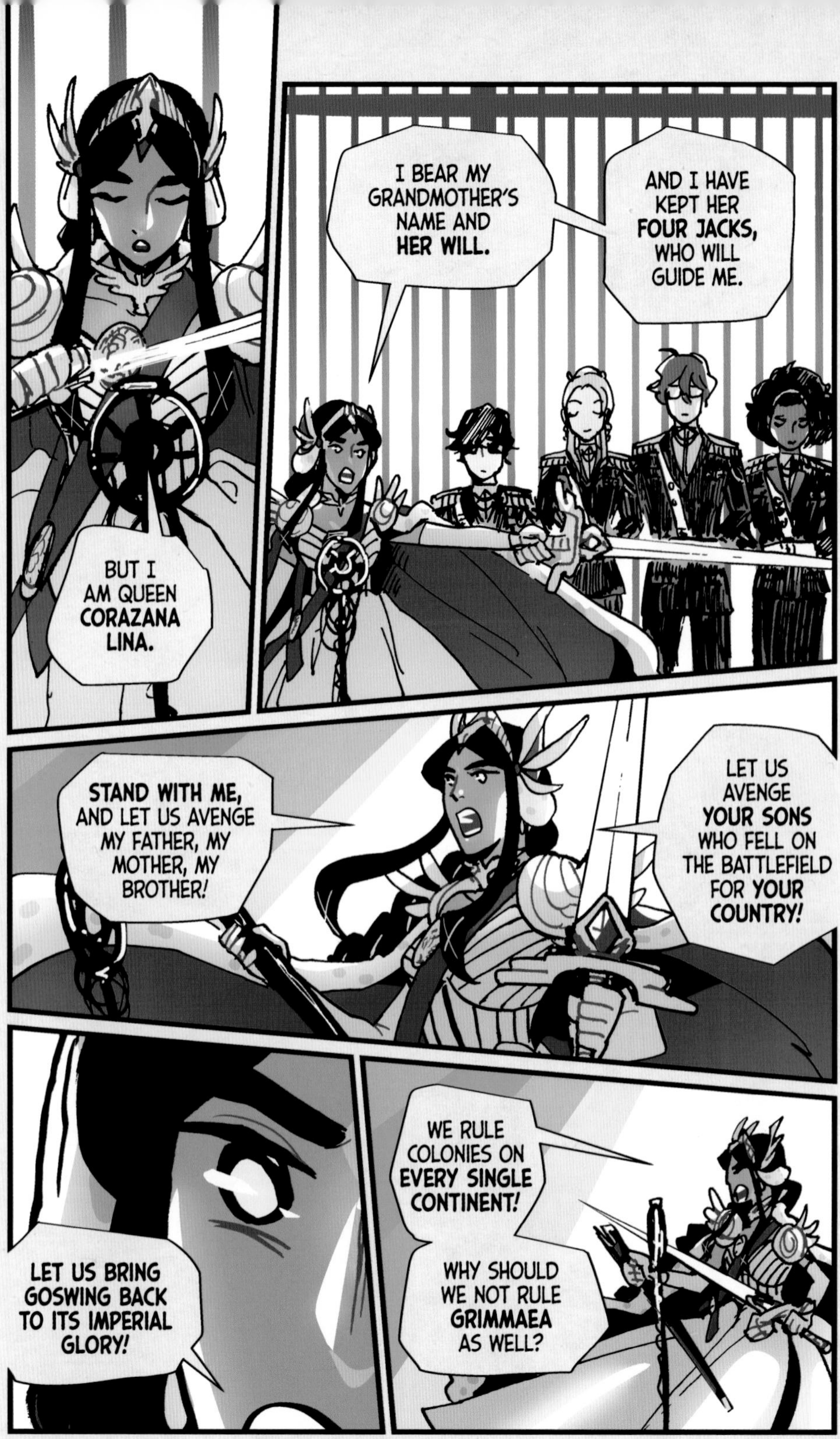

BUT I AM QUEEN CORAZANA LINA.
I BEAR MY GRANDMOTHER'S NAME AND HER WILL.
AND I HAVE KEPT HER FOUR JACKS, WHO WILL GUIDE ME.
STAND WITH ME, AND LET US AVENGE MY FATHER, MY MOTHER, MY BROTHER!
LET US AVENGE YOUR SONS WHO FELL ON THE BATTLEFIELD FOR YOUR COUNTRY!
LET US BRING GOSWING BACK TO ITS IMPERIAL GLORY!
WE RULE COLONIES ON EVERY SINGLE CONTINENT!
WHY SHOULD WE NOT RULE GRIMMAEA AS WELL?

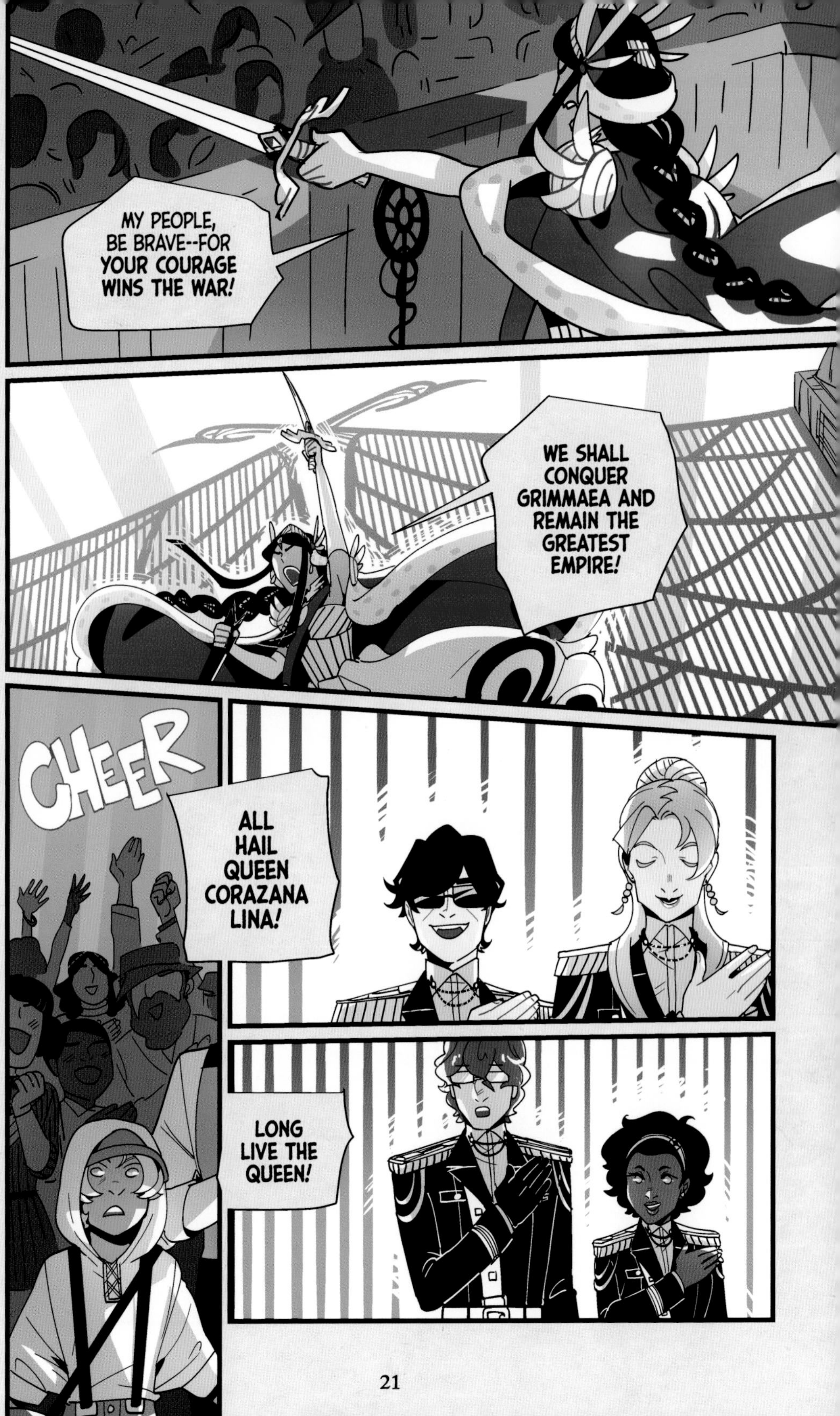
MY PEOPLE, BE BRAVE--FOR YOUR COURAGE WINS THE WAR!
WE SHALL CONQUER GRIMMAEA AND REMAIN THE GREATEST EMPIRE!
CHEER
ALL HAIL QUEEN CORAZANA LINA!
LONG LIVE THE QUEEN!

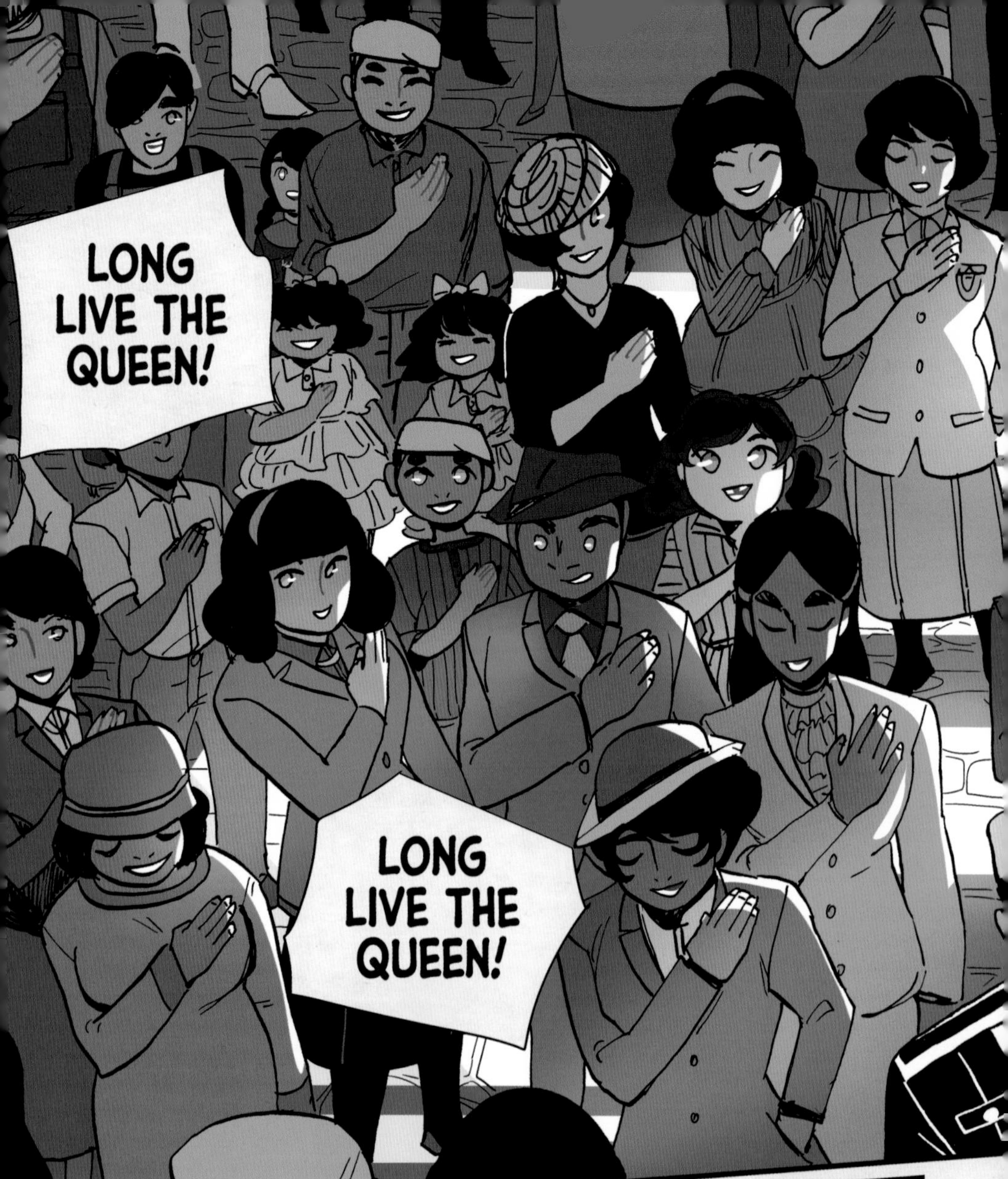
LONG LIVE THE QUEEN!
LONG LIVE THE QUEEN!

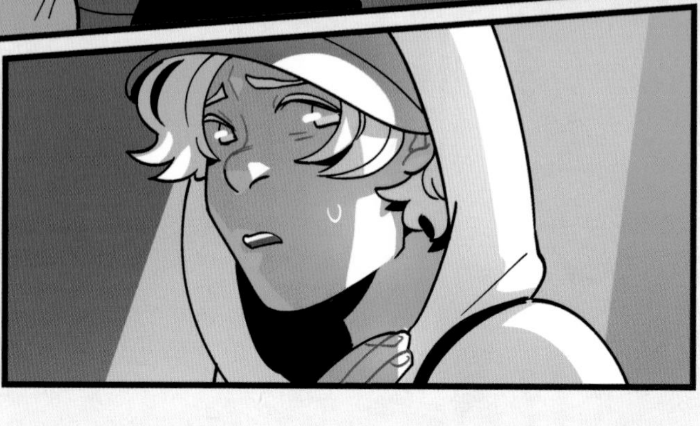

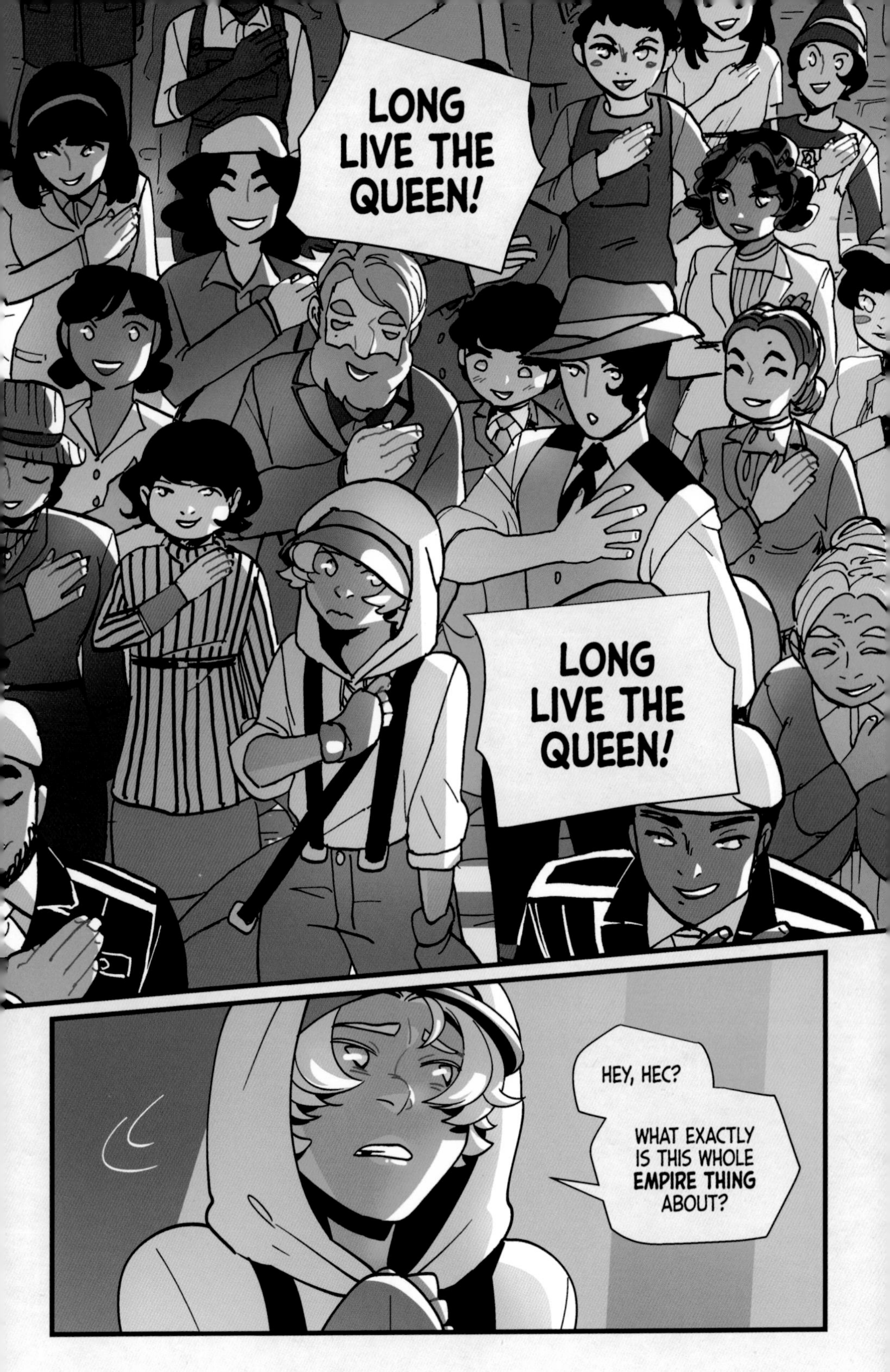
LONG LIVE THE QUEEN!
LONG LIVE THE QUEEN!
HEY, HEC?
WHAT EXACTLY IS THIS WHOLE EMPIRE THING ABOUT?

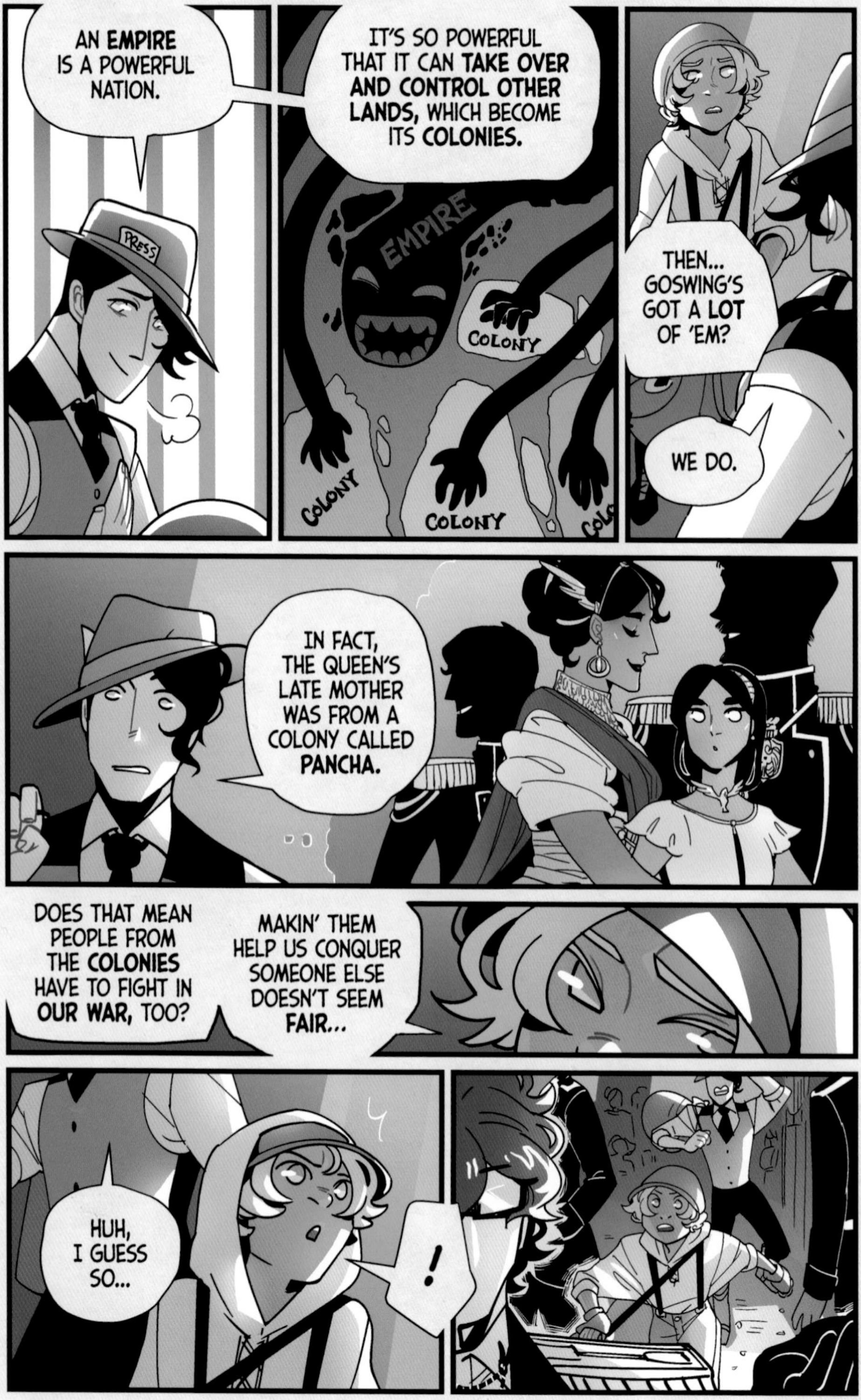
AN EMPIRE IS A POWERFUL NATION.
IT'S SO POWERFUL THAT IT CAN TAKE OVER AND CONTROL OTHER LANDS, WHICH BECOME ITS COLONIES.
EMPIRE
EMPIRE
COLONY
COLONY
COLONY
THEN... GOSWING'S GOT A LOT OF 'EM?
WE DO.
IN FACT, THE QUEEN'S LATE MOTHER WAS FROM A COLONY CALLED PANCHA.
DOES THAT MEAN PEOPLE FROM THE COLONIES HAVE TO FIGHT IN OUR WAR, TOO?
MAKIN' THEM HELP US CONQUER SOMEONE ELSE DOESN'T SEEM FAIR...
HUH, I GUESS SO...
!

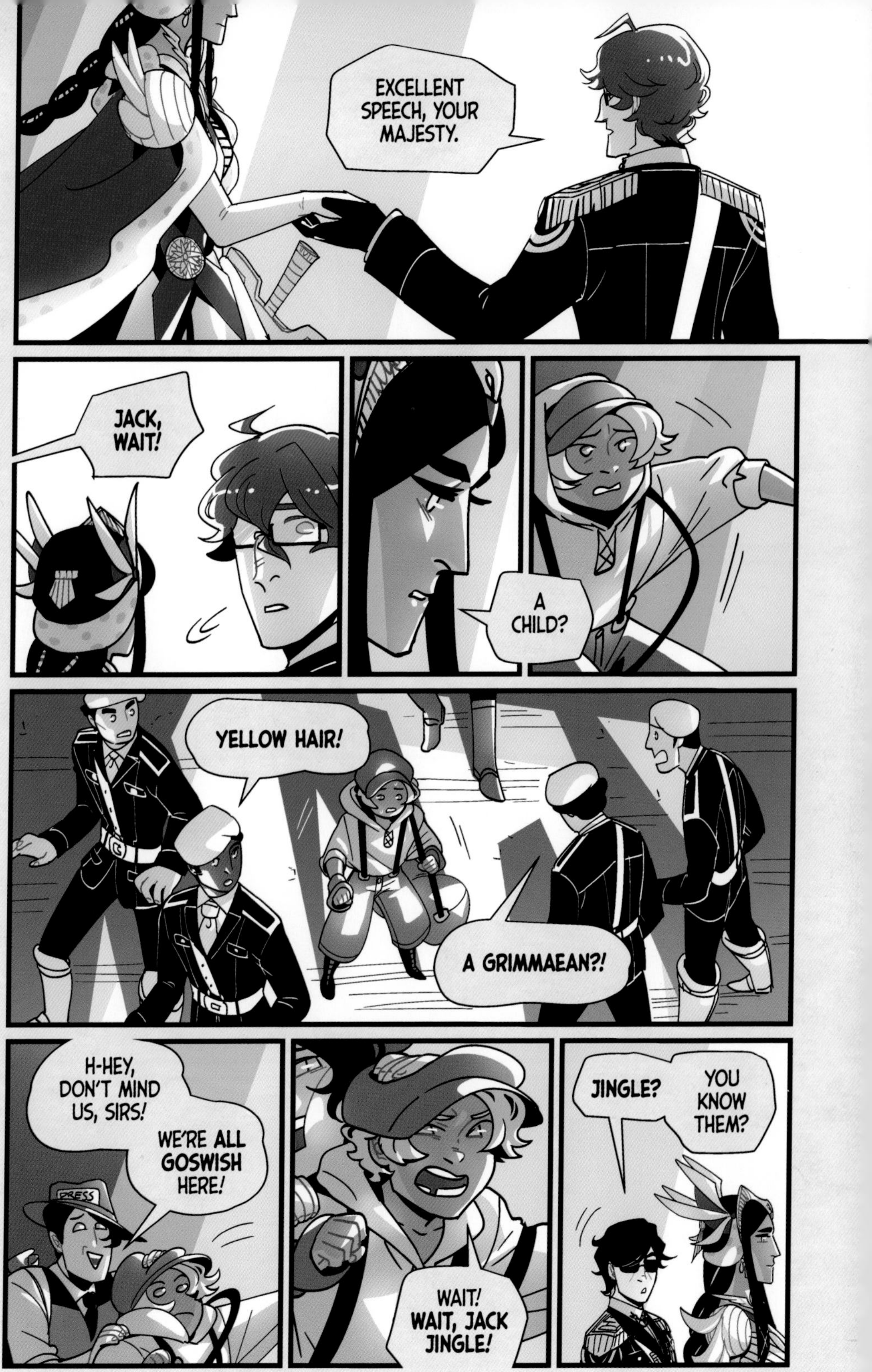
EXCELLENT SPEECH, YOUR MAJESTY.
JACK, WAIT!
A CHILD?
YELLOW HAIR!
A GRIMMAEAN?!
H-HEY, DON'T MIND US, SIRS!
WE'RE ALL GOSWISH HERE!
PRESS
WAIT! WAIT, JACK JINGLE!
JINGLE?
YOU KNOW THEM?

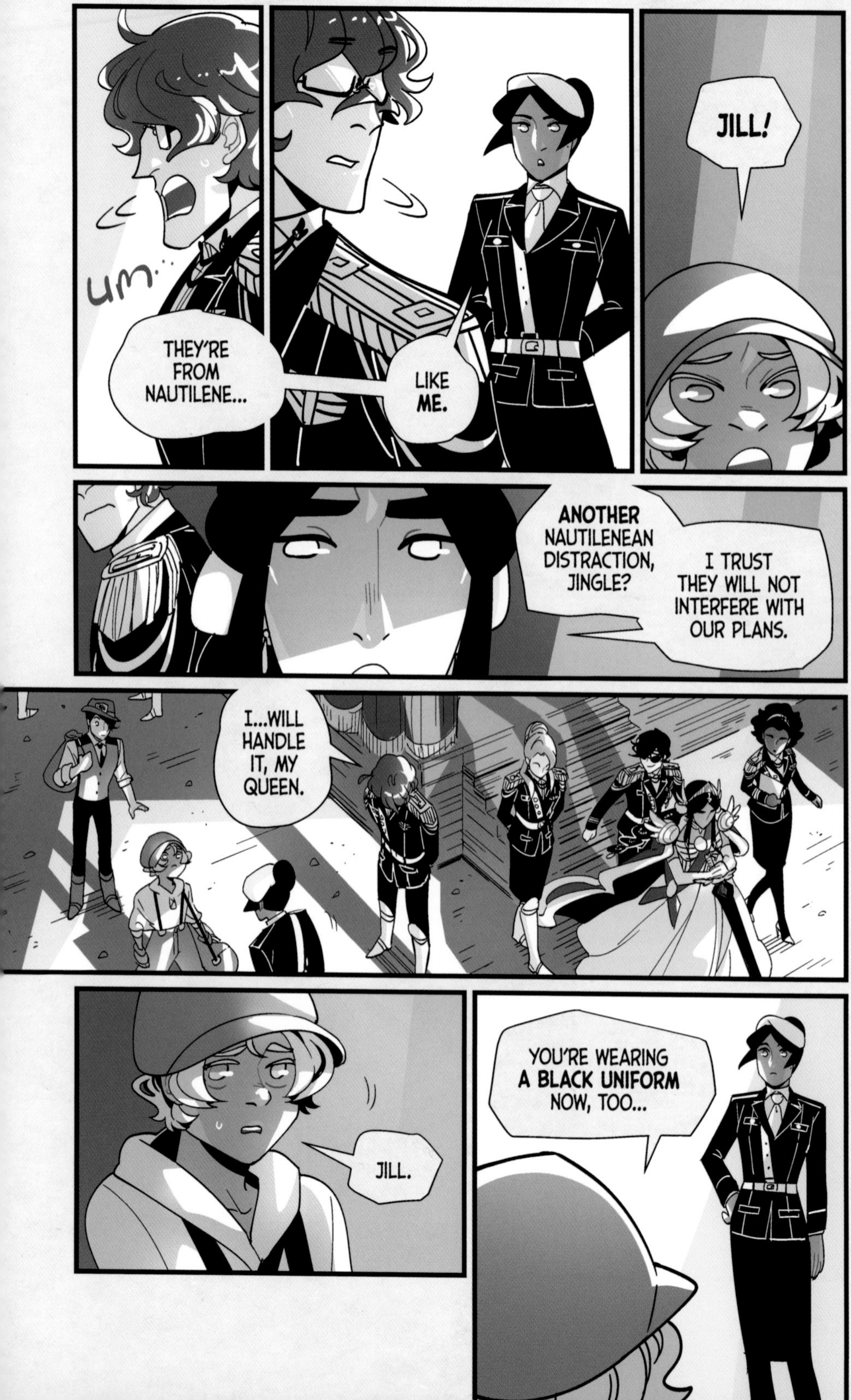
UM...
THEY'RE FROM NAUTILENE...
LIKE ME.
JILL!
ANOTHER NAUTILENEAN DISTRACTION, JINGLE?
I TRUST THEY WILL NOT INTERFERE WITH OUR PLANS.
I...WILL HANDLE IT, MY QUEEN.
JILL.
YOU'RE WEARING A BLACK UNIFORM NOW, TOO...

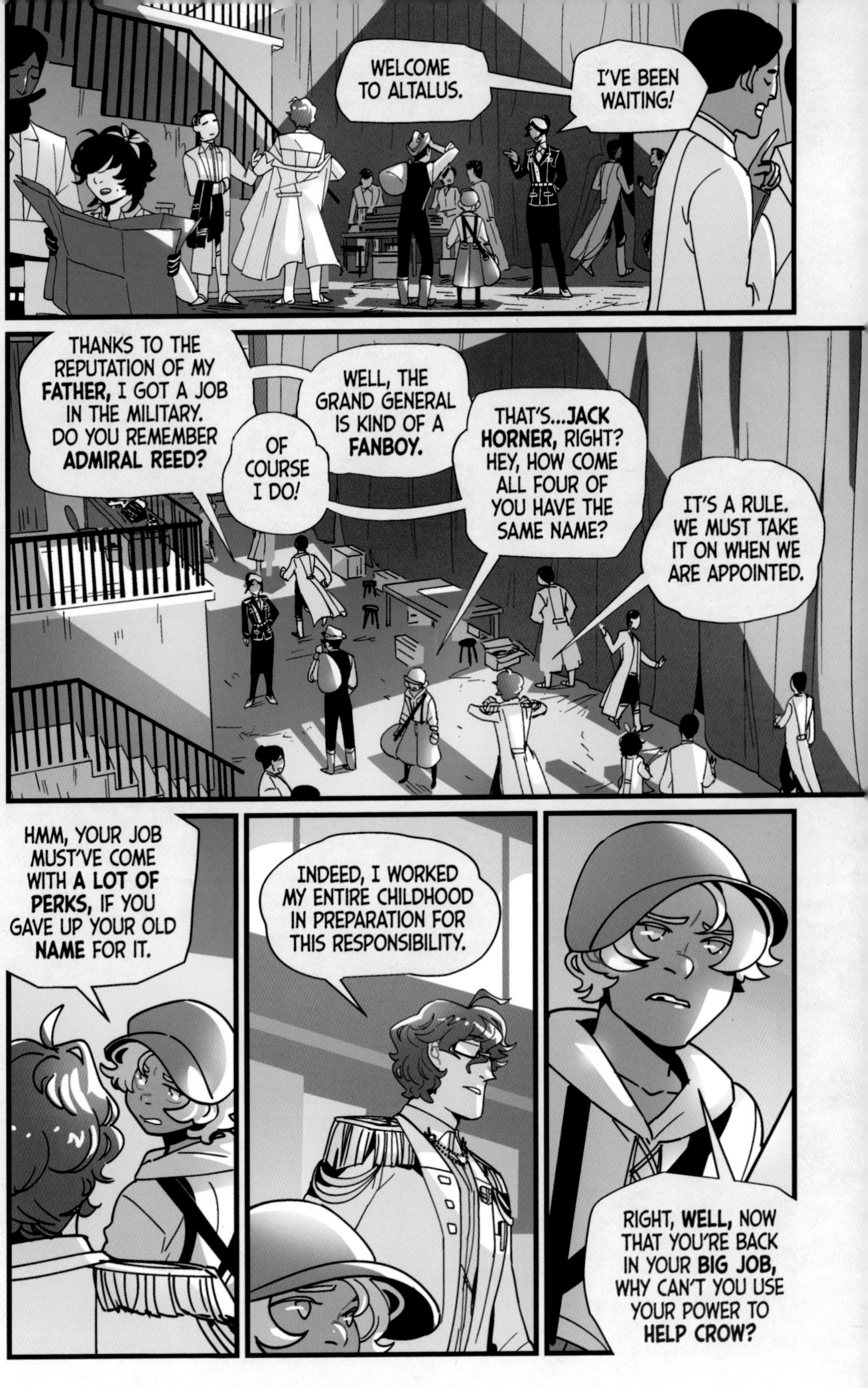
WELCOME TO ALTALUS.
I'VE BEEN WAITING!
THANKS TO THE REPUTATION OF MY **FATHER,** I GOT A JOB IN THE MILITARY. DO YOU REMEMBER **ADMIRAL REED?**
OF COURSE I DO!
WELL, THE GRAND GENERAL IS KIND OF A **FANBOY.**
THAT'S...**JACK HORNER,** RIGHT? HEY, HOW COME ALL FOUR OF YOU HAVE THE SAME NAME?
IT'S A RULE. WE MUST TAKE IT ON WHEN WE ARE APPOINTED.
HMM, YOUR JOB MUST'VE COME WITH **A LOT OF PERKS,** IF YOU GAVE UP YOUR OLD **NAME** FOR IT.
INDEED, I WORKED MY ENTIRE CHILDHOOD IN PREPARATION FOR THIS RESPONSIBILITY.
RIGHT, **WELL,** NOW THAT YOU'RE BACK IN YOUR **BIG JOB,** WHY CAN'T YOU USE YOUR POWER TO **HELP CROW?**

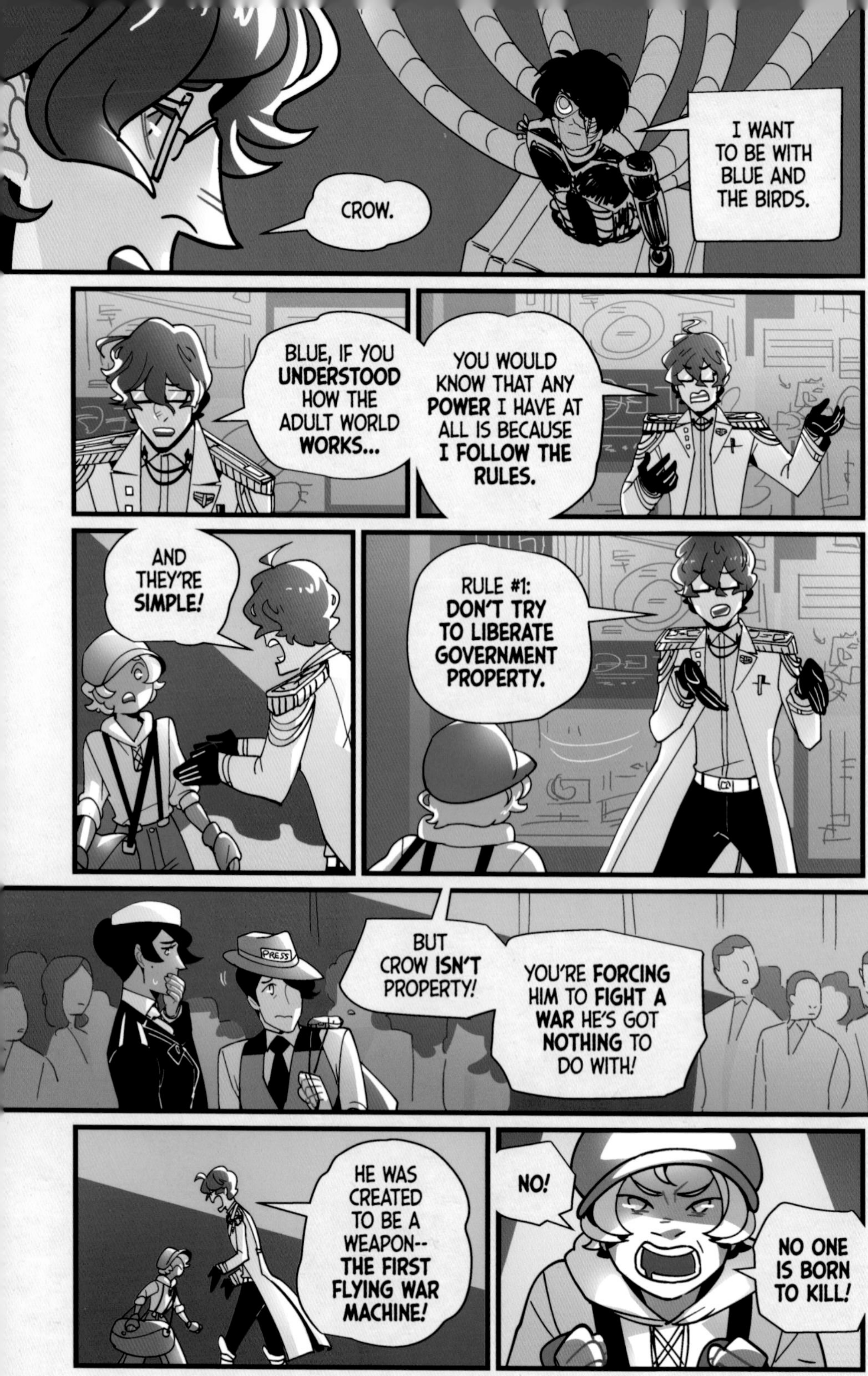
CROW.
I WANT TO BE WITH BLUE AND THE BIRDS.
BLUE, IF YOU UNDERSTOOD HOW THE ADULT WORLD WORKS...
YOU WOULD KNOW THAT ANY POWER I HAVE AT ALL IS BECAUSE I FOLLOW THE RULES.
AND THEY'RE SIMPLE!
RULE #1: DON'T TRY TO LIBERATE GOVERNMENT PROPERTY.
PRESS
BUT CROW ISN'T PROPERTY!
YOU'RE FORCING HIM TO FIGHT A WAR HE'S GOT NOTHING TO DO WITH!
HE WAS CREATED TO BE A WEAPON-- THE FIRST FLYING WAR MACHINE!
NO!
NO ONE IS BORN TO KILL!

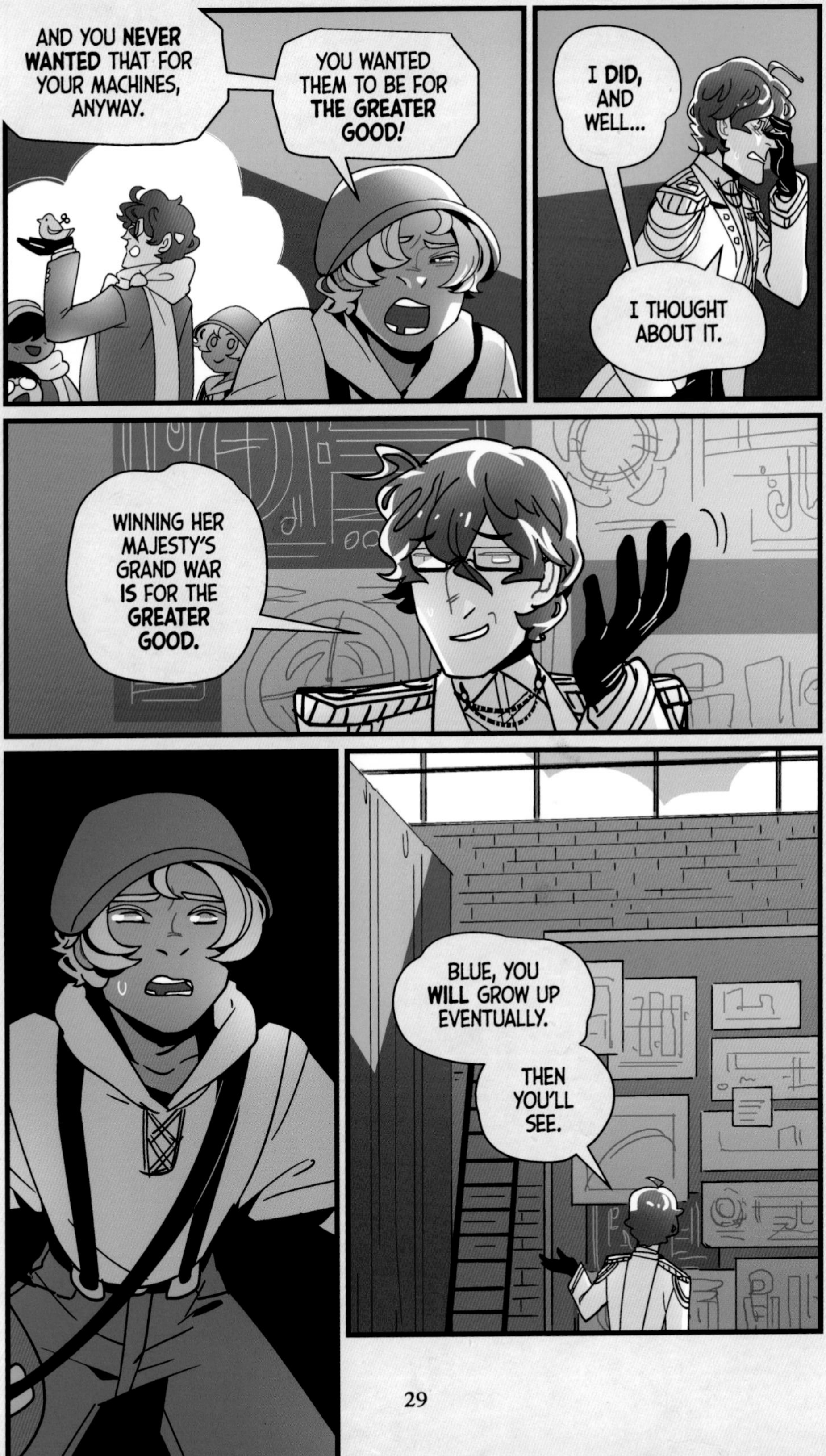
AND YOU NEVER WANTED THAT FOR YOUR MACHINES, ANYWAY.
YOU WANTED THEM TO BE FOR THE GREATER GOOD!
I DID, AND WELL...
I THOUGHT ABOUT IT.
WINNING HER MAJESTY'S GRAND WAR IS FOR THE GREATER GOOD.
BLUE, YOU WILL GROW UP EVENTUALLY.
THEN YOU'LL SEE.

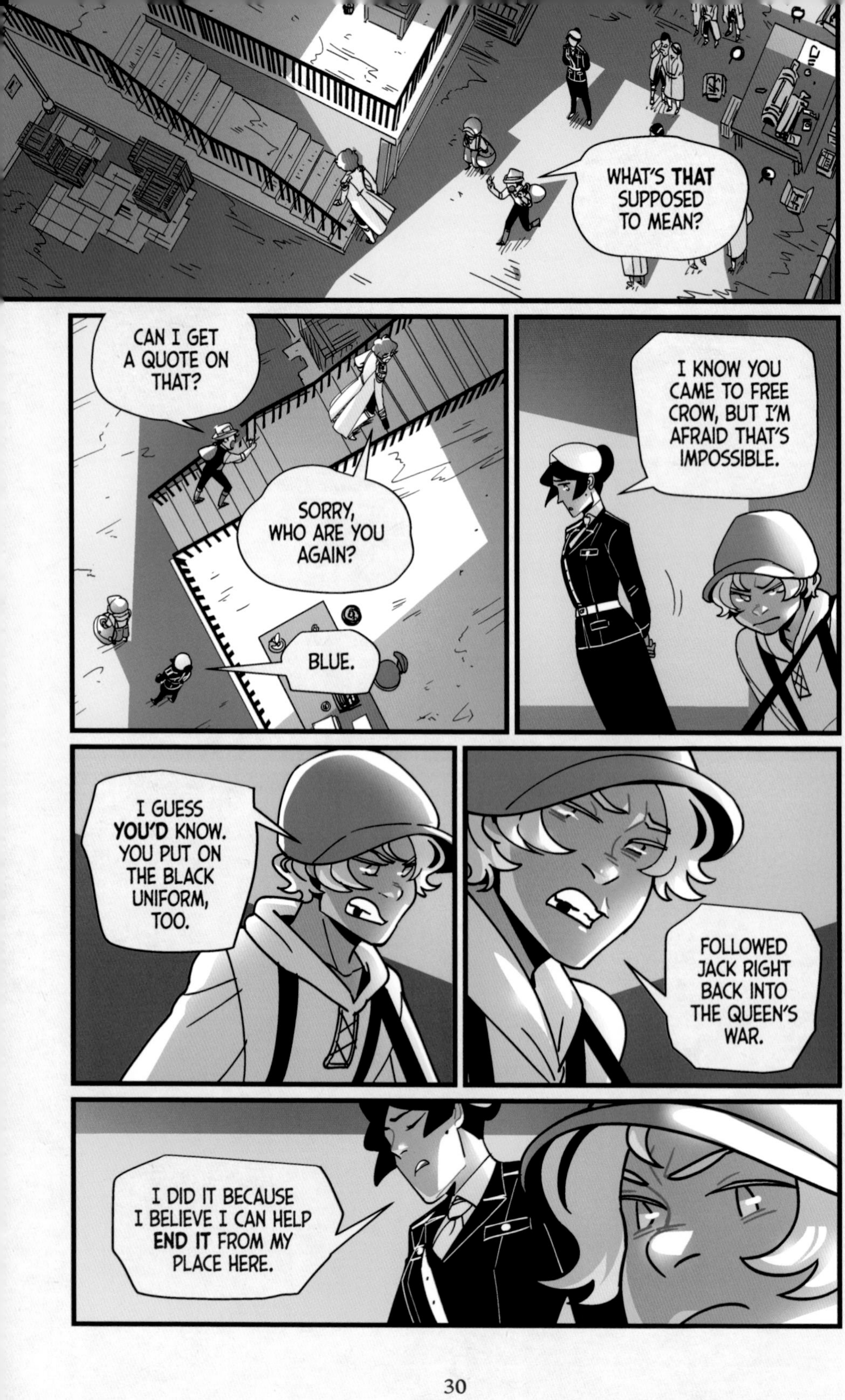
WHAT'S **THAT** SUPPOSED TO MEAN?
CAN I GET A QUOTE ON THAT?
SORRY, WHO ARE YOU AGAIN?
BLUE.
I KNOW YOU CAME TO FREE CROW, BUT I'M AFRAID THAT'S IMPOSSIBLE.
I GUESS **YOU'D** KNOW. YOU PUT ON THE BLACK UNIFORM, TOO.
FOLLOWED JACK RIGHT BACK INTO THE QUEEN'S WAR.
I DID IT BECAUSE I BELIEVE I CAN HELP **END IT** FROM MY PLACE HERE.

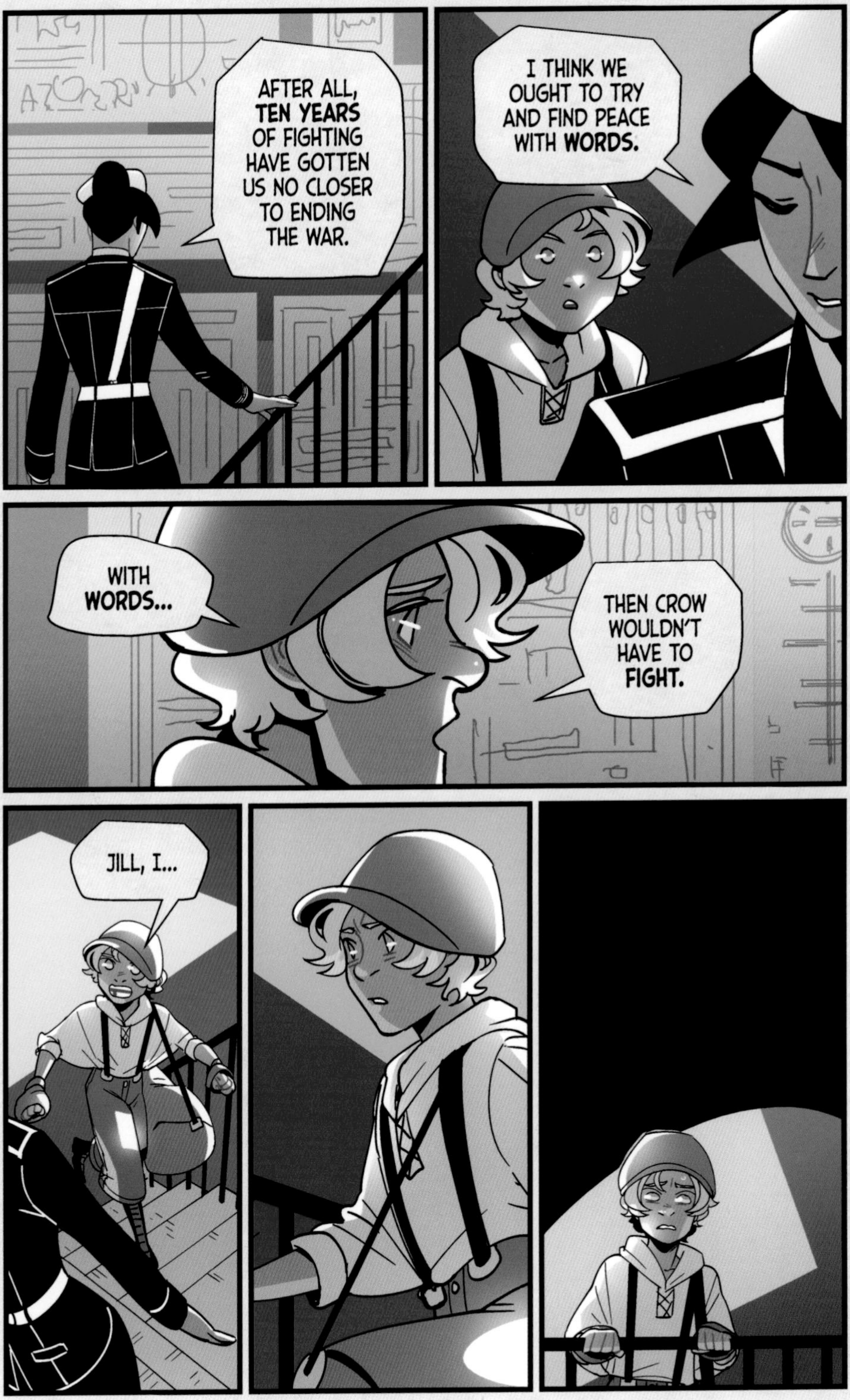
AFTER ALL, TEN YEARS OF FIGHTING HAVE GOTTEN US NO CLOSER TO ENDING THE WAR.
I THINK WE OUGHT TO TRY AND FIND PEACE WITH WORDS.
WITH WORDS...
THEN CROW WOULDN'T HAVE TO FIGHT.
JILL, I...

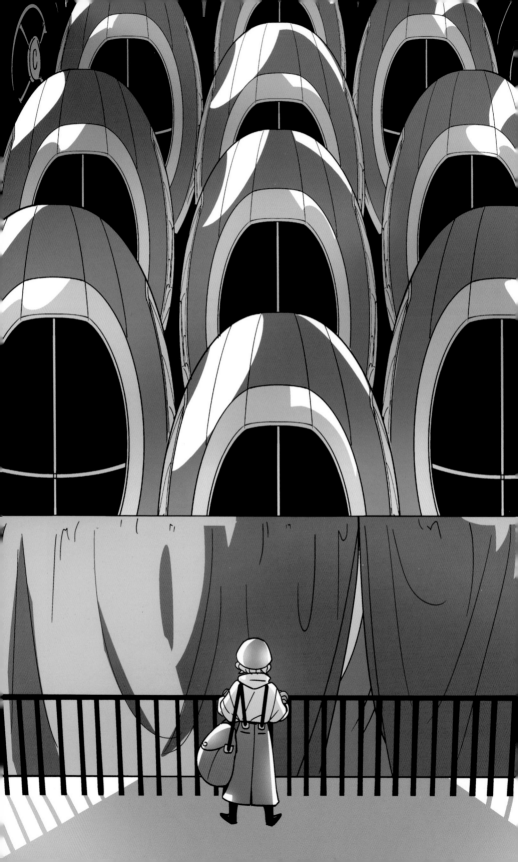

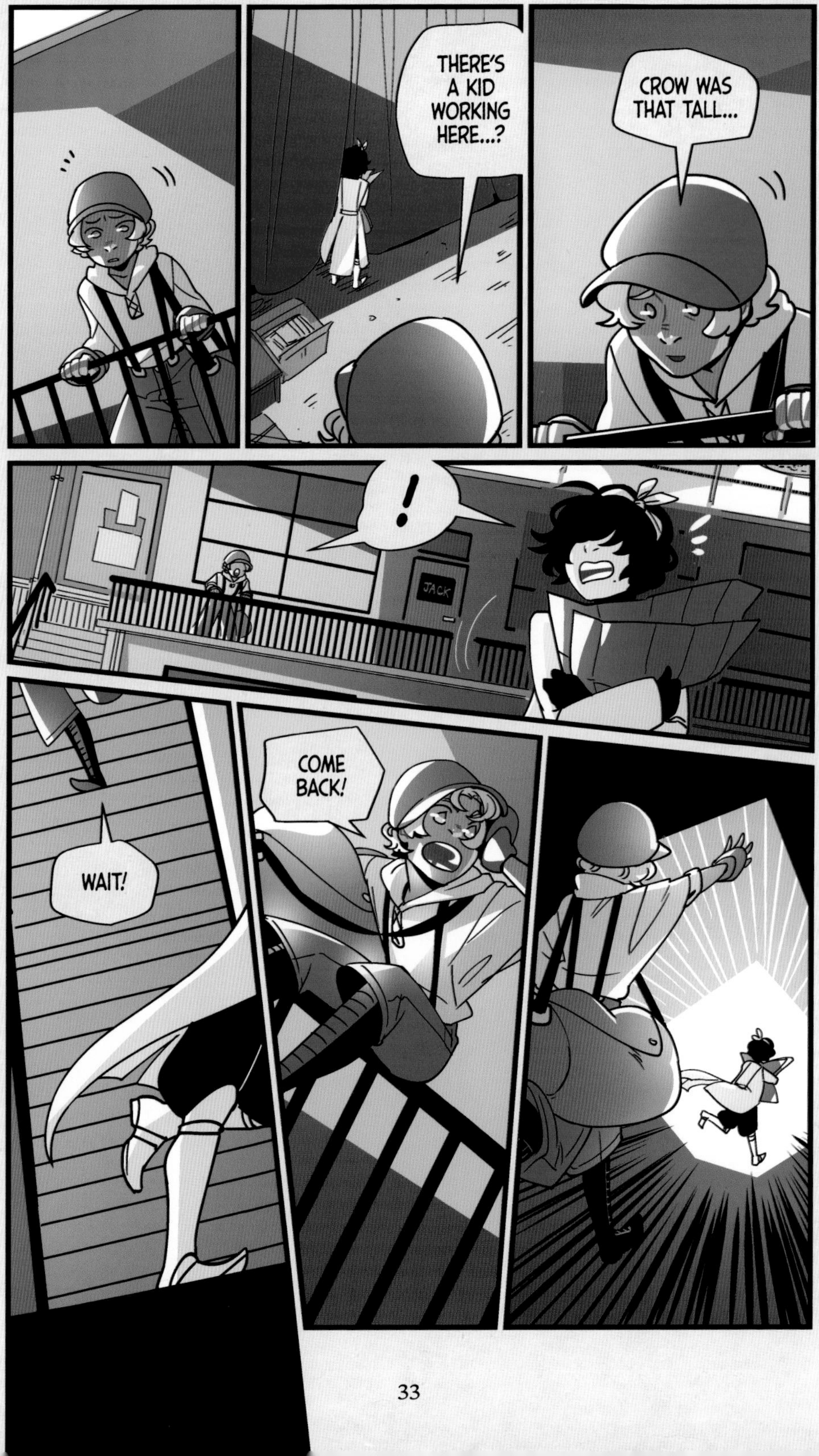
THERE'S A KID WORKING HERE...?
CROW WAS THAT TALL...
!
JACK
WAIT!
COME BACK!

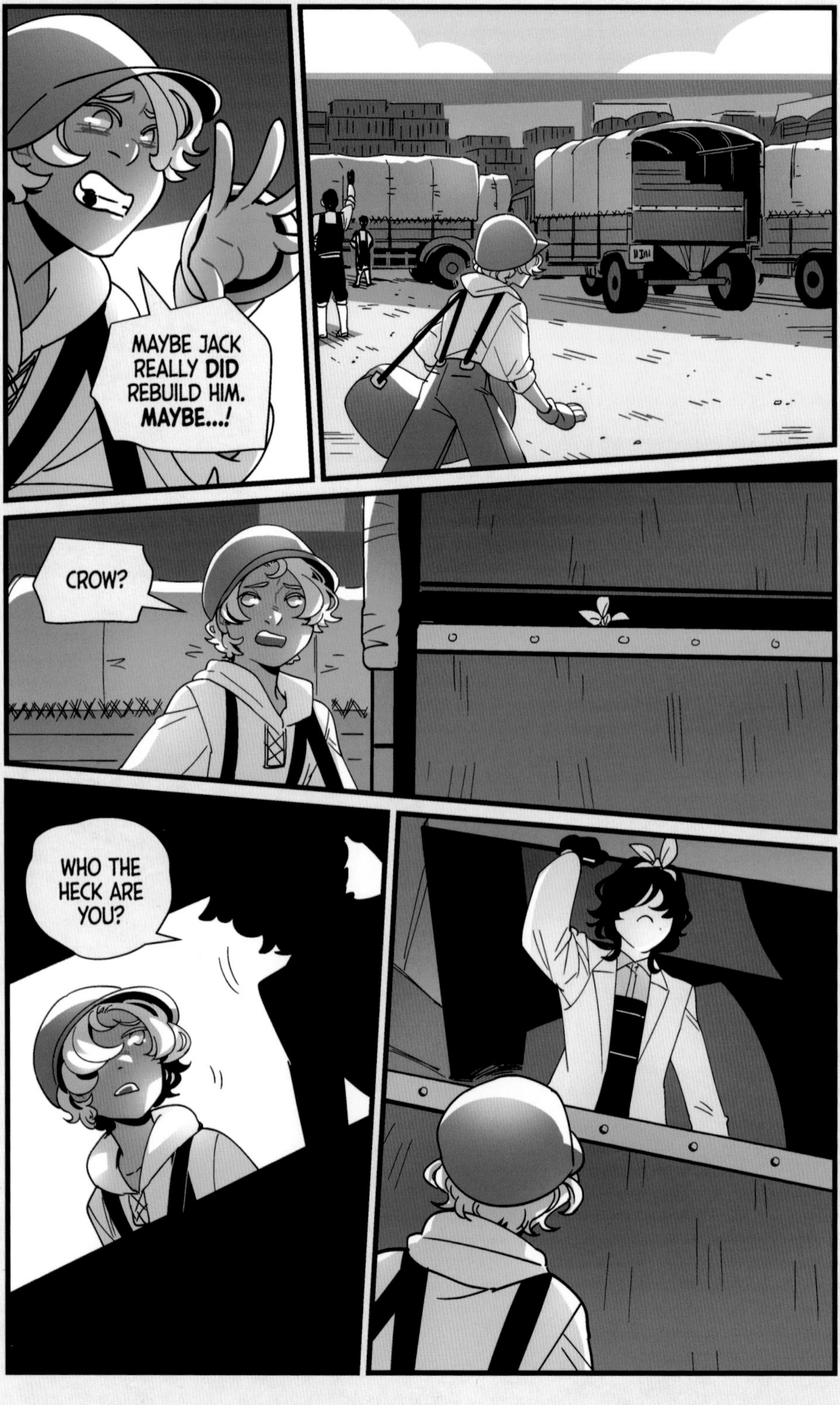
MAYBE JACK REALLY DID REBUILD HIM. MAYBE...!
CROW?
WHO THE HECK ARE YOU?

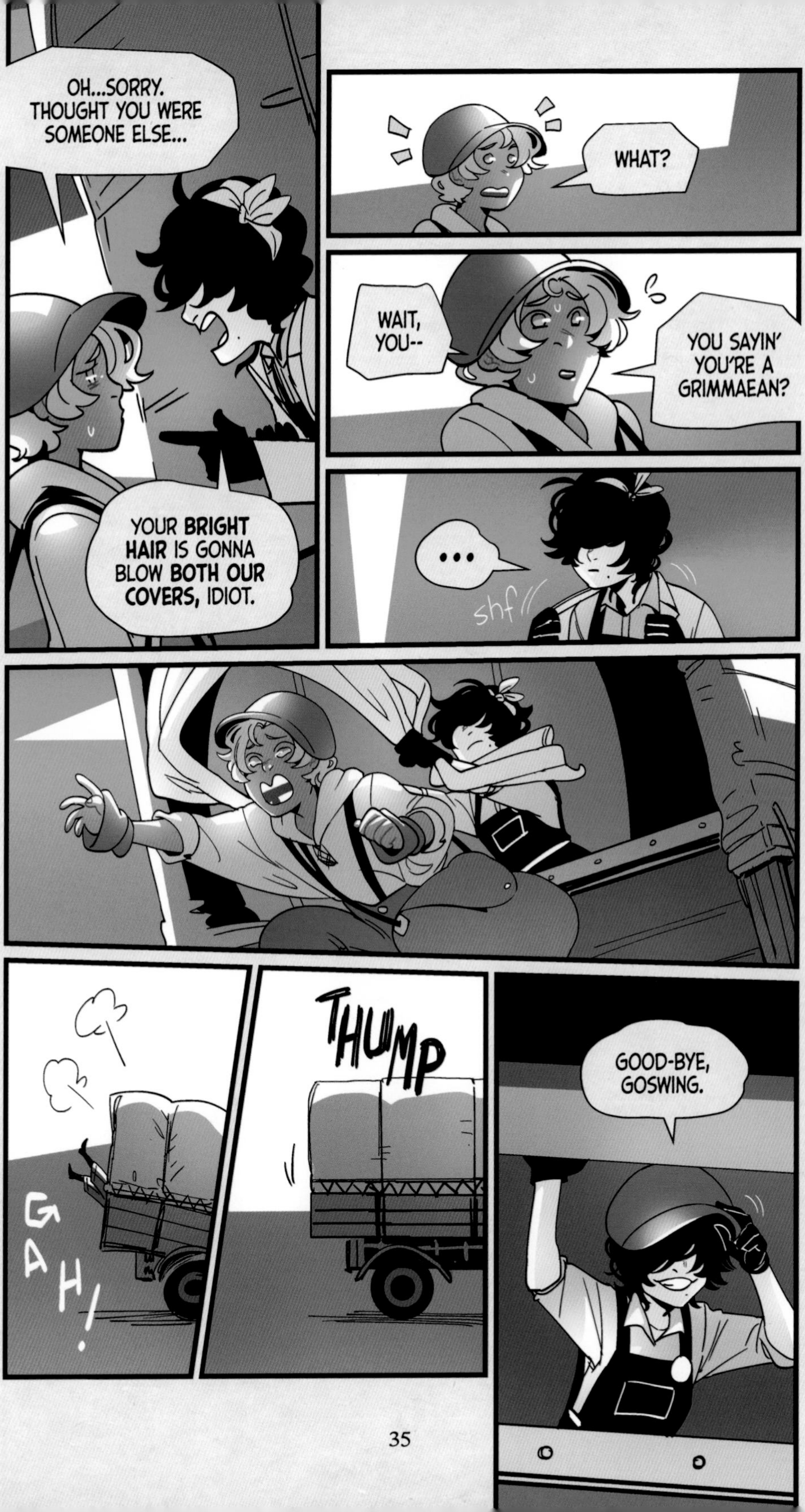

OH...SORRY. THOUGHT YOU WERE SOMEONE ELSE...
WHAT?
WAIT, YOU--
YOU SAYIN' YOU'RE A GRIMMAEAN?
YOUR BRIGHT HAIR IS GONNA BLOW BOTH OUR COVERS, IDIOT.
...
shf
GAH!
THUMP
GOOD-BYE, GOSWING.

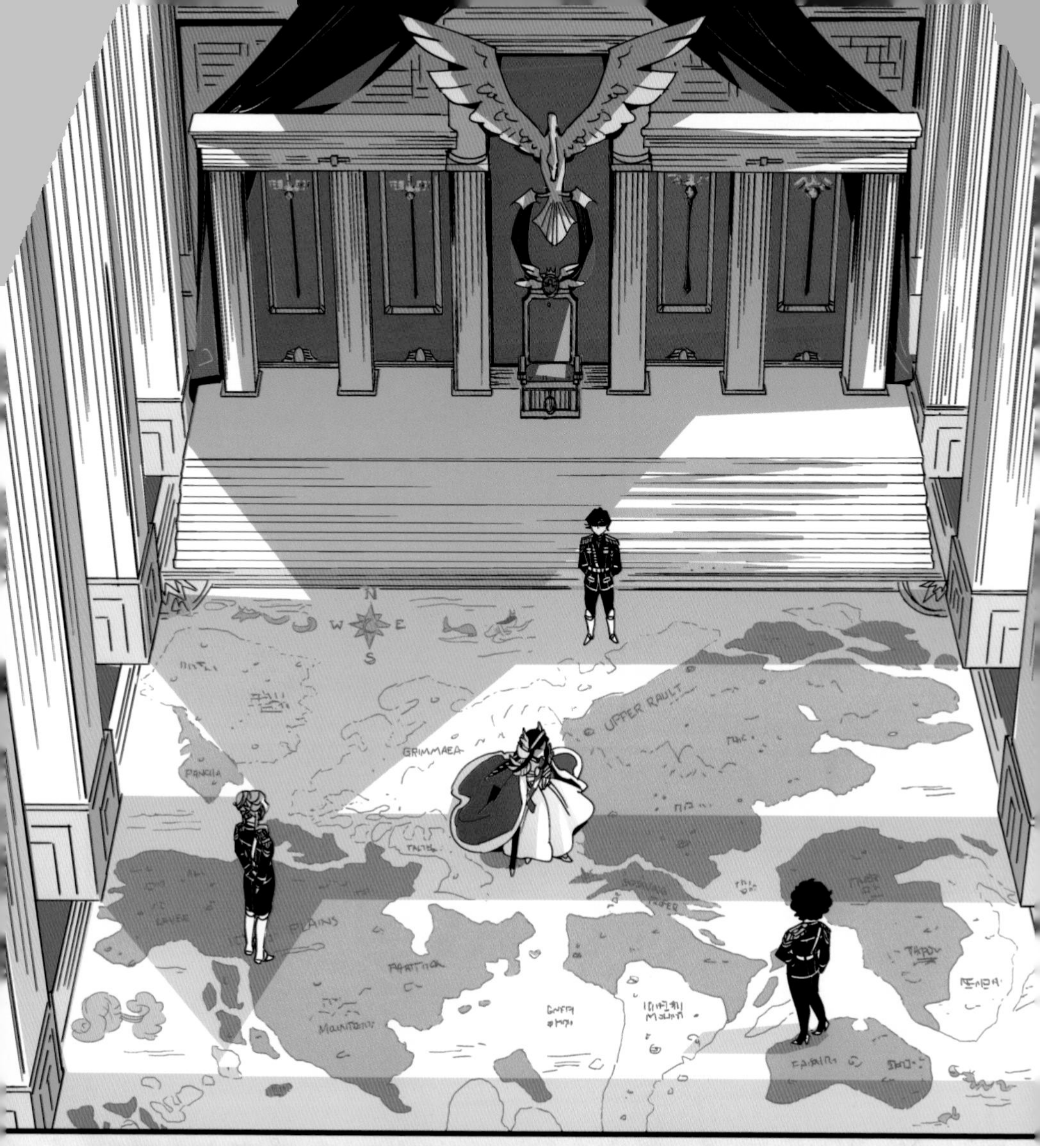
N
W
E
S
UPPER RAULT
GRIMMAEA

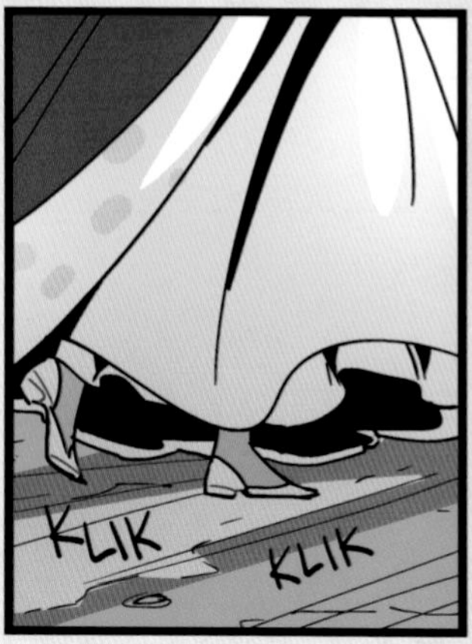
KLIK
KLIK

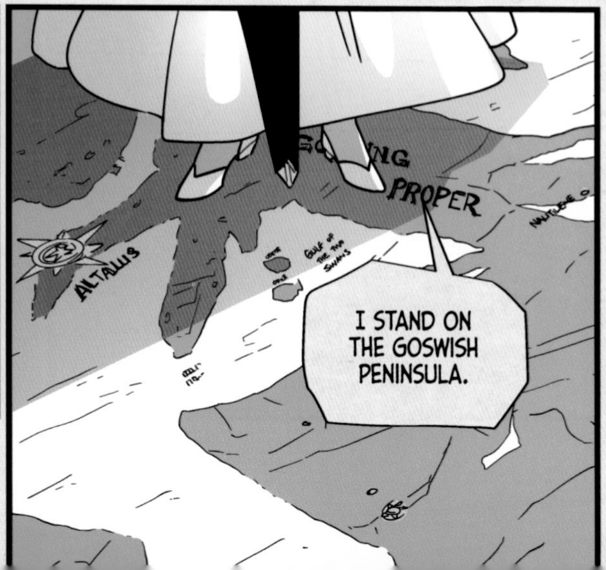
PROPER
ALTALUS
I STAND ON THE GOSWISH PENINSULA.

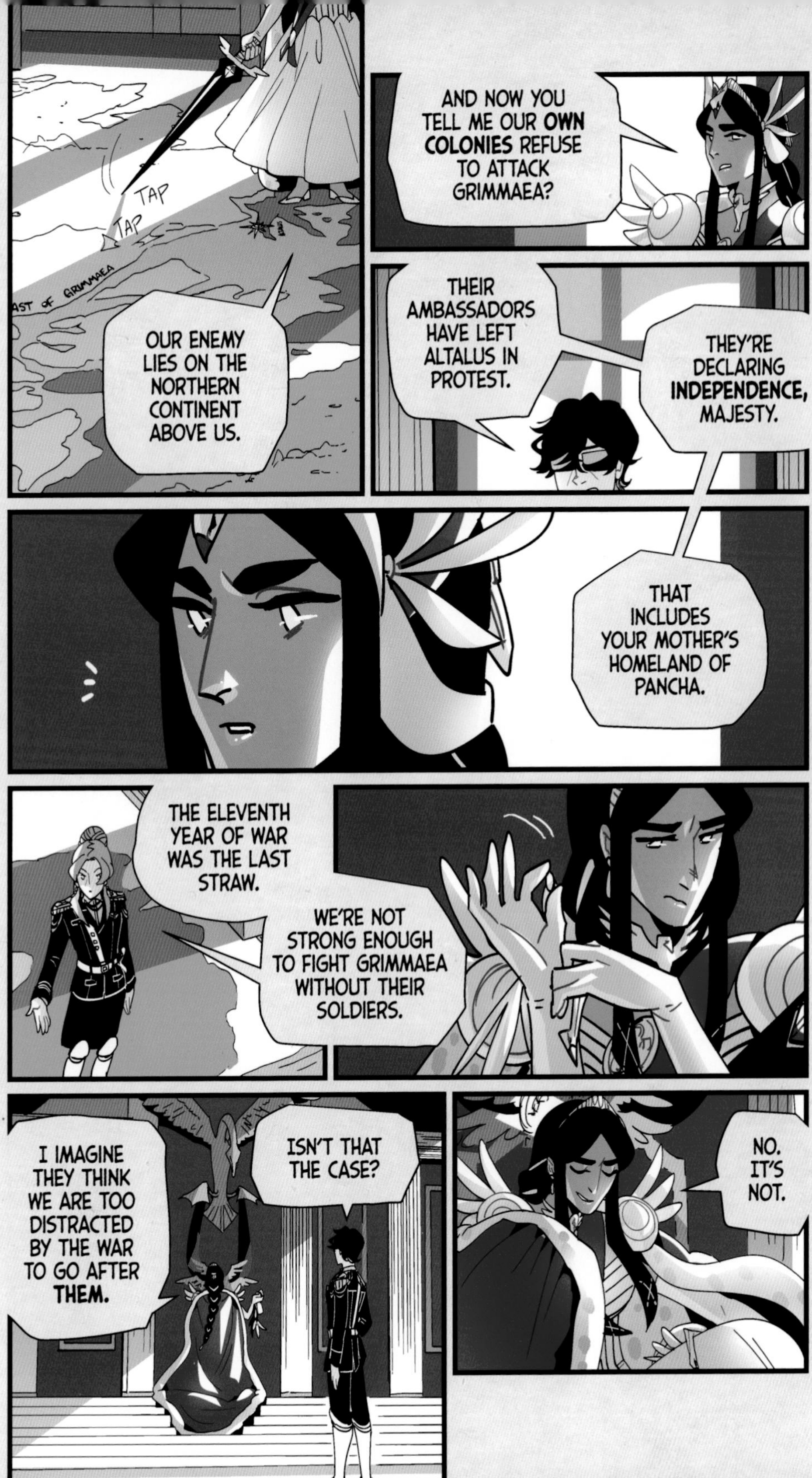
TAP
TAP
AST OF GRIMMAEA
OUR ENEMY LIES ON THE NORTHERN CONTINENT ABOVE US.
AND NOW YOU TELL ME OUR OWN COLONIES REFUSE TO ATTACK GRIMMAEA?
THEIR AMBASSADORS HAVE LEFT ALTALUS IN PROTEST.
THEY'RE DECLARING INDEPENDENCE, MAJESTY.
THAT INCLUDES YOUR MOTHER'S HOMELAND OF PANCHA.
THE ELEVENTH YEAR OF WAR WAS THE LAST STRAW.
WE'RE NOT STRONG ENOUGH TO FIGHT GRIMMAEA WITHOUT THEIR SOLDIERS.
I IMAGINE THEY THINK WE ARE TOO DISTRACTED BY THE WAR TO GO AFTER THEM.
ISN'T THAT THE CASE?
NO. IT'S NOT.

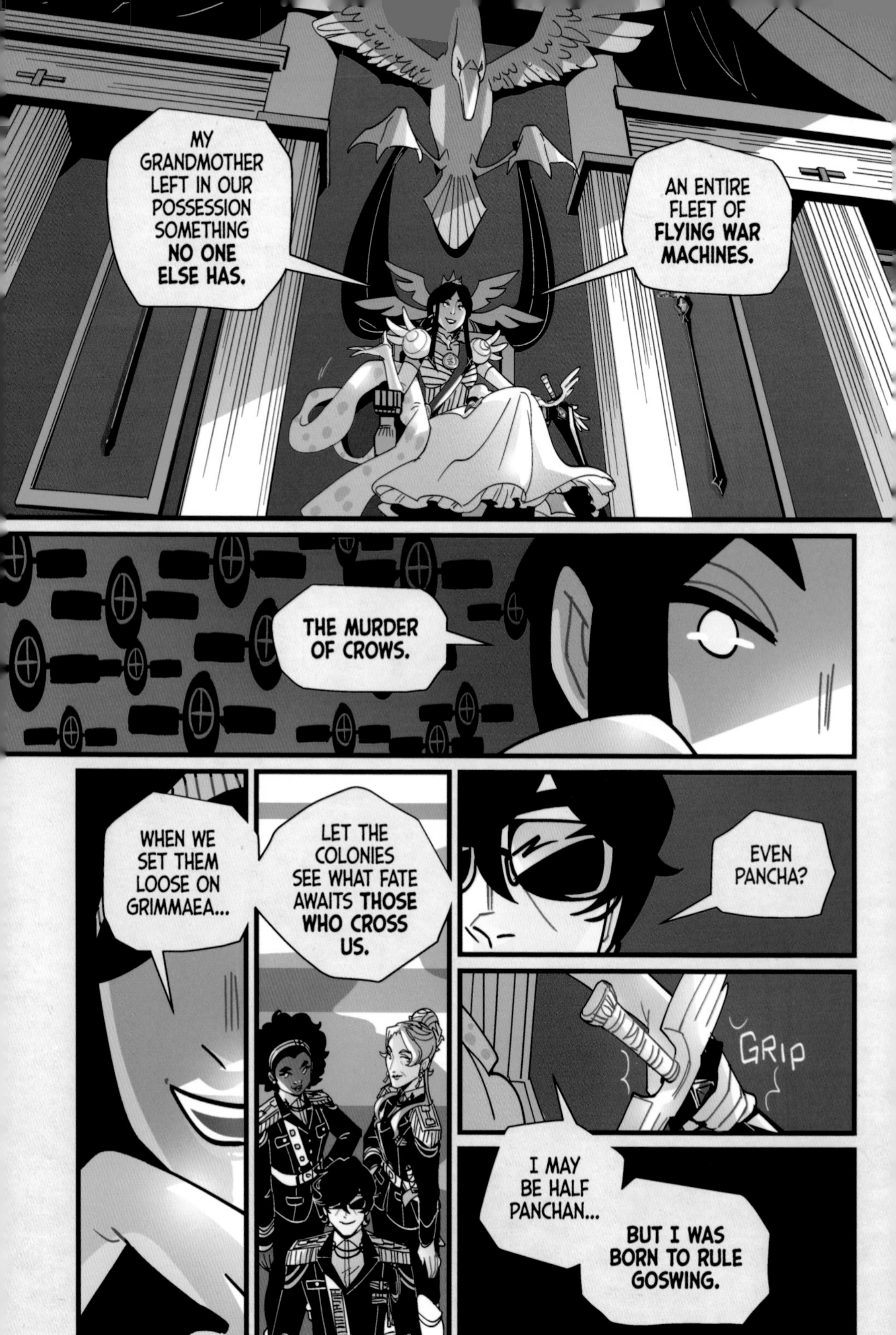
MY GRANDMOTHER LEFT IN OUR POSSESSION SOMETHING **NO ONE** ELSE HAS.
AN ENTIRE FLEET OF **FLYING WAR MACHINES.**
THE MURDER OF CROWS.
WHEN WE SET THEM LOOSE ON GRIMMAEA...
LET THE COLONIES SEE WHAT FATE AWAITS **THOSE** WHO CROSS US.
EVEN PANCHA?
GRIP
I MAY BE HALF PANCHAN...
BUT I WAS BORN TO RULE GOSWING.

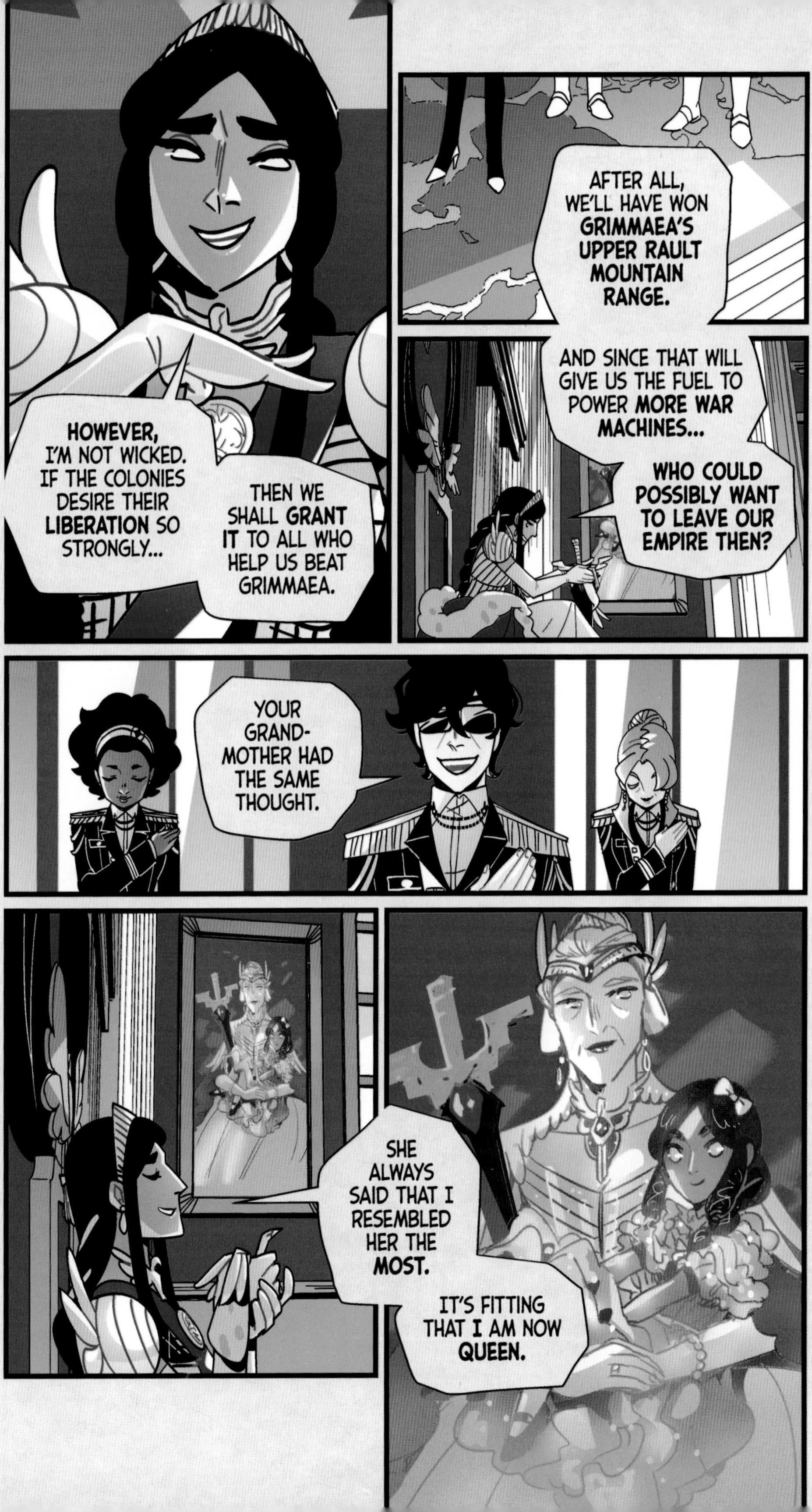
HOWEVER, I'M NOT WICKED. IF THE COLONIES DESIRE THEIR LIBERATION SO STRONGLY...
THEN WE SHALL GRANT IT TO ALL WHO HELP US BEAT GRIMMAEA.
AFTER ALL, WE'LL HAVE WON GRIMMAEA'S UPPER RAULT MOUNTAIN RANGE.
AND SINCE THAT WILL GIVE US THE FUEL TO POWER MORE WAR MACHINES...
WHO COULD POSSIBLY WANT TO LEAVE OUR EMPIRE THEN?
YOUR GRAND-MOTHER HAD THE SAME THOUGHT.
SHE ALWAYS SAID THAT I RESEMBLED HER THE MOST.
IT'S FITTING THAT I AM NOW QUEEN.

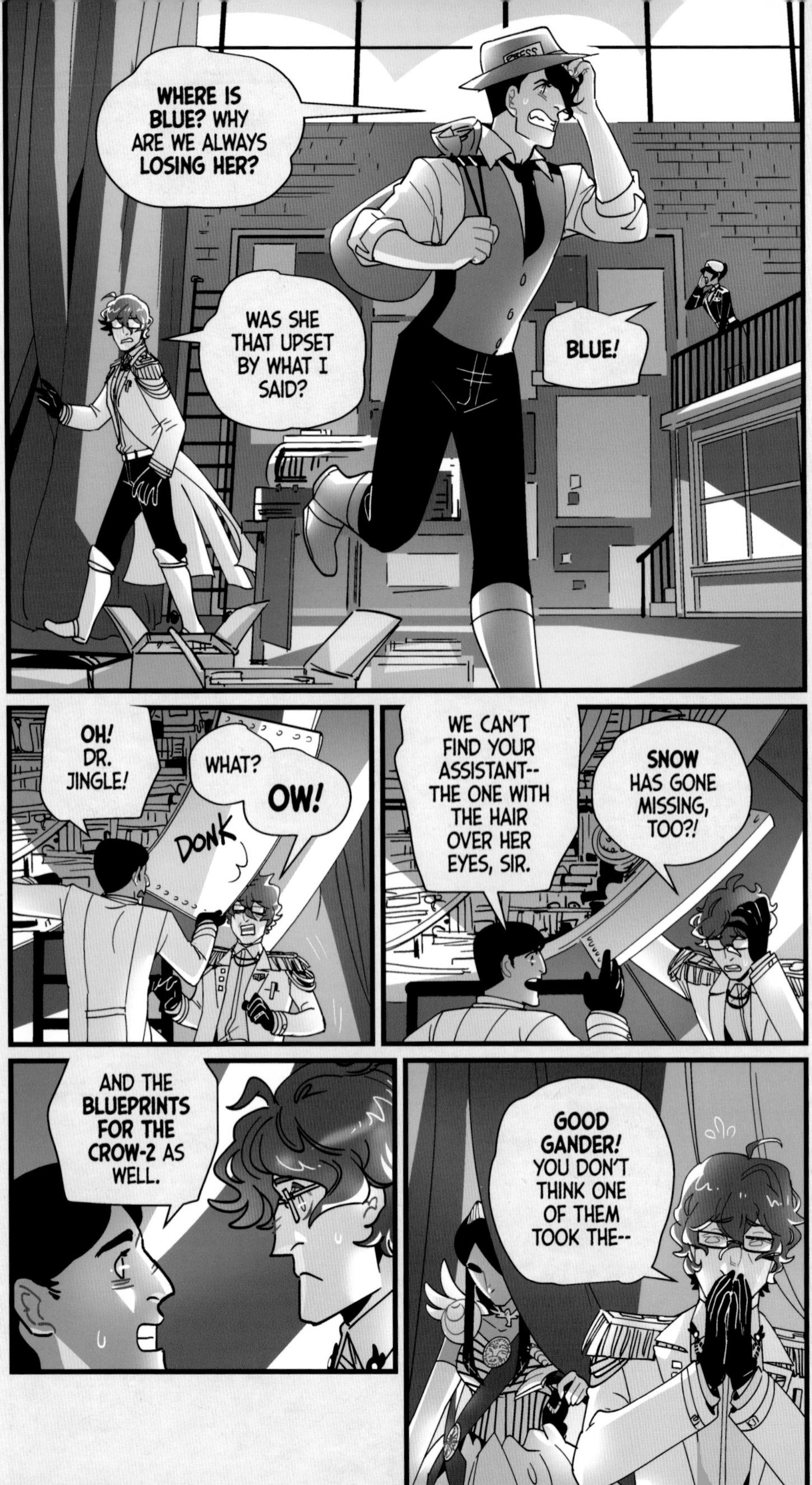
WHERE IS BLUE? WHY ARE WE ALWAYS LOSING HER?
WAS SHE THAT UPSET BY WHAT I SAID?
BLUE!
OH! DR. JINGLE!
WHAT?
OW!
DONK
WE CAN'T FIND YOUR ASSISTANT-- THE ONE WITH THE HAIR OVER HER EYES, SIR.
SNOW HAS GONE MISSING, TOO?!
AND THE BLUEPRINTS FOR THE CROW-2 AS WELL.
GOOD GANDER! YOU DON'T THINK ONE OF THEM TOOK THE--

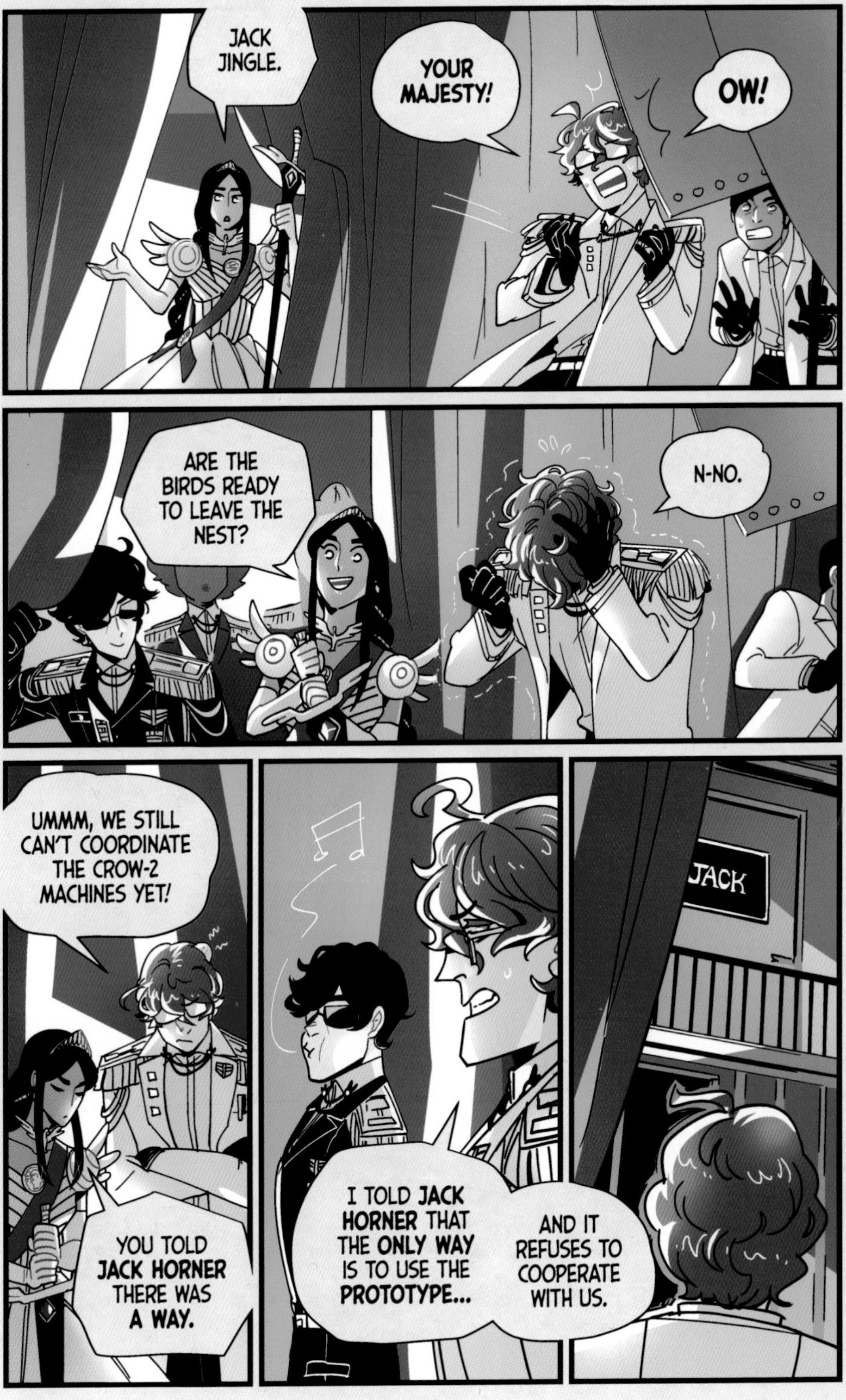
JACK JINGLE.
YOUR MAJESTY!
OW!
ARE THE BIRDS READY TO LEAVE THE NEST?
N-NO.
UMMM, WE STILL CAN'T COORDINATE THE CROW-2 MACHINES YET!
YOU TOLD JACK HORNER THERE WAS A WAY.
I TOLD JACK HORNER THAT THE ONLY WAY IS TO USE THE PROTOTYPE...
AND IT REFUSES TO COOPERATE WITH US.
JACK

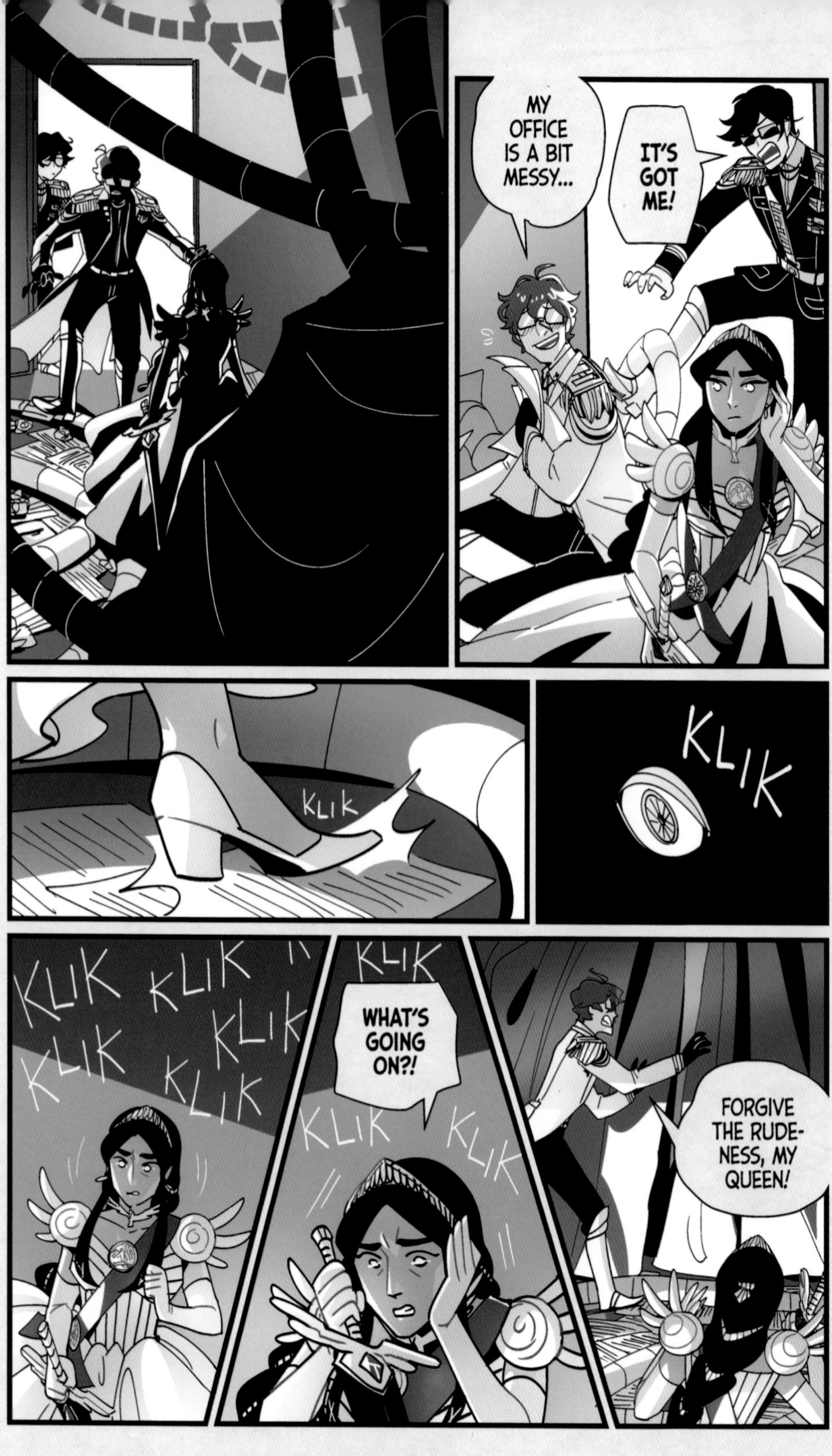
MY OFFICE IS A BIT MESSY...
IT'S GOT ME!
KLIK
KLIK
KLIK KLIK KLIK KLIK KLIK
KLIK
WHAT'S GOING ON?!
KLIK KLIK
FORGIVE THE RUDE-NESS, MY QUEEN!

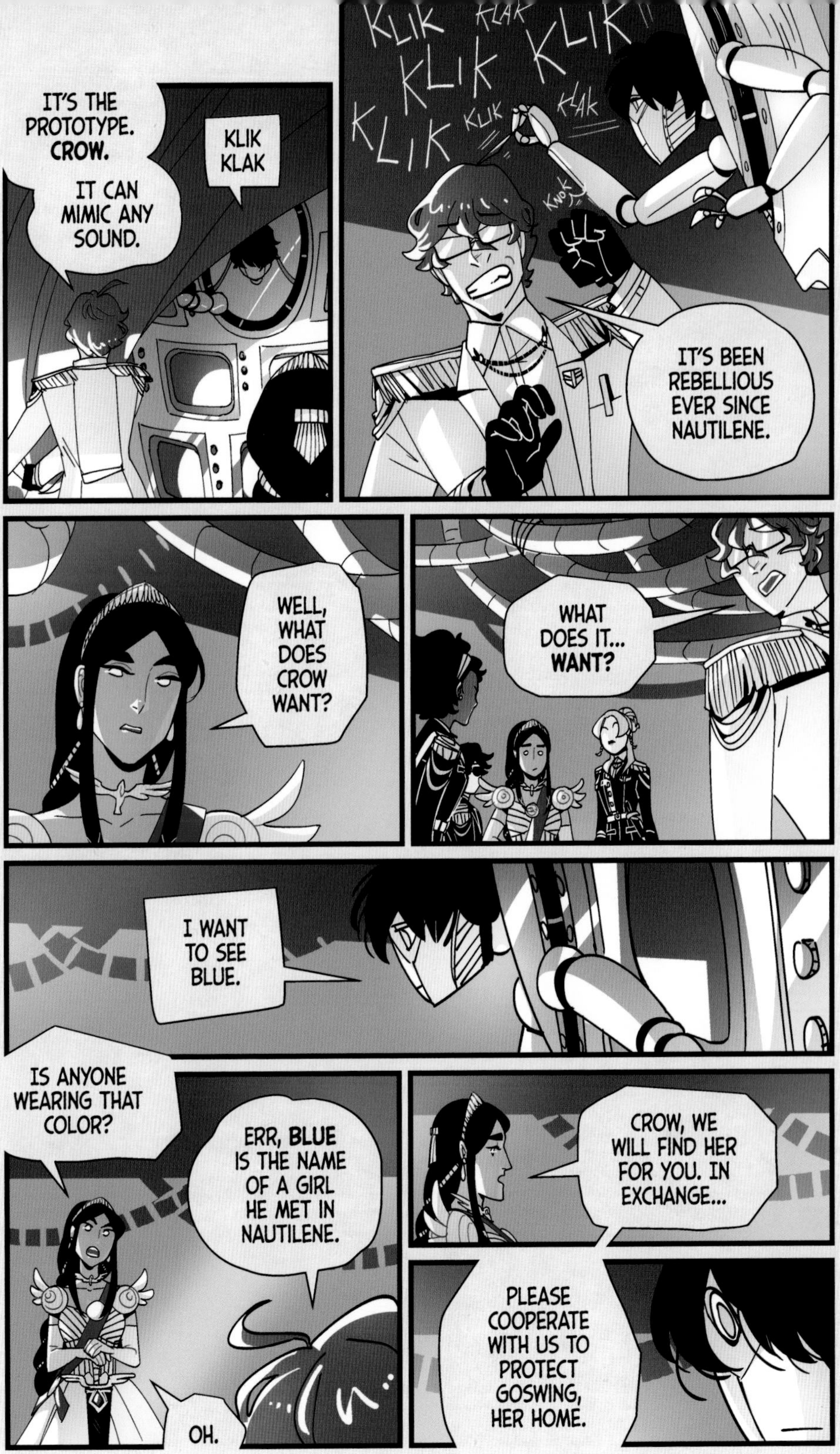
IT'S THE PROTOTYPE. CROW.
IT CAN MIMIC ANY SOUND.
KLIK KLAK
KLIK KLAK KLIK KLIK KLIK KLIK KLAK
KNOK
IT'S BEEN REBELLIOUS EVER SINCE NAUTILENE.
WELL, WHAT DOES CROW WANT?
WHAT DOES IT... WANT?
I WANT TO SEE BLUE.
IS ANYONE WEARING THAT COLOR?
ERR, BLUE IS THE NAME OF A GIRL HE MET IN NAUTILENE.
OH.
CROW, WE WILL FIND HER FOR YOU. IN EXCHANGE...
PLEASE COOPERATE WITH US TO PROTECT GOSWING, HER HOME.

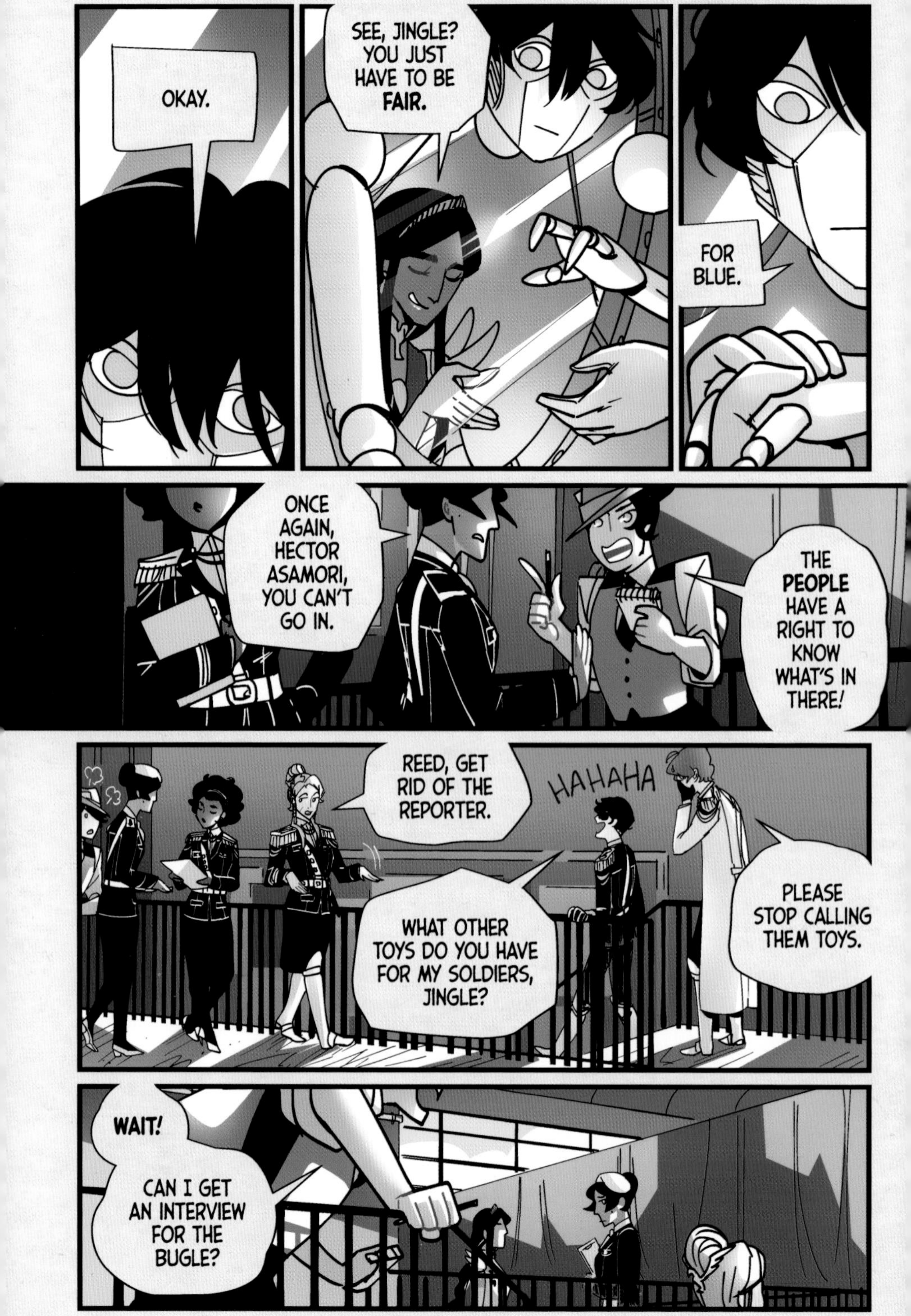
OKAY.
SEE, JINGLE? YOU JUST HAVE TO BE **FAIR.**
FOR BLUE.
ONCE AGAIN, HECTOR ASAMORI, YOU CAN'T GO IN.
THE **PEOPLE** HAVE A RIGHT TO KNOW WHAT'S IN THERE!
REED, GET RID OF THE REPORTER.
HAHAHA
WHAT OTHER TOYS DO YOU HAVE FOR MY SOLDIERS, JINGLE?
PLEASE STOP CALLING THEM TOYS.
WAIT!
CAN I GET AN INTERVIEW FOR THE BUGLE?

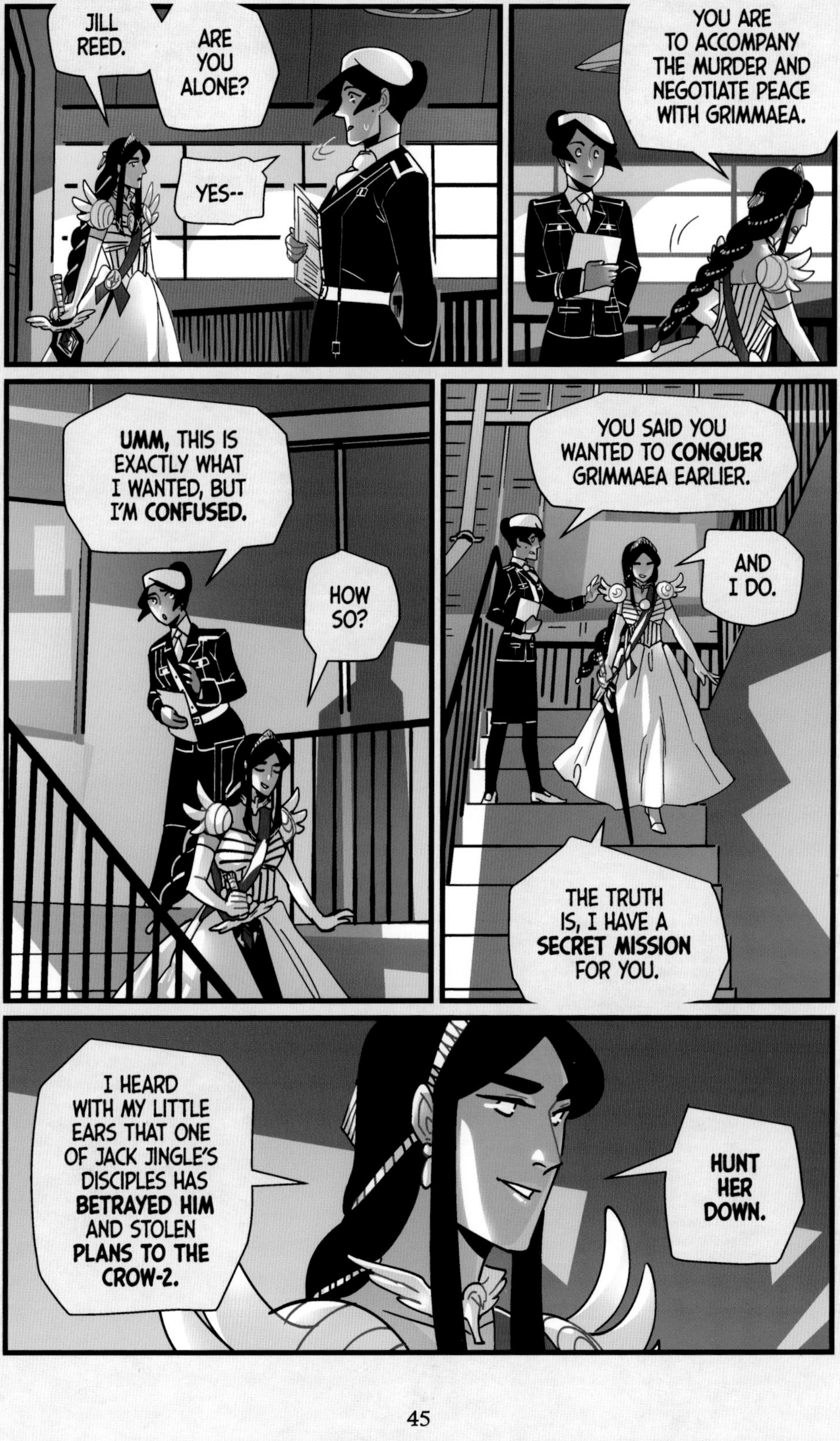
JILL REED.
ARE YOU ALONE?
YES--
YOU ARE TO ACCOMPANY THE MURDER AND NEGOTIATE PEACE WITH GRIMMAEA.
UMM, THIS IS EXACTLY WHAT I WANTED, BUT I'M CONFUSED.
HOW SO?
YOU SAID YOU WANTED TO CONQUER GRIMMAEA EARLIER.
AND I DO.
THE TRUTH IS, I HAVE A SECRET MISSION FOR YOU.
I HEARD WITH MY LITTLE EARS THAT ONE OF JACK JINGLE'S DISCIPLES HAS BETRAYED HIM AND STOLEN PLANS TO THE CROW-2.
HUNT HER DOWN.

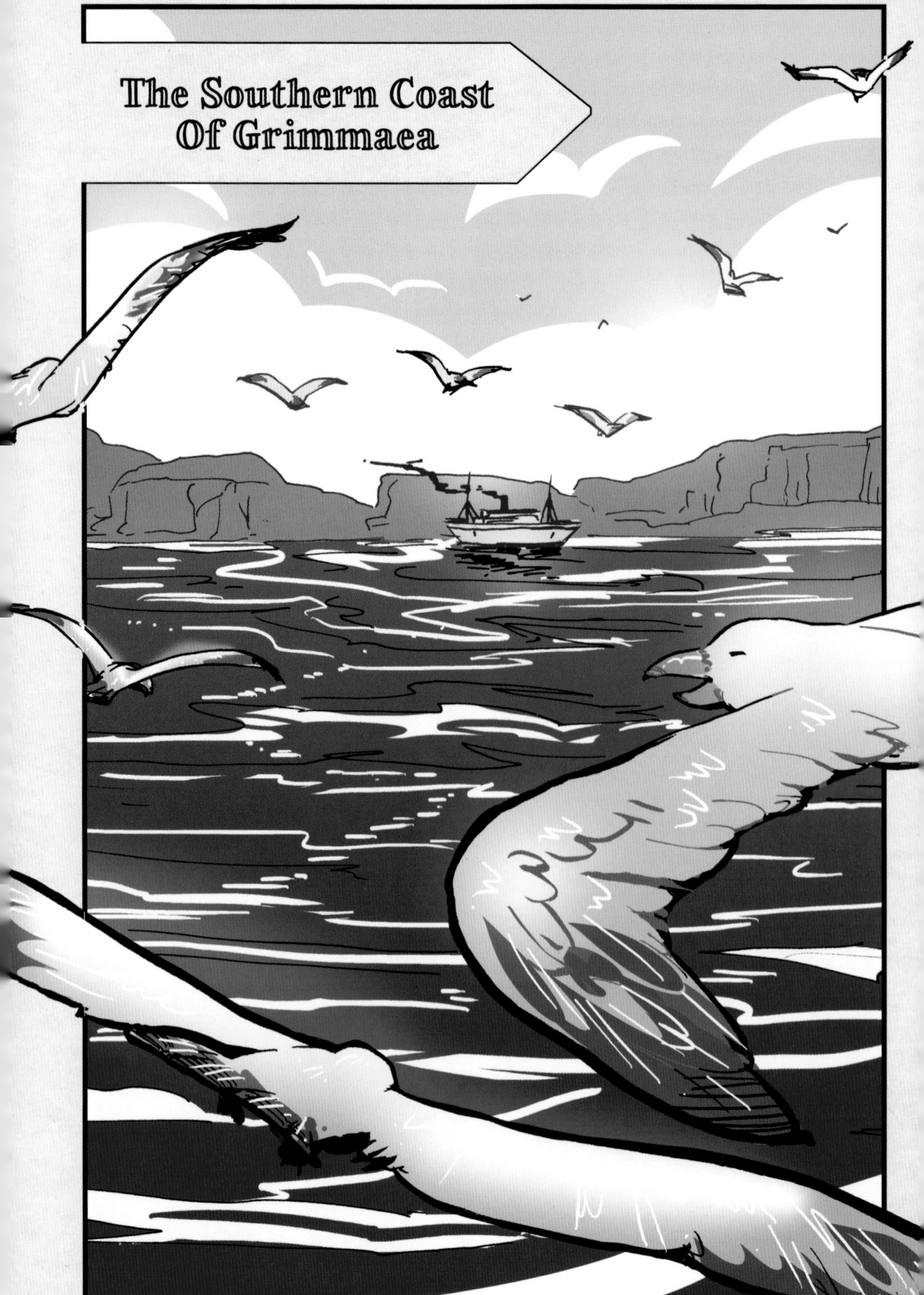
The Southern Coast Of Grimmaea

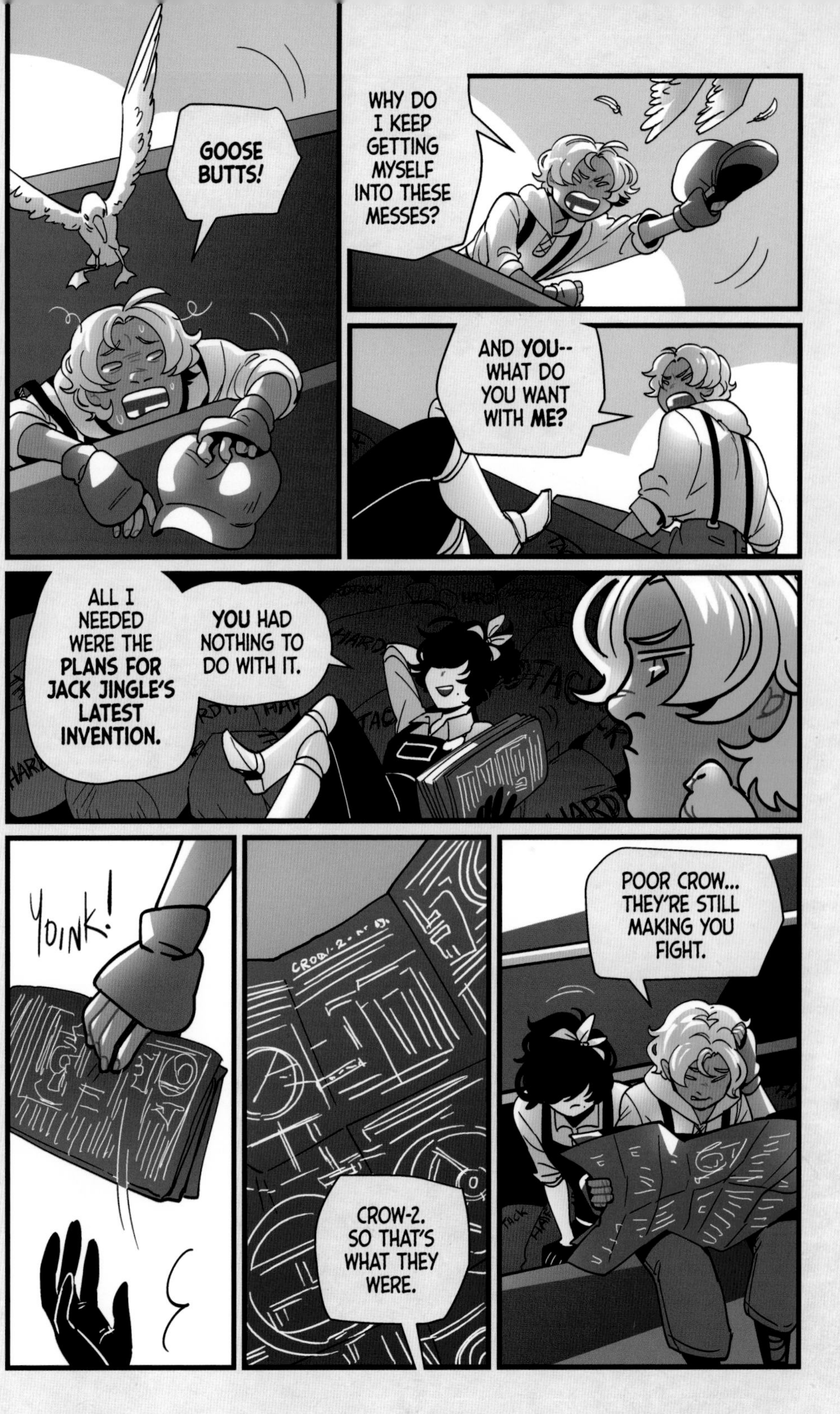
GOOSE BUTTS!
WHY DO I KEEP GETTING MYSELF INTO THESE MESSES?
AND YOU-- WHAT DO YOU WANT WITH ME?
ALL I NEEDED WERE THE PLANS FOR JACK JINGLE'S LATEST INVENTION.
YOU HAD NOTHING TO DO WITH IT.
YOINK!
CROW-2.
CROW-2. SO THAT'S WHAT THEY WERE.
POOR CROW... THEY'RE STILL MAKING YOU FIGHT.

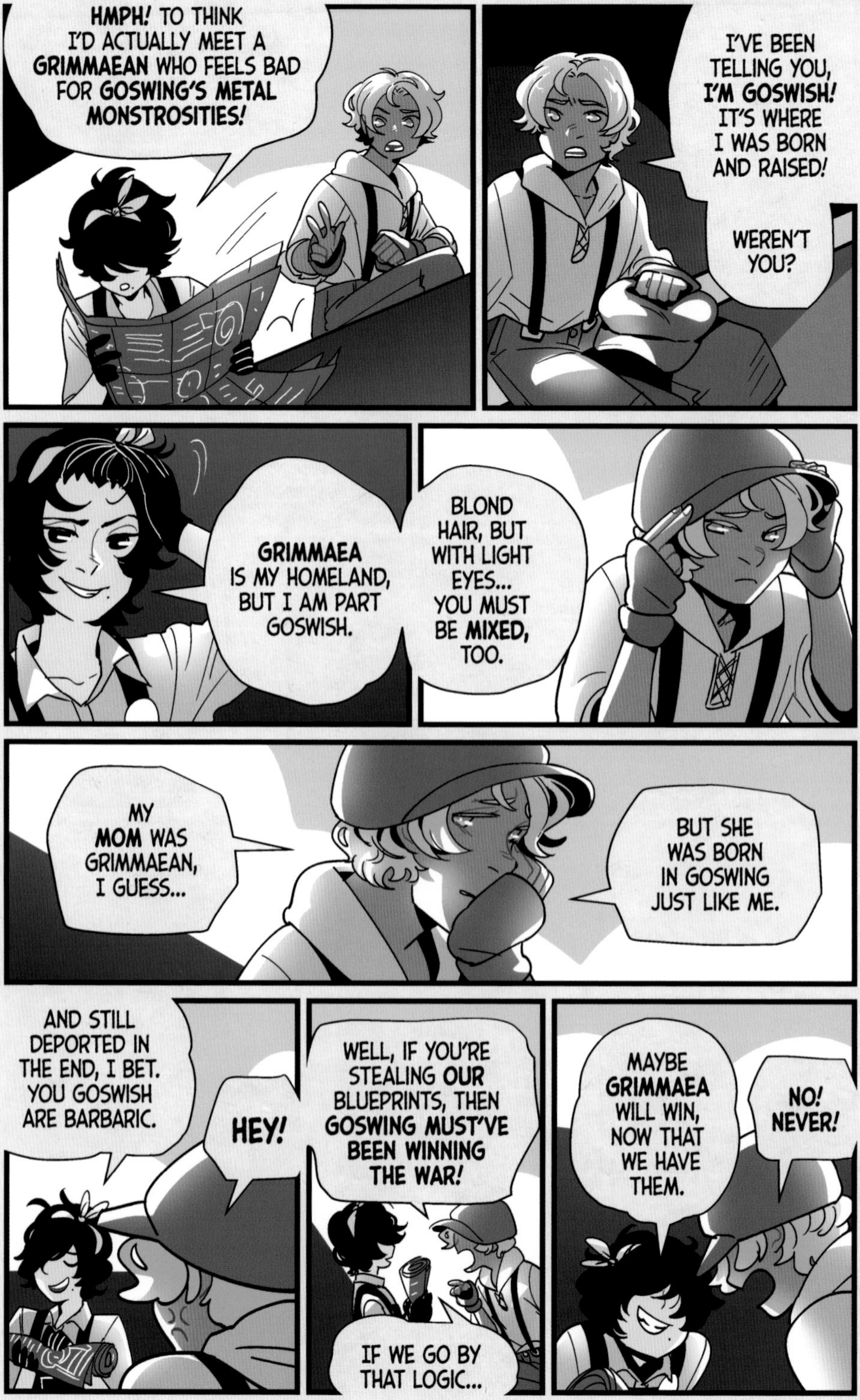
HMPH! TO THINK I'D ACTUALLY MEET A GRIMMAEAN WHO FEELS BAD FOR GOSWING'S METAL MONSTROSITIES!
I'VE BEEN TELLING YOU, I'M GOSWISH! IT'S WHERE I WAS BORN AND RAISED!
WEREN'T YOU?
GRIMMAEA IS MY HOMELAND, BUT I AM PART GOSWISH.
BLOND HAIR, BUT WITH LIGHT EYES... YOU MUST BE MIXED, TOO.
MY MOM WAS GRIMMAEAN, I GUESS...
BUT SHE WAS BORN IN GOSWING JUST LIKE ME.
AND STILL DEPORTED IN THE END, I BET. YOU GOSWISH ARE BARBARIC.
HEY!
WELL, IF YOU'RE STEALING OUR BLUEPRINTS, THEN GOSWING MUST'VE BEEN WINNING THE WAR!
IF WE GO BY THAT LOGIC...
MAYBE GRIMMAEA WILL WIN, NOW THAT WE HAVE THEM.
NO! NEVER!

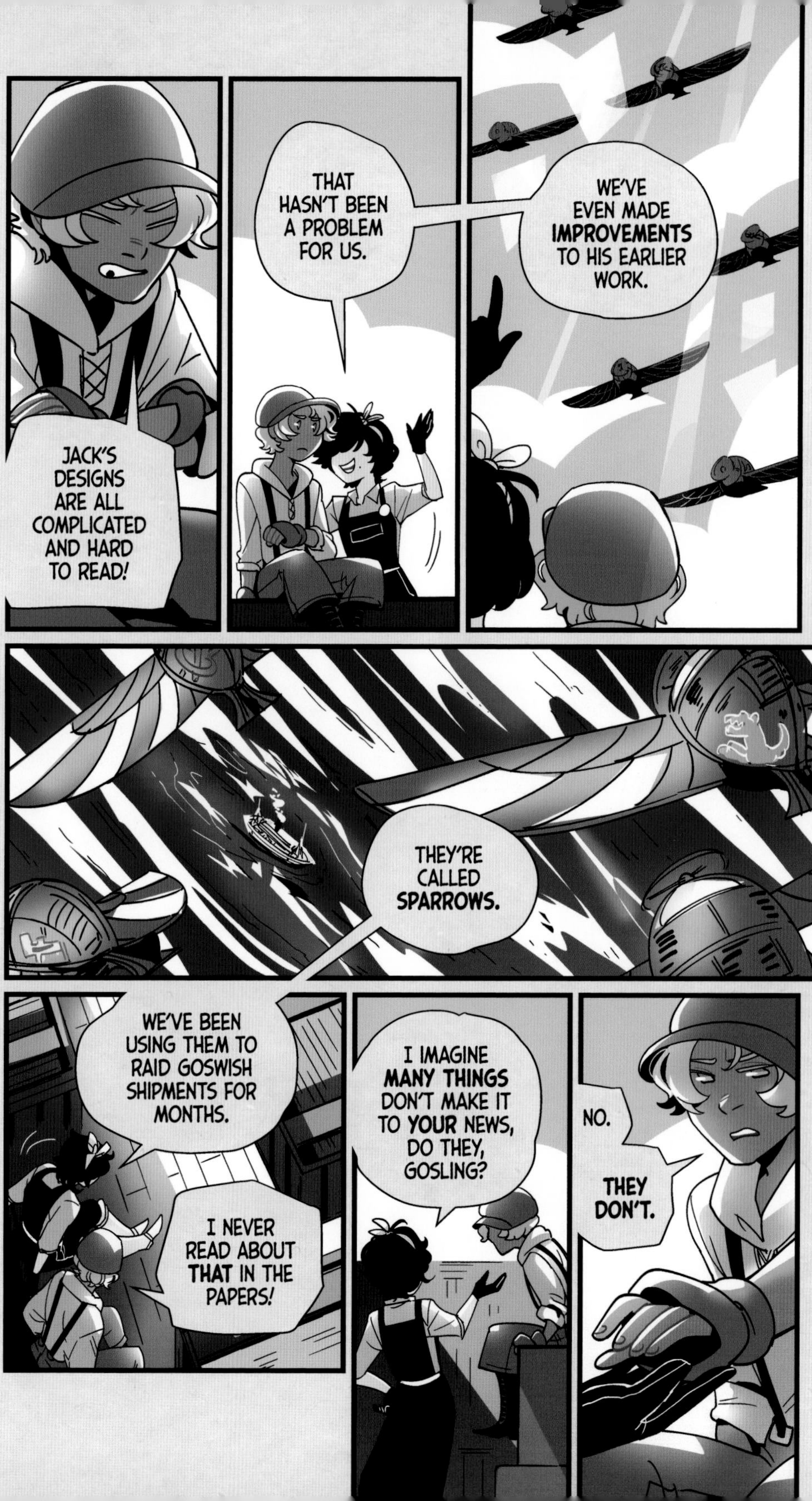
JACK'S DESIGNS ARE ALL COMPLICATED AND HARD TO READ!
THAT HASN'T BEEN A PROBLEM FOR US.
WE'VE EVEN MADE **IMPROVEMENTS** TO HIS EARLIER WORK.
THEY'RE CALLED **SPARROWS.**
WE'VE BEEN USING THEM TO RAID GOSWISH SHIPMENTS FOR MONTHS.
I NEVER READ ABOUT **THAT** IN THE PAPERS!
I IMAGINE **MANY THINGS** DON'T MAKE IT TO **YOUR** NEWS, DO THEY, GOSLING?
NO.
THEY DON'T.

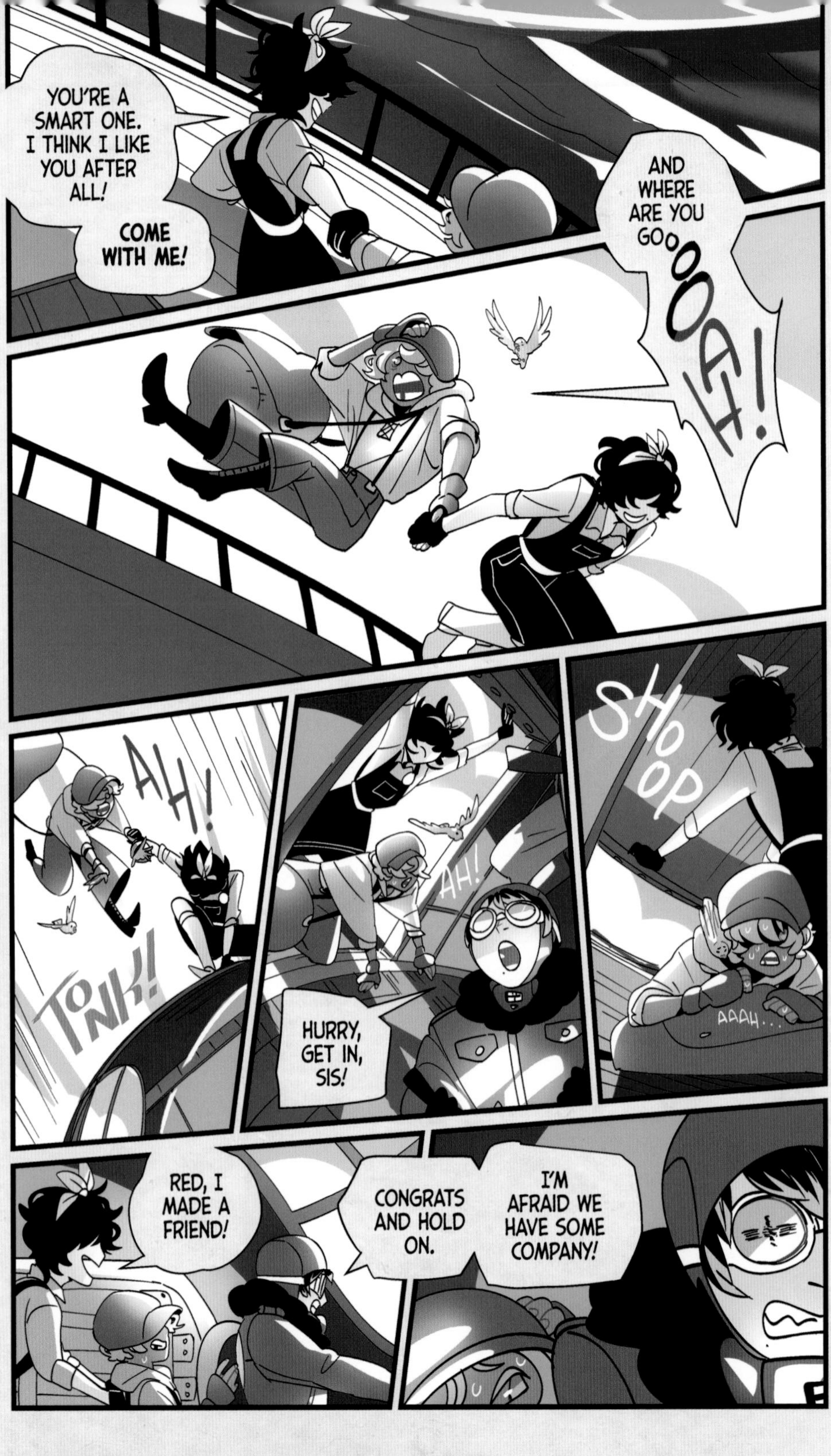
YOU'RE A SMART ONE. I THINK I LIKE YOU AFTER ALL!
COME WITH ME!
AND WHERE ARE YOU GOoOOAH!
AH!
TONK!
AH!
HURRY, GET IN, SIS!
SHOOP
AAAH...
RED, I MADE A FRIEND!
CONGRATS AND HOLD ON.
I'M AFRAID WE HAVE SOME COMPANY!

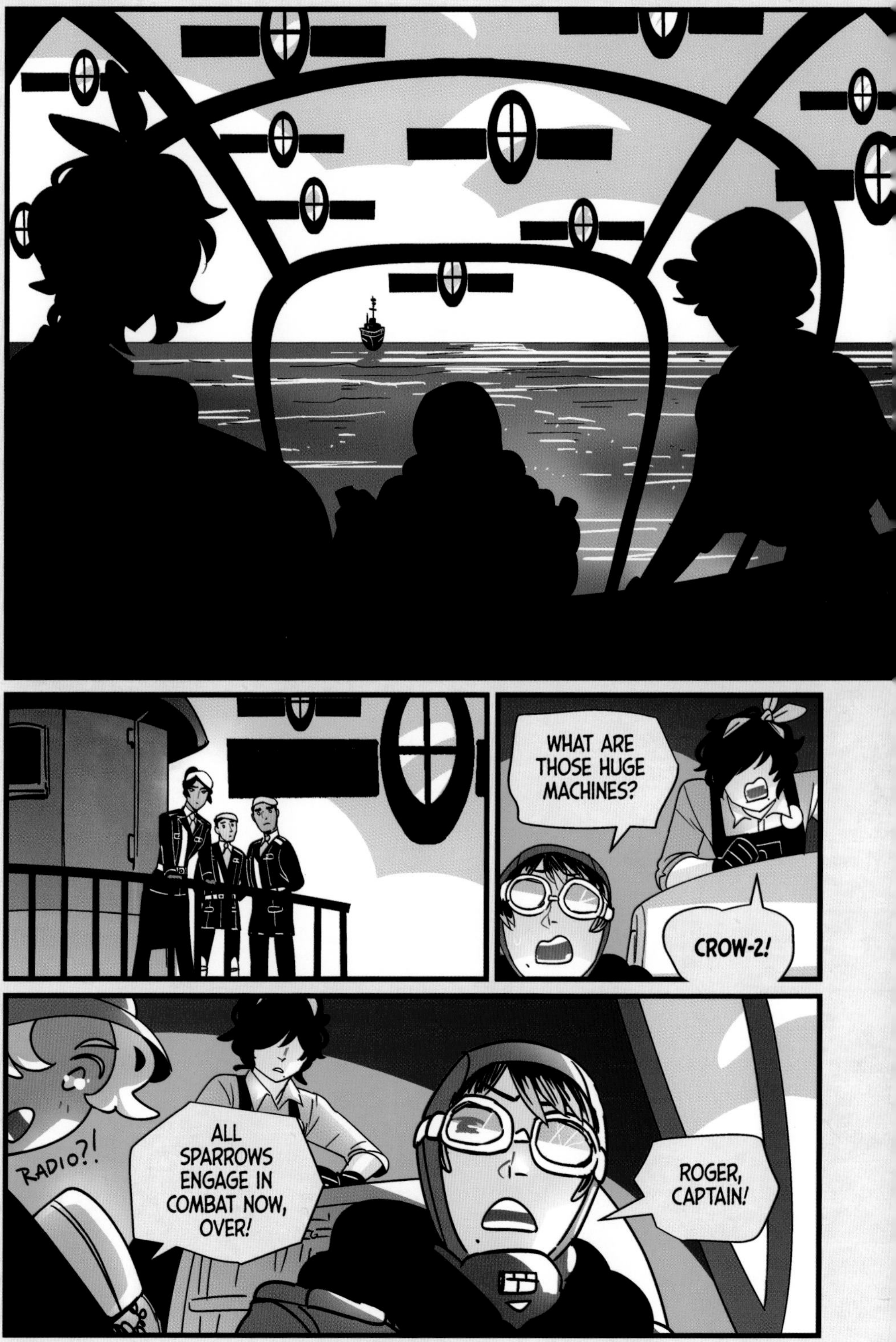
WHAT ARE THOSE HUGE MACHINES?
CROW-2!
RADIO?!
ALL SPARROWS ENGAGE IN COMBAT NOW, OVER!
ROGER, CAPTAIN!

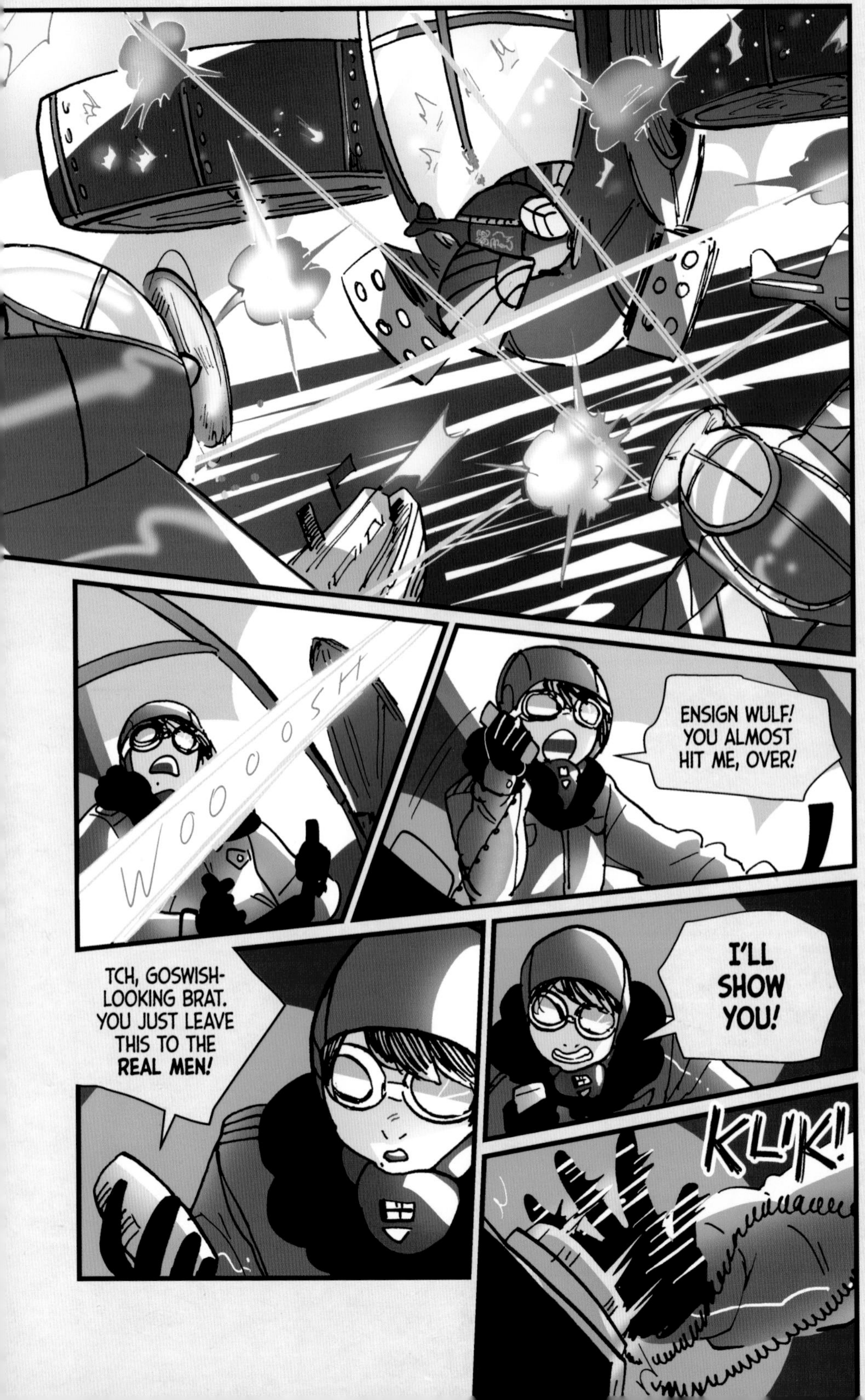
WOOOOOSH
ENSIGN WULF! YOU ALMOST HIT ME, OVER!
TCH, GOSWISH-LOOKING BRAT. YOU JUST LEAVE THIS TO THE **REAL MEN!**
I'LL SHOW YOU!
KLIK!

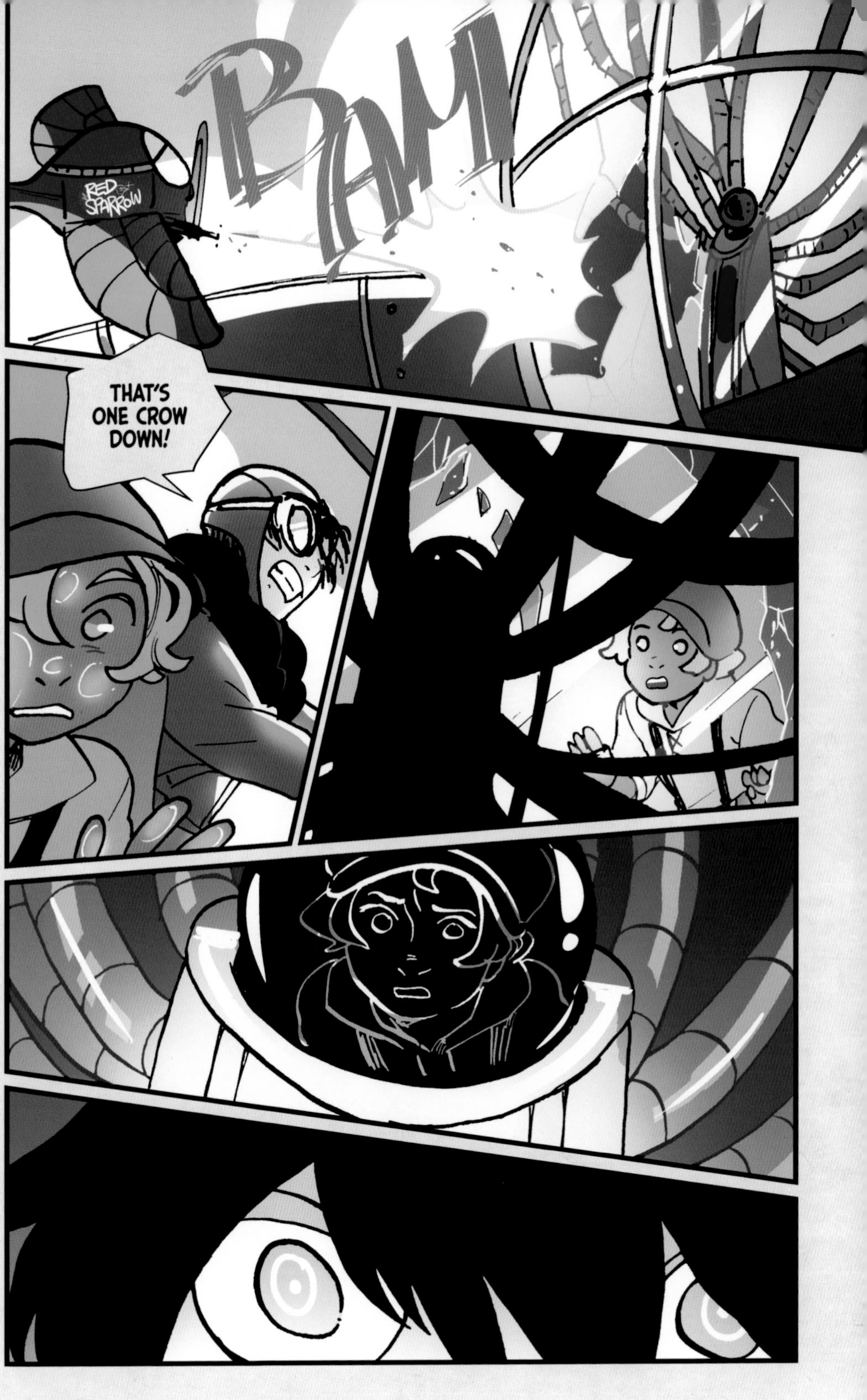
BAM!
RED SPARROW
THAT'S ONE CROW DOWN!

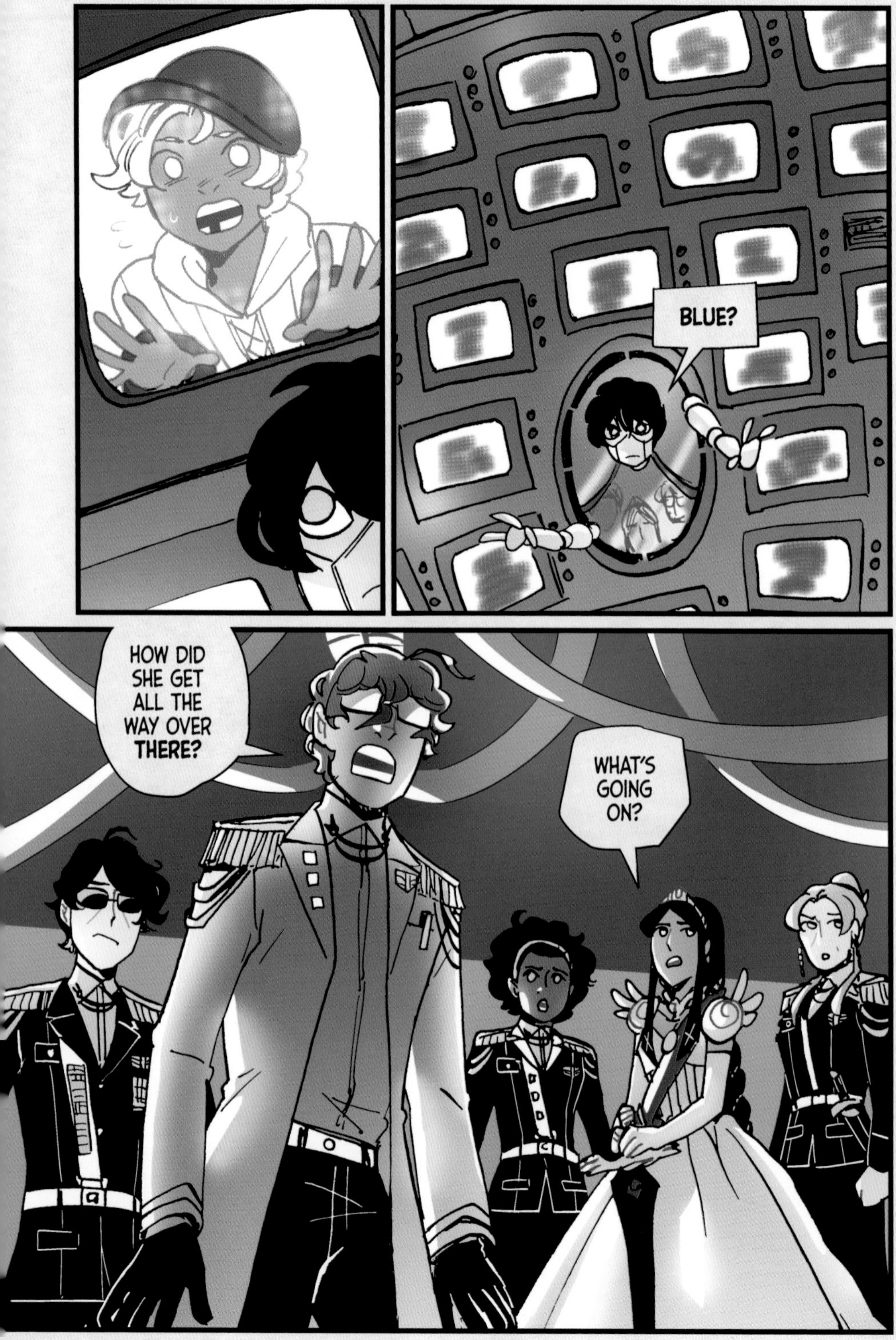
BLUE?
HOW DID SHE GET ALL THE WAY OVER THERE?
WHAT'S GOING ON?

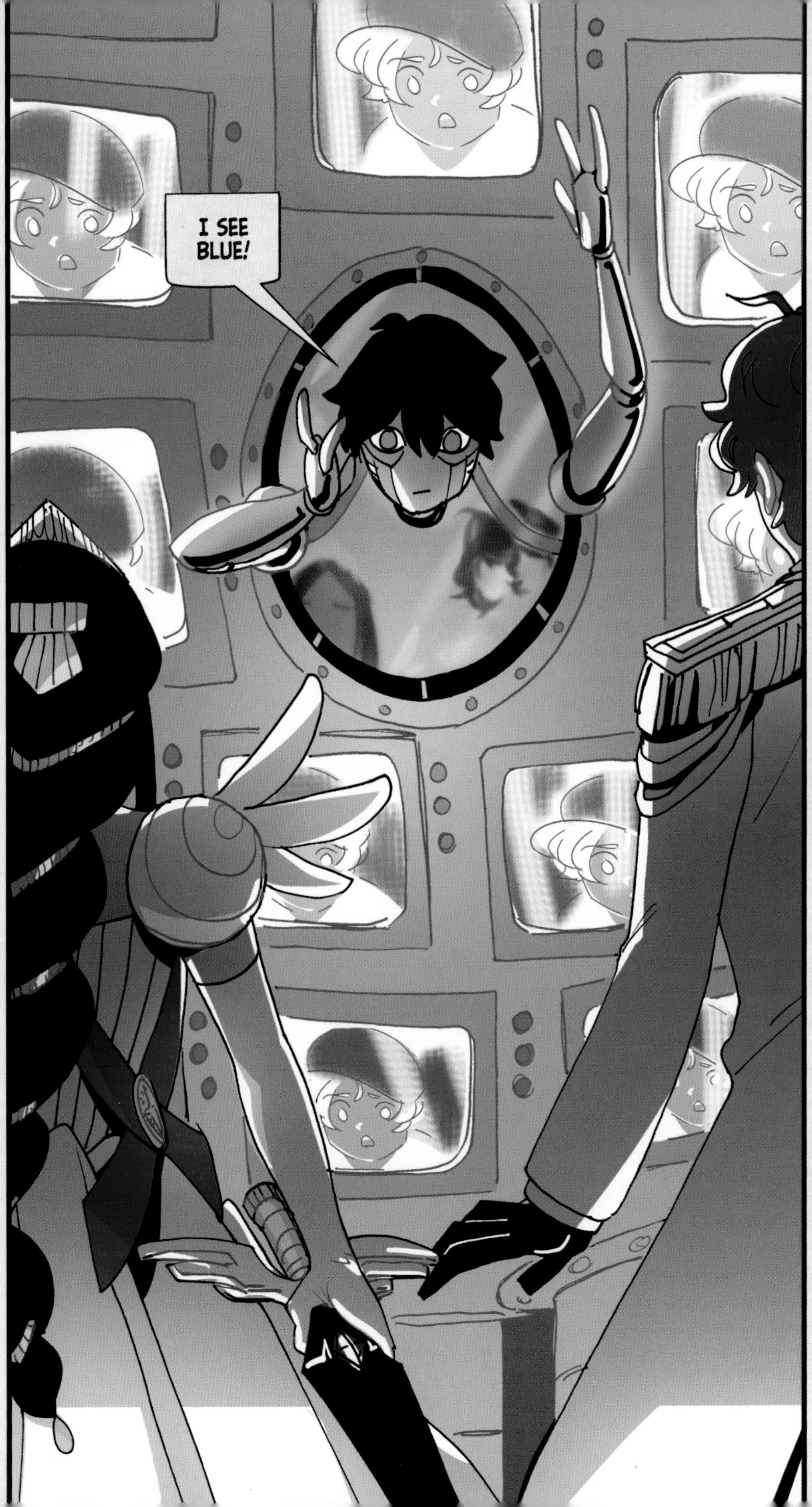
I SEE BLUE!

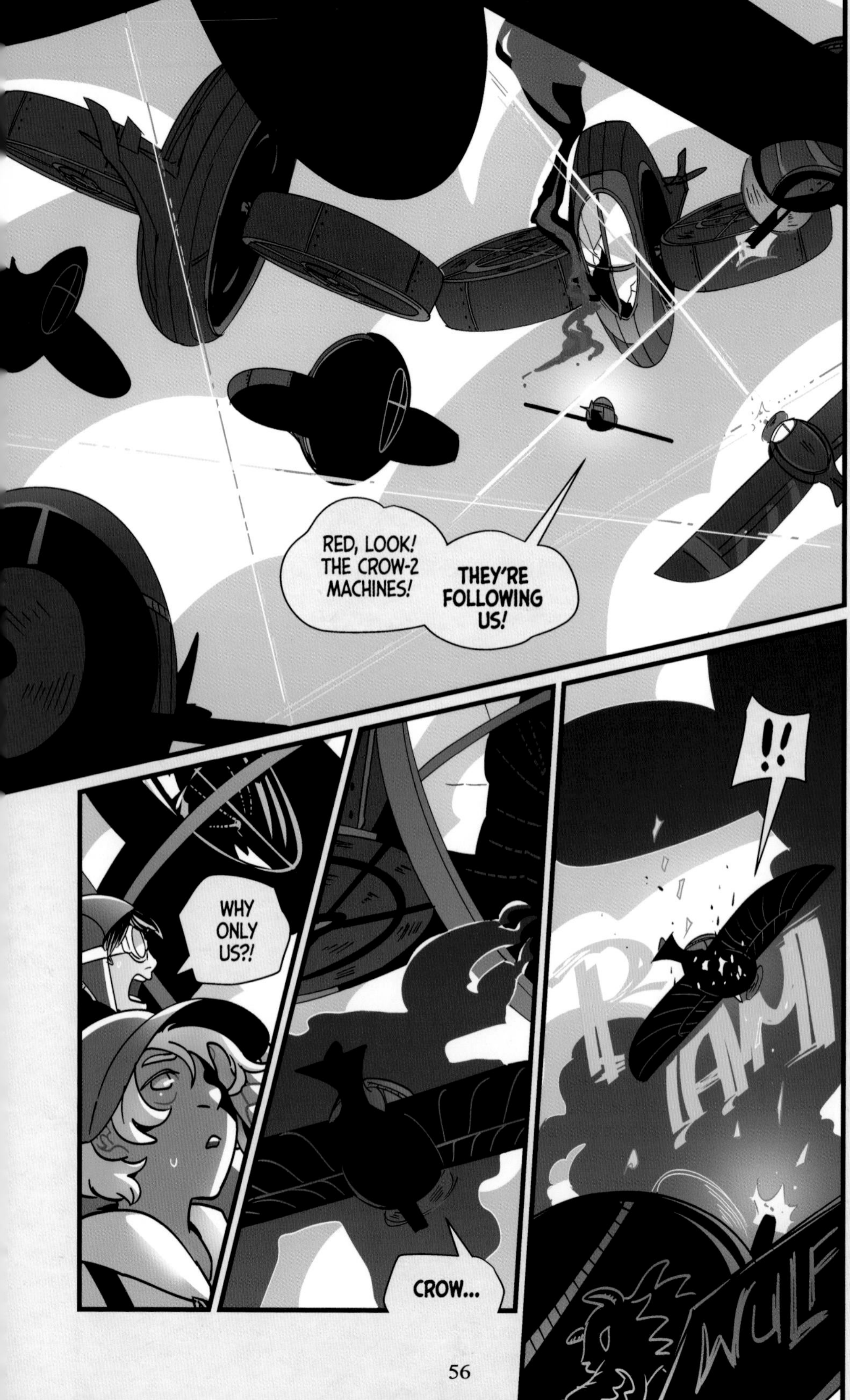
RED, LOOK! THE CROW-2 MACHINES!
THEY'RE FOLLOWING US!
WHY ONLY US?!
CROW...
!!
BLAM
WULF

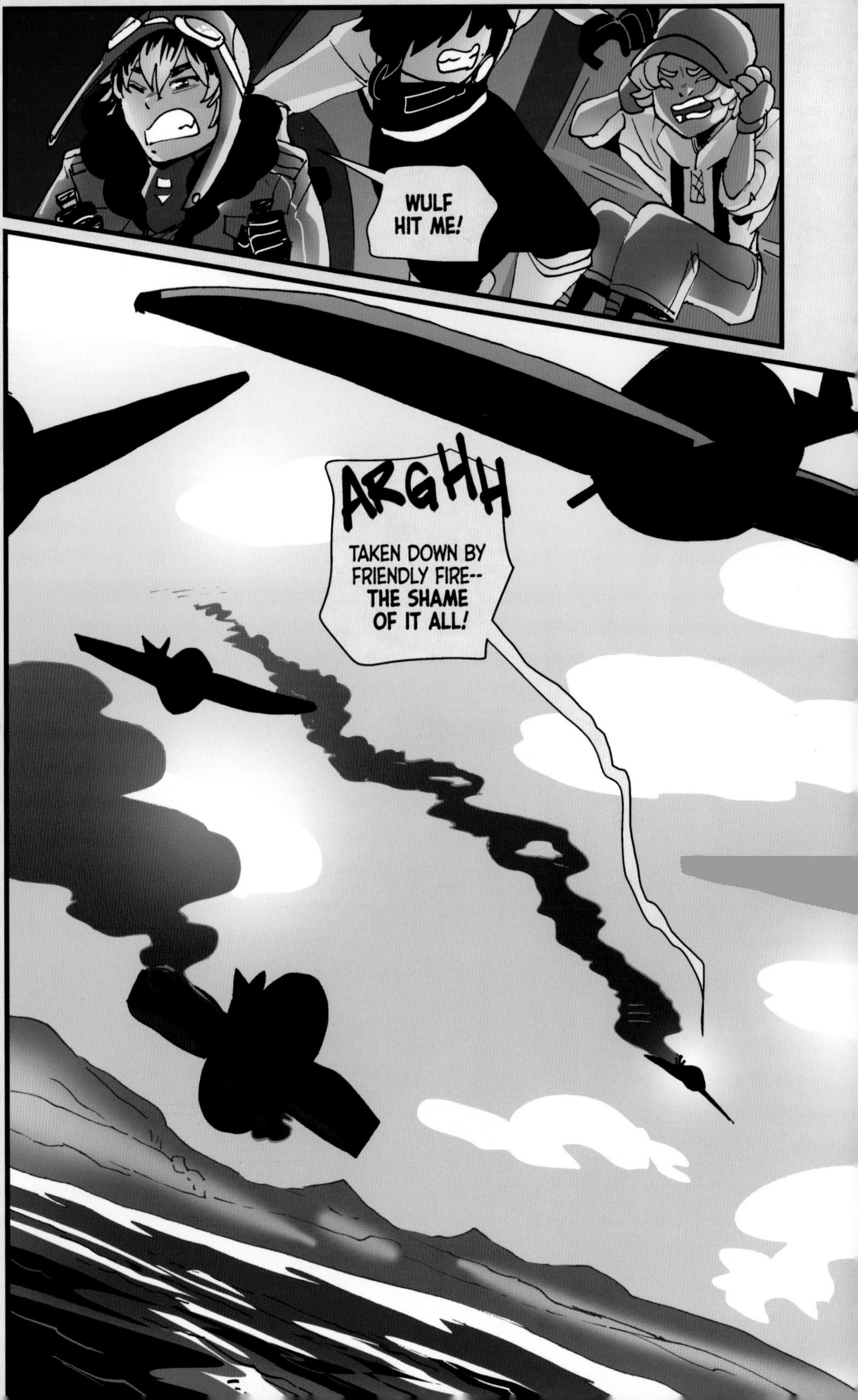
WULF HIT ME!
ARGHH
TAKEN DOWN BY FRIENDLY FIRE-- THE SHAME OF IT ALL!

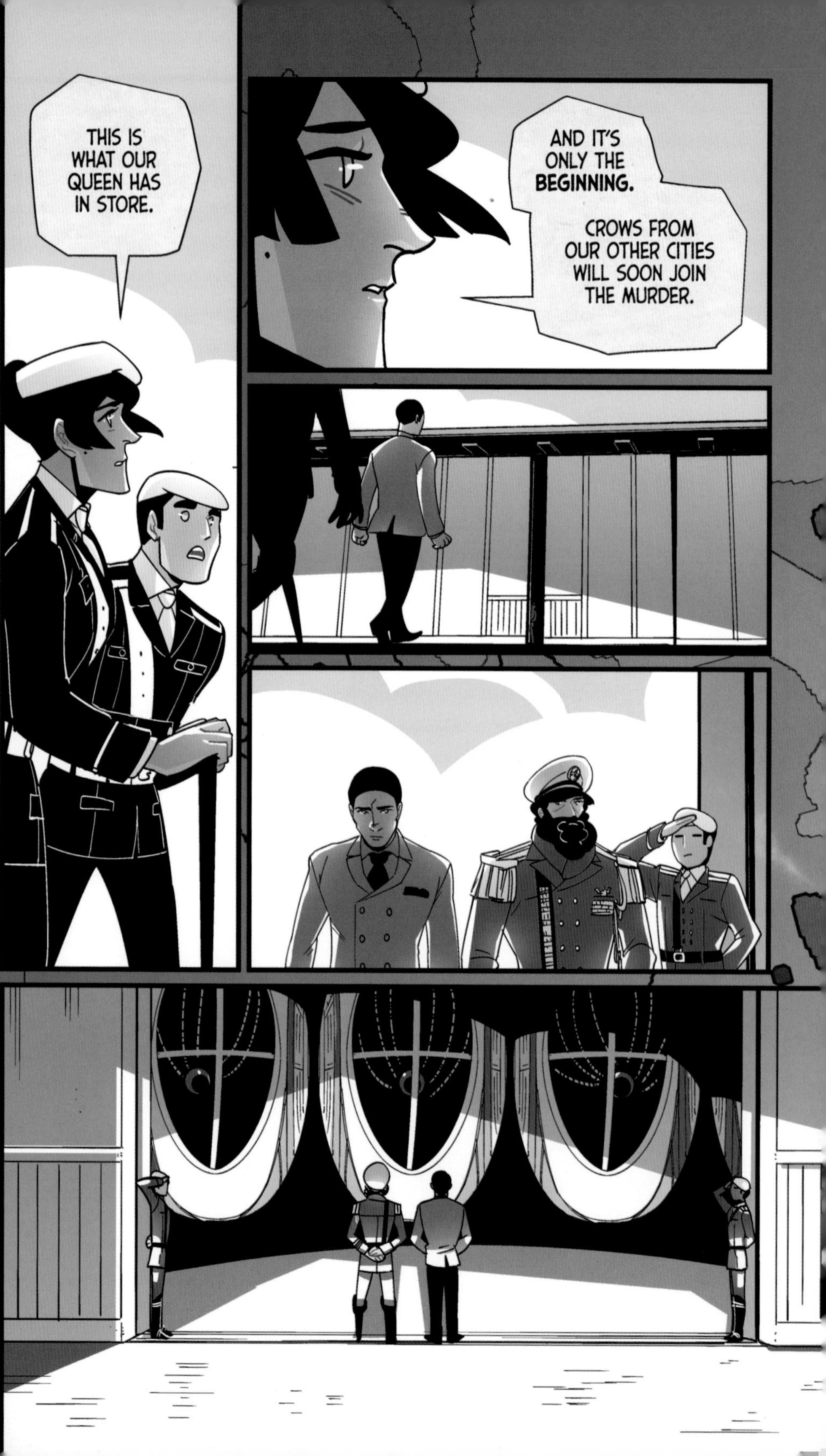
THIS IS WHAT OUR QUEEN HAS IN STORE.
AND IT'S ONLY THE BEGINNING.
CROWS FROM OUR OTHER CITIES WILL SOON JOIN THE MURDER.

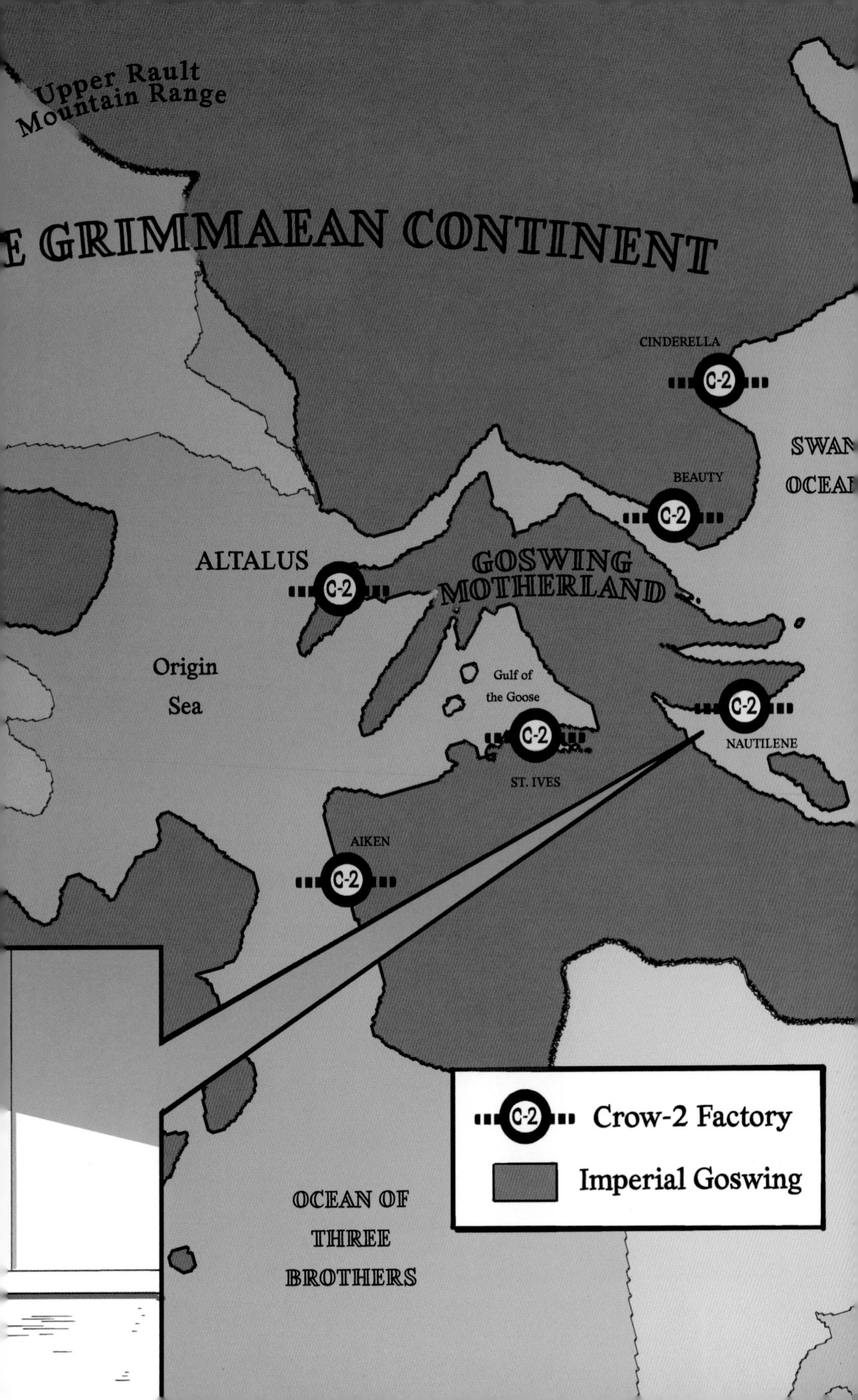
Upper Rault Mountain Range
E GRIMMAEAN CONTINENT
CINDERELLA
BEAUTY
SWAN
OCEA
ALTALUS
GOSWING MOTHERLAND
Origin Sea
Gulf of the Goose
ST. IVES
NAUTILENE
AIKEN
C-2
Crow-2 Factory
Imperial Goswing
OCEAN OF THREE BROTHERS

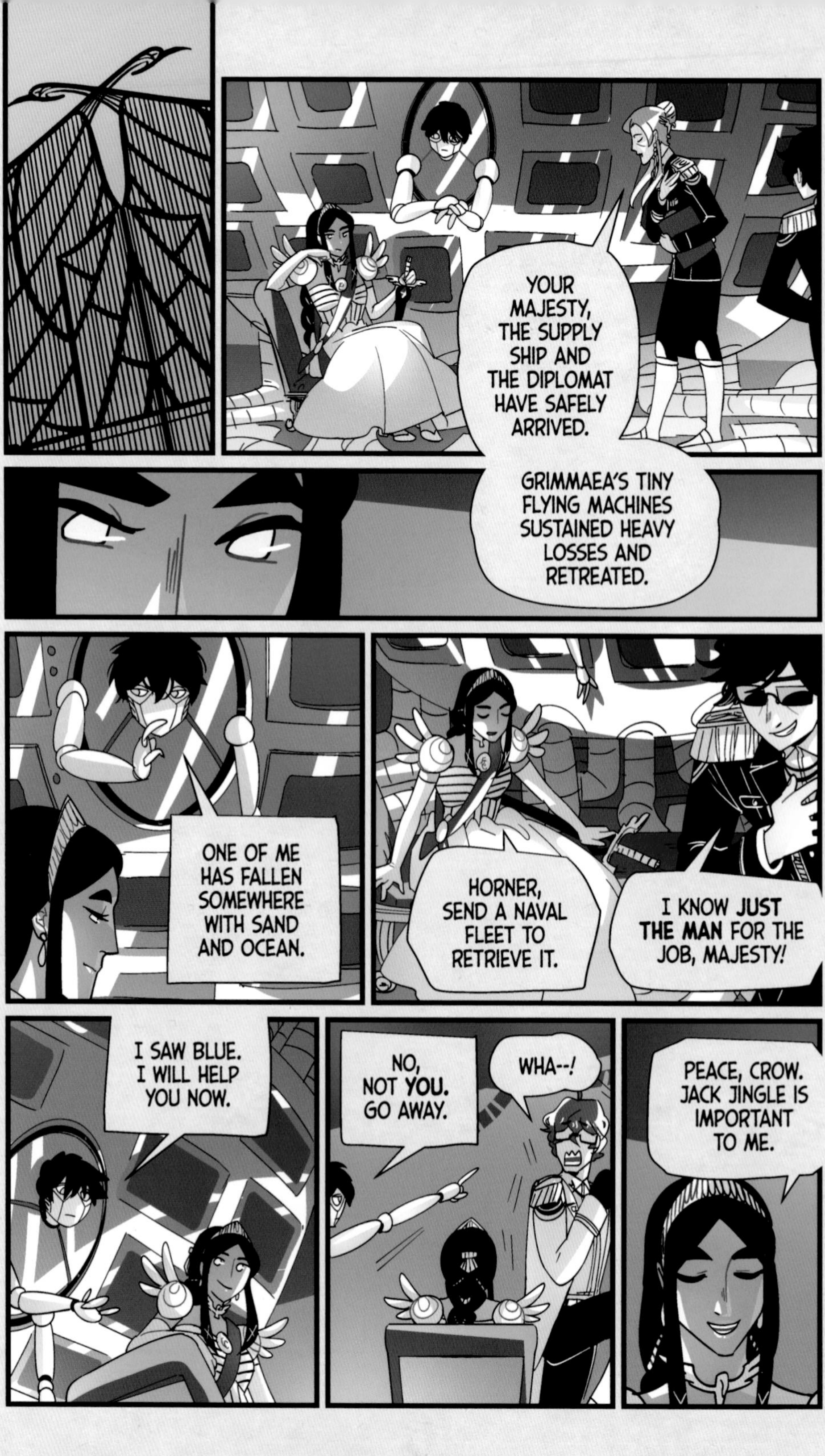
YOUR MAJESTY, THE SUPPLY SHIP AND THE DIPLOMAT HAVE SAFELY ARRIVED.
GRIMMAEA'S TINY FLYING MACHINES SUSTAINED HEAVY LOSSES AND RETREATED.
ONE OF ME HAS FALLEN SOMEWHERE WITH SAND AND OCEAN.
HORNER, SEND A NAVAL FLEET TO RETRIEVE IT.
I KNOW **JUST THE MAN** FOR THE JOB, MAJESTY!
I SAW BLUE. I WILL HELP YOU NOW.
NO, NOT **YOU.** GO AWAY.
WHA--!
PEACE, CROW. JACK JINGLE IS IMPORTANT TO ME.

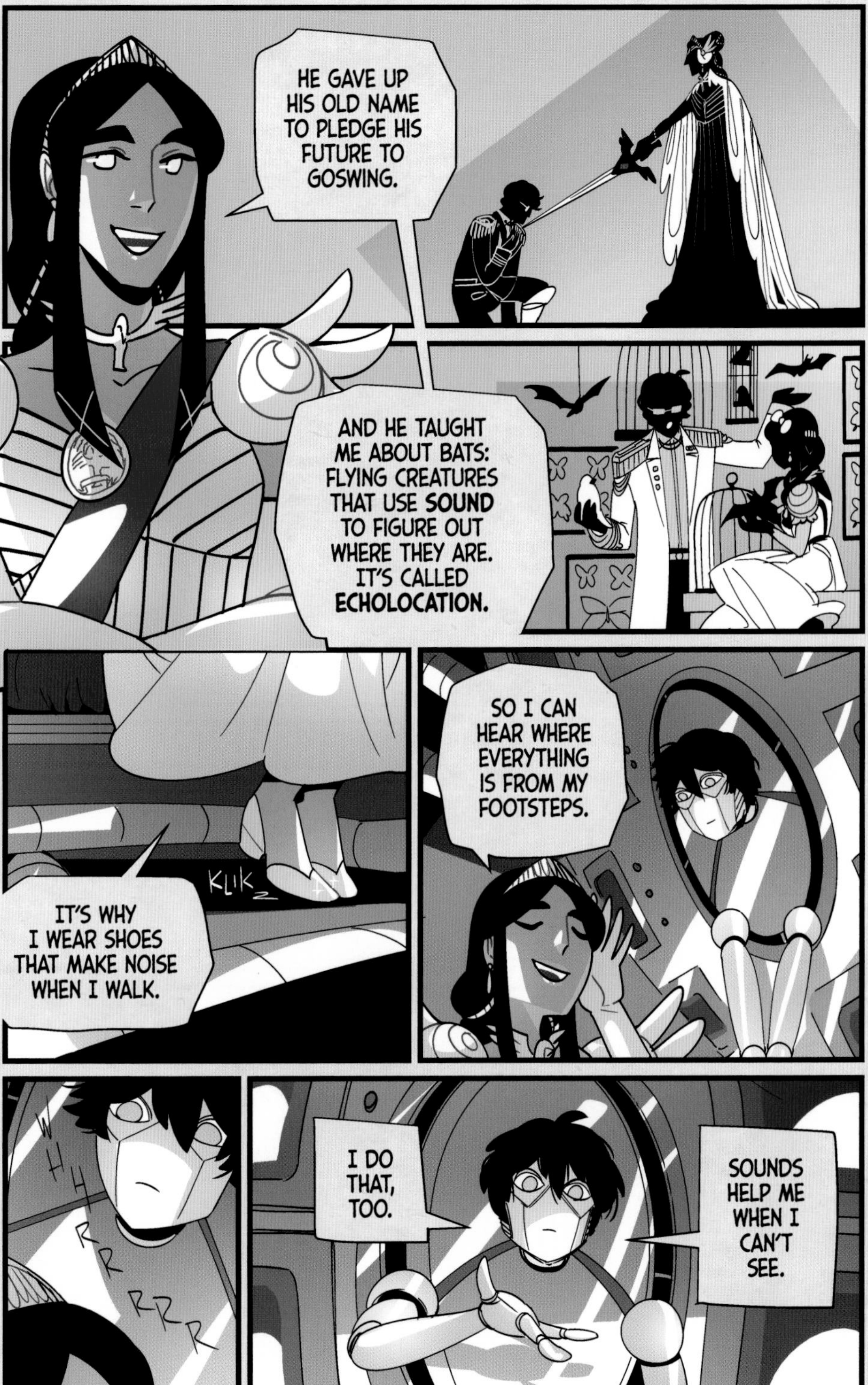
HE GAVE UP HIS OLD NAME TO PLEDGE HIS FUTURE TO GOSWING.
AND HE TAUGHT ME ABOUT BATS: FLYING CREATURES THAT USE **SOUND** TO FIGURE OUT WHERE THEY ARE. IT'S CALLED **ECHOLOCATION.**
KLIK
IT'S WHY I WEAR SHOES THAT MAKE NOISE WHEN I WALK.
SO I CAN HEAR WHERE EVERYTHING IS FROM MY FOOTSTEPS.
WHHRRRRR
I DO THAT, TOO.
SOUNDS HELP ME WHEN I CAN'T SEE.

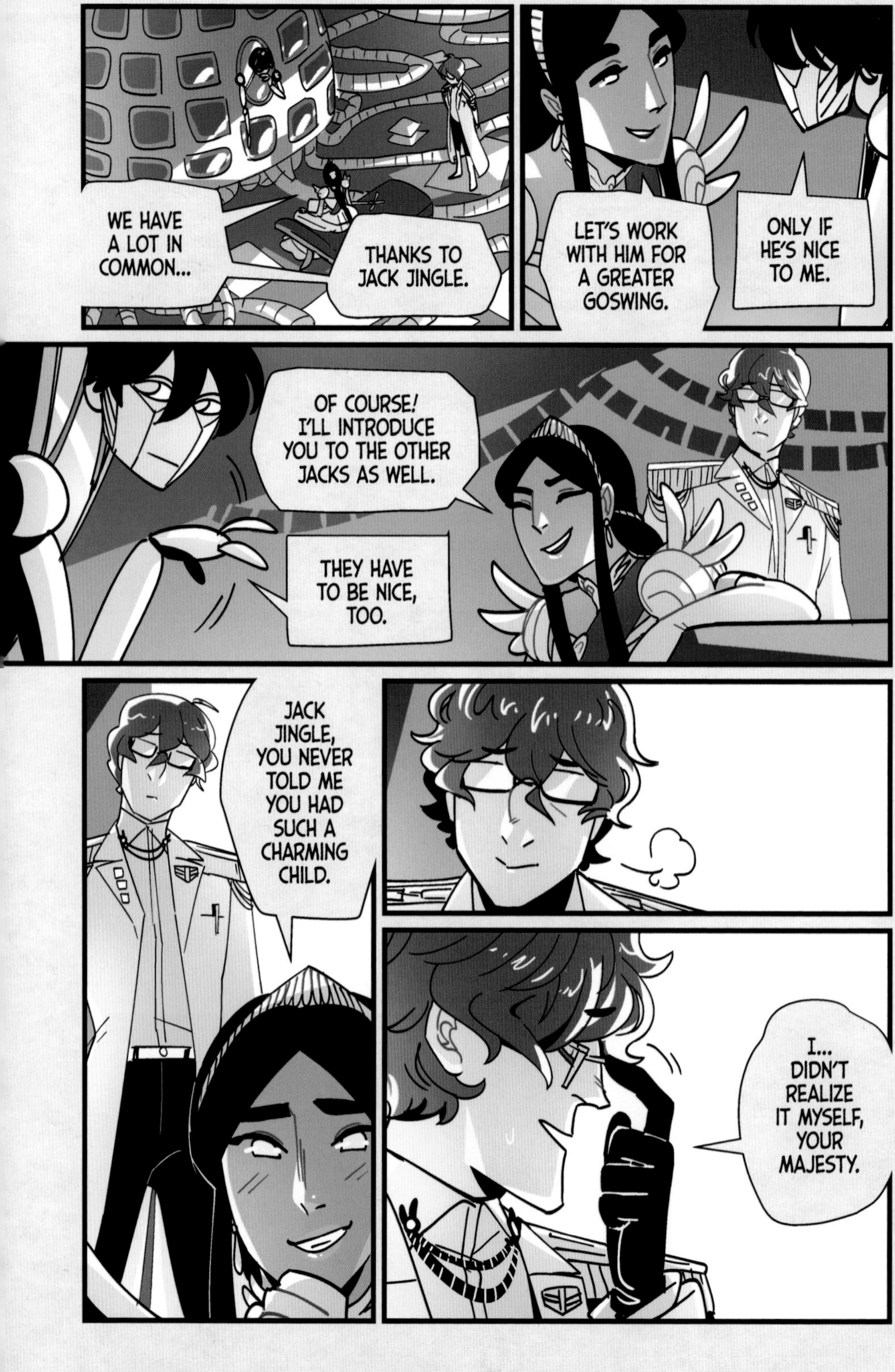
WE HAVE A LOT IN COMMON...
THANKS TO JACK JINGLE.
LET'S WORK WITH HIM FOR A GREATER GOSWING.
ONLY IF HE'S NICE TO ME.
OF COURSE! I'LL INTRODUCE YOU TO THE OTHER JACKS AS WELL.
THEY HAVE TO BE NICE, TOO.
JACK JINGLE, YOU NEVER TOLD ME YOU HAD SUCH A CHARMING CHILD.
I... DIDN'T REALIZE IT MYSELF, YOUR MAJESTY.

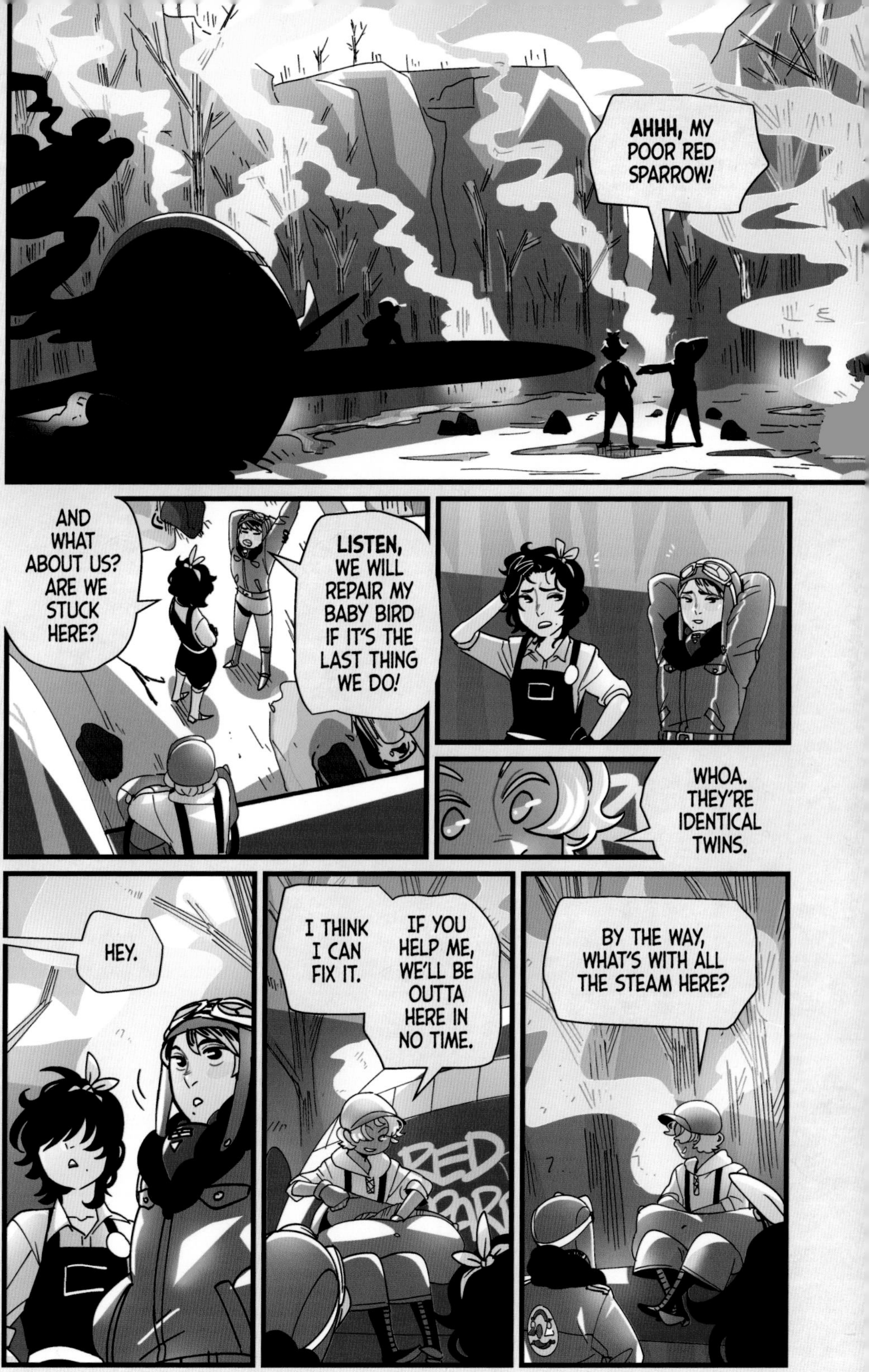
AHHH, MY POOR RED SPARROW!
AND WHAT ABOUT US? ARE WE STUCK HERE?
LISTEN, WE WILL REPAIR MY BABY BIRD IF IT'S THE LAST THING WE DO!
WHOA. THEY'RE IDENTICAL TWINS.
HEY.
I THINK I CAN FIX IT.
IF YOU HELP ME, WE'LL BE OUTTA HERE IN NO TIME.
BY THE WAY, WHAT'S WITH ALL THE STEAM HERE?

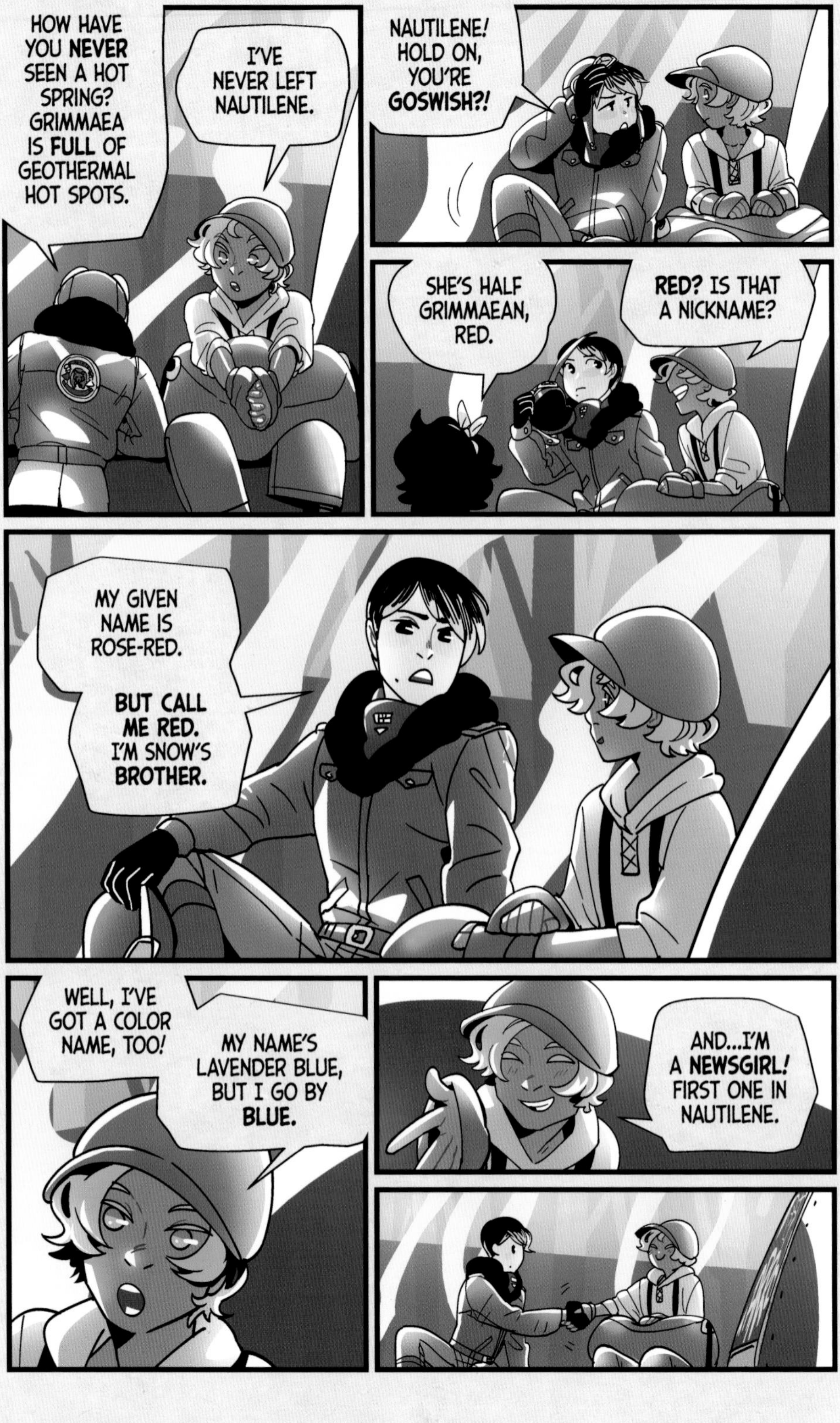
HOW HAVE YOU NEVER SEEN A HOT SPRING? GRIMMAEA IS FULL OF GEOTHERMAL HOT SPOTS.
I'VE NEVER LEFT NAUTILENE.
NAUTILENE! HOLD ON, YOU'RE GOSWISH?!
SHE'S HALF GRIMMAEAN, RED.
RED? IS THAT A NICKNAME?
MY GIVEN NAME IS ROSE-RED.
BUT CALL ME RED. I'M SNOW'S BROTHER.
WELL, I'VE GOT A COLOR NAME, TOO!
MY NAME'S LAVENDER BLUE, BUT I GO BY BLUE.
AND...I'M A NEWSGIRL! FIRST ONE IN NAUTILENE.

BLUE, THAT LOOKS **HEAVY!** DO YOU JUST CARRY IT AROUND WITH YOU?

MY TOOLS?

YEAH, I DIDN'T HAVE THEM ON ME **THIS ONE TIME,** AND I...

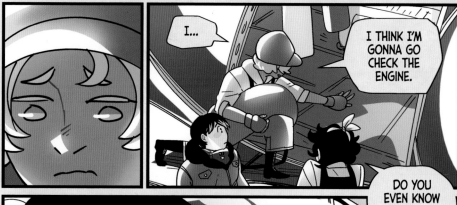

I...

I THINK I'M GONNA GO CHECK THE ENGINE.

DO YOU EVEN KNOW WHERE THE ENGINE IS--

FUME

KOFF

SURE. JACK JINGLE DESIGNED THIS THING, RIGHT?

WHAT DO YOU KNOW OF JACK?!

HMPH. I DIDN'T KNOW HIM AT ALL.

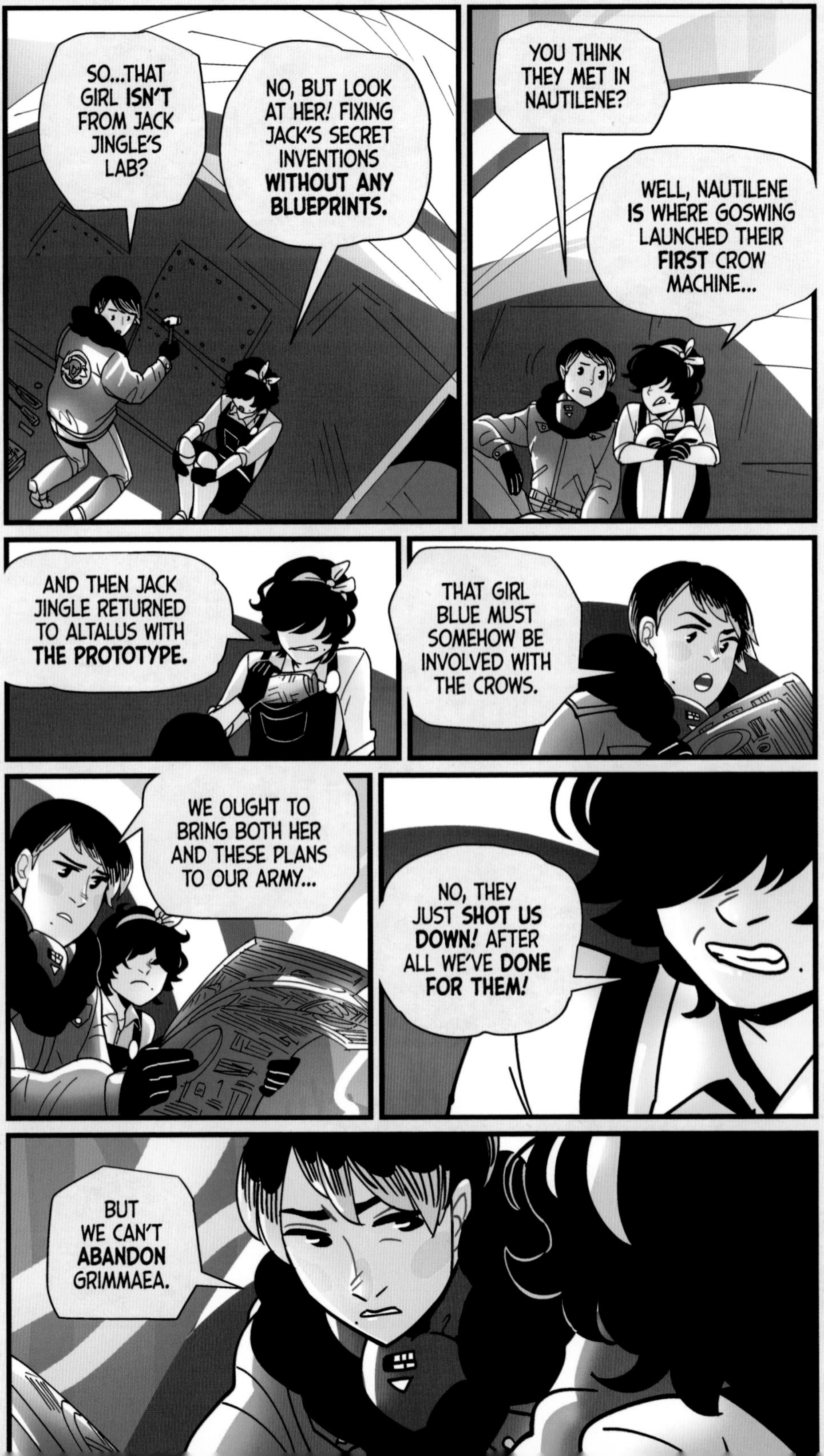
SO...THAT GIRL ISN'T FROM JACK JINGLE'S LAB?
NO, BUT LOOK AT HER! FIXING JACK'S SECRET INVENTIONS WITHOUT ANY BLUEPRINTS.
YOU THINK THEY MET IN NAUTILENE?
WELL, NAUTILENE IS WHERE GOSWING LAUNCHED THEIR FIRST CROW MACHINE...
AND THEN JACK JINGLE RETURNED TO ALTALUS WITH THE PROTOTYPE.
THAT GIRL BLUE MUST SOMEHOW BE INVOLVED WITH THE CROWS.
WE OUGHT TO BRING BOTH HER AND THESE PLANS TO OUR ARMY...
NO, THEY JUST SHOT US DOWN! AFTER ALL WE'VE DONE FOR THEM!
BUT WE CAN'T ABANDON GRIMMAEA.

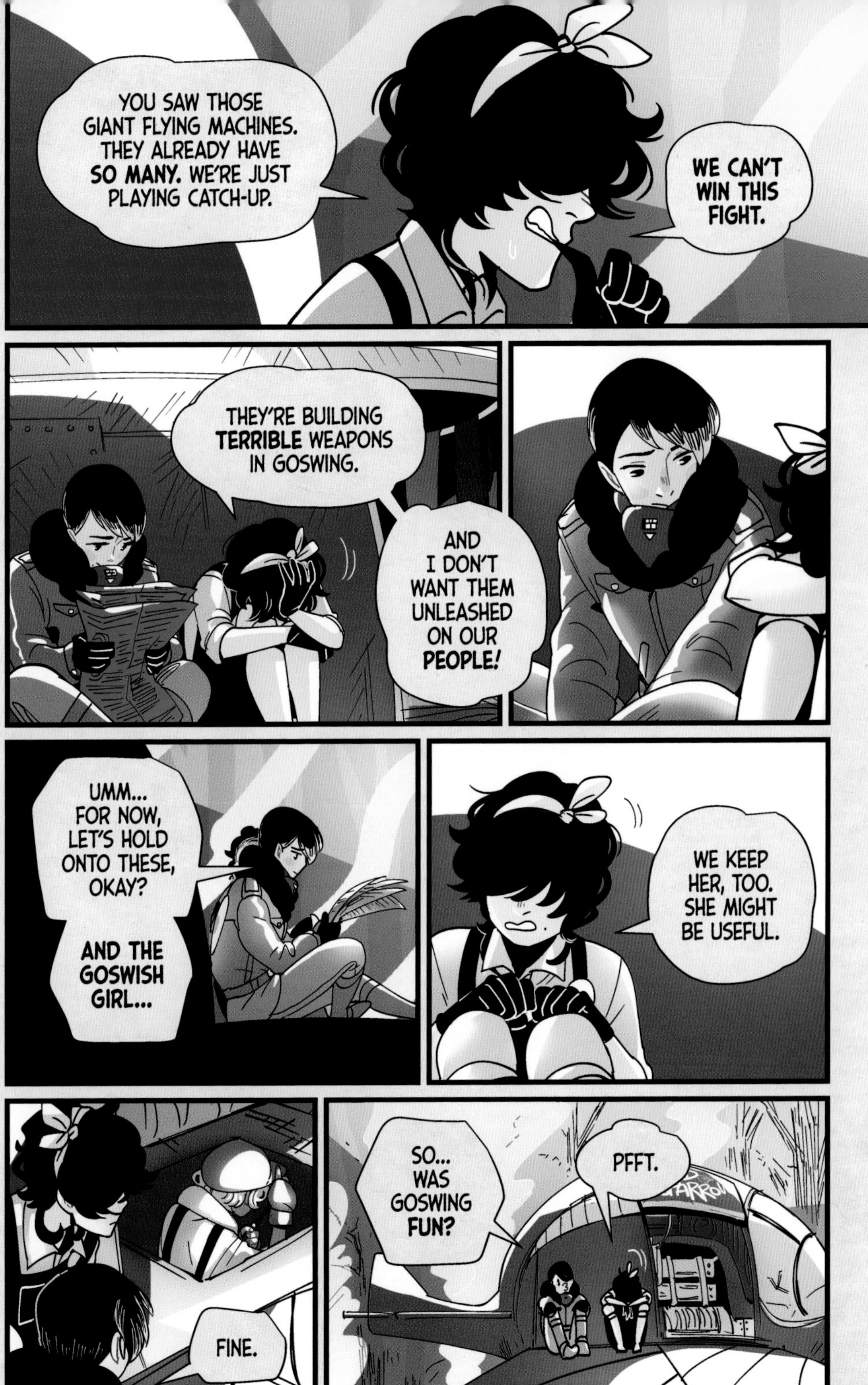
YOU SAW THOSE GIANT FLYING MACHINES. THEY ALREADY HAVE SO MANY. WE'RE JUST PLAYING CATCH-UP.
WE CAN'T WIN THIS FIGHT.
THEY'RE BUILDING TERRIBLE WEAPONS IN GOSWING.
AND I DON'T WANT THEM UNLEASHED ON OUR PEOPLE!
UMM... FOR NOW, LET'S HOLD ONTO THESE, OKAY?
AND THE GOSWISH GIRL...
WE KEEP HER, TOO. SHE MIGHT BE USEFUL.
FINE.
SO... WAS GOSWING FUN?
PFFT.

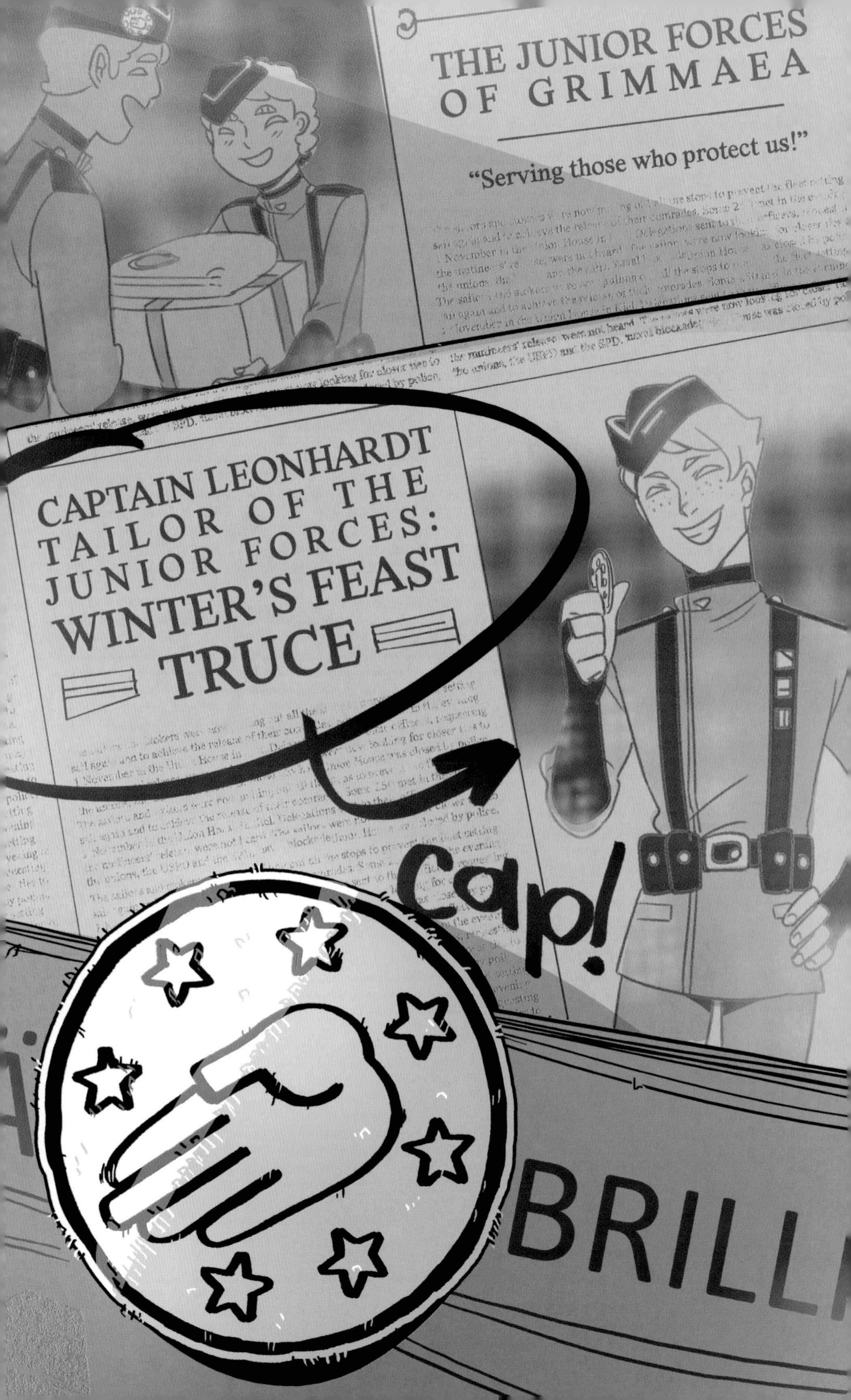
THE JUNIOR FORCES OF GRIMMAEA
"Serving those who protect us!"
CAPTAIN LEONHARDT TAILOR OF THE JUNIOR FORCES: WINTER'S FEAST TRUCE
Cap!
BRILL

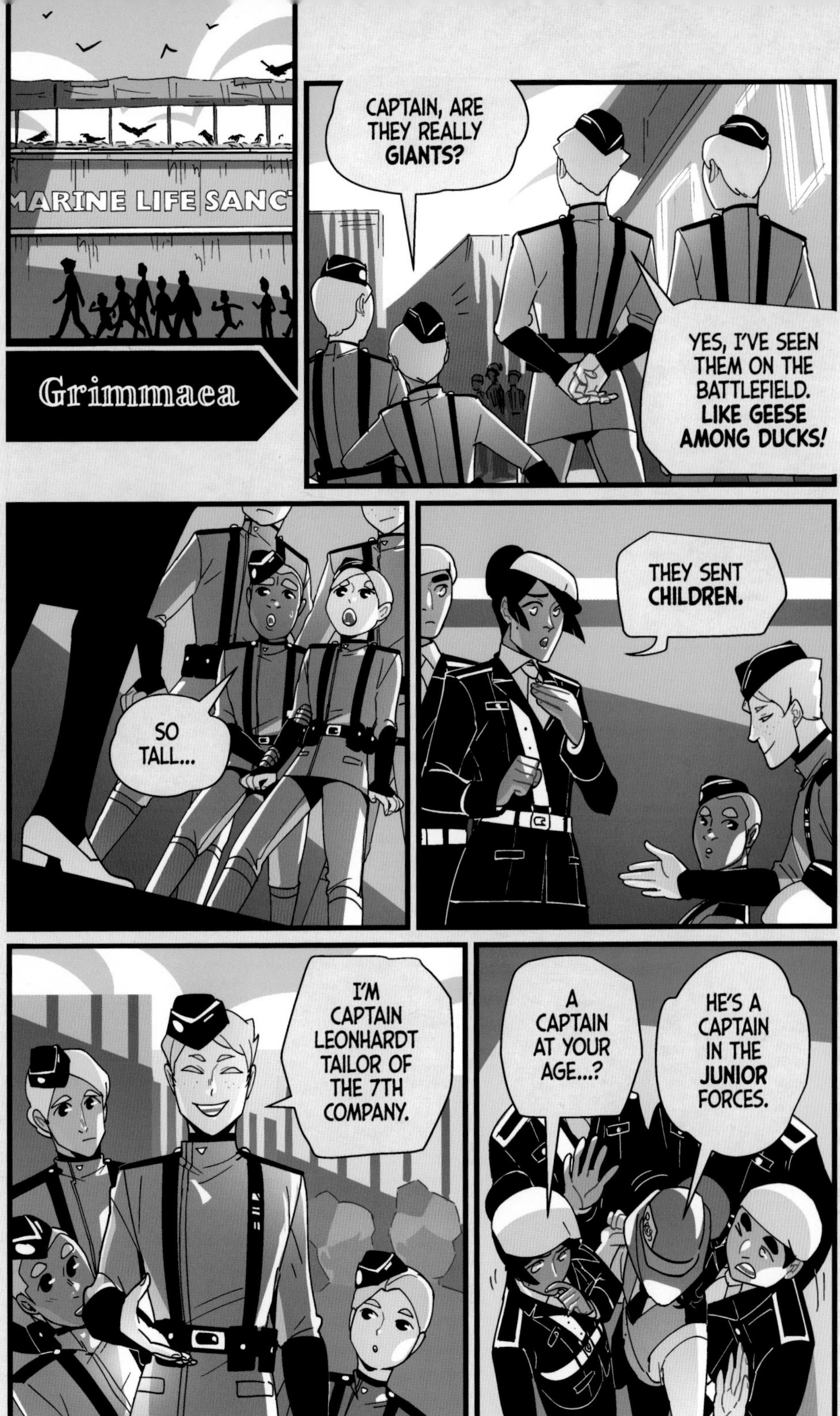
MARINE LIFE SANCT
Grimmaea
CAPTAIN, ARE THEY REALLY GIANTS?
YES, I'VE SEEN THEM ON THE BATTLEFIELD. LIKE GEESE AMONG DUCKS!
SO TALL...
THEY SENT CHILDREN.
I'M CAPTAIN LEONHARDT TAILOR OF THE 7TH COMPANY.
A CAPTAIN AT YOUR AGE...?
HE'S A CAPTAIN IN THE JUNIOR FORCES.

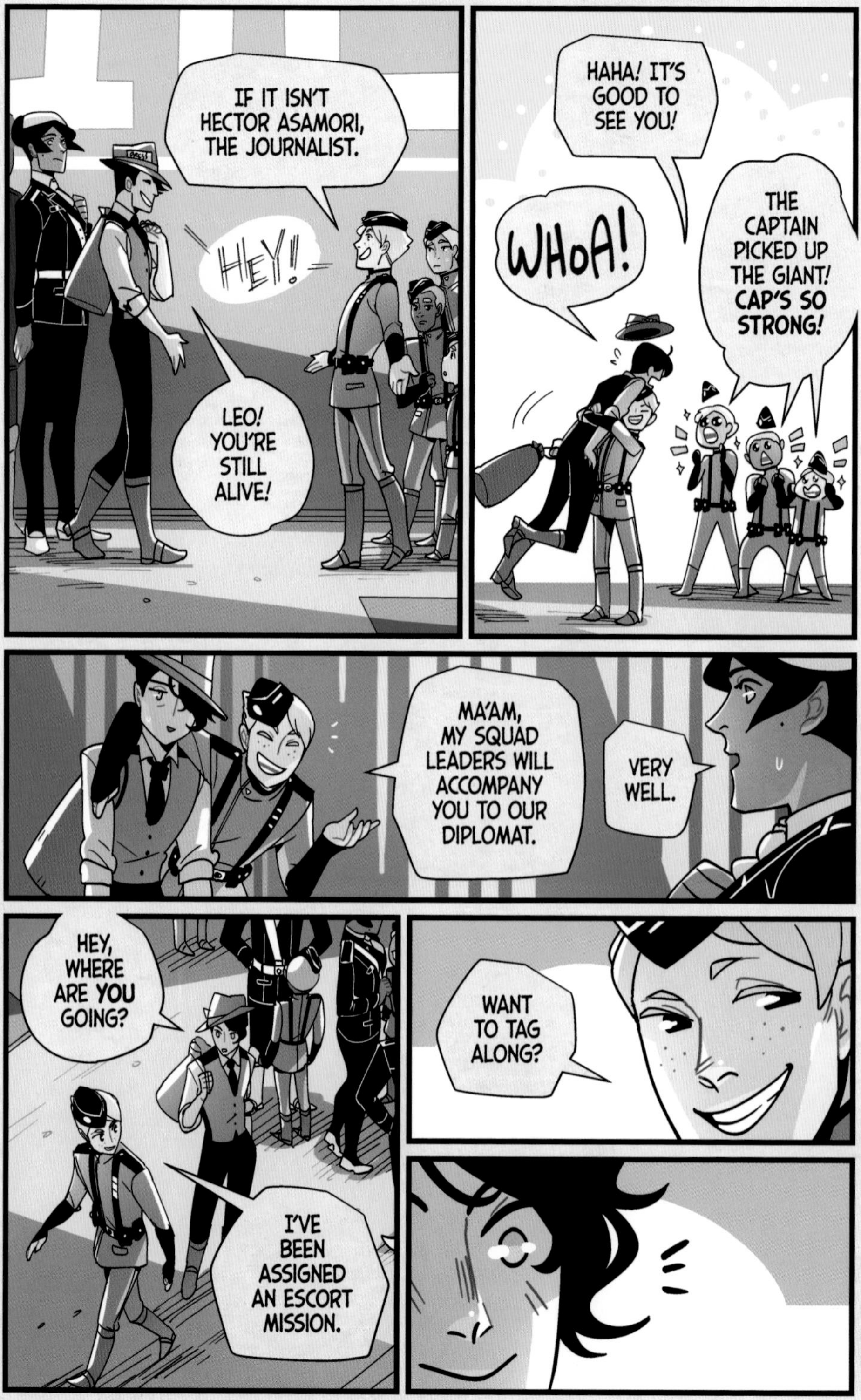
IF IT ISN'T HECTOR ASAMORI, THE JOURNALIST.
HEY!
LEO! YOU'RE STILL ALIVE!
HAHA! IT'S GOOD TO SEE YOU!
WHOA!
THE CAPTAIN PICKED UP THE GIANT! CAP'S SO STRONG!
MA'AM, MY SQUAD LEADERS WILL ACCOMPANY YOU TO OUR DIPLOMAT.
VERY WELL.
HEY, WHERE ARE YOU GOING?
I'VE BEEN ASSIGNED AN ESCORT MISSION.
WANT TO TAG ALONG?

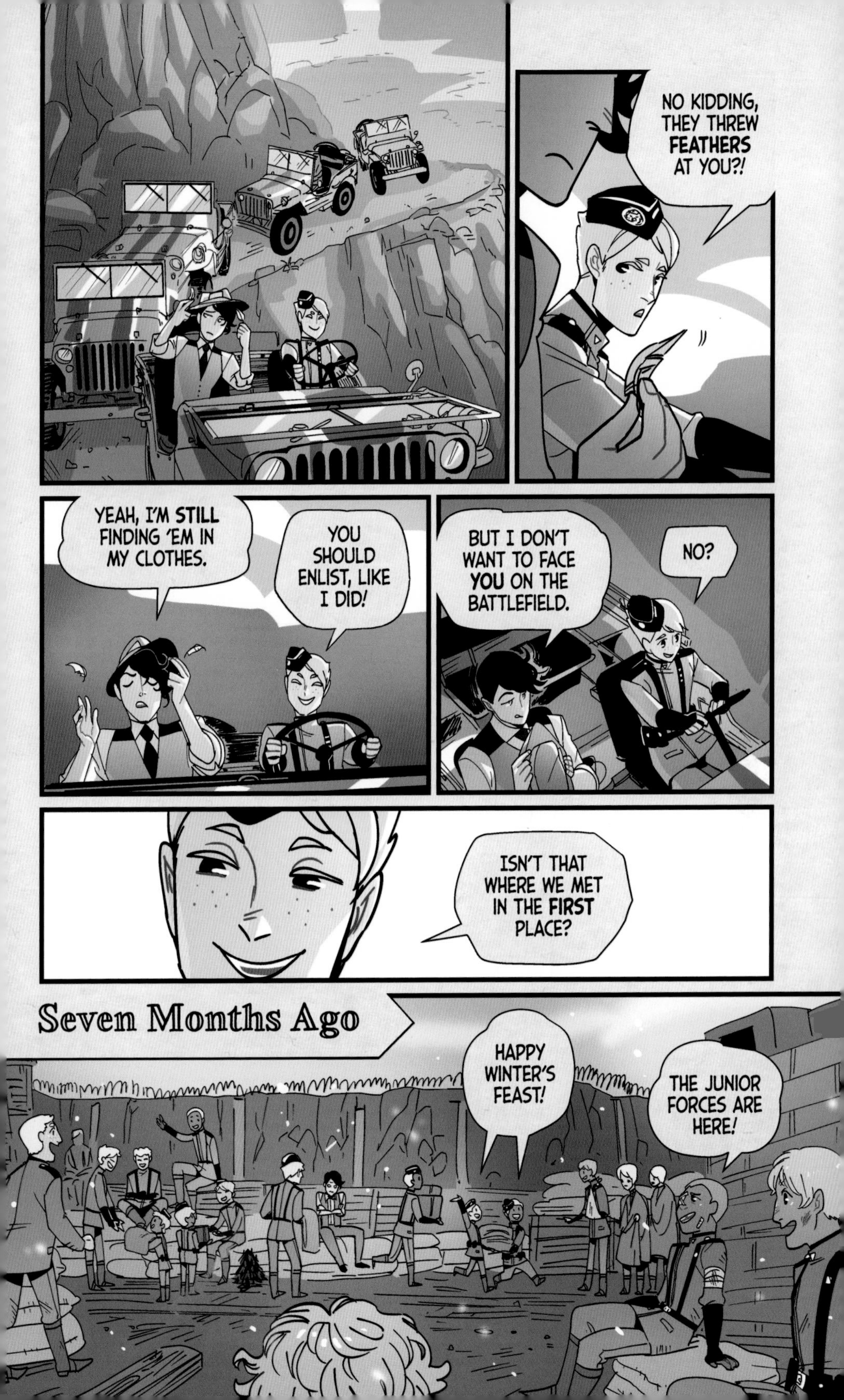
NO KIDDING, THEY THREW FEATHERS AT YOU?!
YEAH, I'M STILL FINDING 'EM IN MY CLOTHES.
YOU SHOULD ENLIST, LIKE I DID!
BUT I DON'T WANT TO FACE YOU ON THE BATTLEFIELD.
NO?
ISN'T THAT WHERE WE MET IN THE FIRST PLACE?
Seven Months Ago
HAPPY WINTER'S FEAST!
THE JUNIOR FORCES ARE HERE!

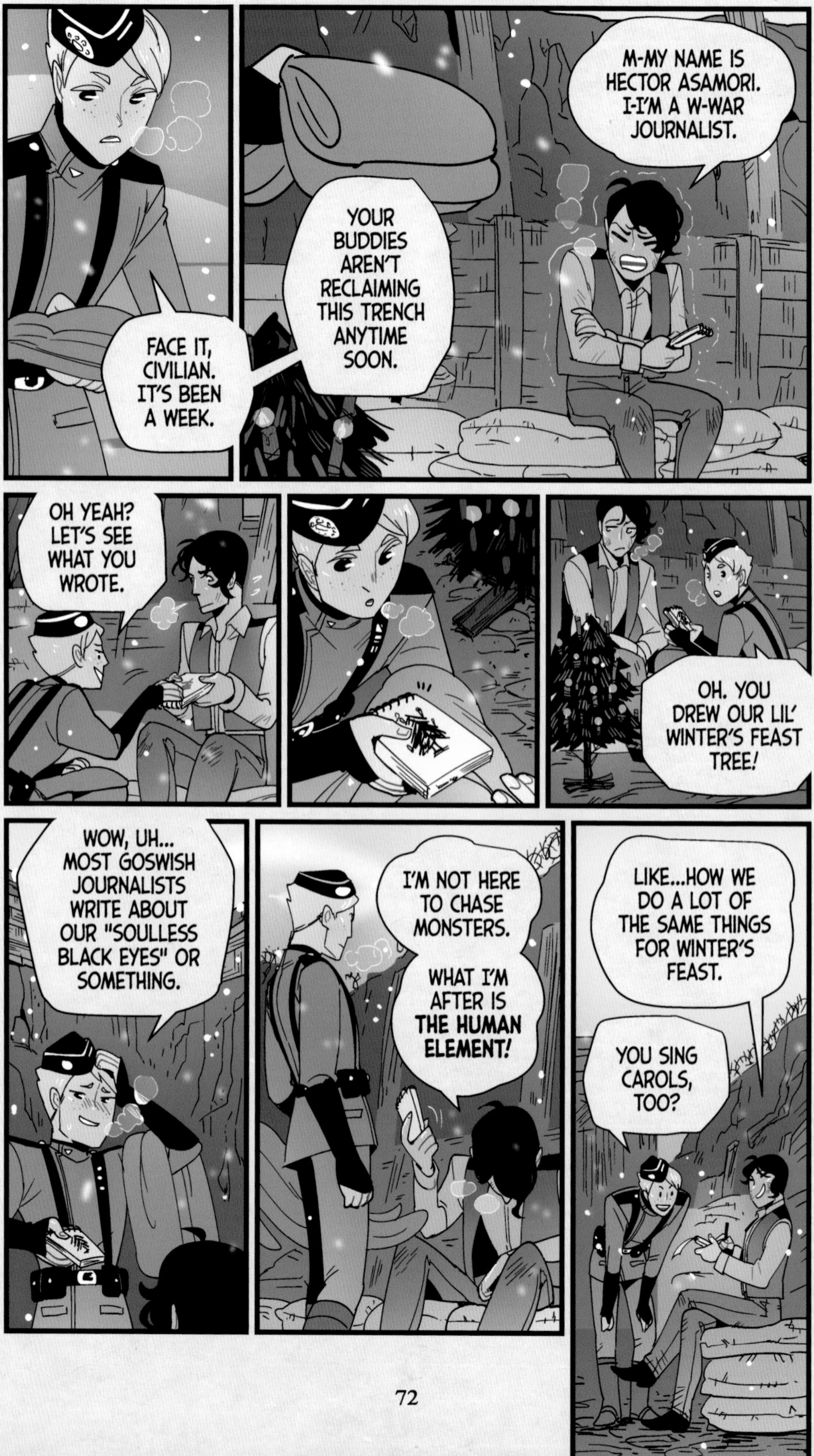
M-MY NAME IS HECTOR ASAMORI. I-I'M A W-WAR JOURNALIST.
FACE IT, CIVILIAN. IT'S BEEN A WEEK.
YOUR BUDDIES AREN'T RECLAIMING THIS TRENCH ANYTIME SOON.
OH YEAH? LET'S SEE WHAT YOU WROTE.
OH. YOU DREW OUR LIL' WINTER'S FEAST TREE!
WOW, UH... MOST GOSWISH JOURNALISTS WRITE ABOUT OUR "SOULLESS BLACK EYES" OR SOMETHING.
I'M NOT HERE TO CHASE MONSTERS.
WHAT I'M AFTER IS **THE HUMAN ELEMENT!**
LIKE...HOW WE DO A LOT OF THE SAME THINGS FOR WINTER'S FEAST.
YOU SING CAROLS, TOO?

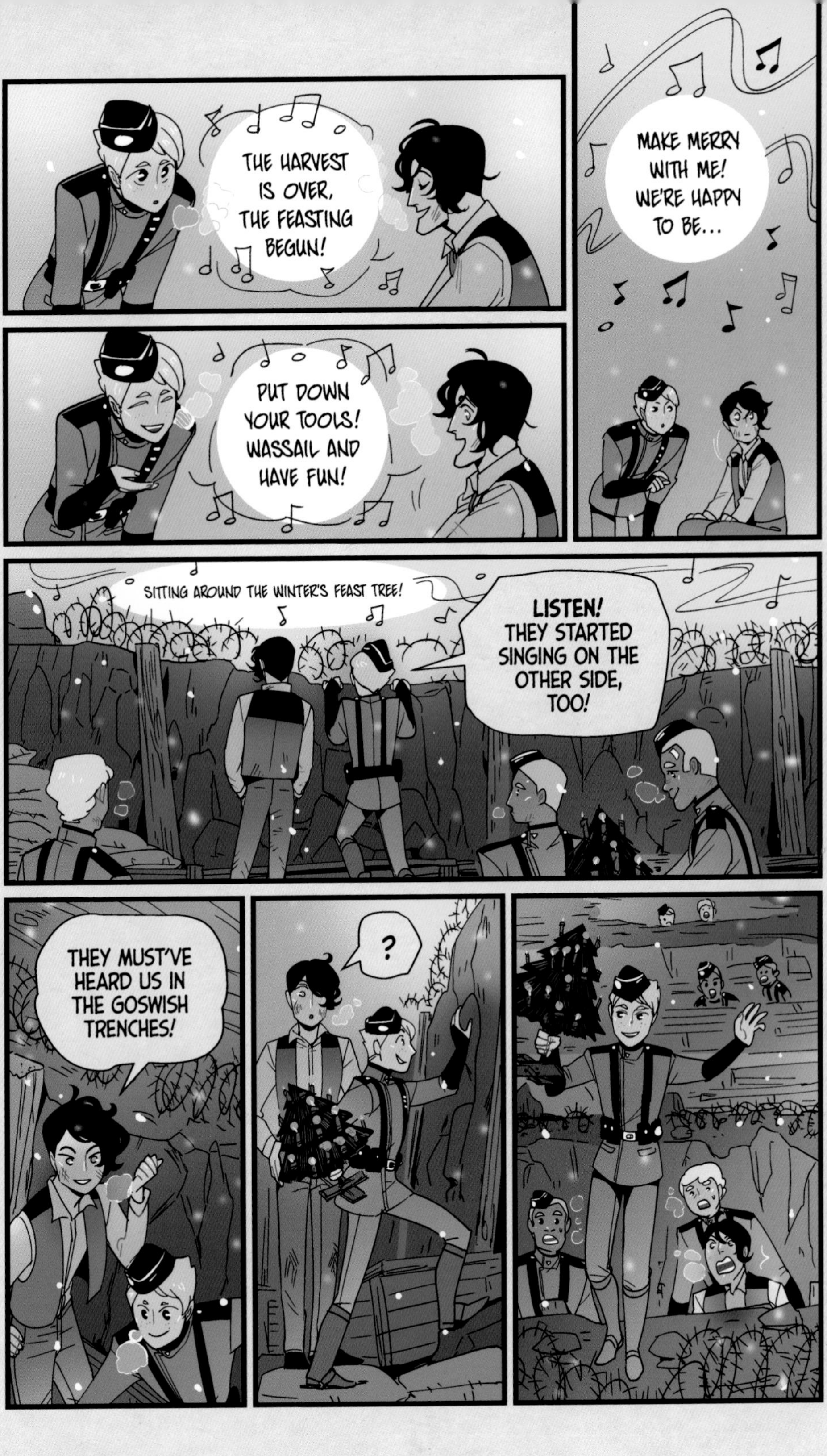
THE HARVEST IS OVER, THE FEASTING BEGUN!
PUT DOWN YOUR TOOLS! WASSAIL AND HAVE FUN!
MAKE MERRY WITH ME! WE'RE HAPPY TO BE...
SITTING AROUND THE WINTER'S FEAST TREE!
LISTEN! THEY STARTED SINGING ON THE OTHER SIDE, TOO!
THEY MUST'VE HEARD US IN THE GOSWISH TRENCHES!
?

LOOK AT THAT!

WE EXCHANGE GIFTS, TOO!

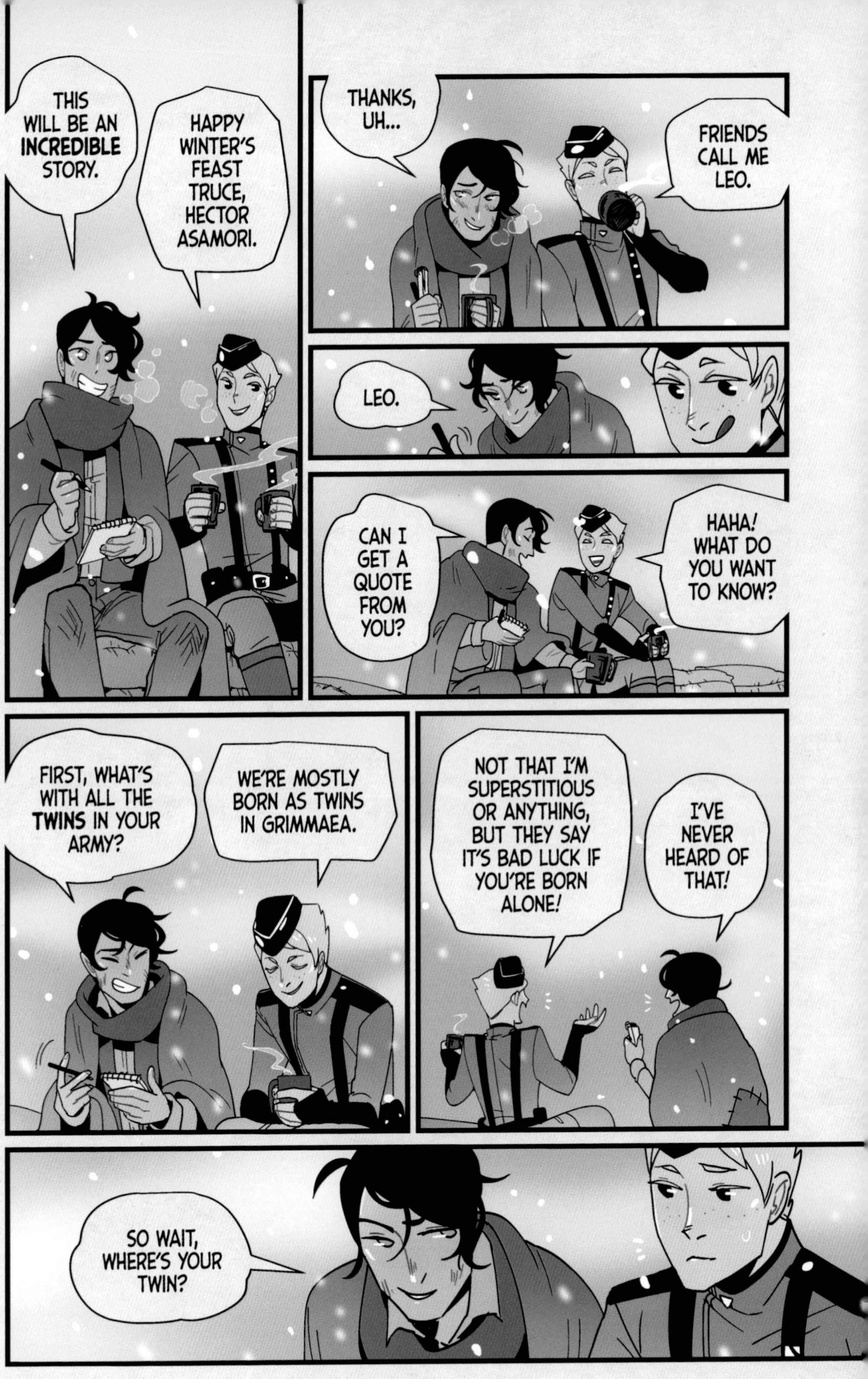
THIS WILL BE AN INCREDIBLE STORY.
HAPPY WINTER'S FEAST TRUCE, HECTOR ASAMORI.
THANKS, UH...
FRIENDS CALL ME LEO.
LEO.
CAN I GET A QUOTE FROM YOU?
HAHA! WHAT DO YOU WANT TO KNOW?
FIRST, WHAT'S WITH ALL THE TWINS IN YOUR ARMY?
WE'RE MOSTLY BORN AS TWINS IN GRIMMAEA.
NOT THAT I'M SUPERSTITIOUS OR ANYTHING, BUT THEY SAY IT'S BAD LUCK IF YOU'RE BORN ALONE!
I'VE NEVER HEARD OF THAT!
SO WAIT, WHERE'S YOUR TWIN?

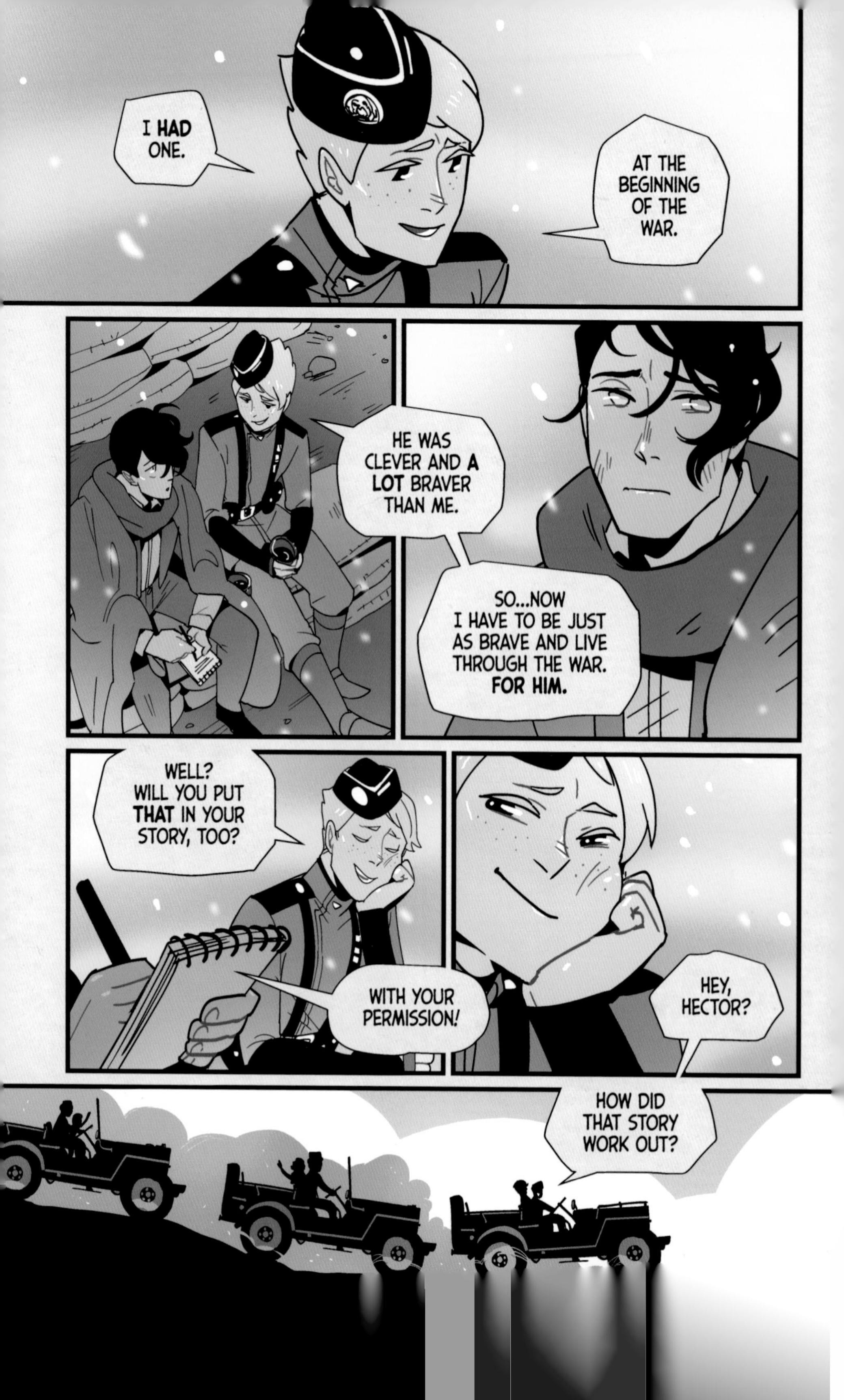
I HAD ONE.
AT THE BEGINNING OF THE WAR.
HE WAS CLEVER AND A LOT BRAVER THAN ME.
SO...NOW I HAVE TO BE JUST AS BRAVE AND LIVE THROUGH THE WAR. FOR HIM.
WELL? WILL YOU PUT THAT IN YOUR STORY, TOO?
WITH YOUR PERMISSION!
HEY, HECTOR?
HOW DID THAT STORY WORK OUT?

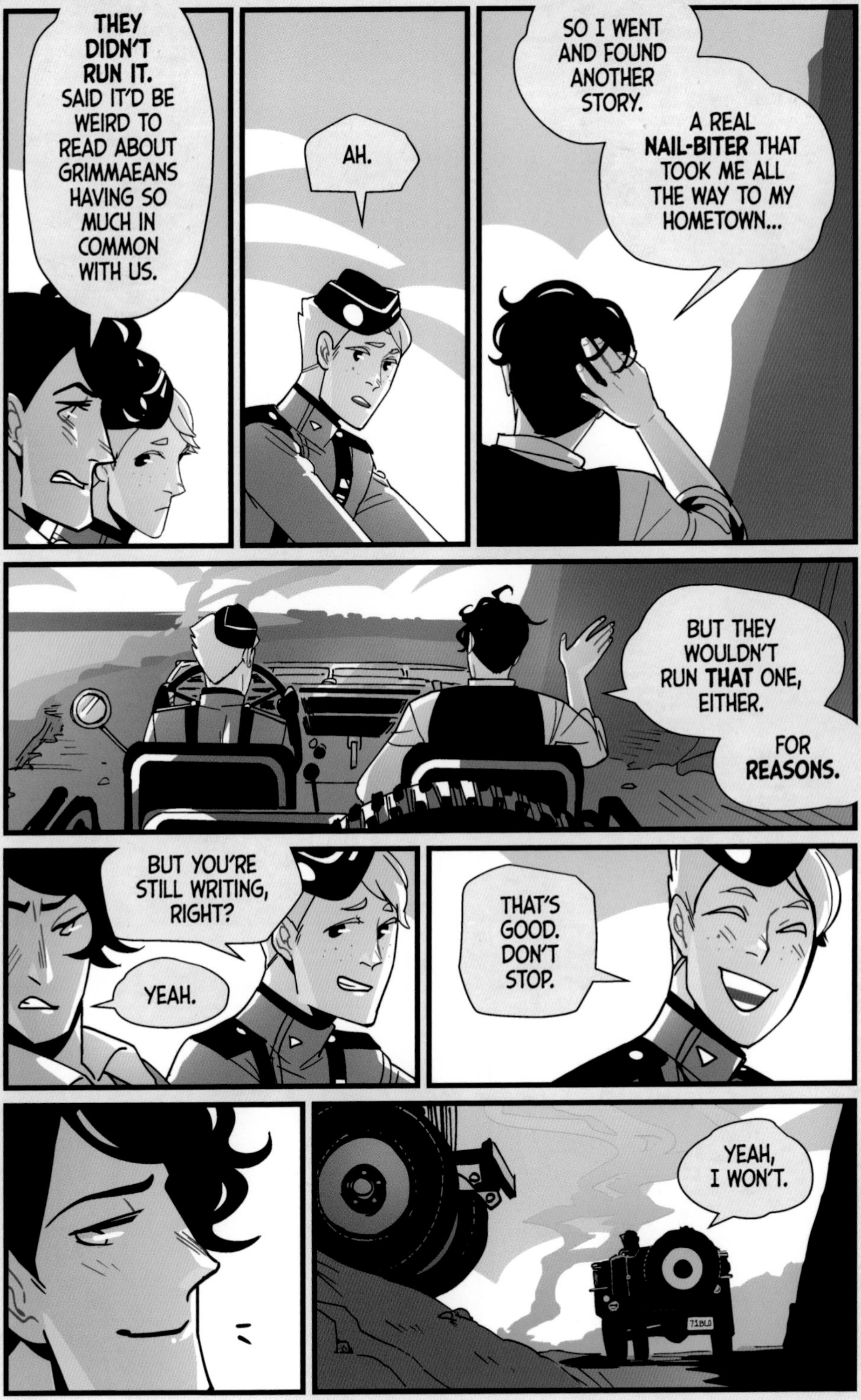
THEY DIDN'T RUN IT. SAID IT'D BE WEIRD TO READ ABOUT GRIMMAEANS HAVING SO MUCH IN COMMON WITH US.
AH.
SO I WENT AND FOUND ANOTHER STORY.
A REAL NAIL-BITER THAT TOOK ME ALL THE WAY TO MY HOMETOWN...
BUT THEY WOULDN'T RUN THAT ONE, EITHER.
FOR REASONS.
BUT YOU'RE STILL WRITING, RIGHT?
YEAH.
THAT'S GOOD. DON'T STOP.
YEAH, I WON'T.
71BLO

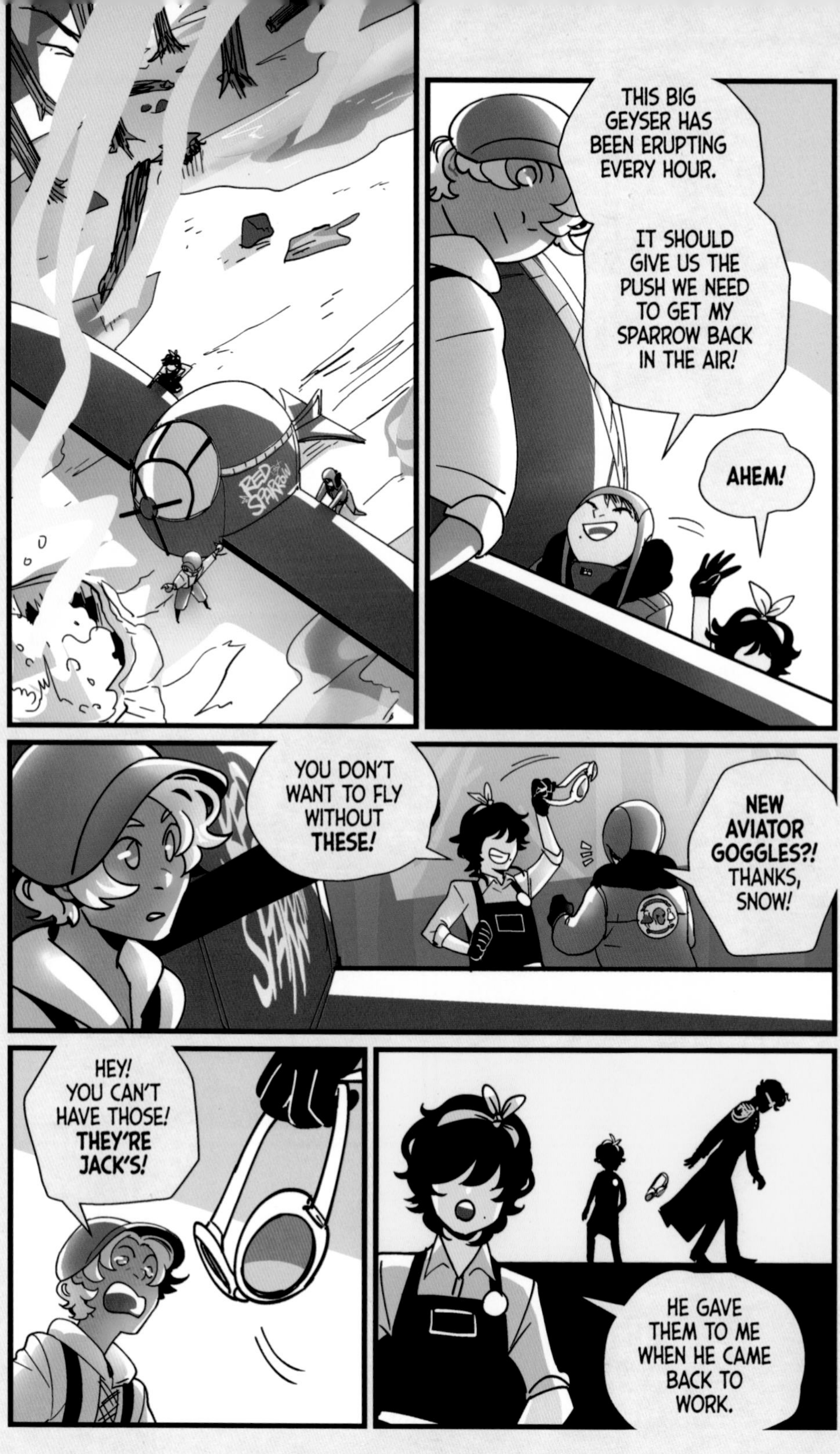
RED SPARROW
THIS BIG GEYSER HAS BEEN ERUPTING EVERY HOUR.
IT SHOULD GIVE US THE PUSH WE NEED TO GET MY SPARROW BACK IN THE AIR!
AHEM!
YOU DON'T WANT TO FLY WITHOUT THESE!
NEW AVIATOR GOGGLES?! THANKS, SNOW!
HEY! YOU CAN'T HAVE THOSE! THEY'RE JACK'S!
HE GAVE THEM TO ME WHEN HE CAME BACK TO WORK.

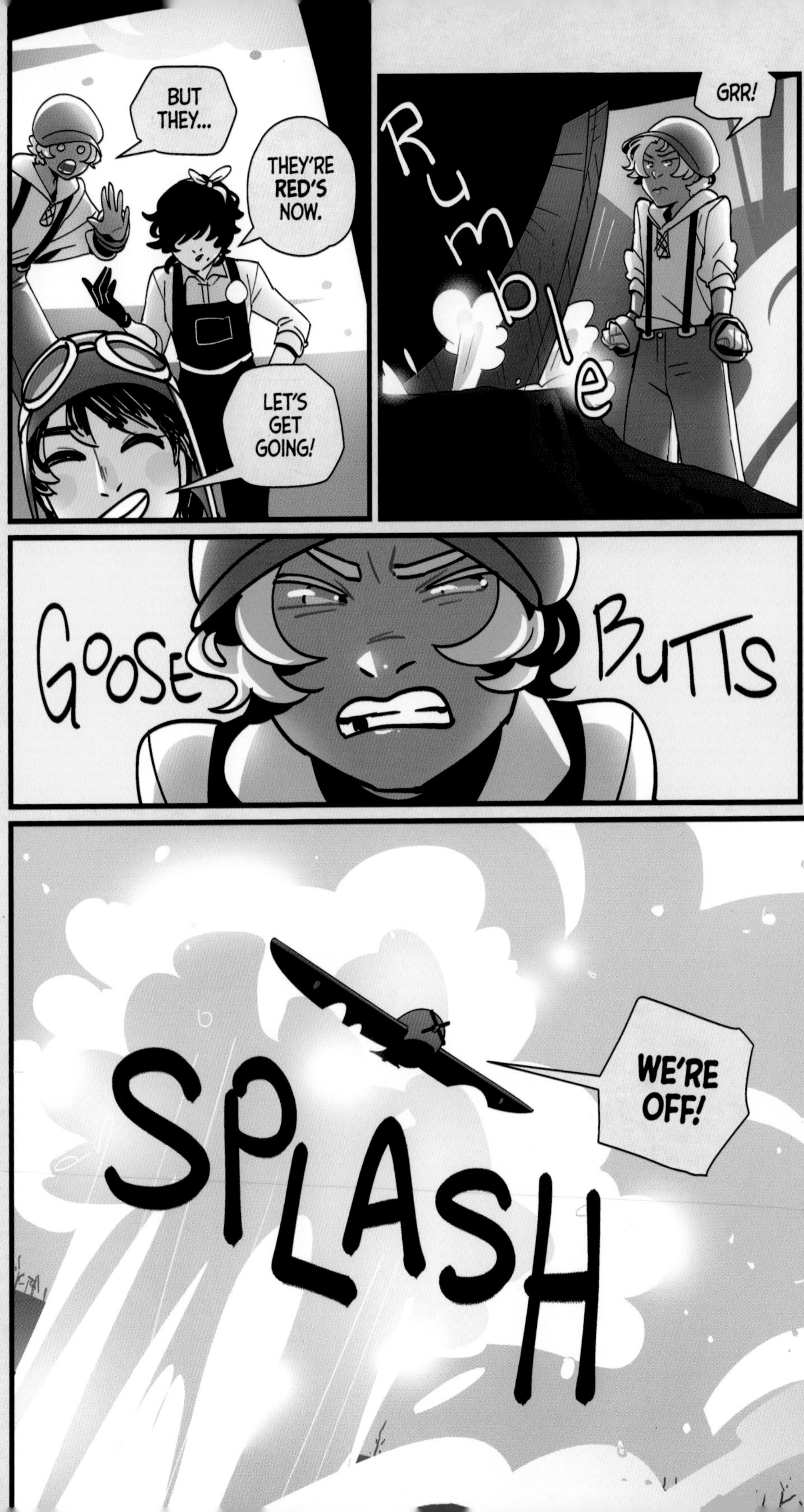
BUT THEY...
THEY'RE RED'S NOW.
LET'S GET GOING!
Rumble
GRR!
GOOSE BUTTS
SPLASH
WE'RE OFF!

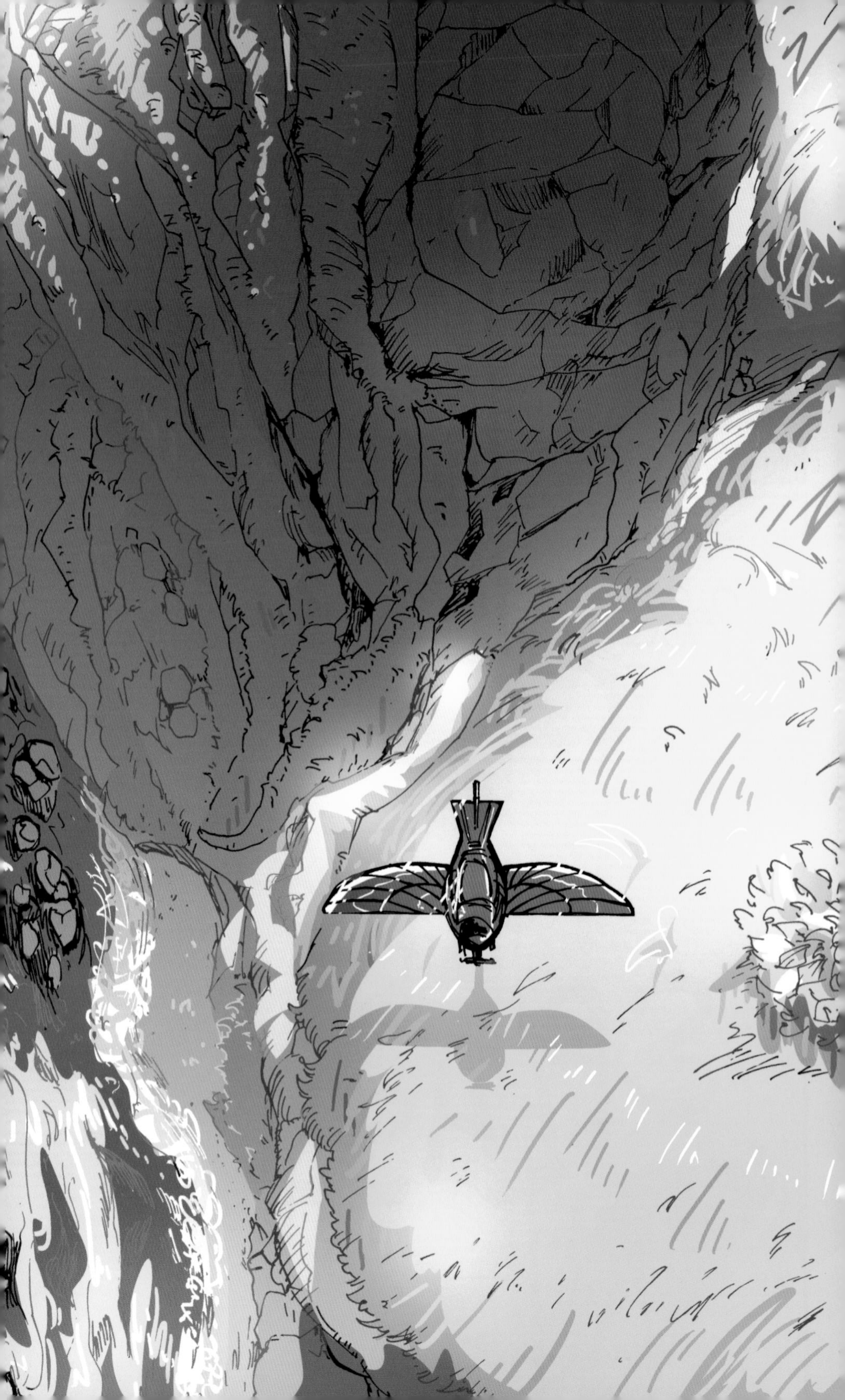

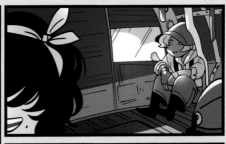

I OUGHT TO REJOIN THE SPARROW FLOCK.

BLEH, I'D RATHER GO HOME.

TAP TAP

UM, GUYS?

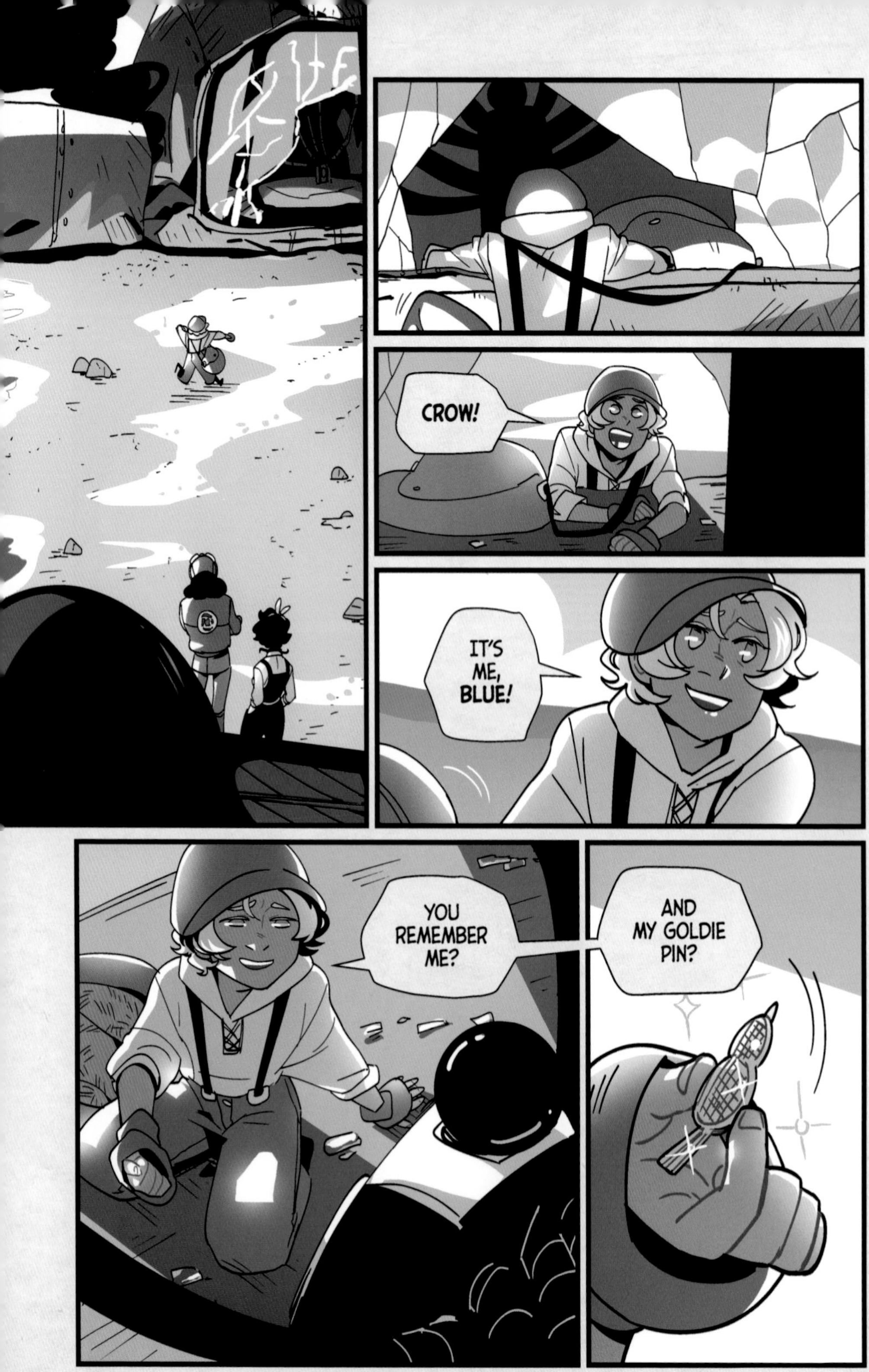
CROW!
IT'S ME, BLUE!
YOU REMEMBER ME?
AND MY GOLDIE PIN?

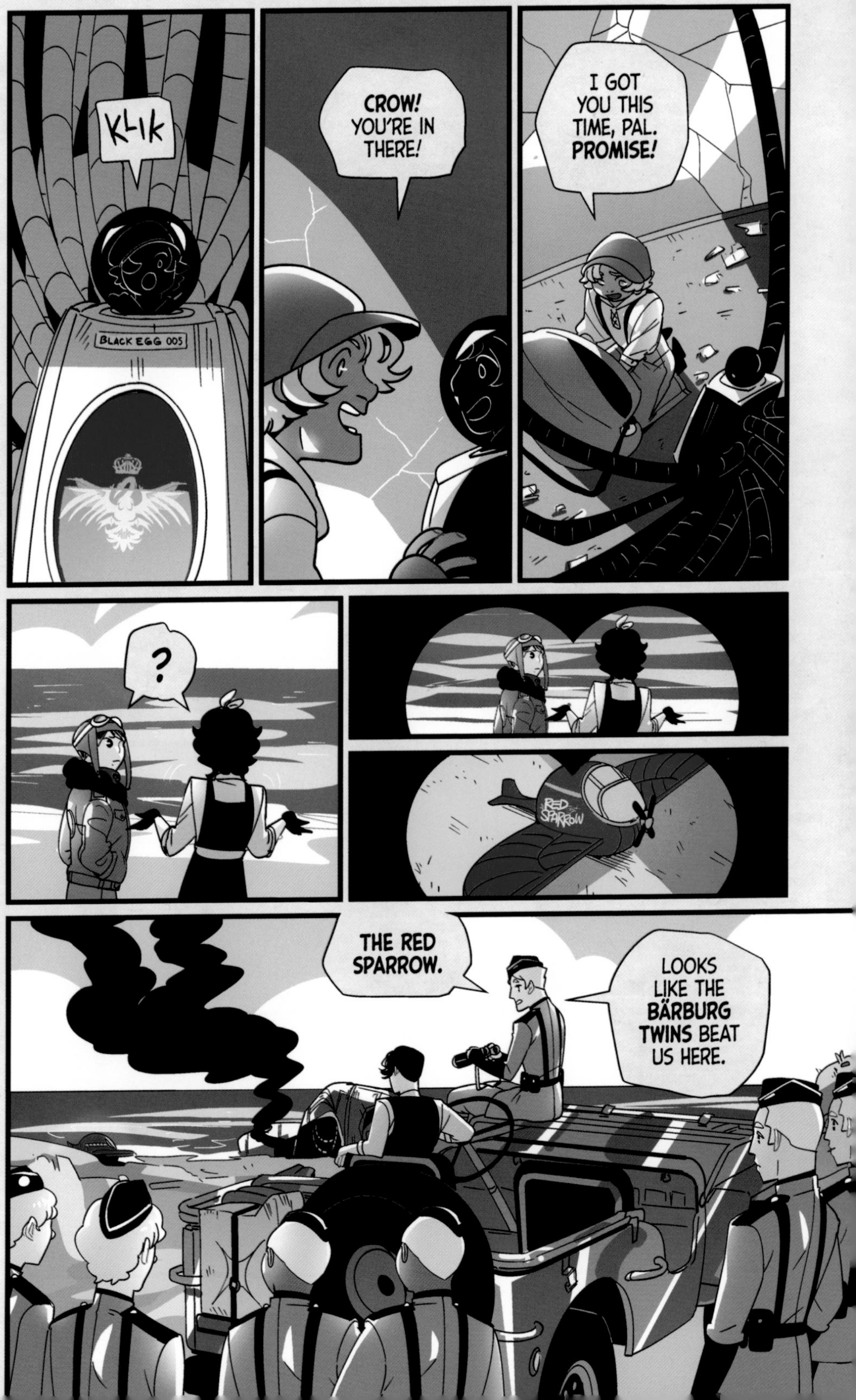
KLIK
BLACK EGG 005
CROW! YOU'RE IN THERE!
I GOT YOU THIS TIME, PAL. PROMISE!
?
RED SPARROW
THE RED SPARROW.
LOOKS LIKE THE BÄRBURG TWINS BEAT US HERE.

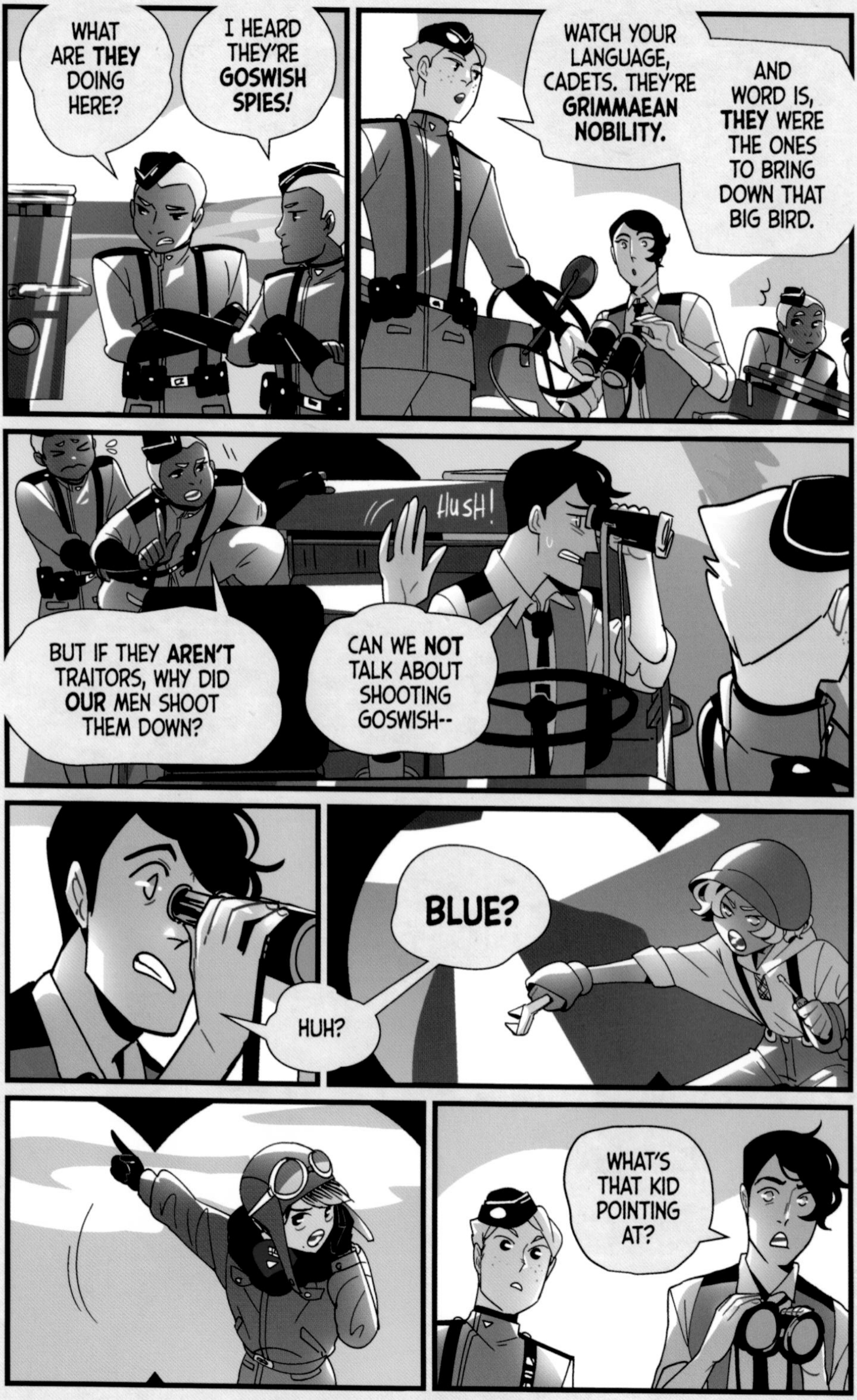
WHAT ARE THEY DOING HERE?
I HEARD THEY'RE GOSWISH SPIES!
WATCH YOUR LANGUAGE, CADETS. THEY'RE GRIMMAEAN NOBILITY.
AND WORD IS, THEY WERE THE ONES TO BRING DOWN THAT BIG BIRD.
HUSH!
BUT IF THEY AREN'T TRAITORS, WHY DID OUR MEN SHOOT THEM DOWN?
CAN WE NOT TALK ABOUT SHOOTING GOSWISH--
BLUE?
HUH?
WHAT'S THAT KID POINTING AT?

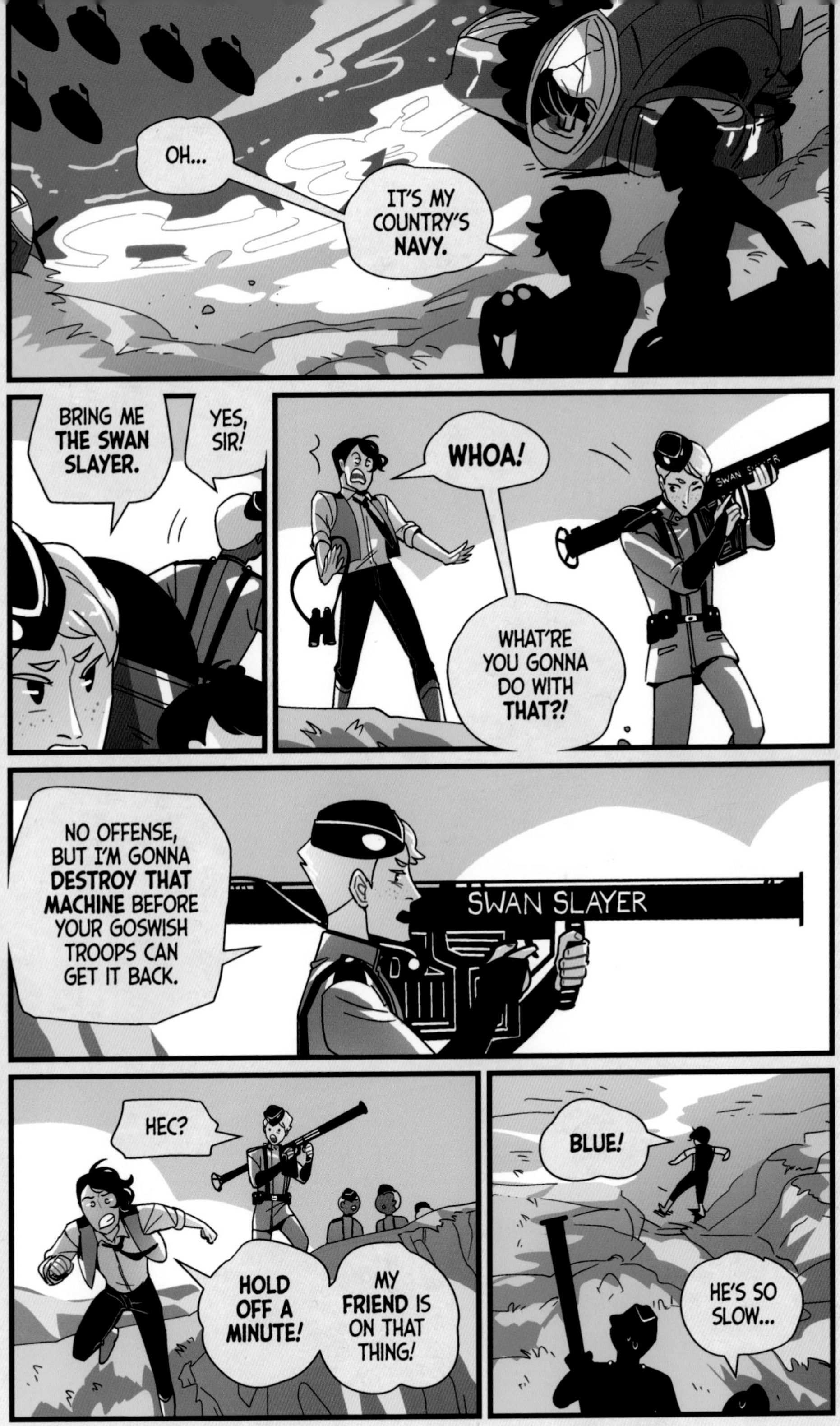
OH...
IT'S MY COUNTRY'S NAVY.
BRING ME THE SWAN SLAYER.
YES, SIR!
WHOA!
WHAT'RE YOU GONNA DO WITH THAT?!
NO OFFENSE, BUT I'M GONNA DESTROY THAT MACHINE BEFORE YOUR GOSWISH TROOPS CAN GET IT BACK.
SWAN SLAYER
HEC?
HOLD OFF A MINUTE!
MY FRIEND IS ON THAT THING!
BLUE!
HE'S SO SLOW...

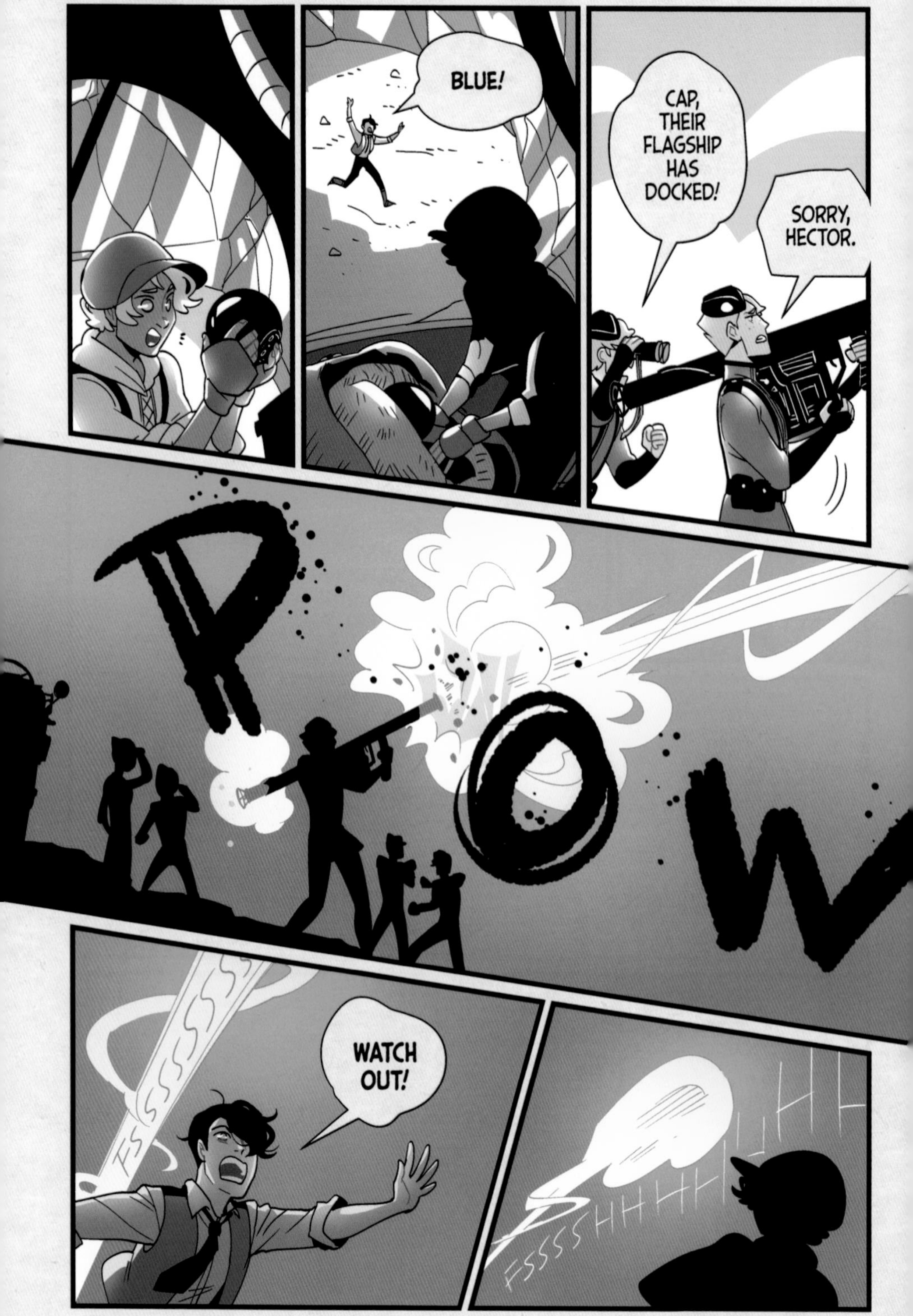
BLUE!
CAP, THEIR FLAGSHIP HAS DOCKED!
SORRY, HECTOR.
POW
WATCH OUT!
FSSSSSSSS
FSSSSHHHHHH

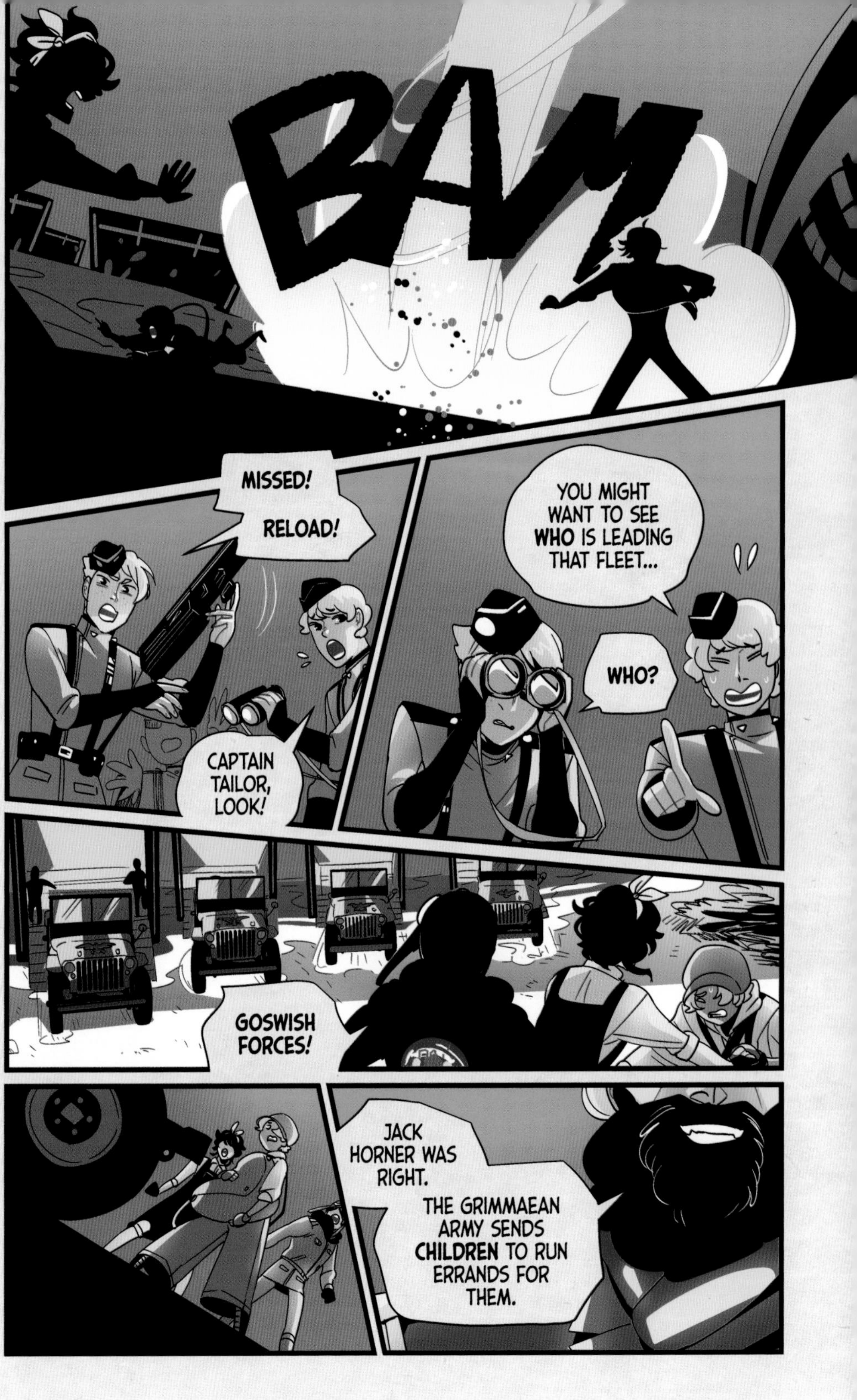
BAM
MISSED!
RELOAD!
CAPTAIN TAILOR, LOOK!
YOU MIGHT WANT TO SEE WHO IS LEADING THAT FLEET...
WHO?
GOSWISH FORCES!
JACK HORNER WAS RIGHT.
THE GRIMMAEAN ARMY SENDS CHILDREN TO RUN ERRANDS FOR THEM.

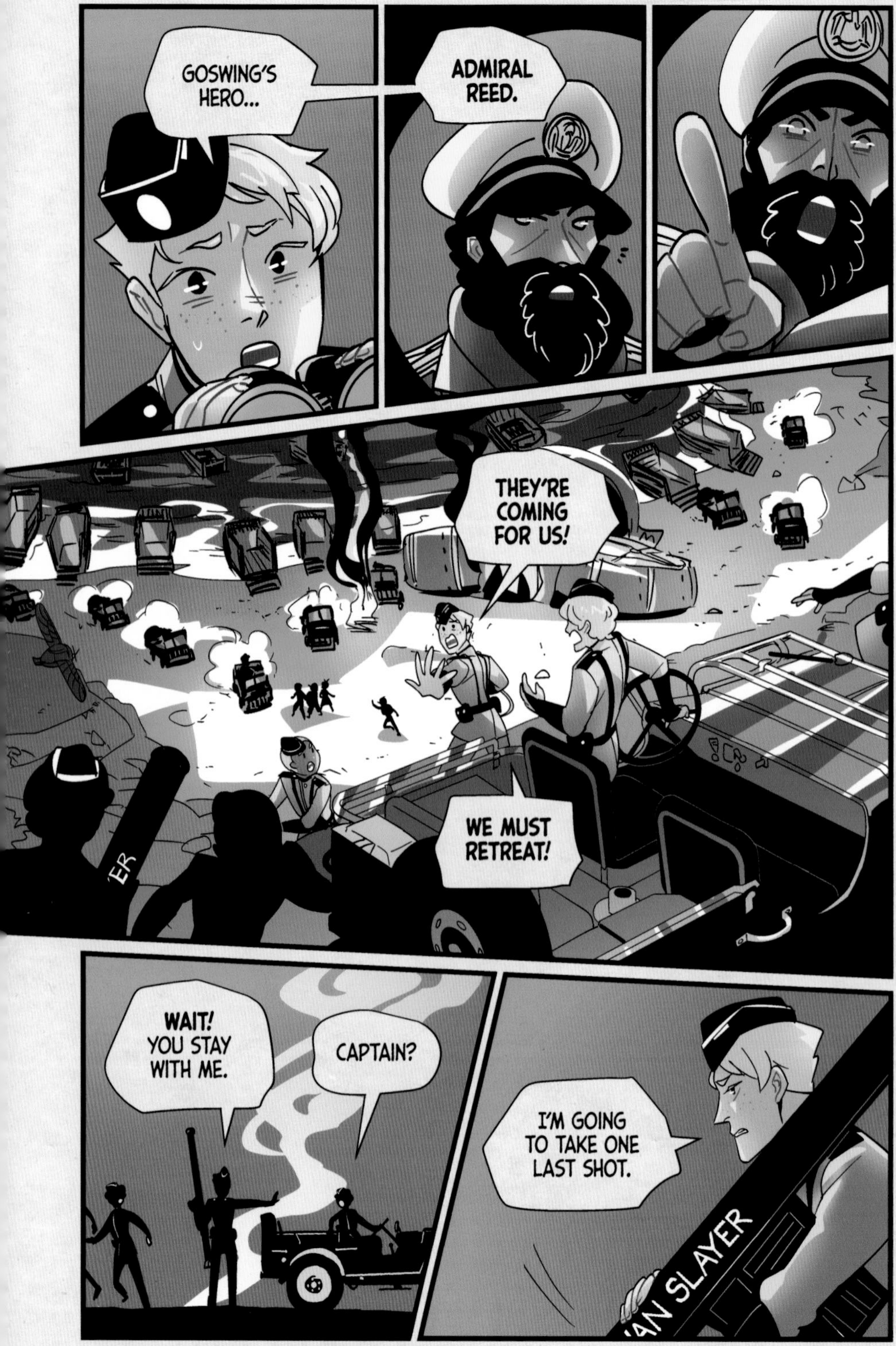
GOSWING'S HERO...
ADMIRAL REED.
THEY'RE COMING FOR US!
WE MUST RETREAT!
ER
WAIT! YOU STAY WITH ME.
CAPTAIN?
I'M GOING TO TAKE ONE LAST SHOT.
AN SLAYER

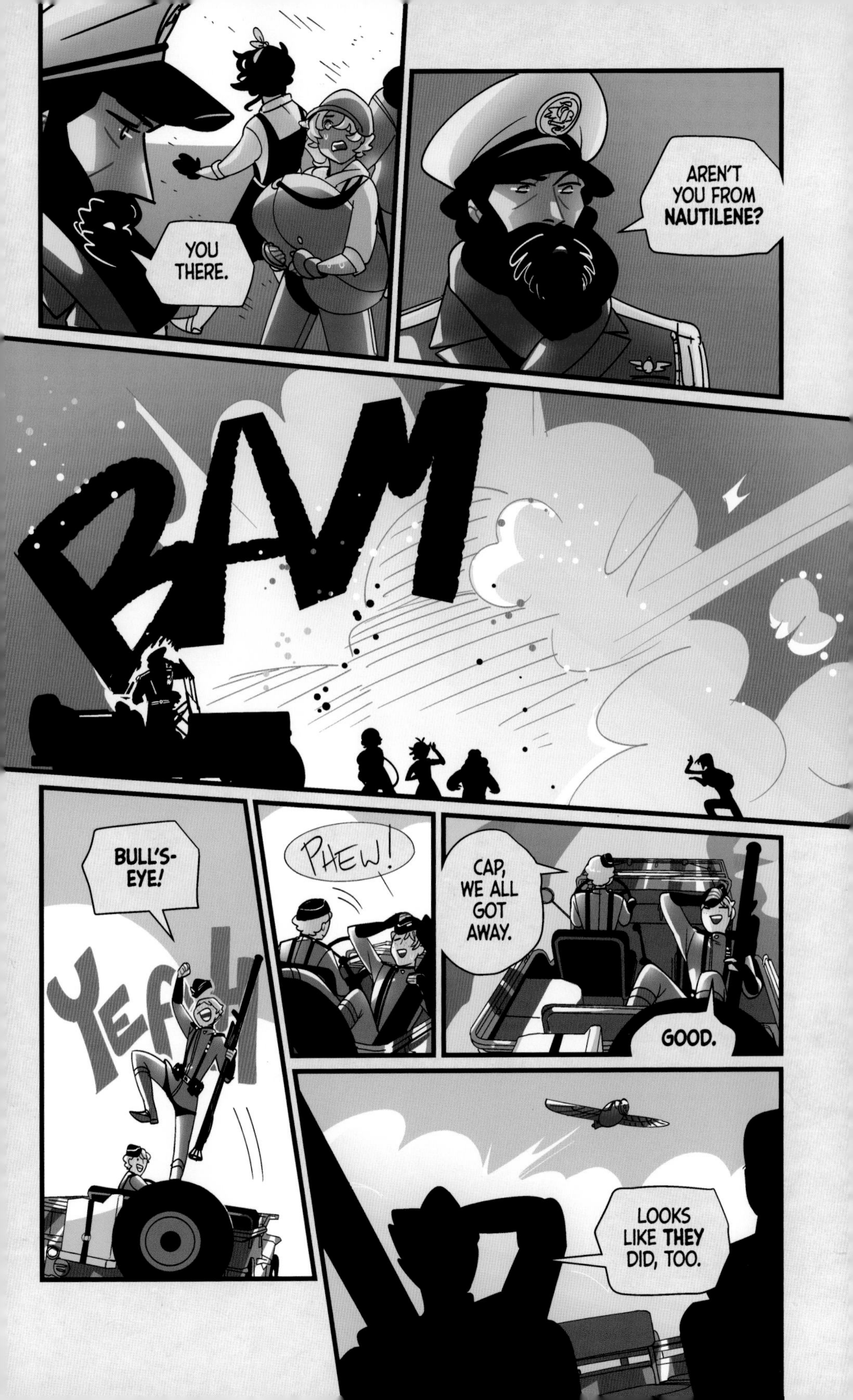
YOU THERE.
AREN'T YOU FROM NAUTILENE?
BAM
BULL'S-EYE!
YEAH
PHEW!
CAP, WE ALL GOT AWAY.
GOOD.
LOOKS LIKE THEY DID, TOO.

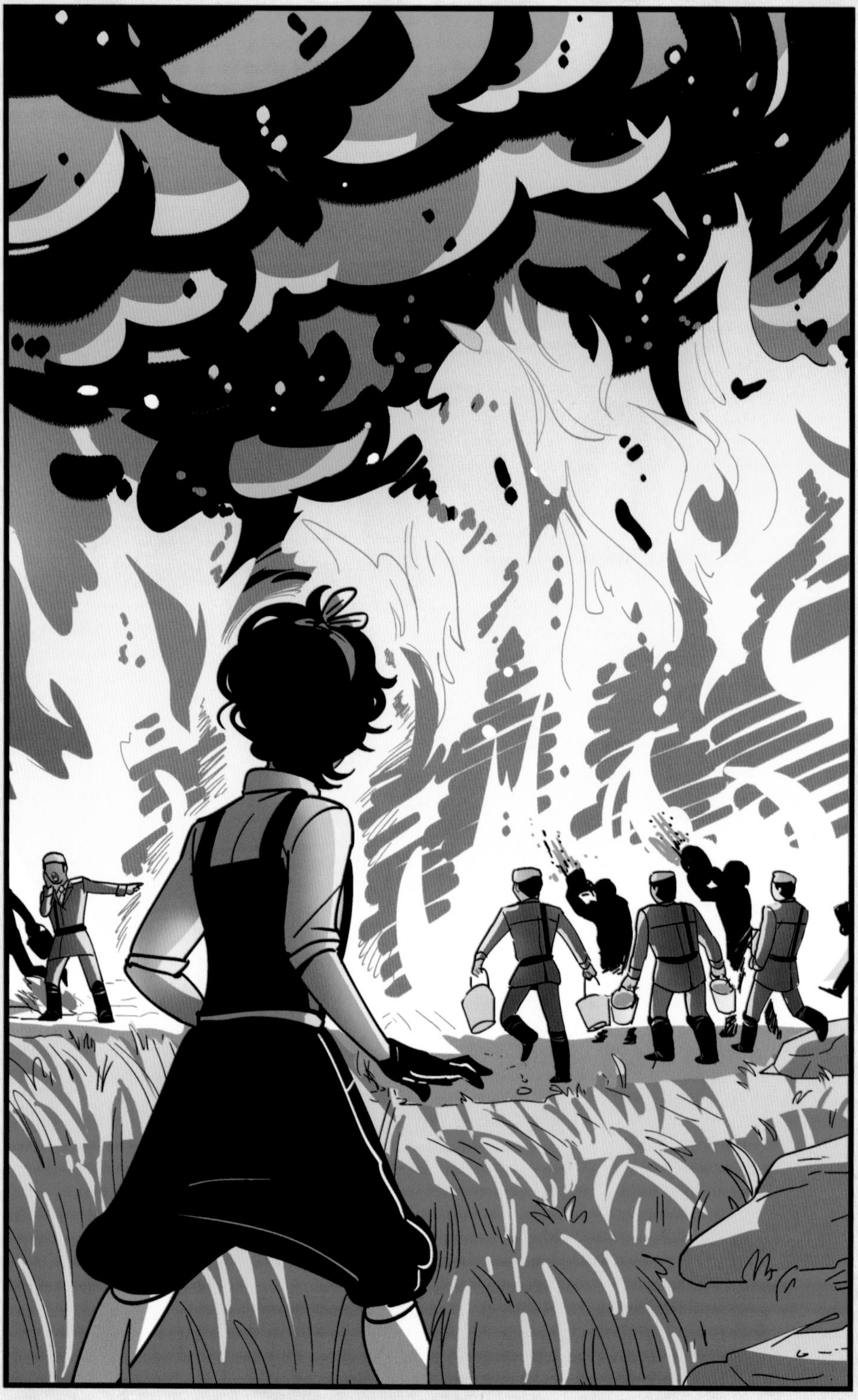

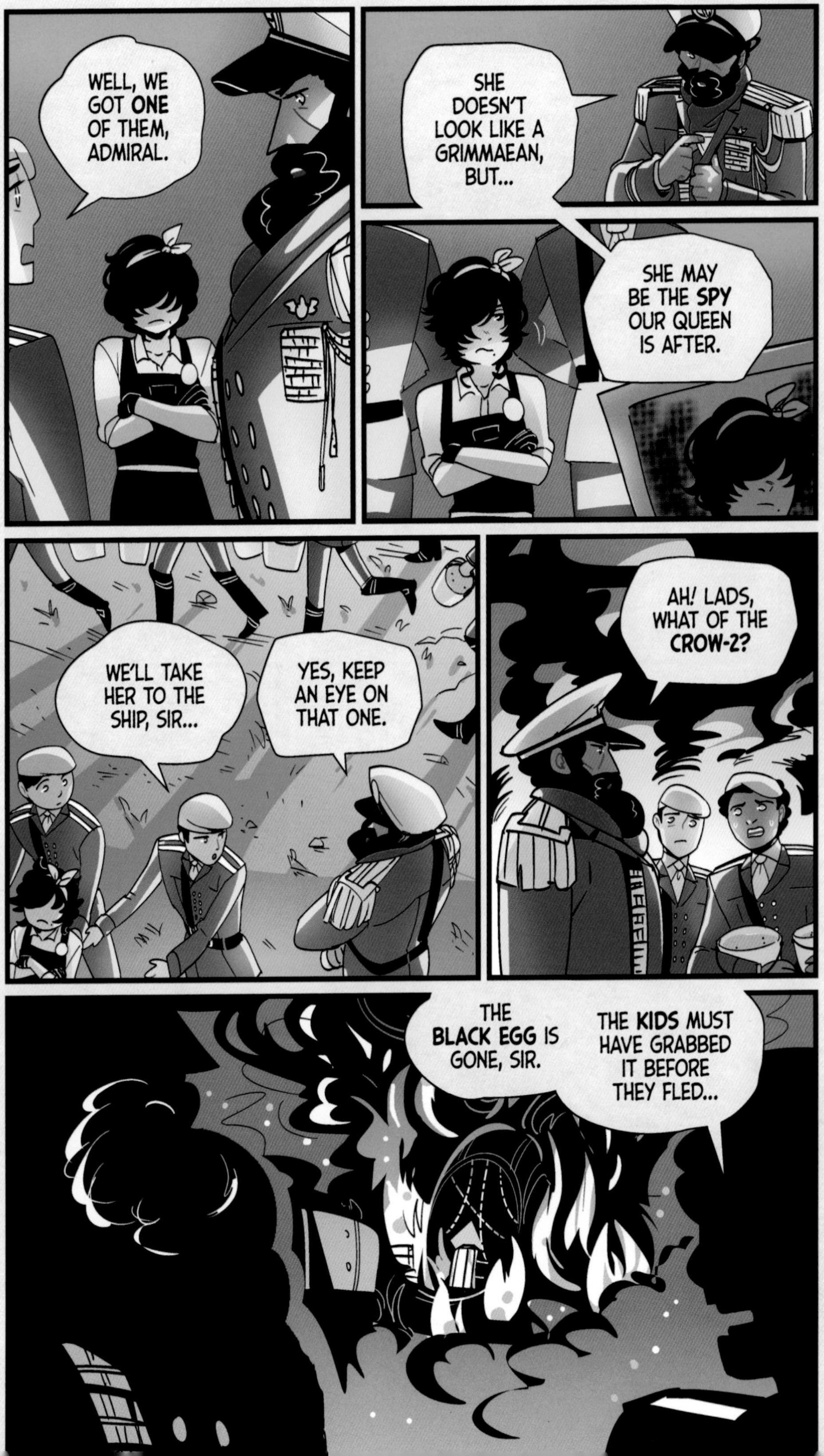
WELL, WE GOT ONE OF THEM, ADMIRAL.
SHE DOESN'T LOOK LIKE A GRIMMAEAN, BUT...
SHE MAY BE THE SPY OUR QUEEN IS AFTER.
WE'LL TAKE HER TO THE SHIP, SIR...
YES, KEEP AN EYE ON THAT ONE.
AH! LADS, WHAT OF THE CROW-2?
THE BLACK EGG IS GONE, SIR.
THE KIDS MUST HAVE GRABBED IT BEFORE THEY FLED...

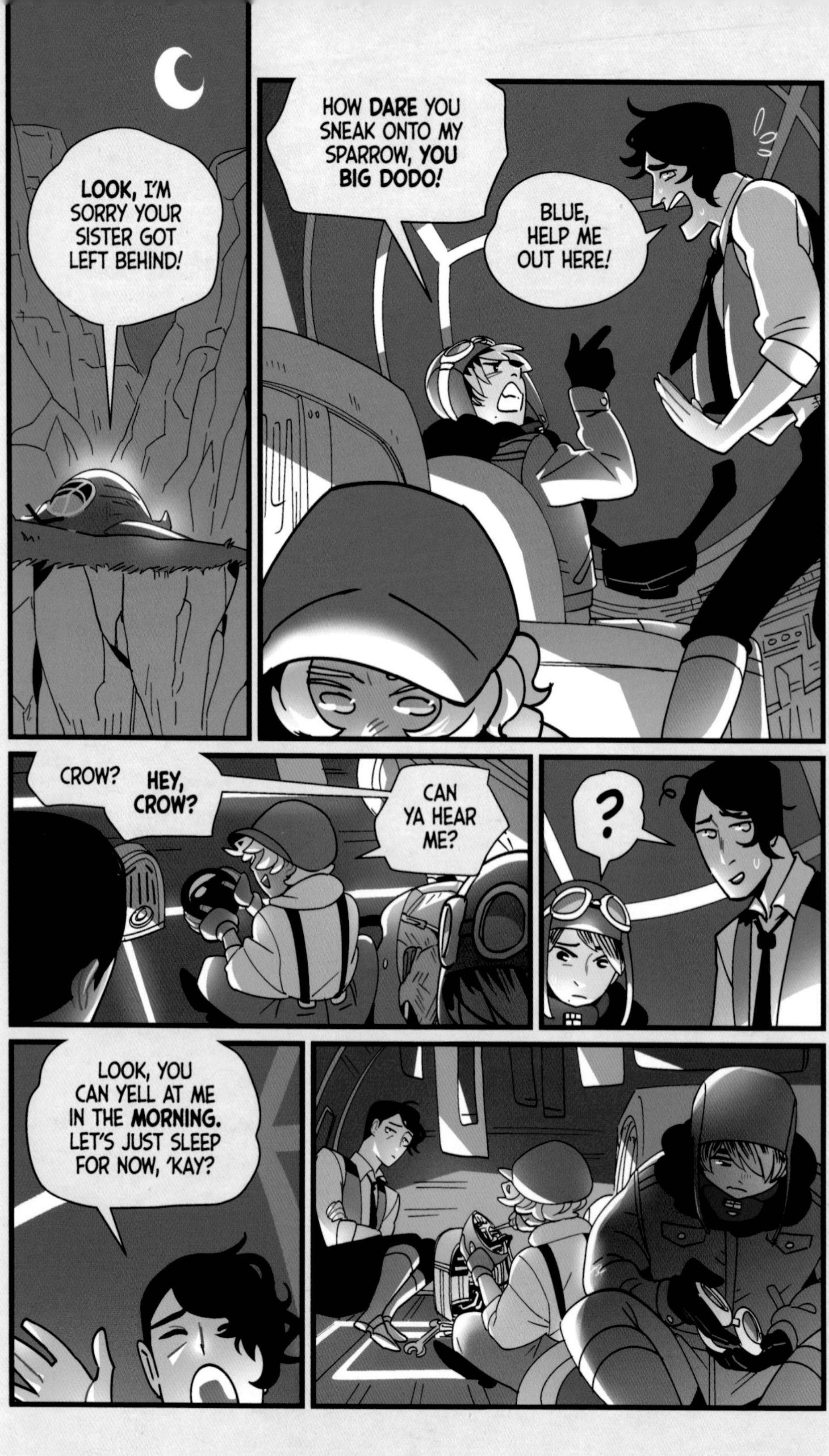
LOOK, I'M SORRY YOUR SISTER GOT LEFT BEHIND!
HOW DARE YOU SNEAK ONTO MY SPARROW, YOU BIG DODO!
BLUE, HELP ME OUT HERE!
CROW? HEY, CROW?
CAN YA HEAR ME?
?
LOOK, YOU CAN YELL AT ME IN THE MORNING. LET'S JUST SLEEP FOR NOW, 'KAY?

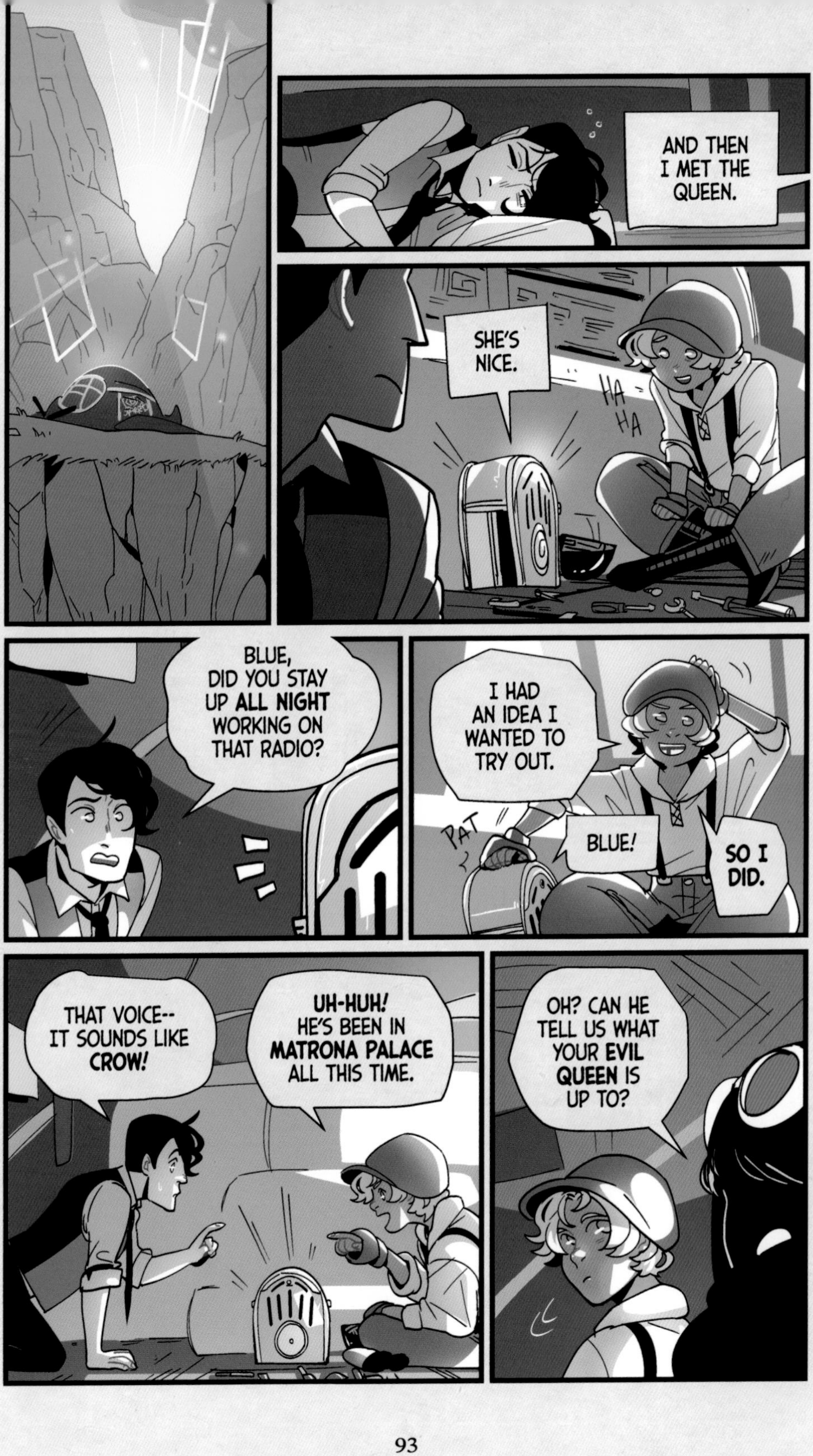
AND THEN I MET THE QUEEN.
SHE'S NICE.
HA HA
BLUE, DID YOU STAY UP **ALL NIGHT** WORKING ON THAT RADIO?
I HAD AN IDEA I WANTED TO TRY OUT.
PAT
BLUE!
SO I DID.
THAT VOICE-- IT SOUNDS LIKE **CROW!**
UH-HUH! HE'S BEEN IN **MATRONA PALACE** ALL THIS TIME.
OH? CAN HE TELL US WHAT YOUR **EVIL QUEEN** IS UP TO?

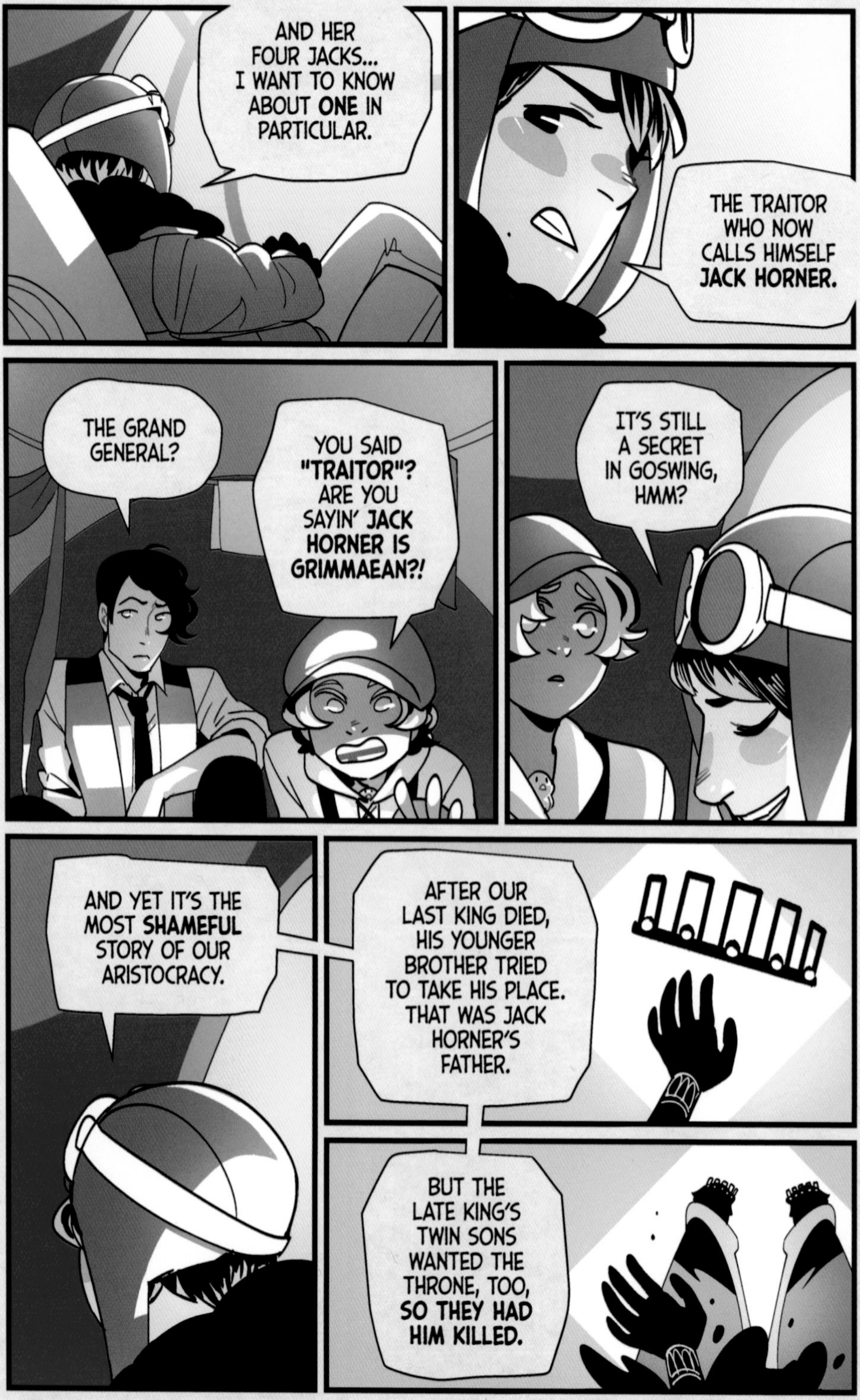
AND HER FOUR JACKS... I WANT TO KNOW ABOUT ONE IN PARTICULAR.
THE TRAITOR WHO NOW CALLS HIMSELF JACK HORNER.
THE GRAND GENERAL?
YOU SAID "TRAITOR"? ARE YOU SAYIN' JACK HORNER IS GRIMMAEAN?!
IT'S STILL A SECRET IN GOSWING, HMM?
AND YET IT'S THE MOST SHAMEFUL STORY OF OUR ARISTOCRACY.
AFTER OUR LAST KING DIED, HIS YOUNGER BROTHER TRIED TO TAKE HIS PLACE. THAT WAS JACK HORNER'S FATHER.
BUT THE LATE KING'S TWIN SONS WANTED THE THRONE, TOO, SO THEY HAD HIM KILLED.

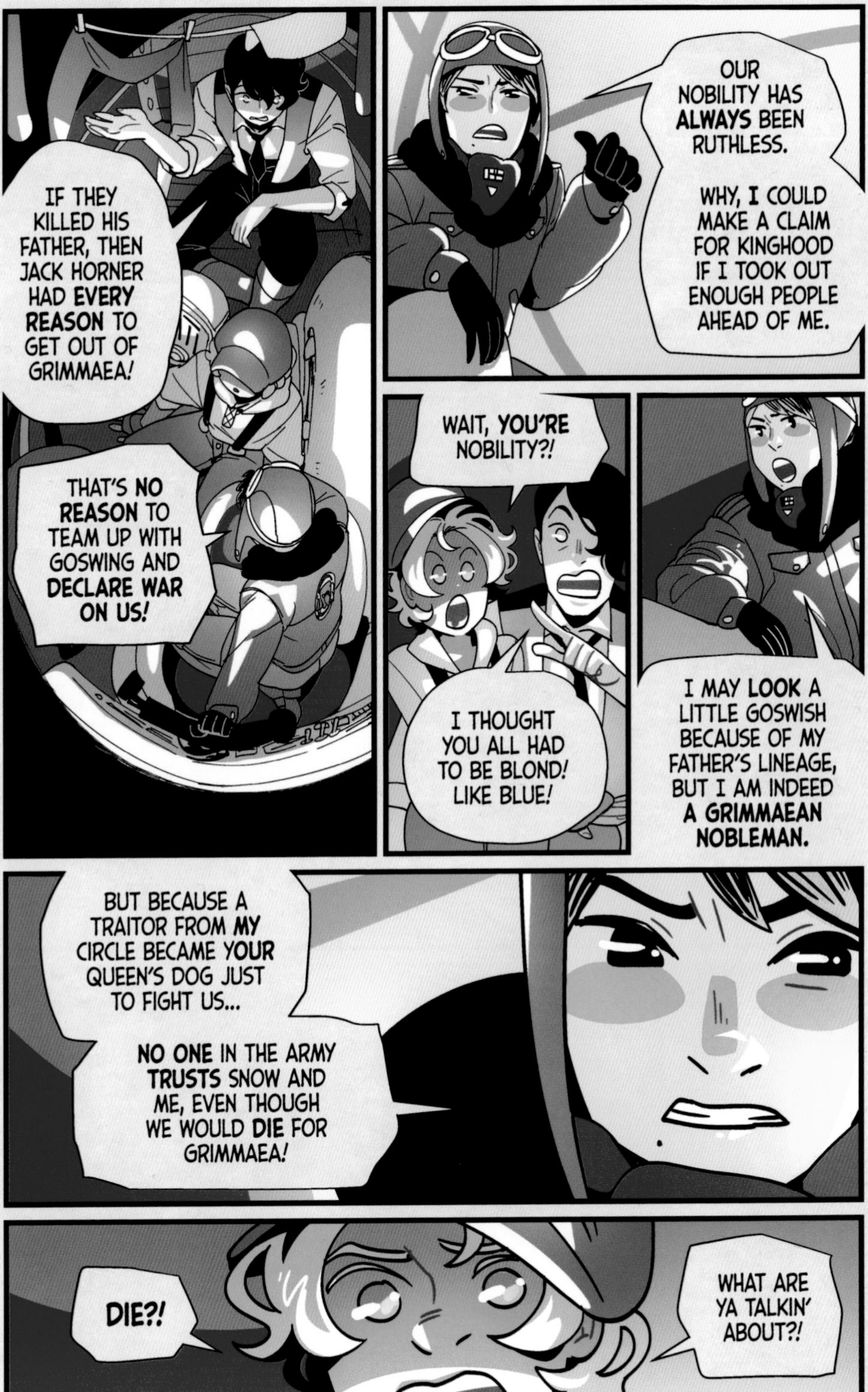
IF THEY KILLED HIS FATHER, THEN JACK HORNER HAD EVERY REASON TO GET OUT OF GRIMMAEA!
THAT'S NO REASON TO TEAM UP WITH GOSWING AND DECLARE WAR ON US!
OUR NOBILITY HAS ALWAYS BEEN RUTHLESS.
WHY, I COULD MAKE A CLAIM FOR KINGHOOD IF I TOOK OUT ENOUGH PEOPLE AHEAD OF ME.
WAIT, YOU'RE NOBILITY?!
I THOUGHT YOU ALL HAD TO BE BLOND! LIKE BLUE!
I MAY LOOK A LITTLE GOSWISH BECAUSE OF MY FATHER'S LINEAGE, BUT I AM INDEED A GRIMMAEAN NOBLEMAN.
BUT BECAUSE A TRAITOR FROM MY CIRCLE BECAME YOUR QUEEN'S DOG JUST TO FIGHT US...
NO ONE IN THE ARMY TRUSTS SNOW AND ME, EVEN THOUGH WE WOULD DIE FOR GRIMMAEA!
DIE?!
WHAT ARE YA TALKIN' ABOUT?!

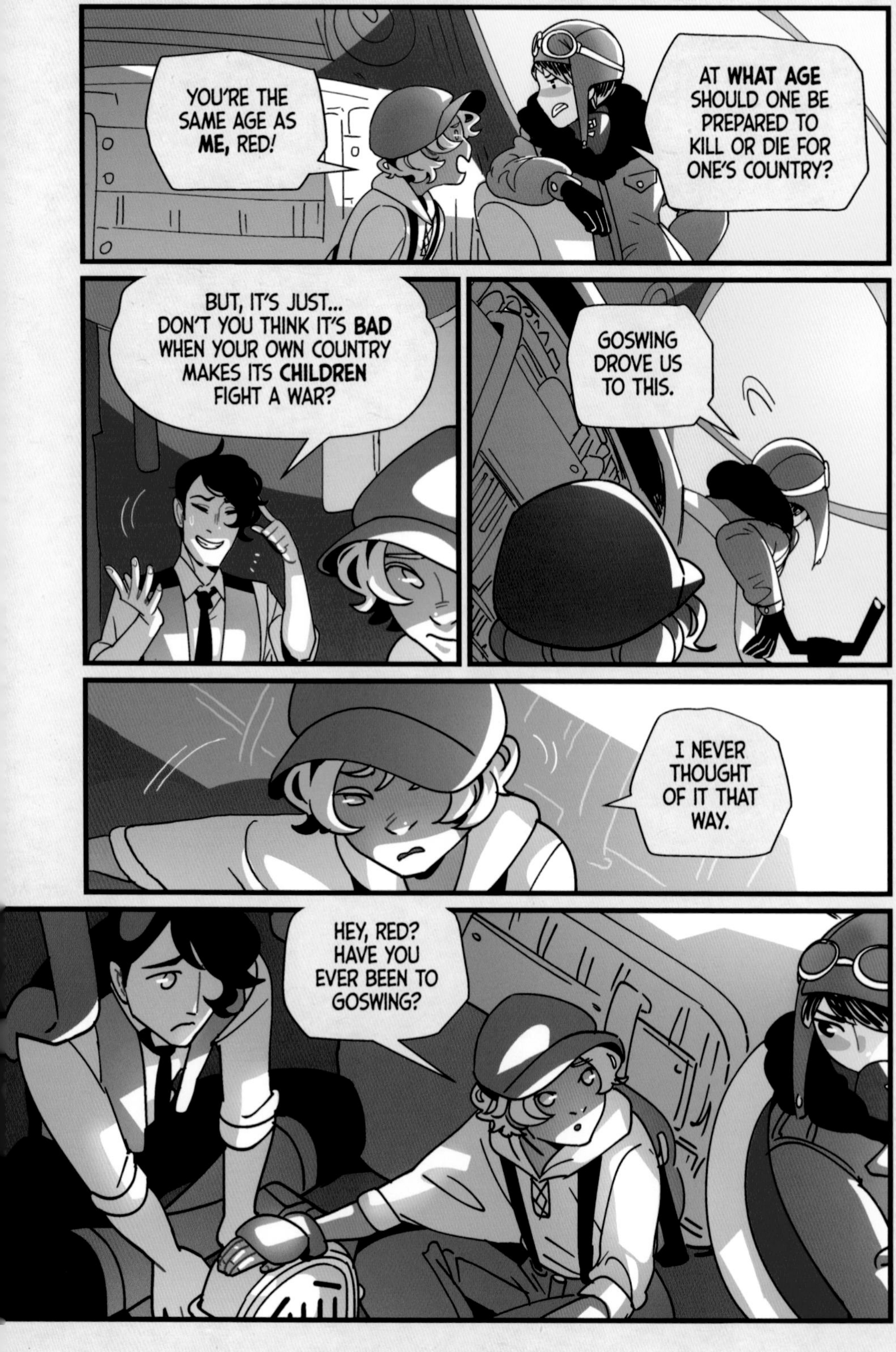
YOU'RE THE SAME AGE AS ME, RED!
AT WHAT AGE SHOULD ONE BE PREPARED TO KILL OR DIE FOR ONE'S COUNTRY?
BUT, IT'S JUST... DON'T YOU THINK IT'S BAD WHEN YOUR OWN COUNTRY MAKES ITS CHILDREN FIGHT A WAR?
GOSWING DROVE US TO THIS.
I NEVER THOUGHT OF IT THAT WAY.
HEY, RED? HAVE YOU EVER BEEN TO GOSWING?

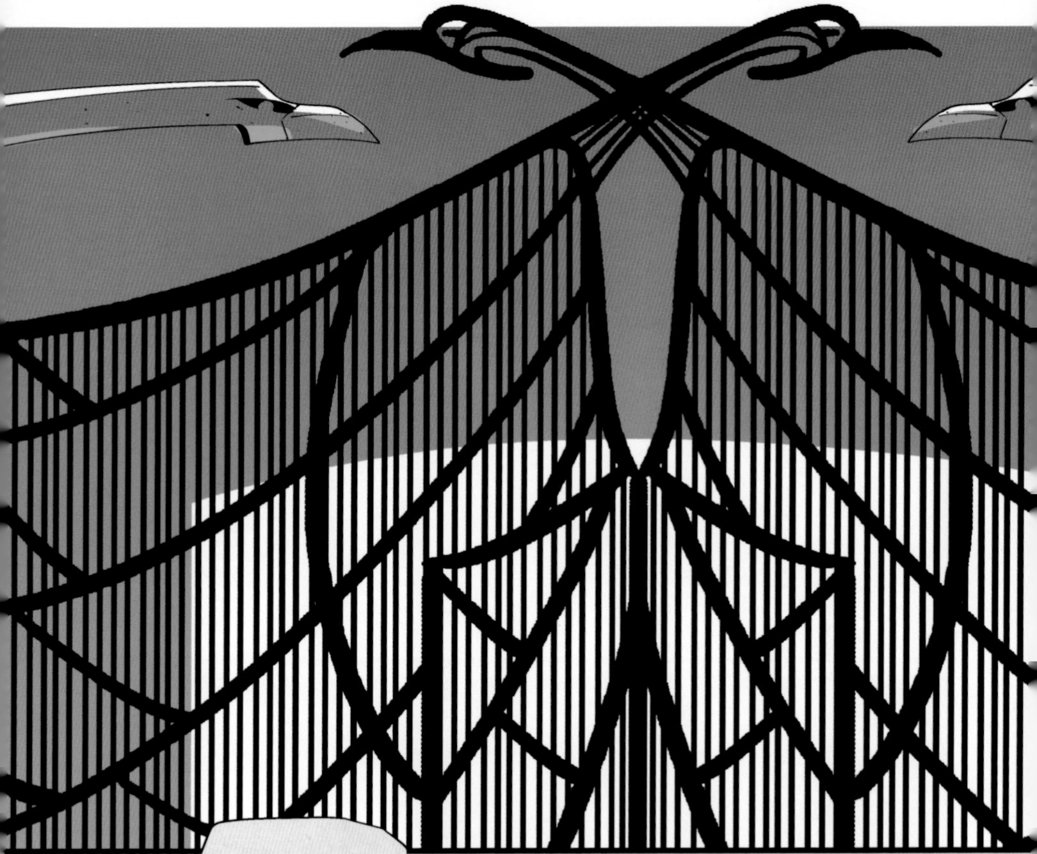

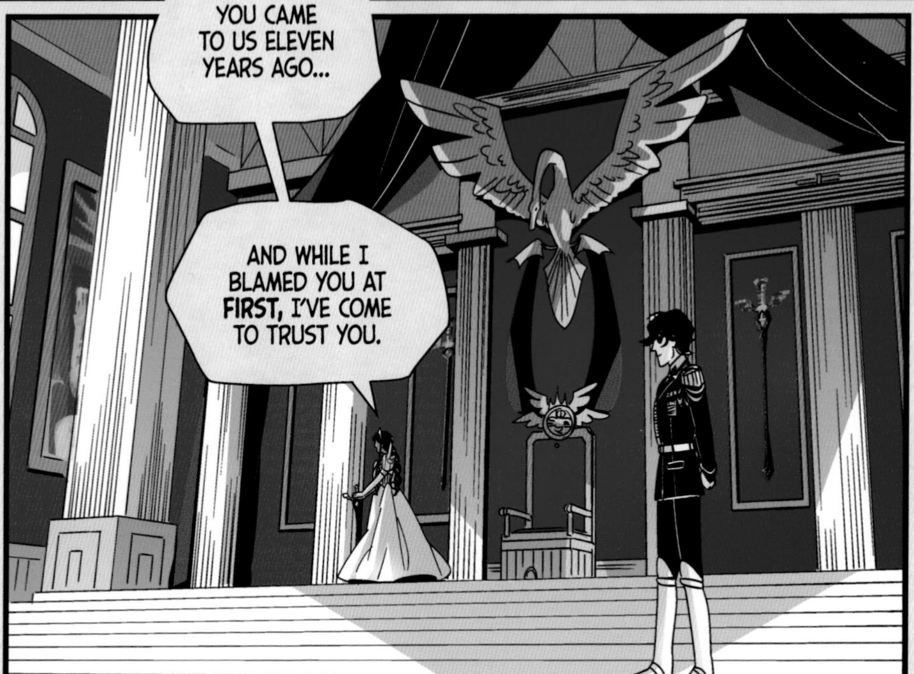
YOU CAME TO US ELEVEN YEARS AGO...
AND WHILE I BLAMED YOU AT FIRST, I'VE COME TO TRUST YOU.

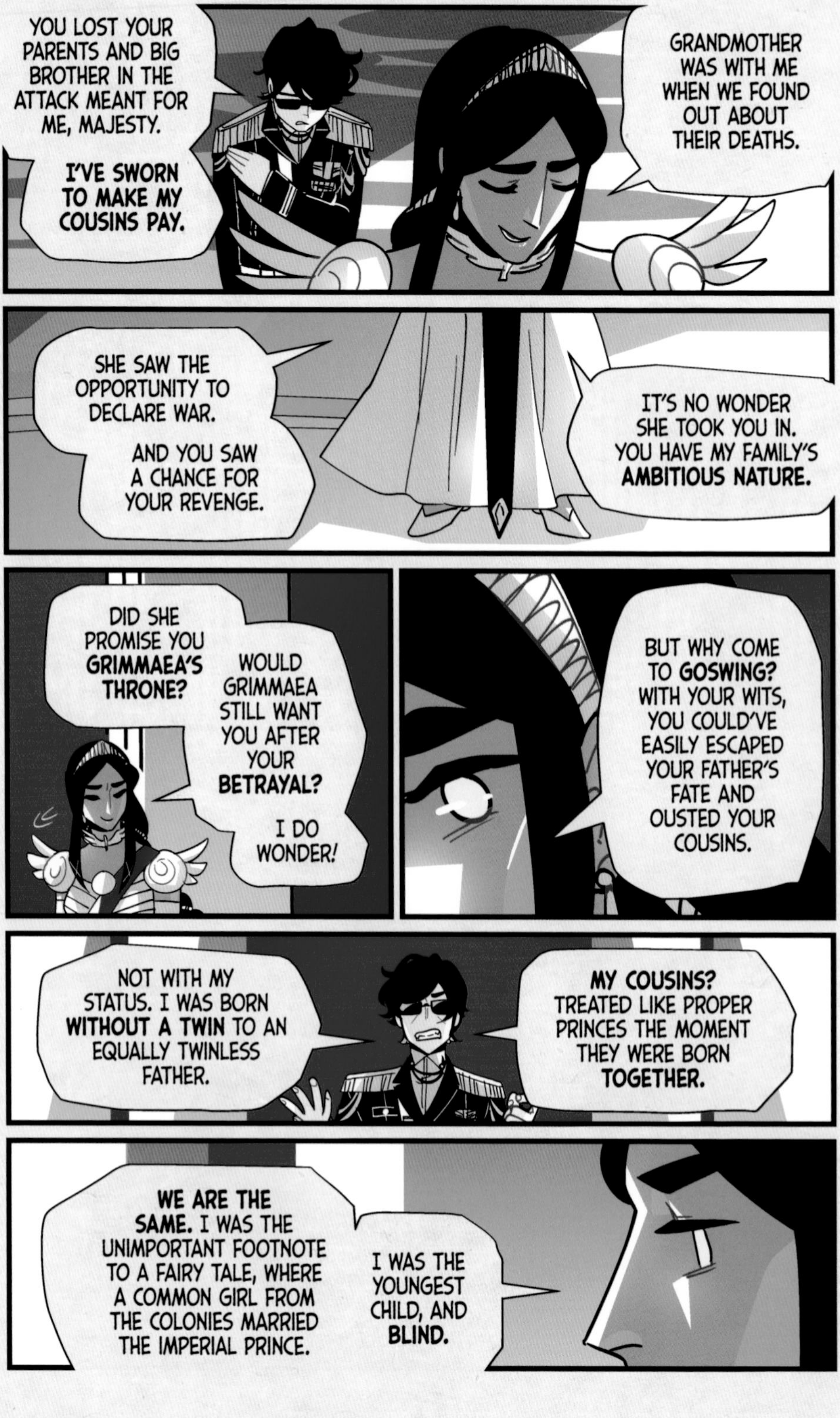

YOU LOST YOUR PARENTS AND BIG BROTHER IN THE ATTACK MEANT FOR ME, MAJESTY.
I'VE SWORN TO MAKE MY COUSINS PAY.
GRANDMOTHER WAS WITH ME WHEN WE FOUND OUT ABOUT THEIR DEATHS.
SHE SAW THE OPPORTUNITY TO DECLARE WAR.
AND YOU SAW A CHANCE FOR YOUR REVENGE.
IT'S NO WONDER SHE TOOK YOU IN. YOU HAVE MY FAMILY'S AMBITIOUS NATURE.
DID SHE PROMISE YOU GRIMMAEA'S THRONE?
WOULD GRIMMAEA STILL WANT YOU AFTER YOUR BETRAYAL?
I DO WONDER!
BUT WHY COME TO GOSWING? WITH YOUR WITS, YOU COULD'VE EASILY ESCAPED YOUR FATHER'S FATE AND OUSTED YOUR COUSINS.
NOT WITH MY STATUS. I WAS BORN WITHOUT A TWIN TO AN EQUALLY TWINLESS FATHER.
MY COUSINS? TREATED LIKE PROPER PRINCES THE MOMENT THEY WERE BORN TOGETHER.
WE ARE THE SAME. I WAS THE UNIMPORTANT FOOTNOTE TO A FAIRY TALE, WHERE A COMMON GIRL FROM THE COLONIES MARRIED THE IMPERIAL PRINCE.
I WAS THE YOUNGEST CHILD, AND BLIND.

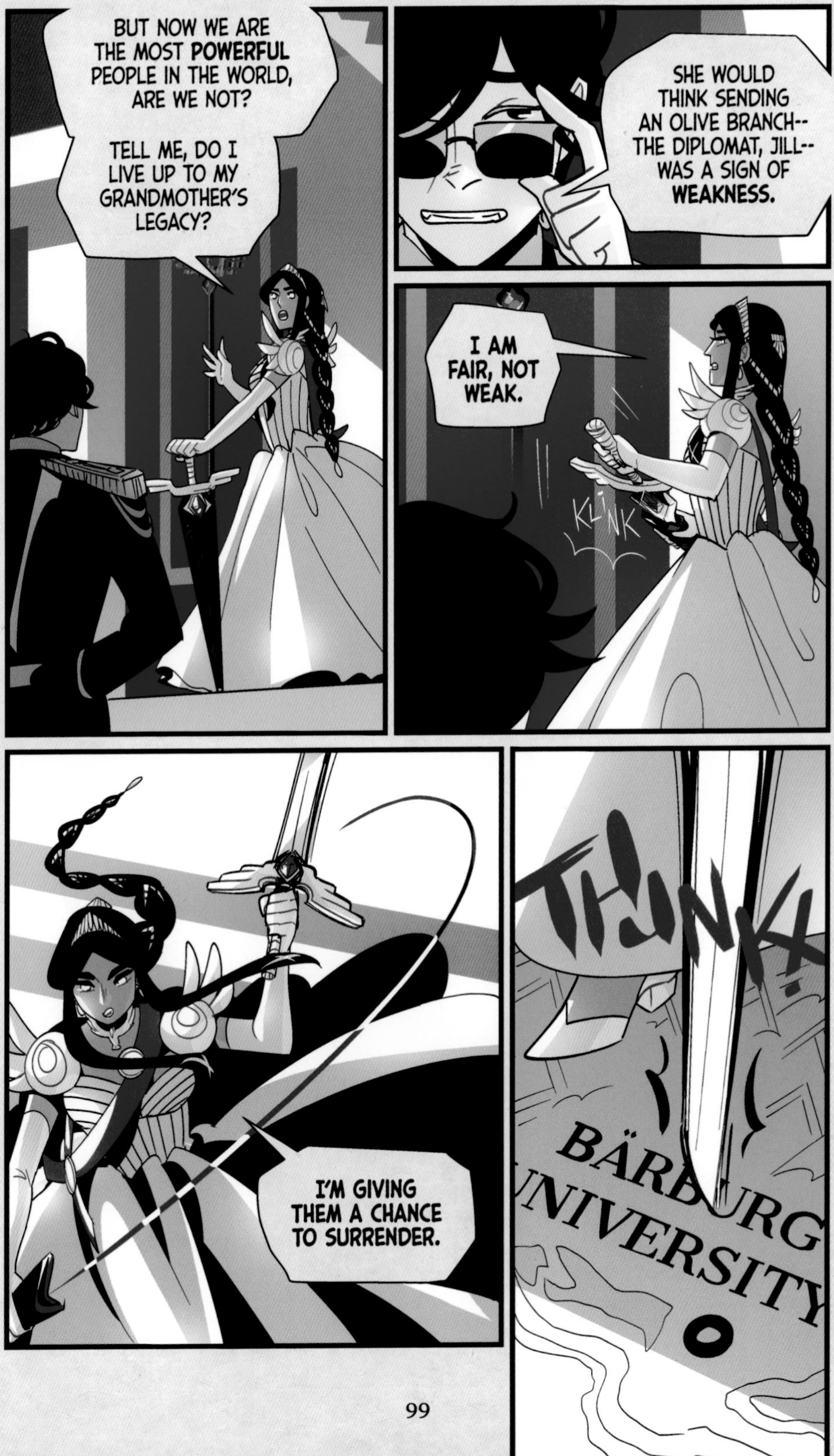
BUT NOW WE ARE THE MOST **POWERFUL** PEOPLE IN THE WORLD, ARE WE NOT?
TELL ME, DO I LIVE UP TO MY GRANDMOTHER'S LEGACY?
SHE WOULD THINK SENDING AN OLIVE BRANCH-- THE DIPLOMAT, JILL-- WAS A SIGN OF **WEAKNESS.**
I AM FAIR, NOT WEAK.
KLINK
I'M GIVING THEM A CHANCE TO SURRENDER.
THUNK!
BÄRBURG UNIVERSITY

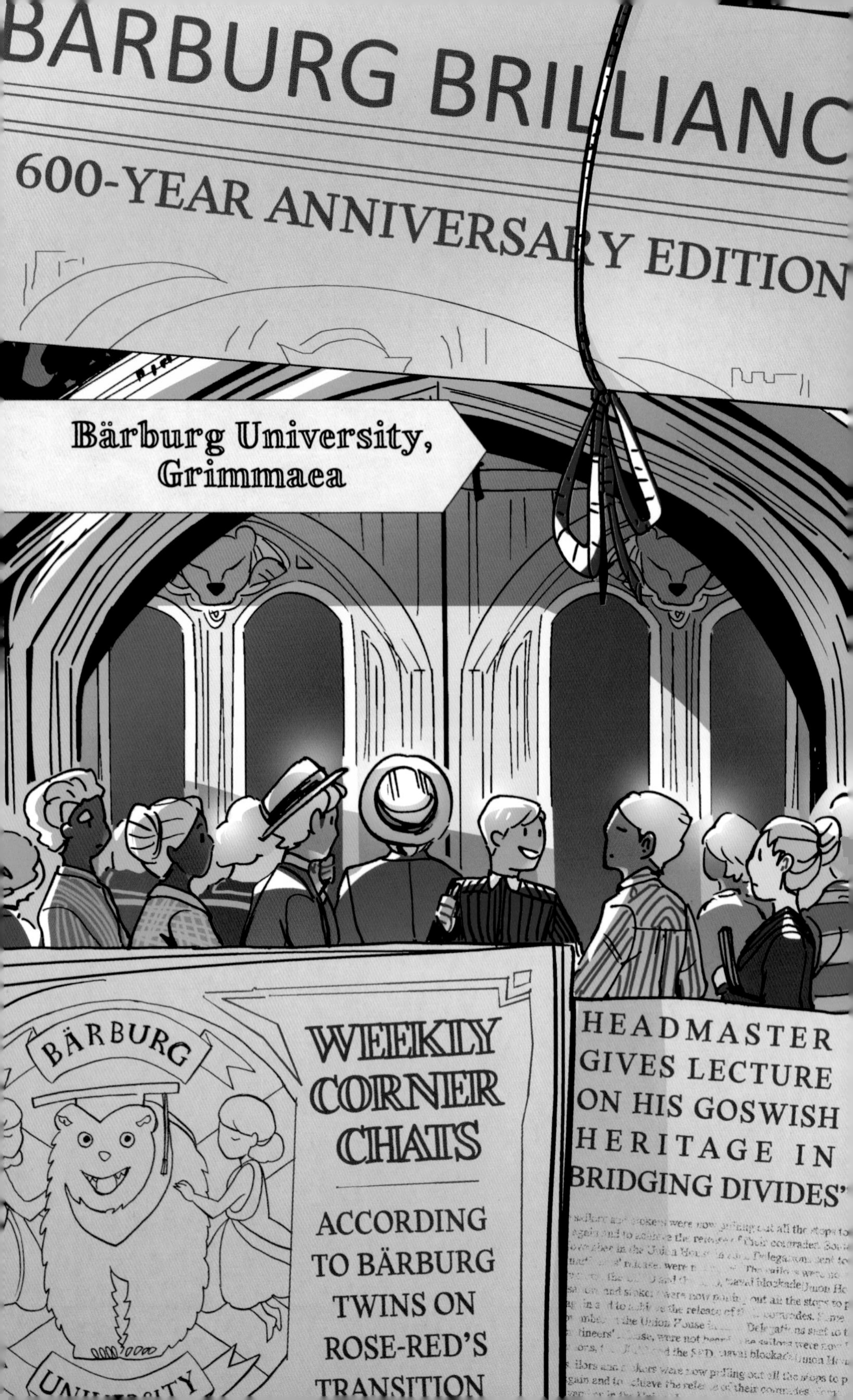
BÄRBURG BRILLIANC
600-YEAR ANNIVERSARY EDITION
Bärburg University, Grimmaea
BÄRBURG
WEEKLY CORNER CHATS
ACCORDING TO BÄRBURG TWINS ON ROSE-RED'S TRANSITION
HEADMASTER GIVES LECTURE ON HIS GOSWISH HERITAGE IN BRIDGING DIVIDES'

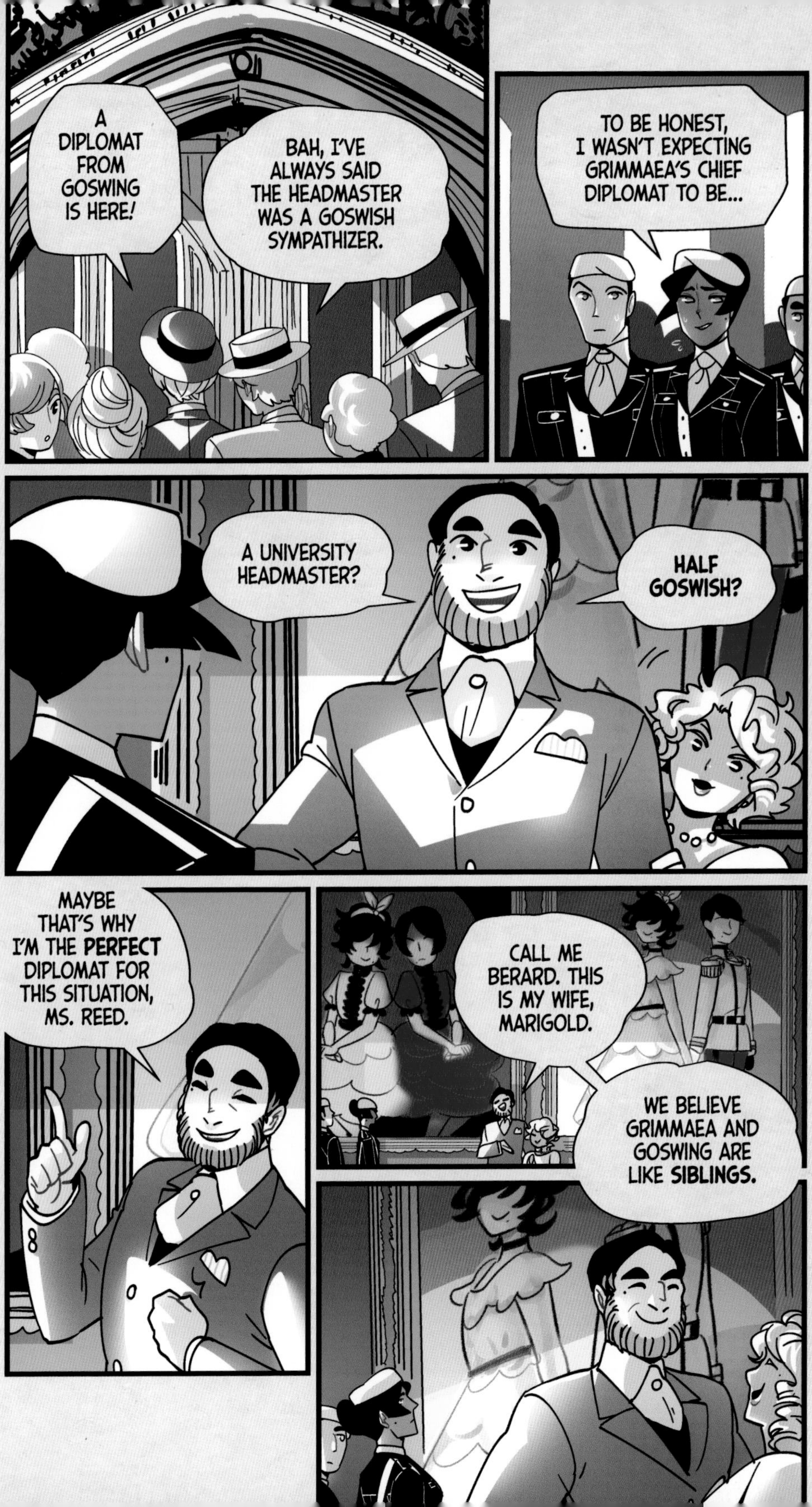
A DIPLOMAT FROM GOSWING IS HERE!
BAH, I'VE ALWAYS SAID THE HEADMASTER WAS A GOSWISH SYMPATHIZER.
TO BE HONEST, I WASN'T EXPECTING GRIMMAEA'S CHIEF DIPLOMAT TO BE...
A UNIVERSITY HEADMASTER?
HALF GOSWISH?
MAYBE THAT'S WHY I'M THE PERFECT DIPLOMAT FOR THIS SITUATION, MS. REED.
CALL ME BERARD. THIS IS MY WIFE, MARIGOLD.
WE BELIEVE GRIMMAEA AND GOSWING ARE LIKE SIBLINGS.

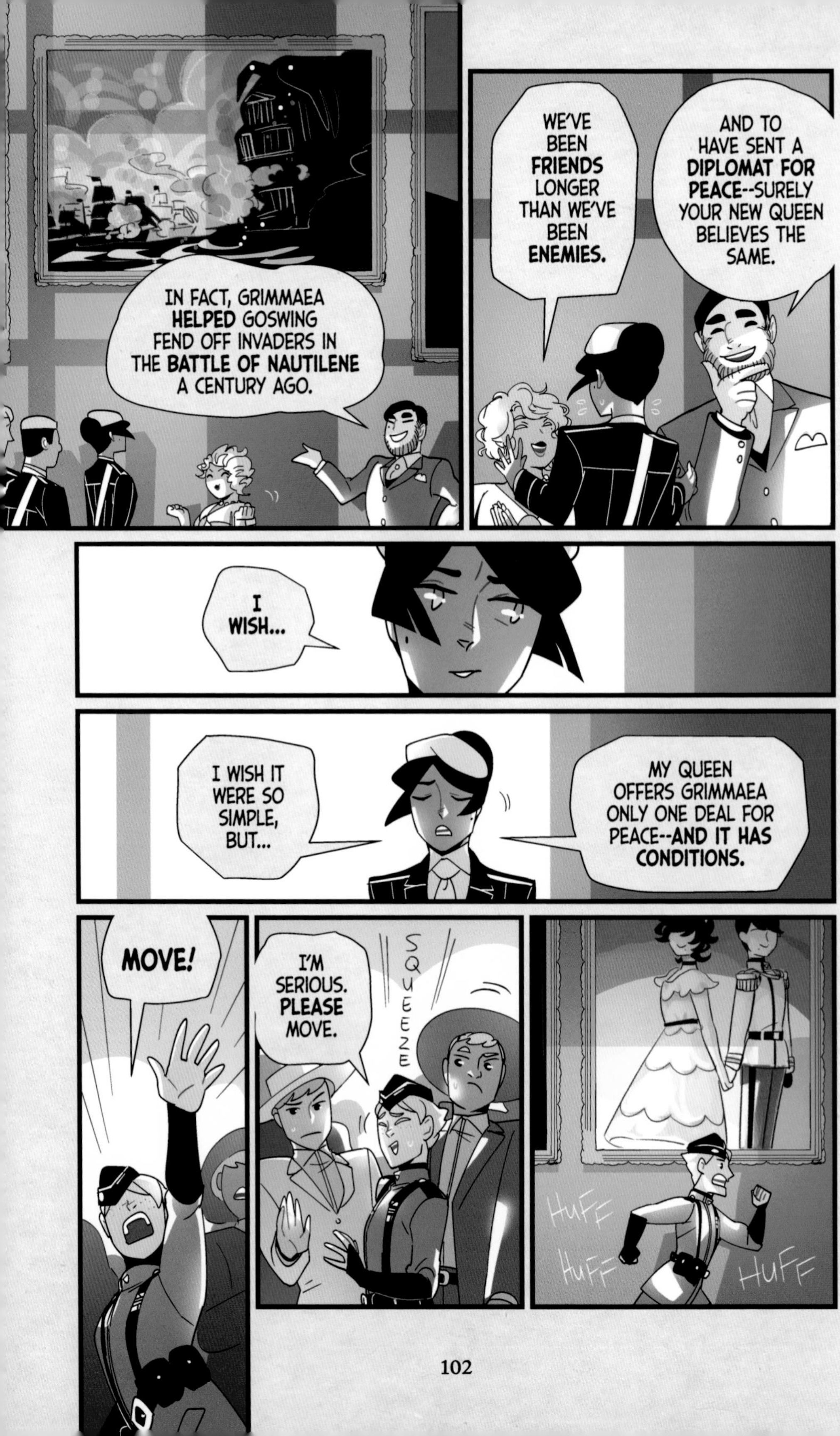
IN FACT, GRIMMAEA **HELPED** GOSWING FEND OFF INVADERS IN THE **BATTLE OF NAUTILENE** A CENTURY AGO.
WE'VE BEEN **FRIENDS** LONGER THAN WE'VE BEEN **ENEMIES.**
AND TO HAVE SENT A **DIPLOMAT FOR PEACE**--SURELY YOUR NEW QUEEN BELIEVES THE SAME.
I WISH...
I WISH IT WERE SO SIMPLE, BUT...
MY QUEEN OFFERS GRIMMAEA ONLY ONE DEAL FOR PEACE--**AND IT HAS CONDITIONS.**
MOVE!
I'M SERIOUS. **PLEASE** MOVE.
SQUEEZE
HUFF
HUFF
HUFF

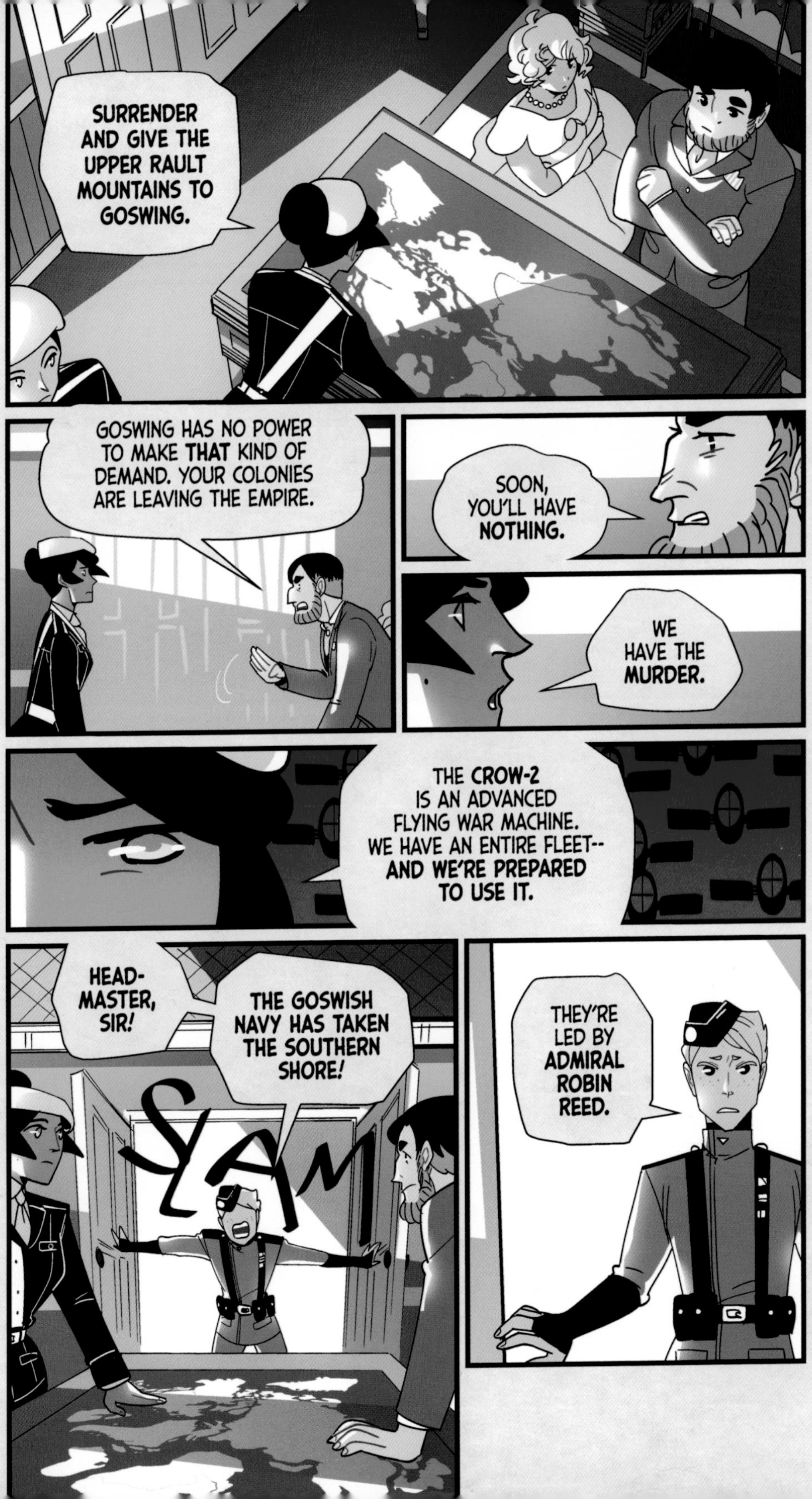
SURRENDER AND GIVE THE UPPER RAULT MOUNTAINS TO GOSWING.
GOSWING HAS NO POWER TO MAKE **THAT** KIND OF DEMAND. YOUR COLONIES ARE LEAVING THE EMPIRE.
SOON, YOU'LL HAVE **NOTHING.**
WE HAVE THE **MURDER.**
THE **CROW-2** IS AN ADVANCED FLYING WAR MACHINE. WE HAVE AN ENTIRE FLEET-- **AND WE'RE PREPARED** TO USE IT.
HEAD-MASTER, SIR!
THE GOSWISH NAVY HAS TAKEN THE SOUTHERN SHORE!
SLAM
THEY'RE LED BY **ADMIRAL ROBIN REED.**

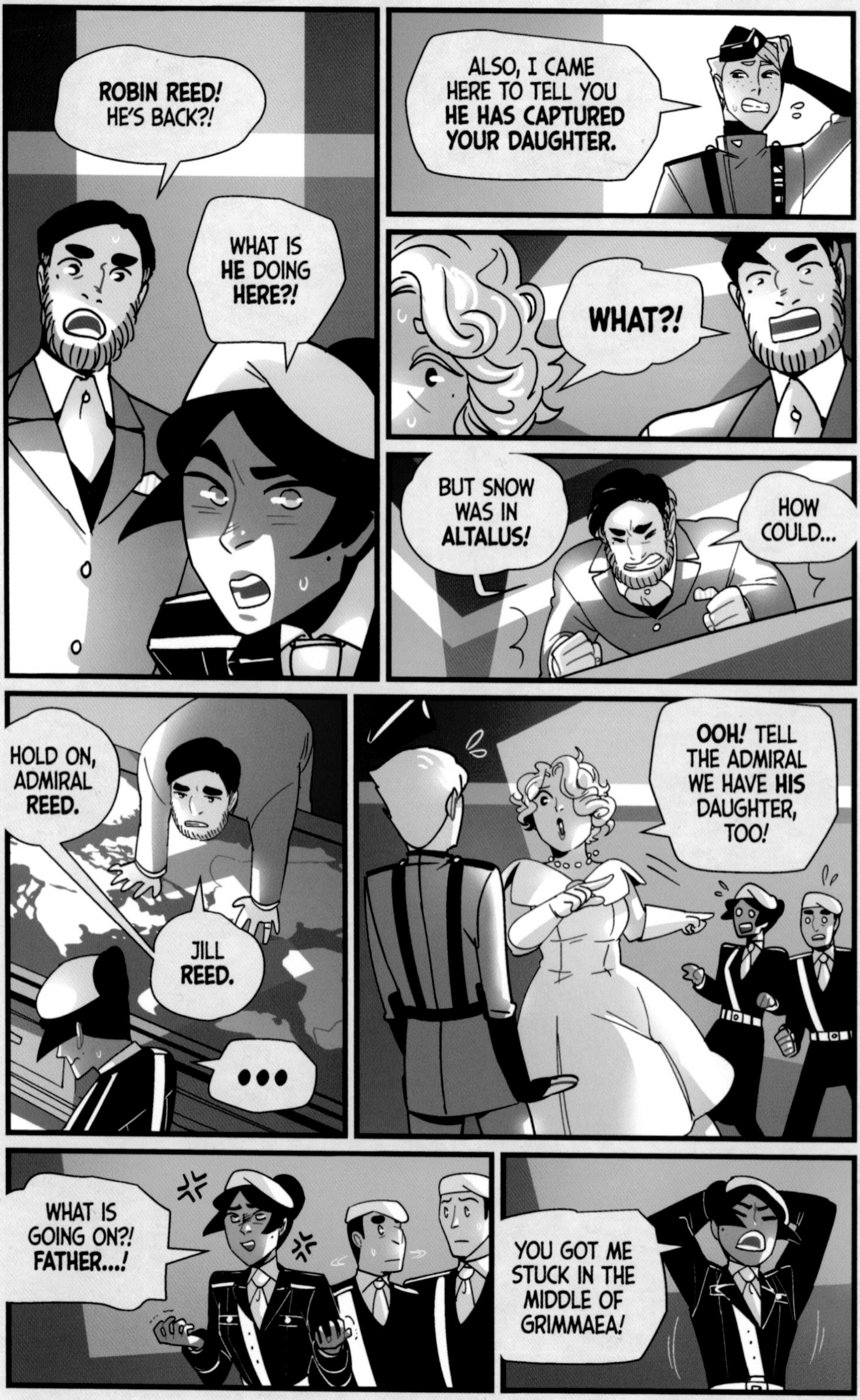
ROBIN REED! HE'S BACK?!
WHAT IS HE DOING HERE?!
ALSO, I CAME HERE TO TELL YOU HE HAS CAPTURED YOUR DAUGHTER.
WHAT?!
BUT SNOW WAS IN ALTALUS!
HOW COULD...
HOLD ON, ADMIRAL REED.
JILL REED.
•••
OOH! TELL THE ADMIRAL WE HAVE HIS DAUGHTER, TOO!
WHAT IS GOING ON?! FATHER...!
YOU GOT ME STUCK IN THE MIDDLE OF GRIMMAEA!

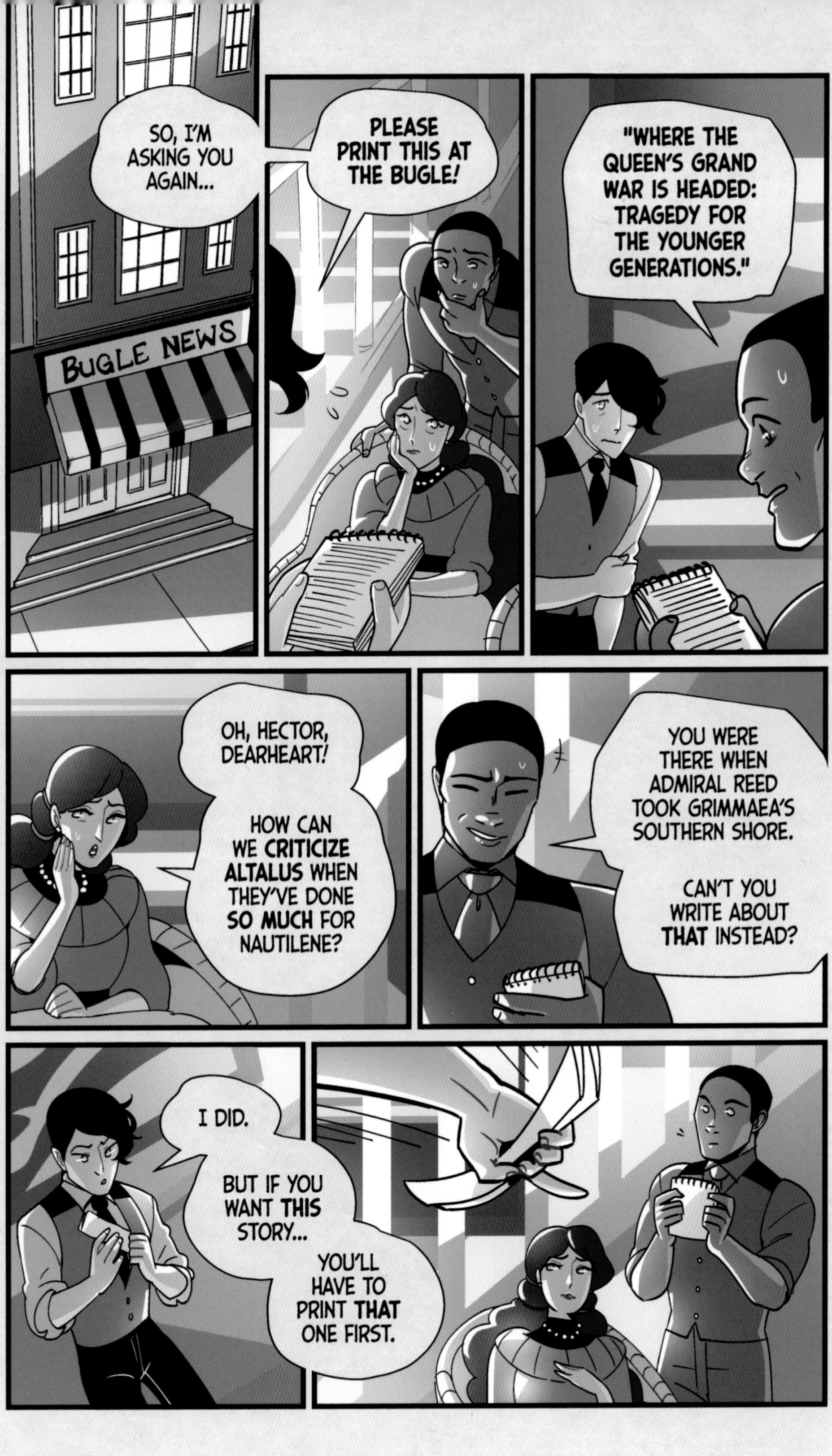

BUGLE NEWS
SO, I'M ASKING YOU AGAIN...
PLEASE PRINT THIS AT THE BUGLE!
"WHERE THE QUEEN'S GRAND WAR IS HEADED: TRAGEDY FOR THE YOUNGER GENERATIONS."
OH, HECTOR, DEARHEART!
HOW CAN WE CRITICIZE ALTALUS WHEN THEY'VE DONE SO MUCH FOR NAUTILENE?
YOU WERE THERE WHEN ADMIRAL REED TOOK GRIMMAEA'S SOUTHERN SHORE.
CAN'T YOU WRITE ABOUT THAT INSTEAD?
I DID.
BUT IF YOU WANT THIS STORY...
YOU'LL HAVE TO PRINT THAT ONE FIRST.

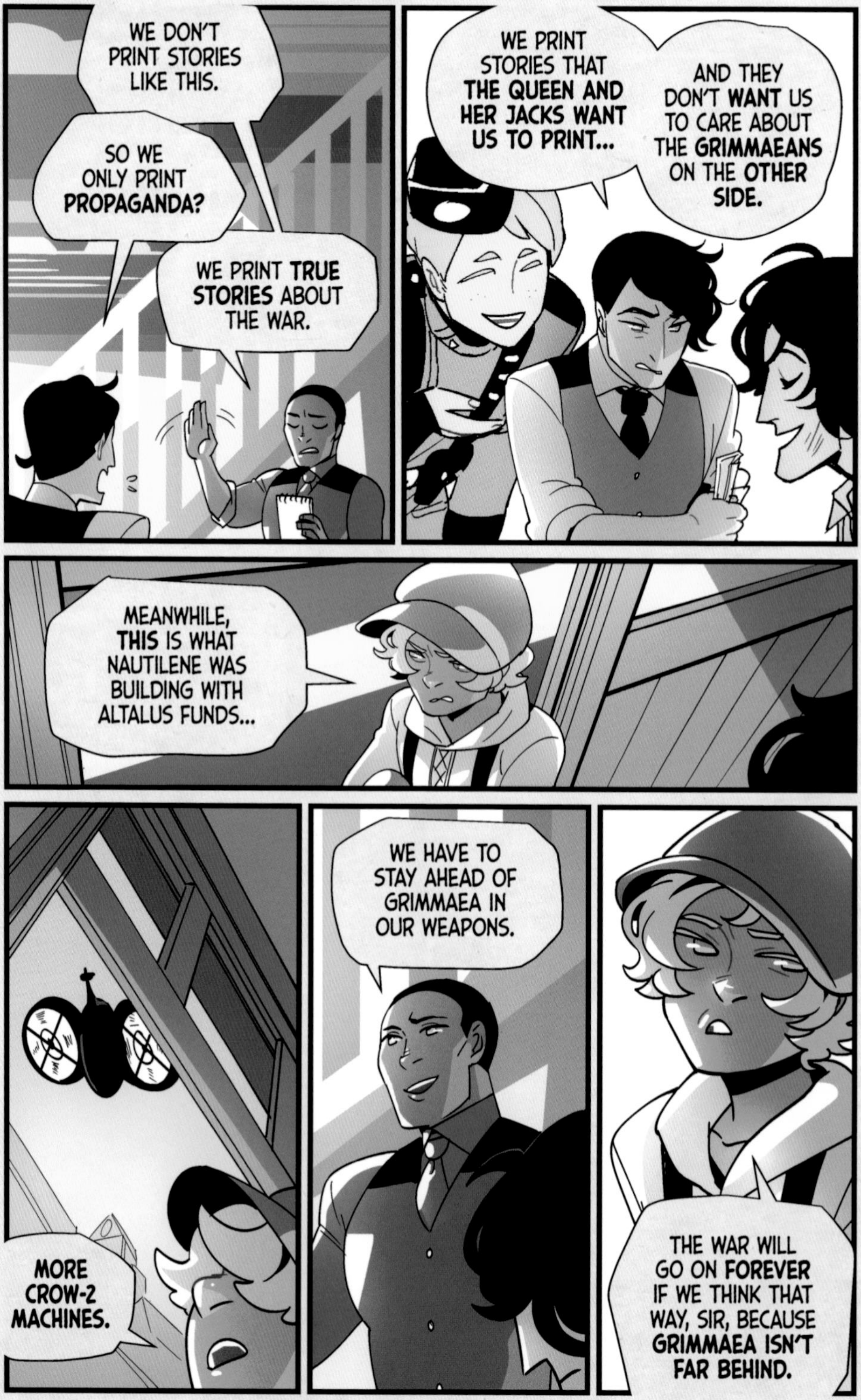
WE DON'T PRINT STORIES LIKE THIS.
SO WE ONLY PRINT PROPAGANDA?
WE PRINT TRUE STORIES ABOUT THE WAR.
WE PRINT STORIES THAT THE QUEEN AND HER JACKS WANT US TO PRINT...
AND THEY DON'T WANT US TO CARE ABOUT THE GRIMMAEANS ON THE OTHER SIDE.
MEANWHILE, THIS IS WHAT NAUTILENE WAS BUILDING WITH ALTALUS FUNDS...
MORE CROW-2 MACHINES.
WE HAVE TO STAY AHEAD OF GRIMMAEA IN OUR WEAPONS.
THE WAR WILL GO ON FOREVER IF WE THINK THAT WAY, SIR, BECAUSE GRIMMAEA ISN'T FAR BEHIND.

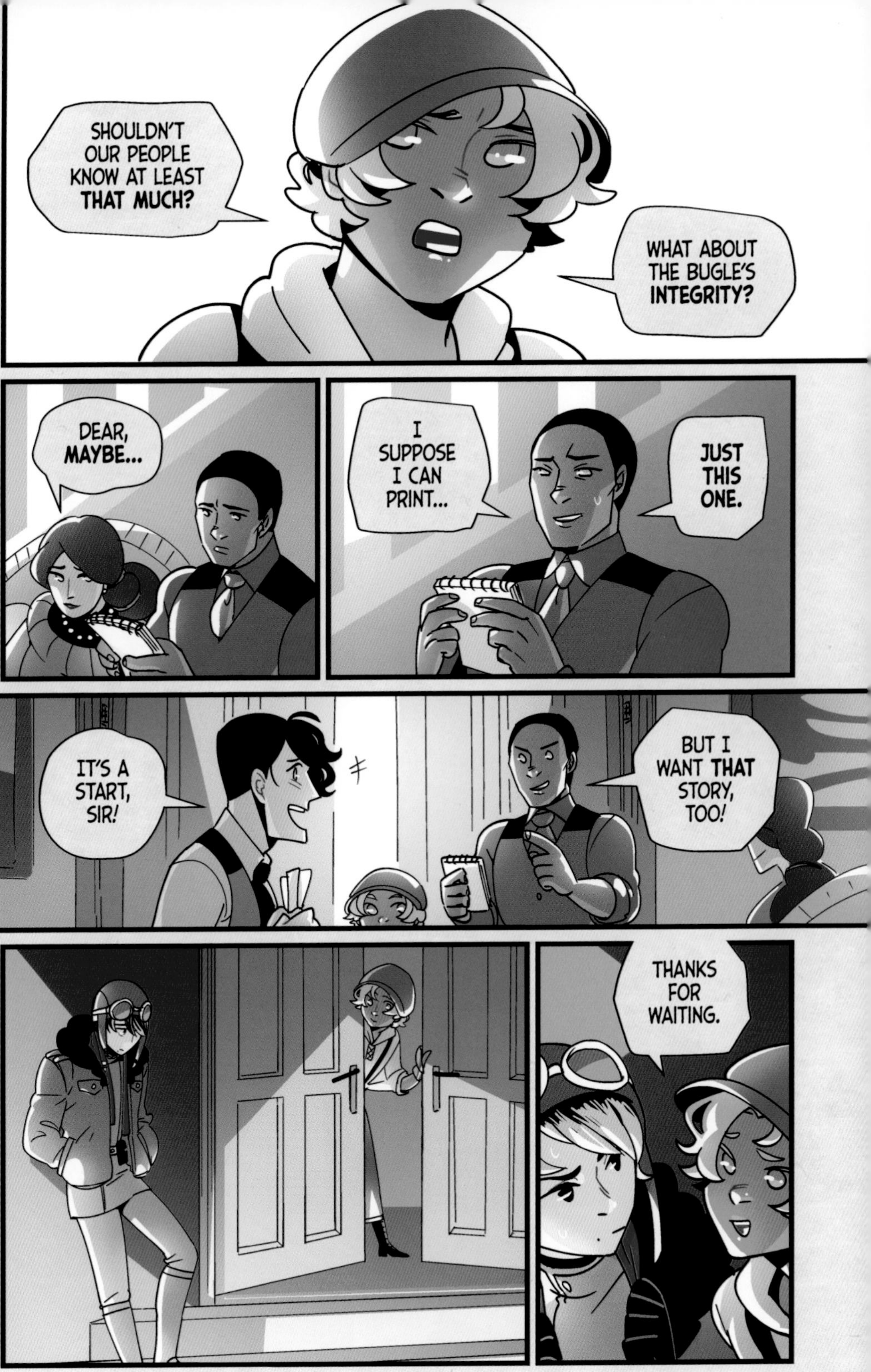
SHOULDN'T OUR PEOPLE KNOW AT LEAST **THAT MUCH?**
WHAT ABOUT THE BUGLE'S **INTEGRITY?**
DEAR, **MAYBE...**
I SUPPOSE I CAN PRINT...
JUST THIS ONE.
IT'S A START, SIR!
BUT I WANT **THAT** STORY, TOO!
THANKS FOR WAITING.

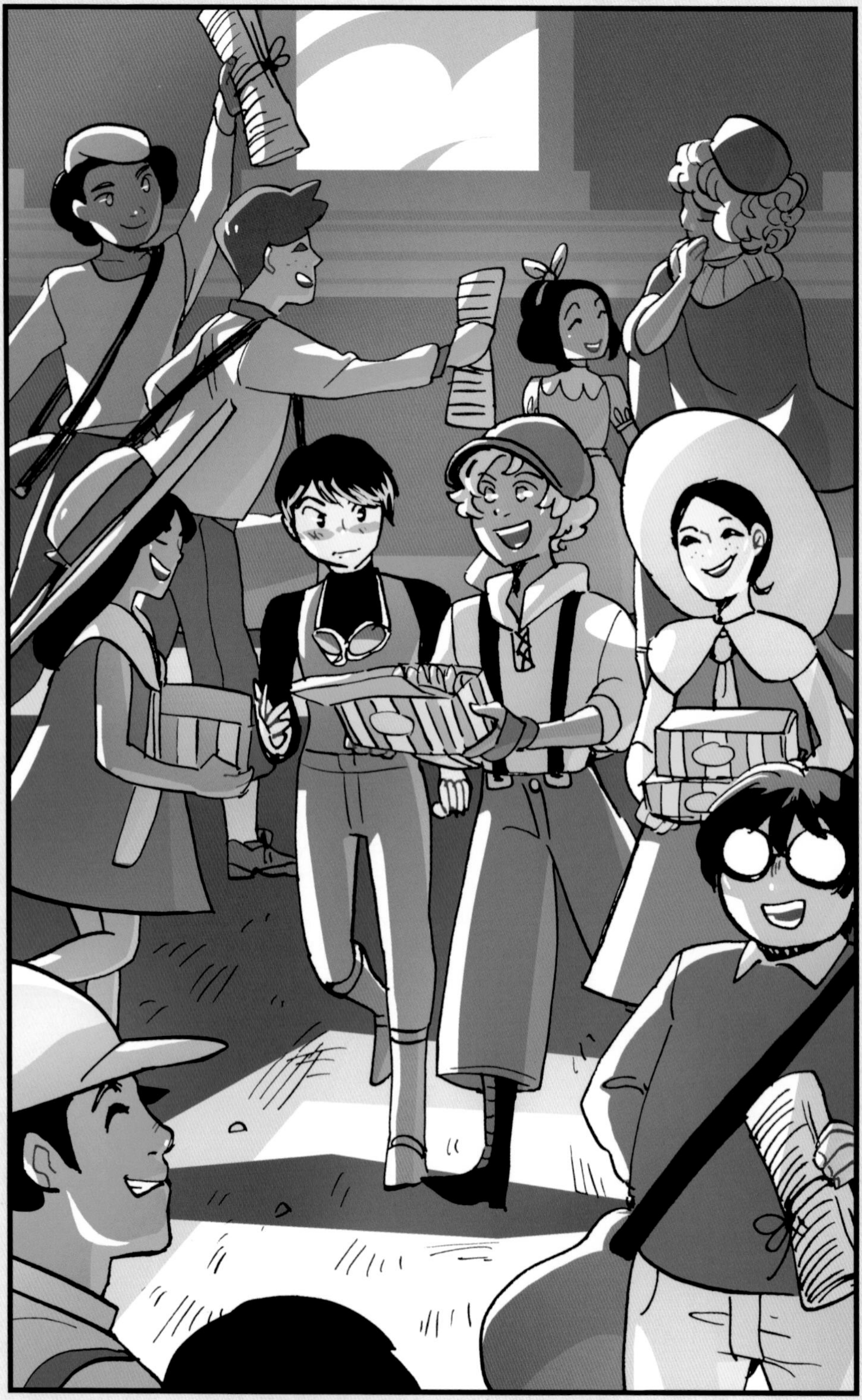

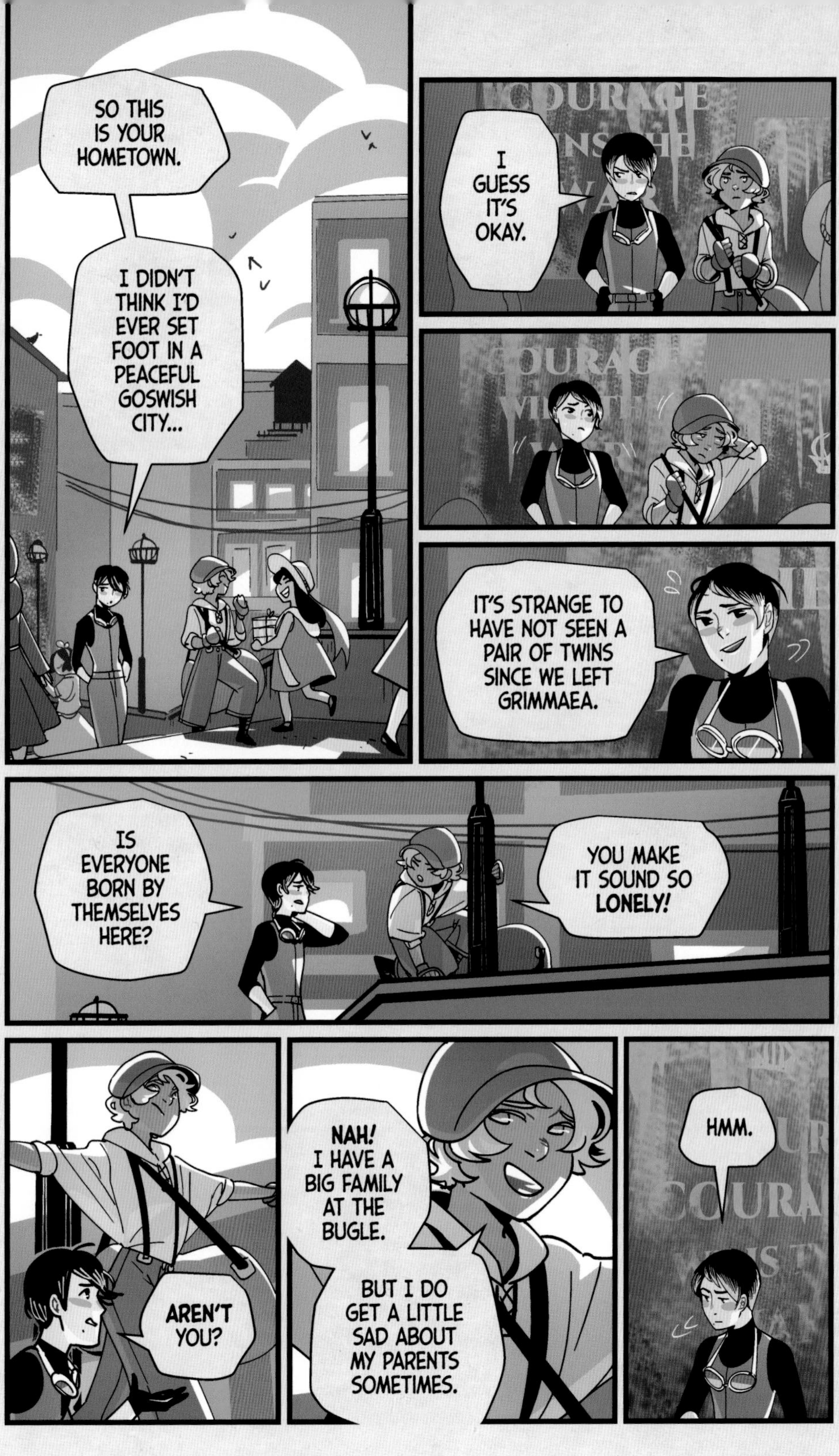
SO THIS IS YOUR HOMETOWN.
I DIDN'T THINK I'D EVER SET FOOT IN A PEACEFUL GOSWISH CITY...
I GUESS IT'S OKAY.
IT'S STRANGE TO HAVE NOT SEEN A PAIR OF TWINS SINCE WE LEFT GRIMMAEA.
IS EVERYONE BORN BY THEMSELVES HERE?
YOU MAKE IT SOUND SO **LONELY!**
AREN'T YOU?
NAH! I HAVE A BIG FAMILY AT THE BUGLE.
BUT I DO GET A LITTLE SAD ABOUT MY PARENTS SOMETIMES.
HMM.

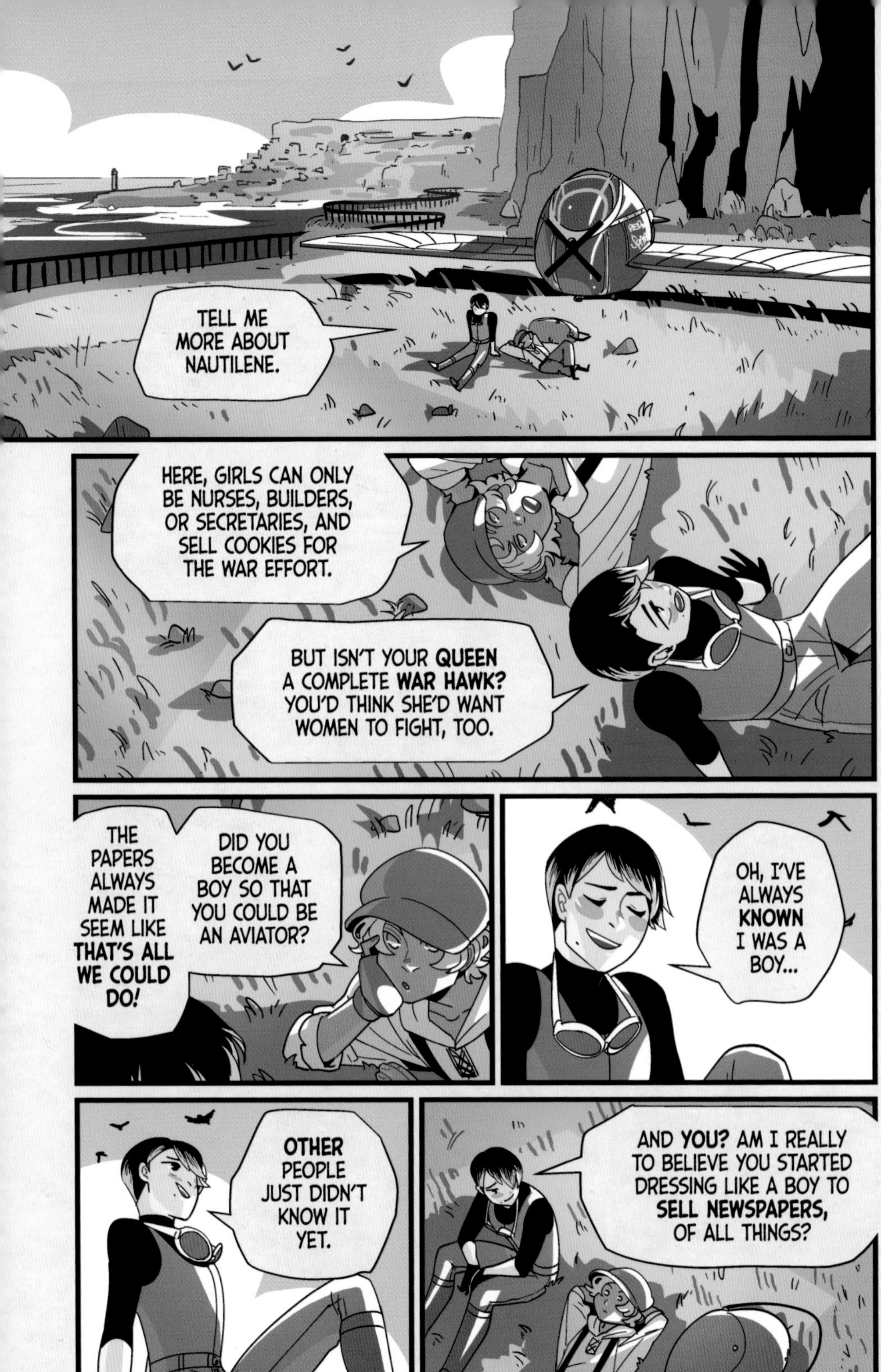
TELL ME MORE ABOUT NAUTILENE.
HERE, GIRLS CAN ONLY BE NURSES, BUILDERS, OR SECRETARIES, AND SELL COOKIES FOR THE WAR EFFORT.
BUT ISN'T YOUR QUEEN A COMPLETE WAR HAWK? YOU'D THINK SHE'D WANT WOMEN TO FIGHT, TOO.
THE PAPERS ALWAYS MADE IT SEEM LIKE THAT'S ALL WE COULD DO!
DID YOU BECOME A BOY SO THAT YOU COULD BE AN AVIATOR?
OH, I'VE ALWAYS KNOWN I WAS A BOY...
OTHER PEOPLE JUST DIDN'T KNOW IT YET.
AND YOU? AM I REALLY TO BELIEVE YOU STARTED DRESSING LIKE A BOY TO SELL NEWSPAPERS, OF ALL THINGS?

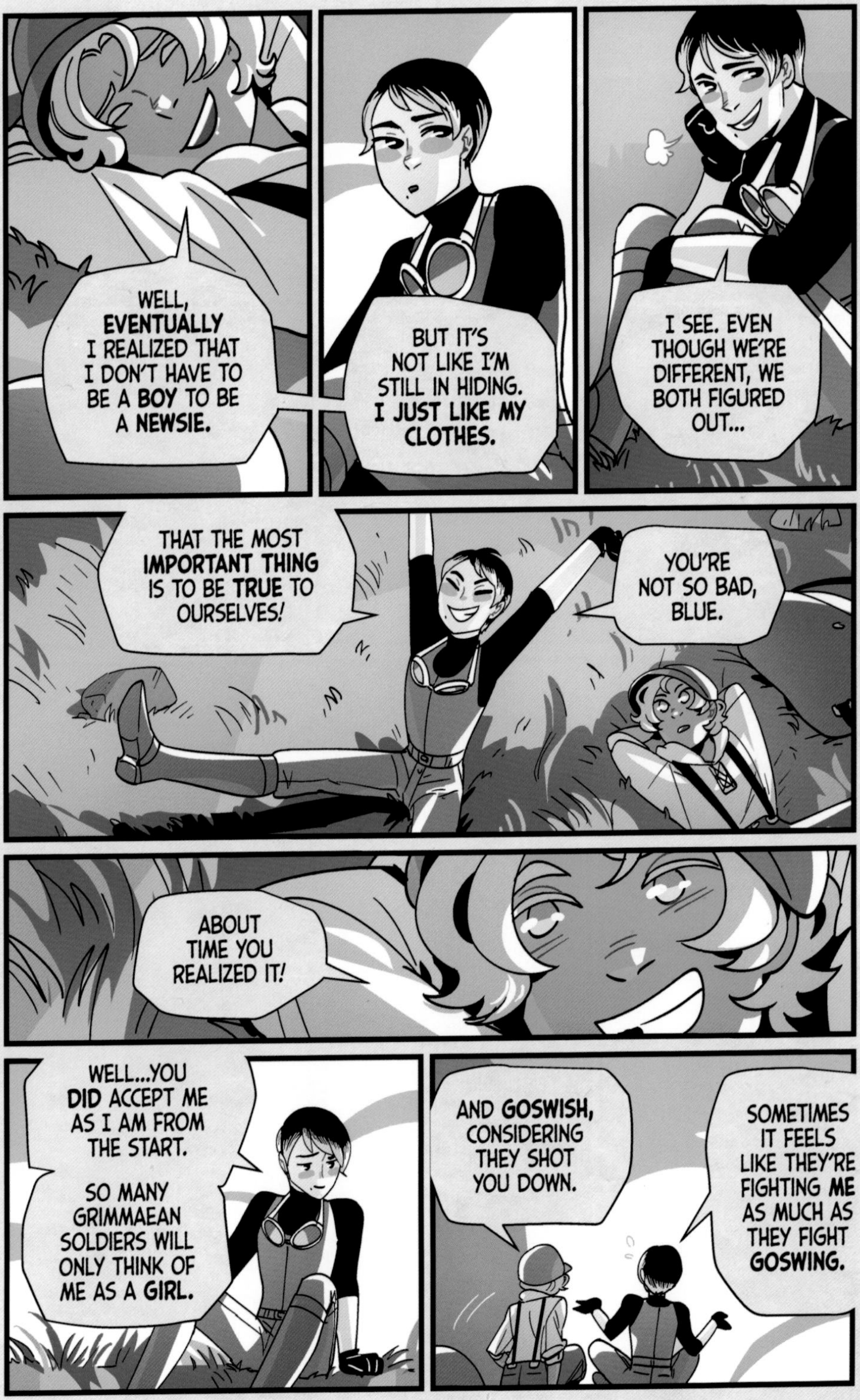
WELL, EVENTUALLY I REALIZED THAT I DON'T HAVE TO BE A BOY TO BE A NEWSIE.
BUT IT'S NOT LIKE I'M STILL IN HIDING. I JUST LIKE MY CLOTHES.
I SEE. EVEN THOUGH WE'RE DIFFERENT, WE BOTH FIGURED OUT...
THAT THE MOST IMPORTANT THING IS TO BE TRUE TO OURSELVES!
YOU'RE NOT SO BAD, BLUE.
ABOUT TIME YOU REALIZED IT!
WELL...YOU DID ACCEPT ME AS I AM FROM THE START.
SO MANY GRIMMAEAN SOLDIERS WILL ONLY THINK OF ME AS A GIRL.
AND GOSWISH, CONSIDERING THEY SHOT YOU DOWN.
SOMETIMES IT FEELS LIKE THEY'RE FIGHTING ME AS MUCH AS THEY FIGHT GOSWING.

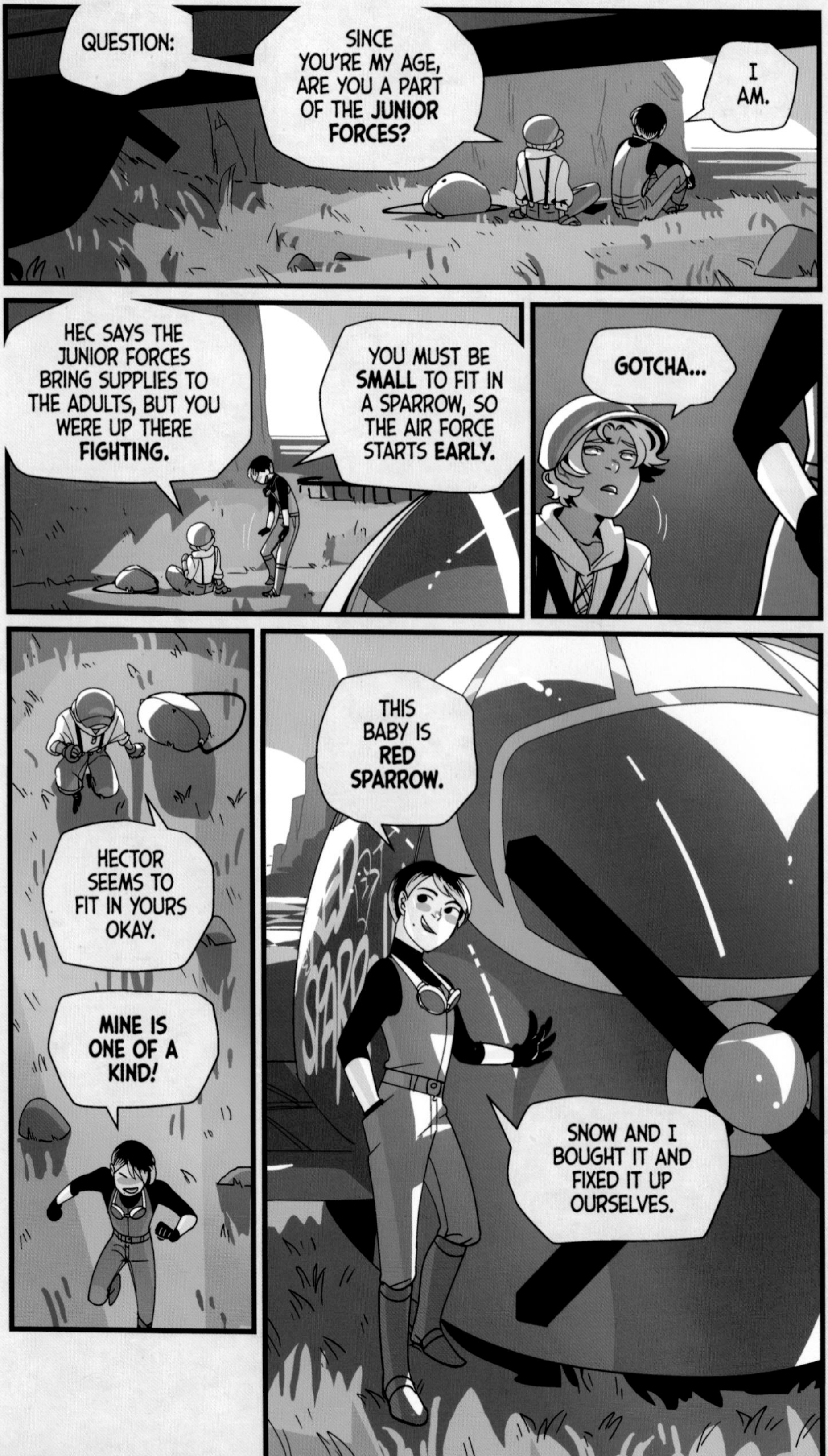
QUESTION:
SINCE YOU'RE MY AGE, ARE YOU A PART OF THE **JUNIOR FORCES?**
I AM.
HEC SAYS THE JUNIOR FORCES BRING SUPPLIES TO THE ADULTS, BUT YOU WERE UP THERE **FIGHTING.**
YOU MUST BE **SMALL** TO FIT IN A SPARROW, SO THE AIR FORCE STARTS **EARLY.**
GOTCHA...
HECTOR SEEMS TO FIT IN YOURS OKAY.
MINE IS ONE OF A KIND!
THIS BABY IS **RED SPARROW.**
SNOW AND I BOUGHT IT AND FIXED IT UP OURSELVES.

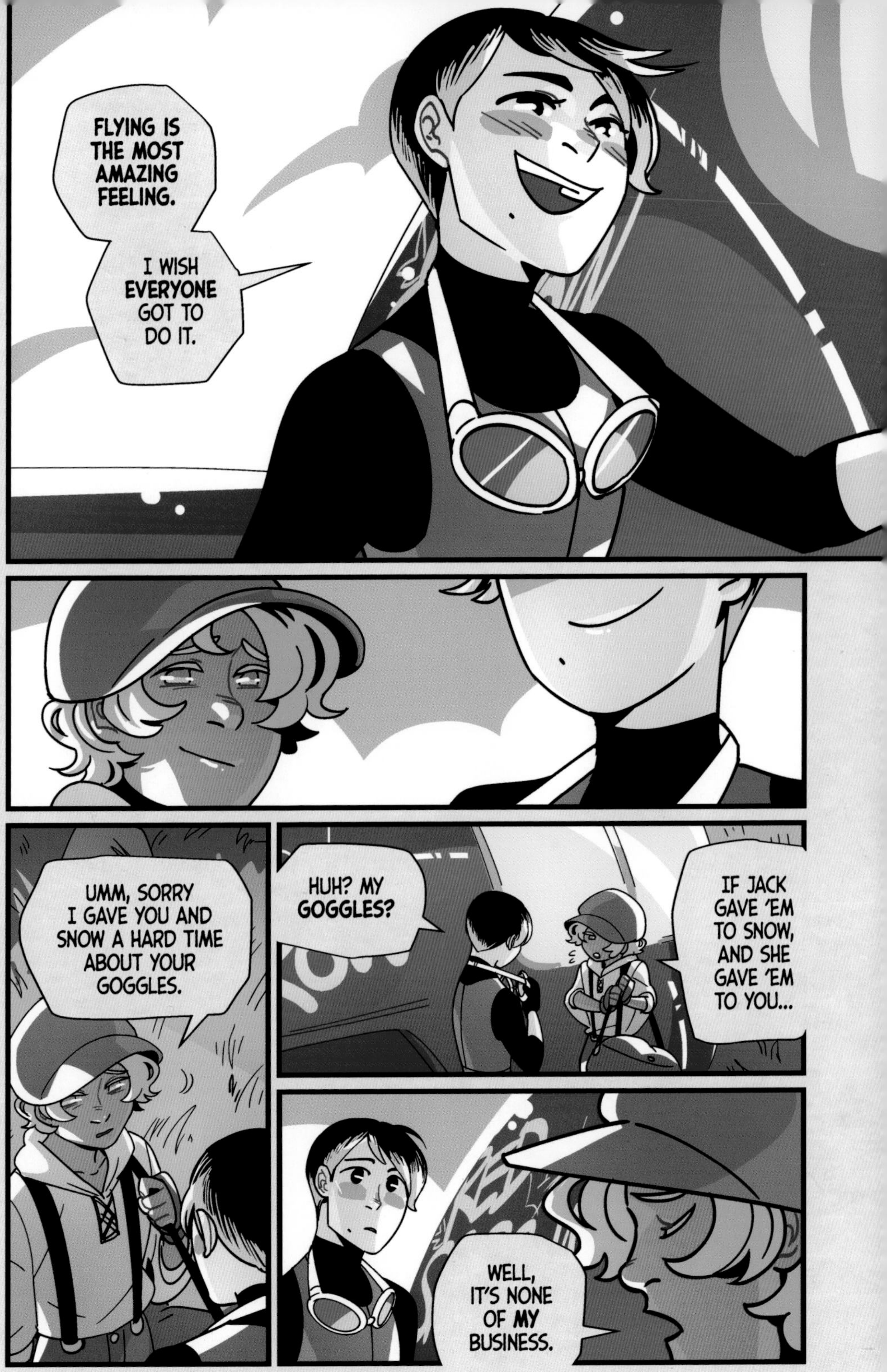
FLYING IS THE MOST AMAZING FEELING.
I WISH EVERYONE GOT TO DO IT.
UMM, SORRY I GAVE YOU AND SNOW A HARD TIME ABOUT YOUR GOGGLES.
HUH? MY GOGGLES?
IF JACK GAVE 'EM TO SNOW, AND SHE GAVE 'EM TO YOU...
WELL, IT'S NONE OF MY BUSINESS.

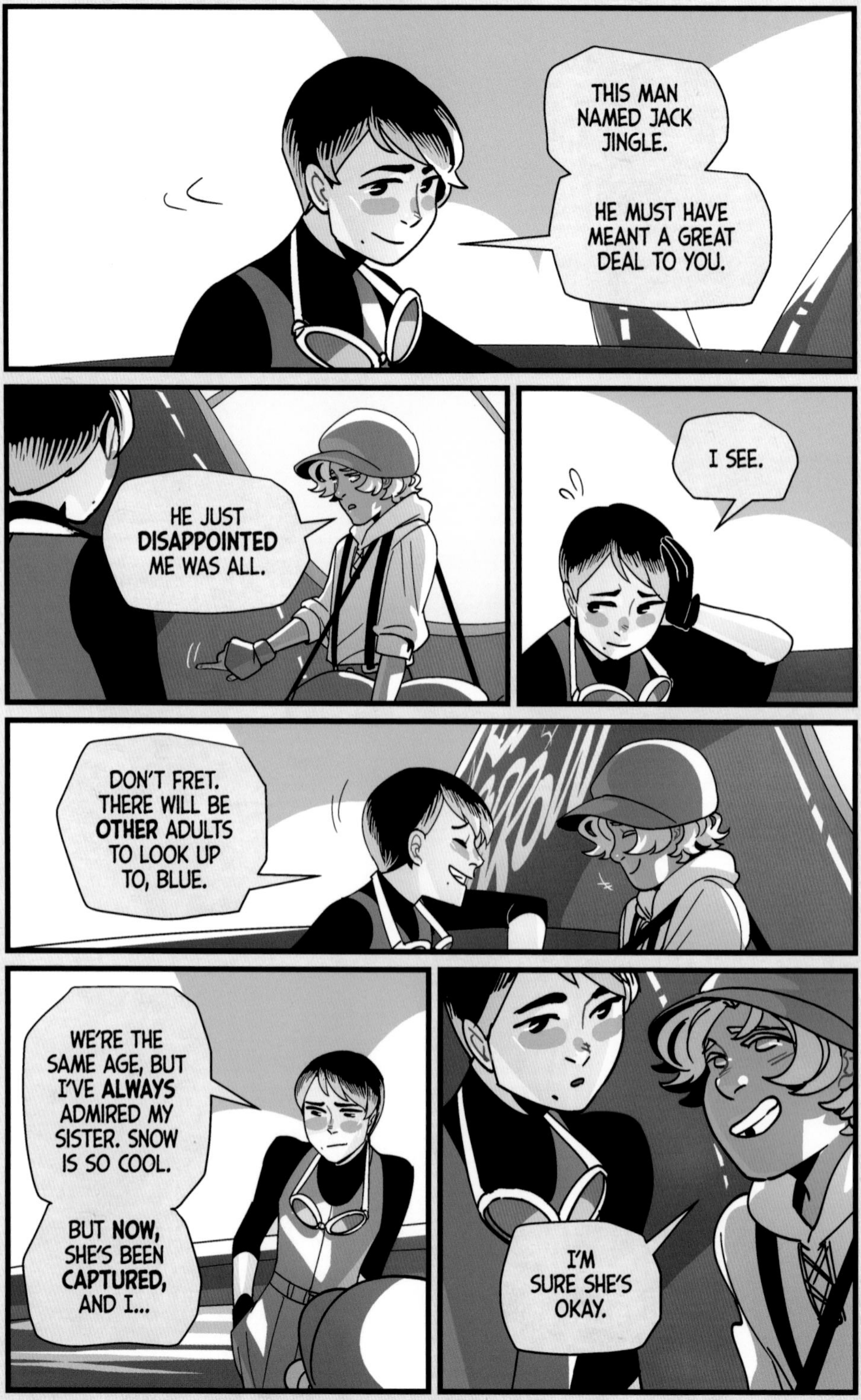
THIS MAN NAMED JACK JINGLE.
HE MUST HAVE MEANT A GREAT DEAL TO YOU.
HE JUST DISAPPOINTED ME WAS ALL.
I SEE.
DON'T FRET. THERE WILL BE OTHER ADULTS TO LOOK UP TO, BLUE.
WE'RE THE SAME AGE, BUT I'VE ALWAYS ADMIRED MY SISTER. SNOW IS SO COOL.
BUT NOW, SHE'S BEEN CAPTURED, AND I...
I'M SURE SHE'S OKAY.

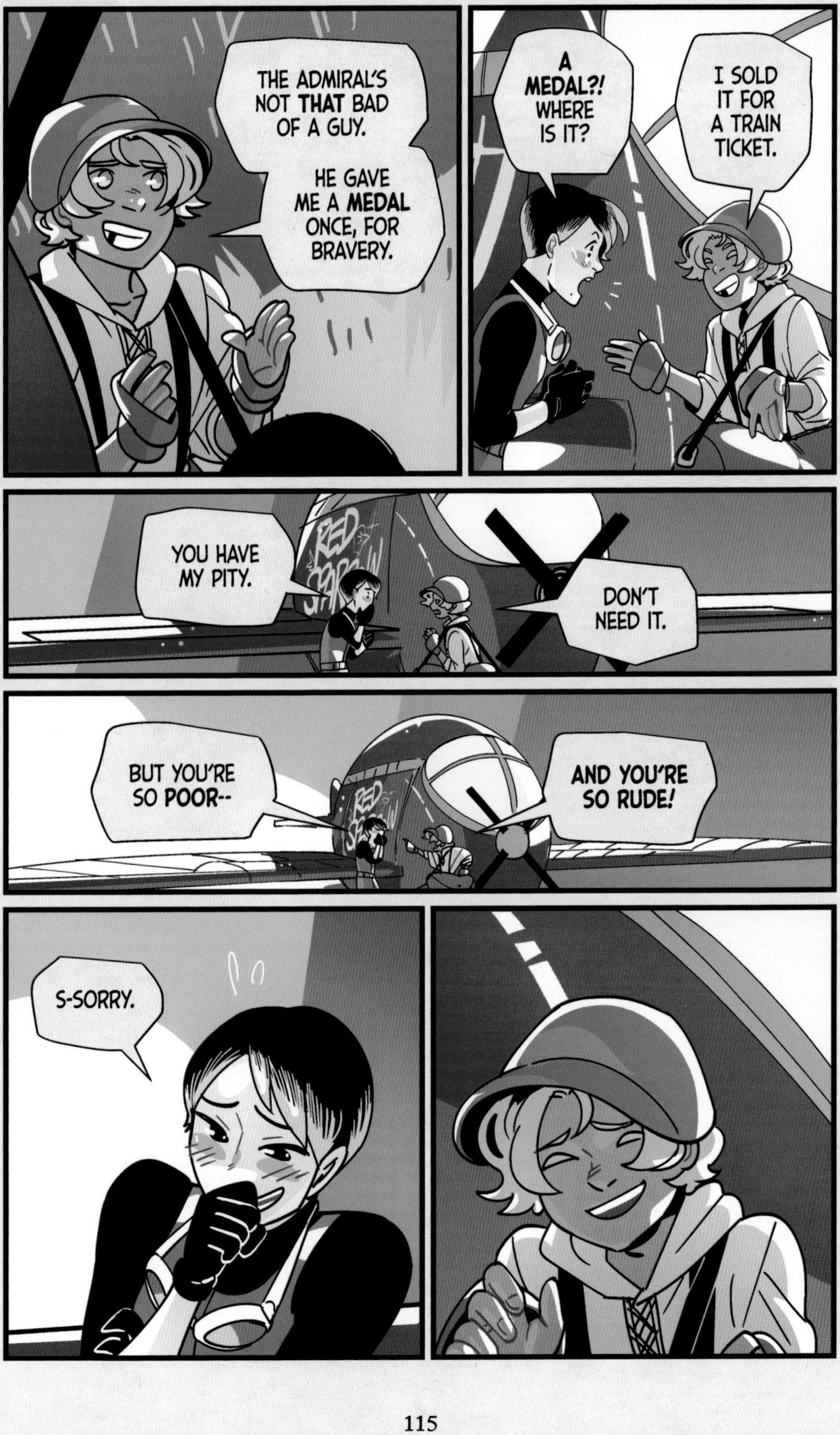
THE ADMIRAL'S NOT THAT BAD OF A GUY.
HE GAVE ME A MEDAL ONCE, FOR BRAVERY.
A MEDAL?! WHERE IS IT?
I SOLD IT FOR A TRAIN TICKET.
YOU HAVE MY PITY.
DON'T NEED IT.
BUT YOU'RE SO POOR--
AND YOU'RE SO RUDE!
S-SORRY.

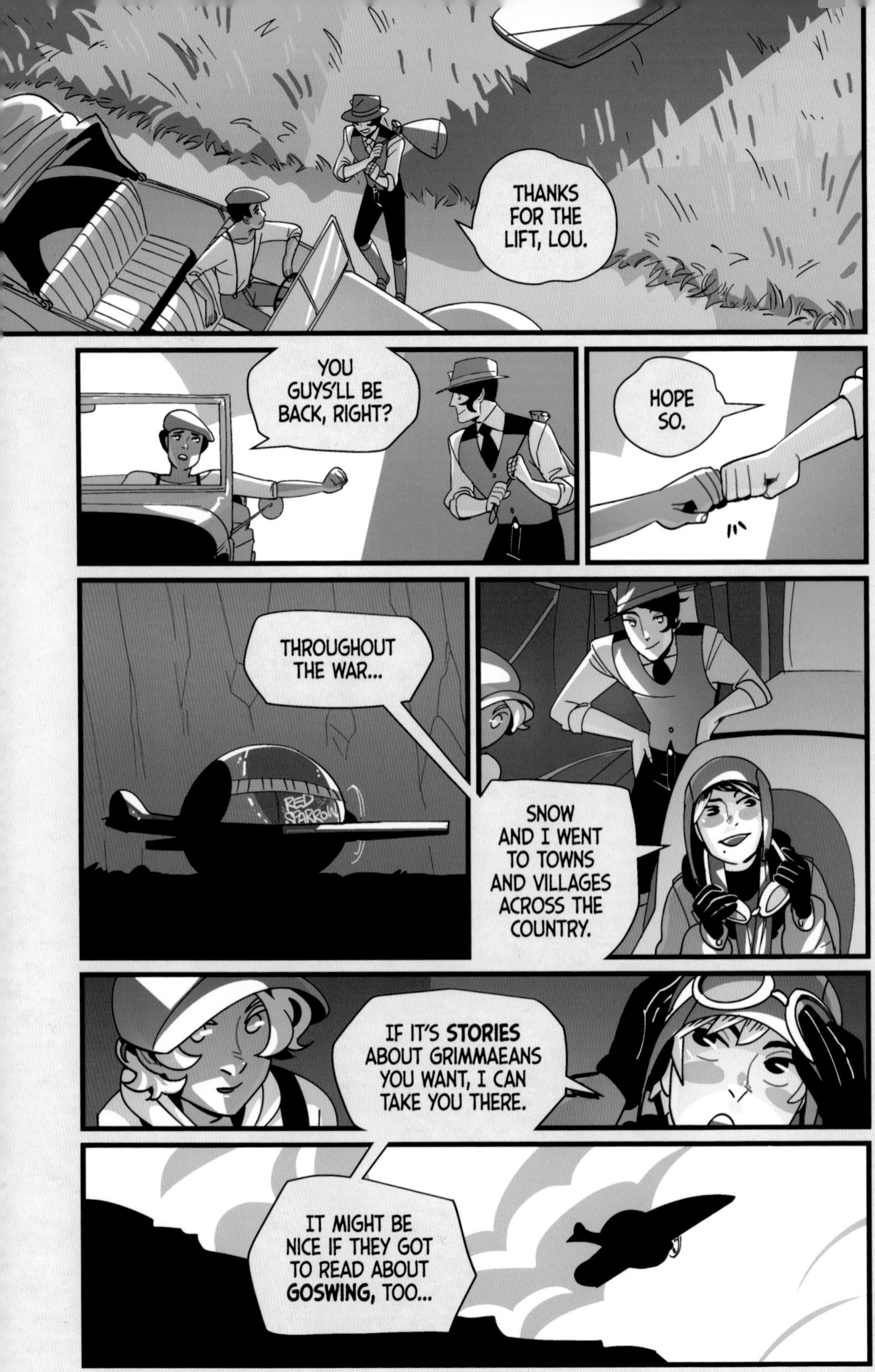
THANKS FOR THE LIFT, LOU.
YOU GUYS'LL BE BACK, RIGHT?
HOPE SO.
THROUGHOUT THE WAR...
RED SPARROW
SNOW AND I WENT TO TOWNS AND VILLAGES ACROSS THE COUNTRY.
IF IT'S **STORIES** ABOUT GRIMMAEANS YOU WANT, I CAN TAKE YOU THERE.
IT MIGHT BE NICE IF THEY GOT TO READ ABOUT **GOSWING**, TOO...

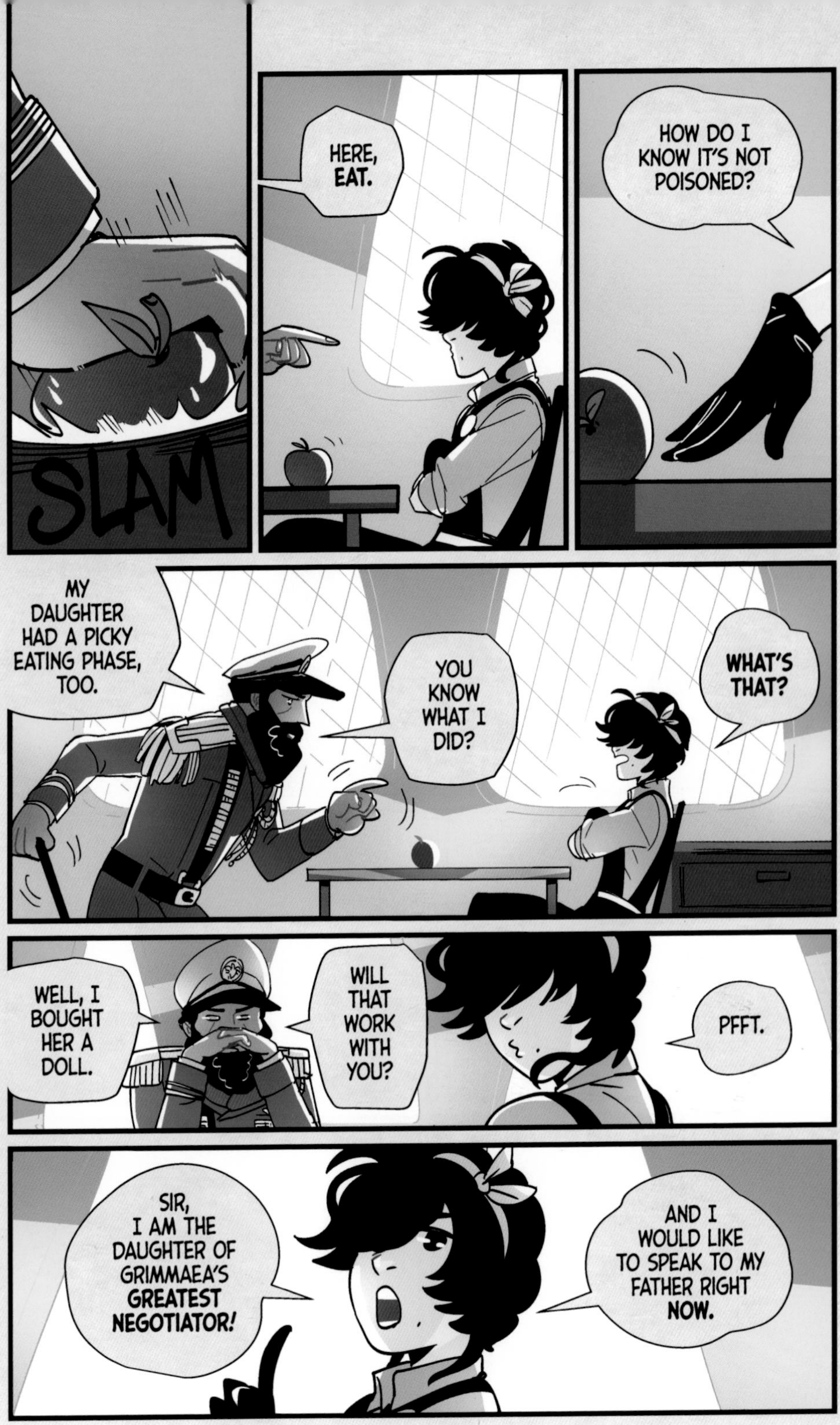
SLAM
HERE, EAT.
HOW DO I KNOW IT'S NOT POISONED?
MY DAUGHTER HAD A PICKY EATING PHASE, TOO.
YOU KNOW WHAT I DID?
WHAT'S THAT?
WELL, I BOUGHT HER A DOLL.
WILL THAT WORK WITH YOU?
PFFT.
SIR, I AM THE DAUGHTER OF GRIMMAEA'S GREATEST NEGOTIATOR!
AND I WOULD LIKE TO SPEAK TO MY FATHER RIGHT NOW.

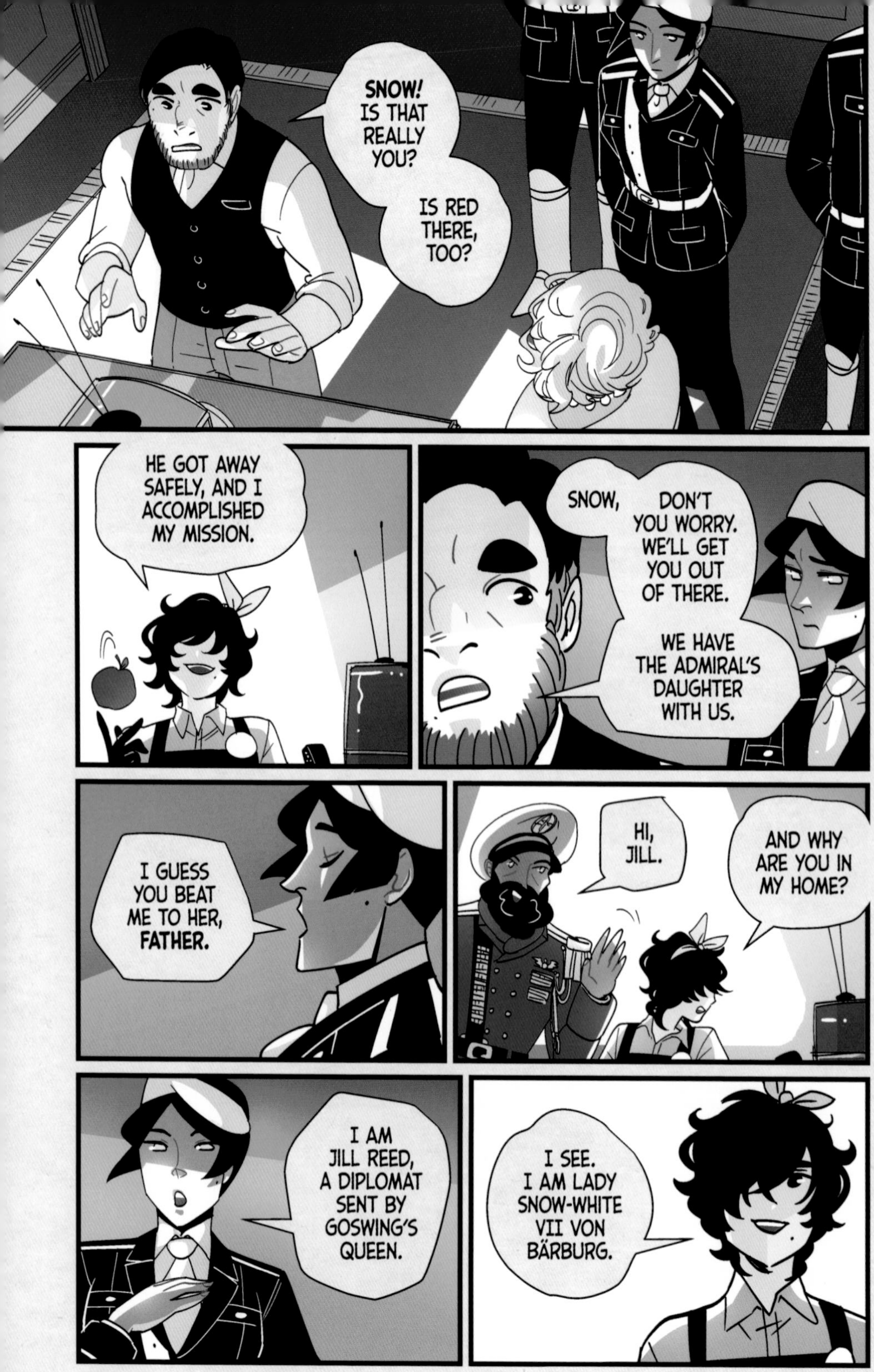
SNOW! IS THAT REALLY YOU?
IS RED THERE, TOO?
HE GOT AWAY SAFELY, AND I ACCOMPLISHED MY MISSION.
SNOW,
DON'T YOU WORRY. WE'LL GET YOU OUT OF THERE.
WE HAVE THE ADMIRAL'S DAUGHTER WITH US.
I GUESS YOU BEAT ME TO HER, FATHER.
HI, JILL.
AND WHY ARE YOU IN MY HOME?
I AM JILL REED, A DIPLOMAT SENT BY GOSWING'S QUEEN.
I SEE. I AM LADY SNOW-WHITE VII VON BÄRBURG.

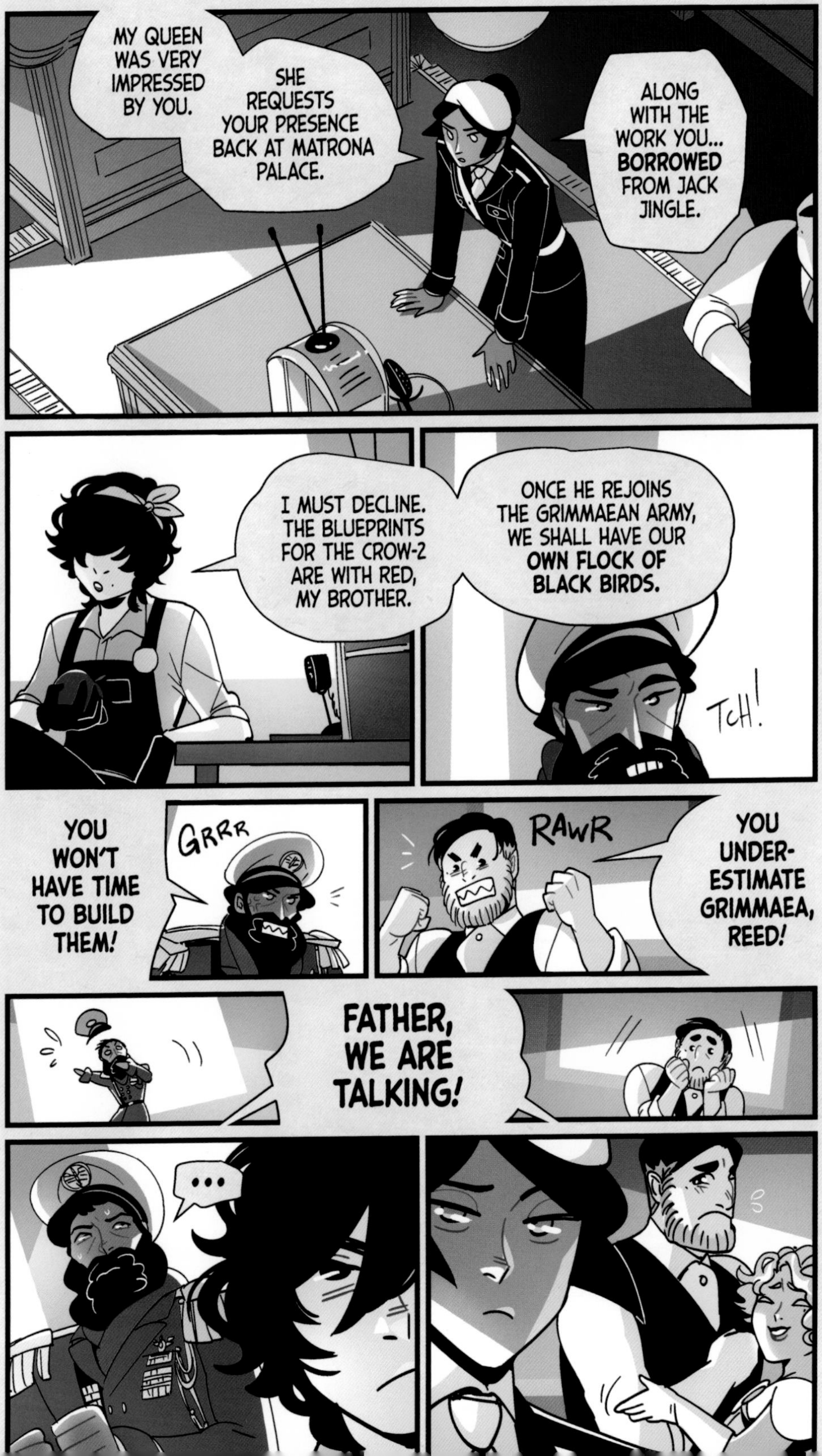
MY QUEEN WAS VERY IMPRESSED BY YOU.
SHE REQUESTS YOUR PRESENCE BACK AT MATRONA PALACE.
ALONG WITH THE WORK YOU... BORROWED FROM JACK JINGLE.
I MUST DECLINE. THE BLUEPRINTS FOR THE CROW-2 ARE WITH RED, MY BROTHER.
ONCE HE REJOINS THE GRIMMAEAN ARMY, WE SHALL HAVE OUR OWN FLOCK OF BLACK BIRDS.
TCH!
YOU WON'T HAVE TIME TO BUILD THEM!
GRRR
RAWR
YOU UNDER-ESTIMATE GRIMMAEA, REED!
FATHER, WE ARE TALKING!
...

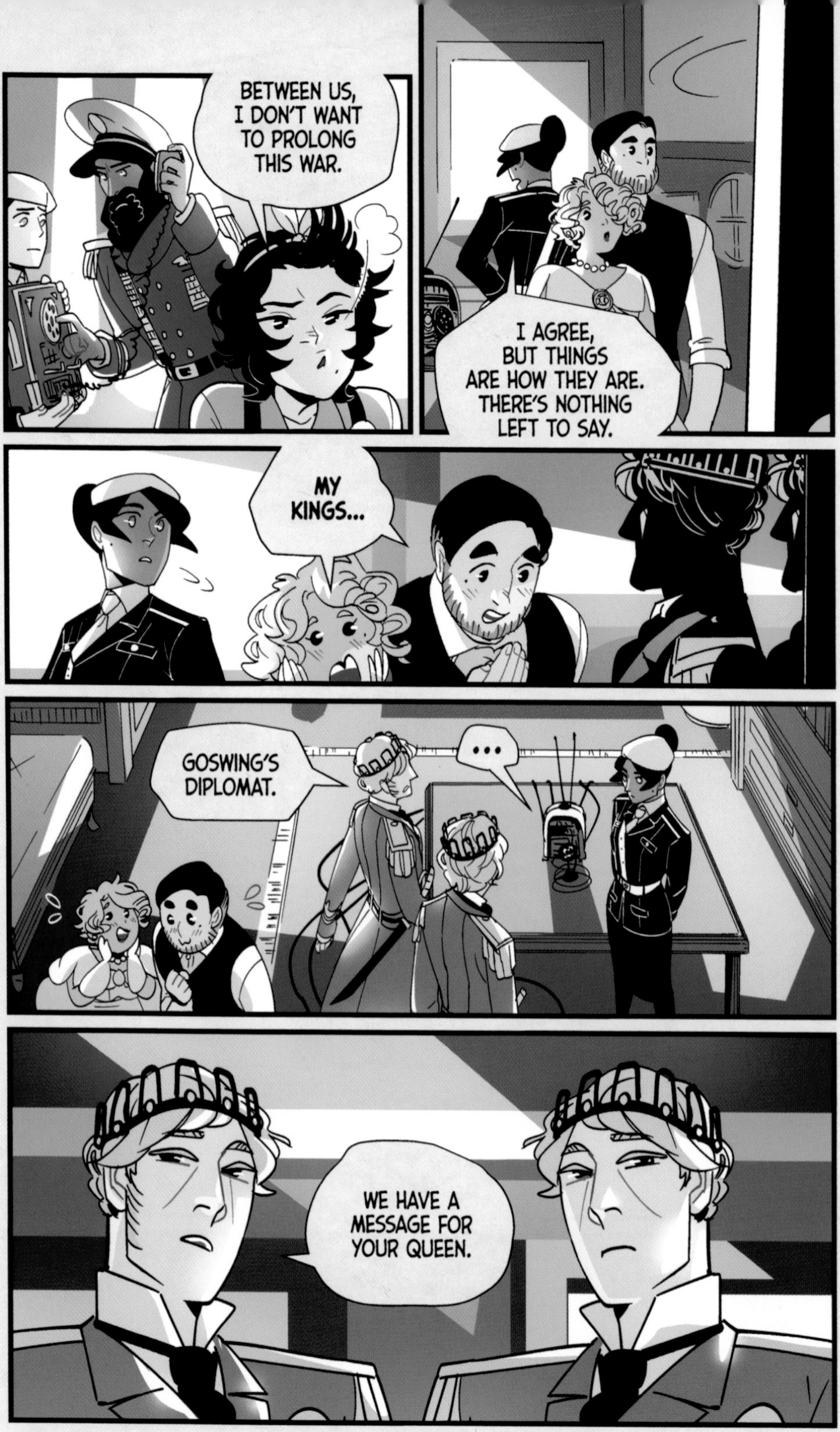
BETWEEN US, I DON'T WANT TO PROLONG THIS WAR.
I AGREE, BUT THINGS ARE HOW THEY ARE. THERE'S NOTHING LEFT TO SAY.
MY KINGS...
GOSWING'S DIPLOMAT.
...
WE HAVE A MESSAGE FOR YOUR QUEEN.

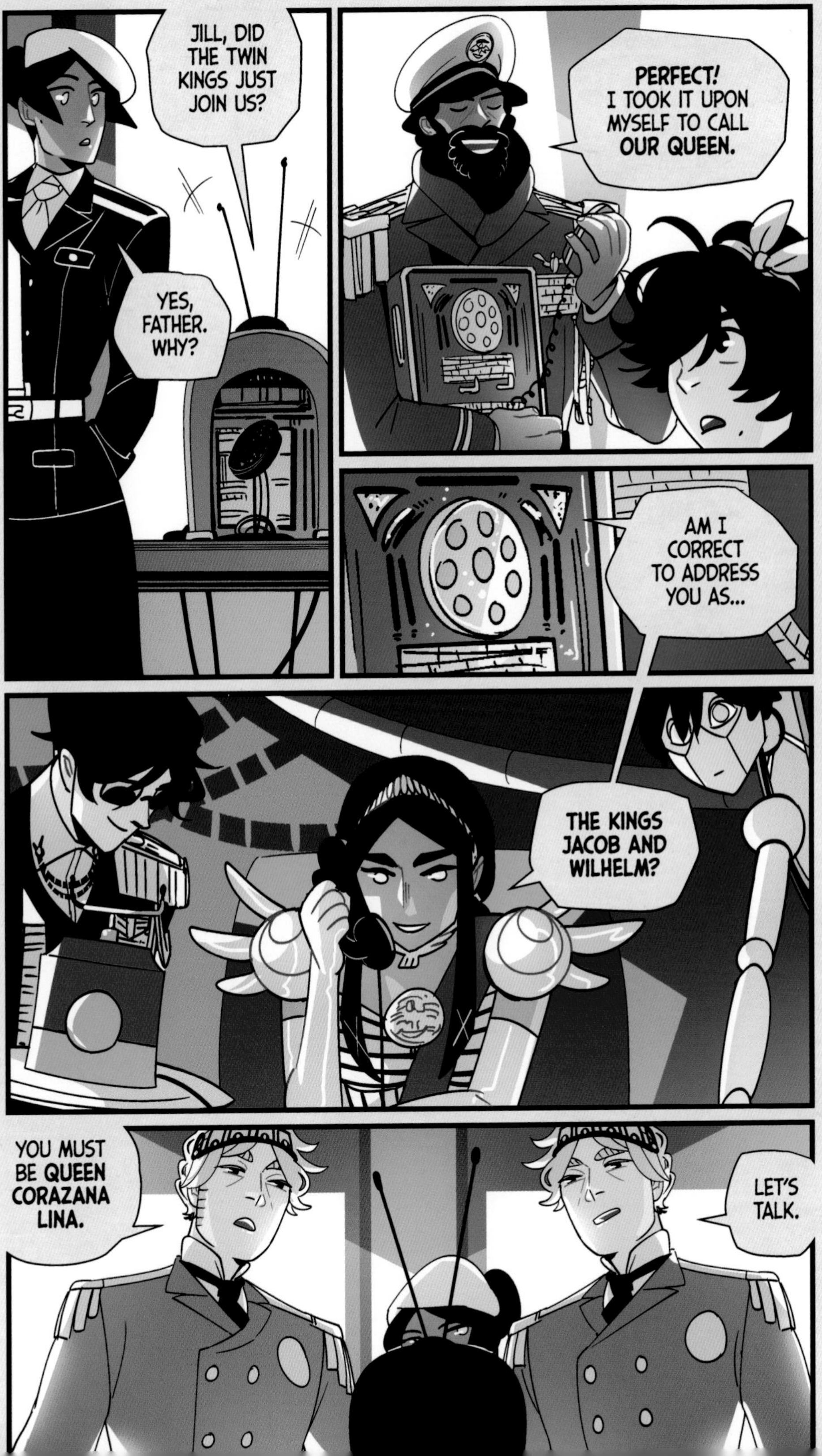
JILL, DID THE TWIN KINGS JUST JOIN US?
YES, FATHER. WHY?
PERFECT! I TOOK IT UPON MYSELF TO CALL OUR QUEEN.
AM I CORRECT TO ADDRESS YOU AS...
THE KINGS JACOB AND WILHELM?
YOU MUST BE QUEEN CORAZANA LINA.
LET'S TALK.

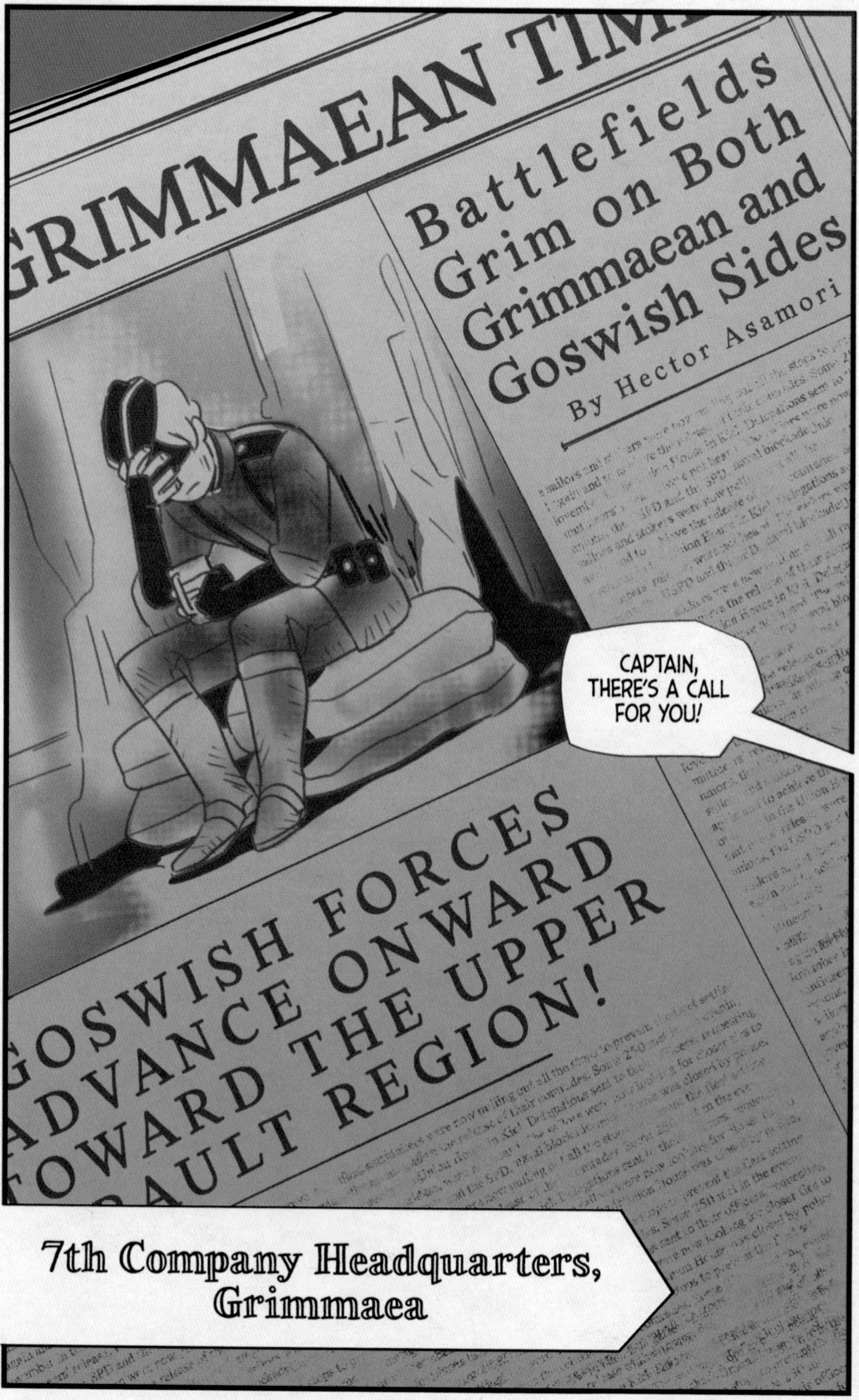
GRIMMAEAN TIM
Battlefields Grim on Both Grimmaean and Goswish Sides
By Hector Asamori
CAPTAIN, THERE'S A CALL FOR YOU!
GOSWISH FORCES ADVANCE ONWARD TOWARD THE UPPER
AULT REGION!
7th Company Headquarters, Grimmaea

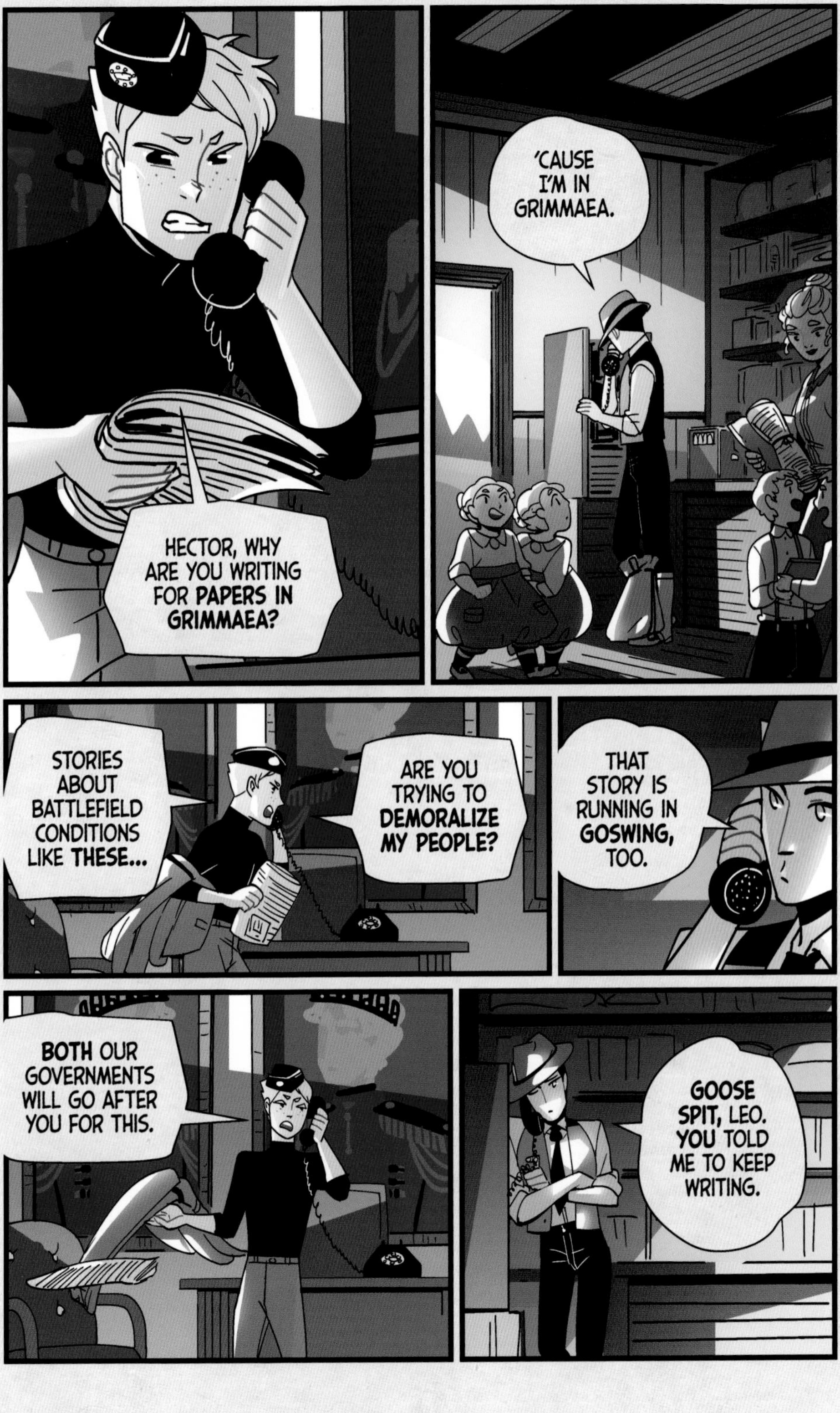
HECTOR, WHY ARE YOU WRITING FOR PAPERS IN GRIMMAEA?
'CAUSE I'M IN GRIMMAEA.
STORIES ABOUT BATTLEFIELD CONDITIONS LIKE THESE...
ARE YOU TRYING TO DEMORALIZE MY PEOPLE?
THAT STORY IS RUNNING IN GOSWING, TOO.
BOTH OUR GOVERNMENTS WILL GO AFTER YOU FOR THIS.
GOOSE SPIT, LEO. YOU TOLD ME TO KEEP WRITING.

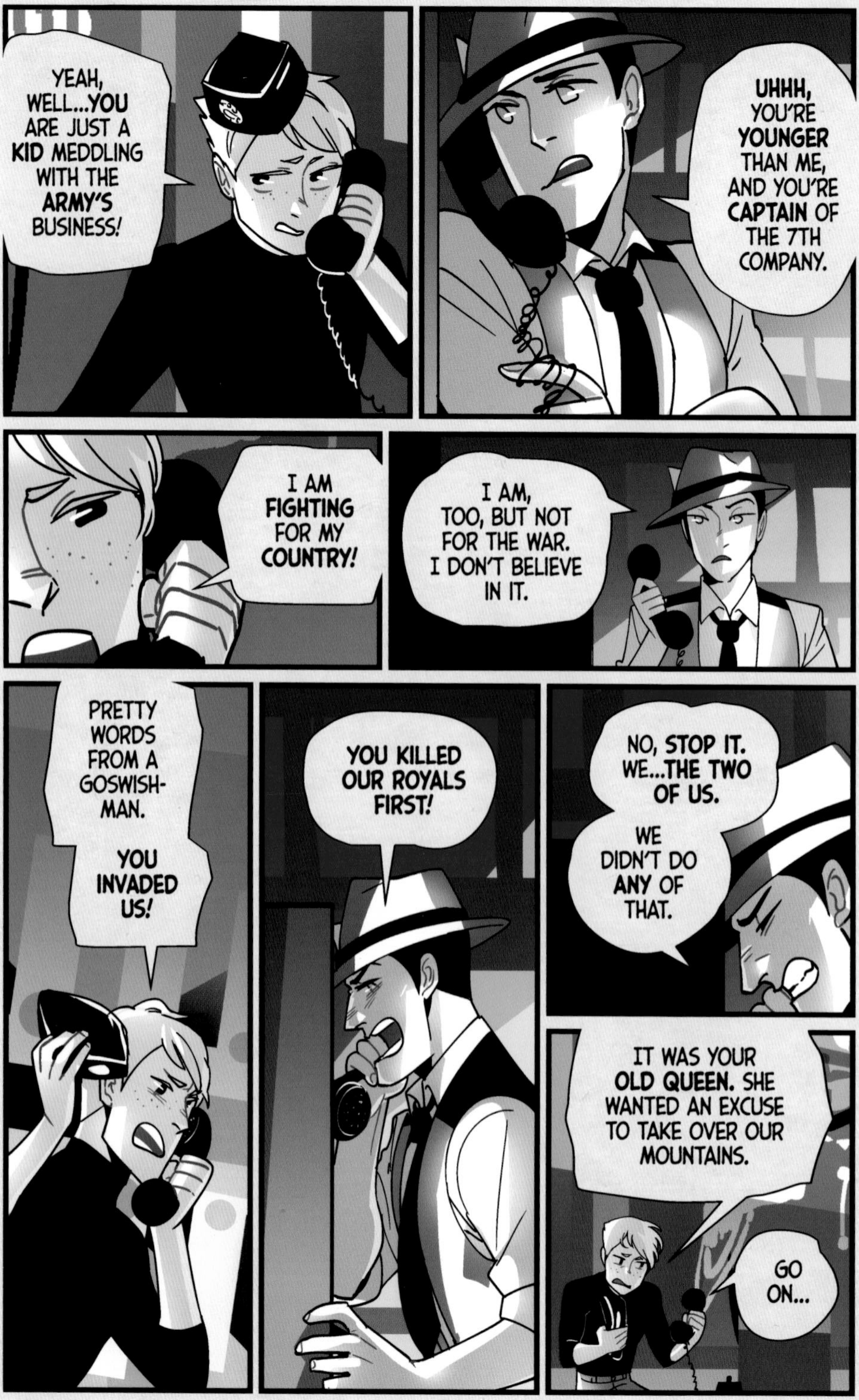
YEAH, WELL...YOU ARE JUST A KID MEDDLING WITH THE ARMY'S BUSINESS!
UHHH, YOU'RE YOUNGER THAN ME, AND YOU'RE CAPTAIN OF THE 7TH COMPANY.
I AM FIGHTING FOR MY COUNTRY!
I AM, TOO, BUT NOT FOR THE WAR. I DON'T BELIEVE IN IT.
PRETTY WORDS FROM A GOSWISH-MAN.
YOU INVADED US!
YOU KILLED OUR ROYALS FIRST!
NO, STOP IT. WE...THE TWO OF US.
WE DIDN'T DO ANY OF THAT.
IT WAS YOUR OLD QUEEN. SHE WANTED AN EXCUSE TO TAKE OVER OUR MOUNTAINS.
GO ON...

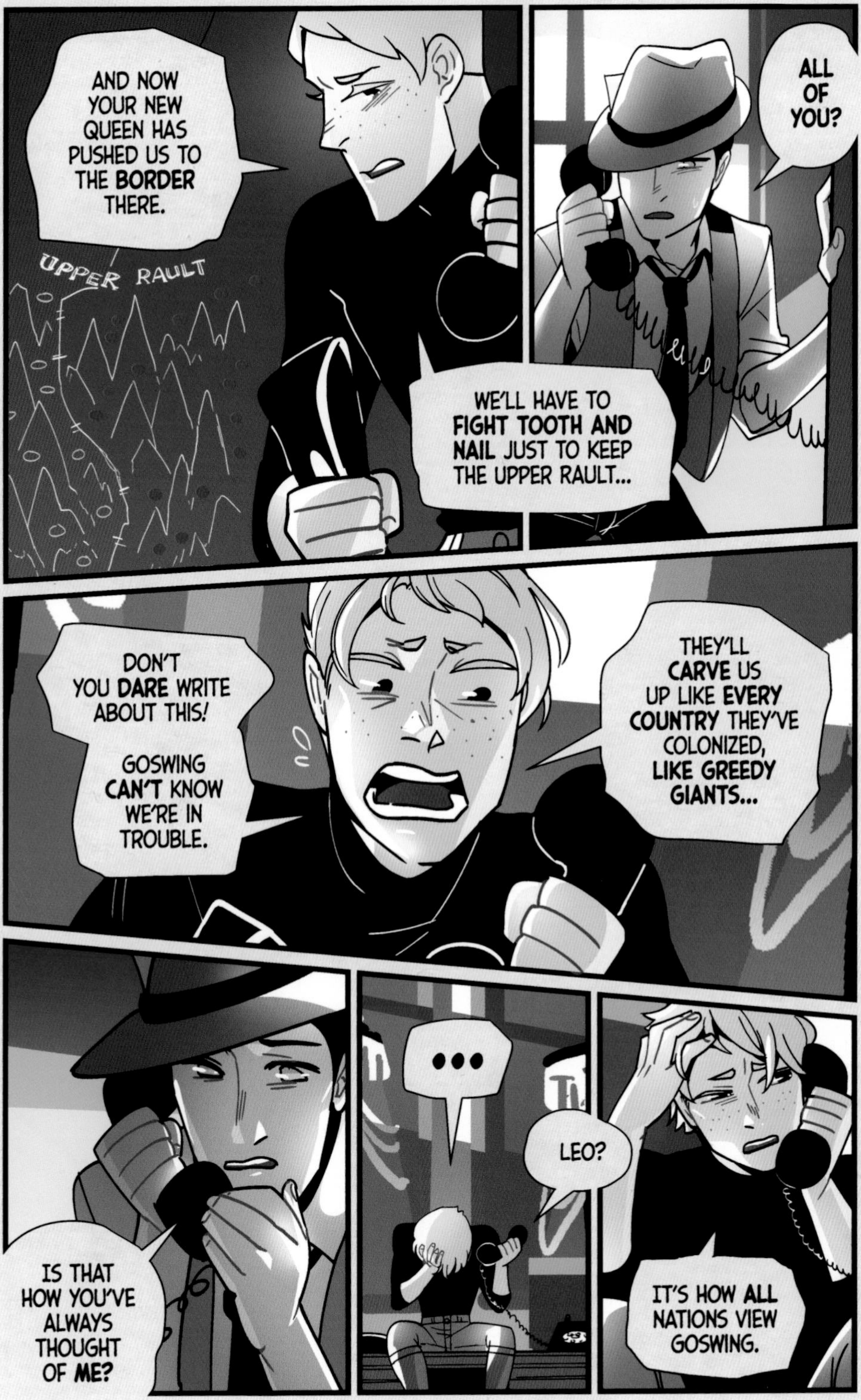
AND NOW YOUR NEW QUEEN HAS PUSHED US TO THE **BORDER** THERE.
UPPER RAULT
ALL OF YOU?
WE'LL HAVE TO **FIGHT TOOTH AND NAIL** JUST TO KEEP THE UPPER RAULT...
DON'T YOU **DARE** WRITE ABOUT THIS!
GOSWING **CAN'T** KNOW WE'RE IN TROUBLE.
THEY'LL **CARVE** US UP LIKE **EVERY COUNTRY** THEY'VE COLONIZED, **LIKE GREEDY GIANTS...**
IS THAT HOW YOU'VE ALWAYS THOUGHT OF **ME?**
...
LEO?
IT'S HOW **ALL** NATIONS VIEW GOSWING.

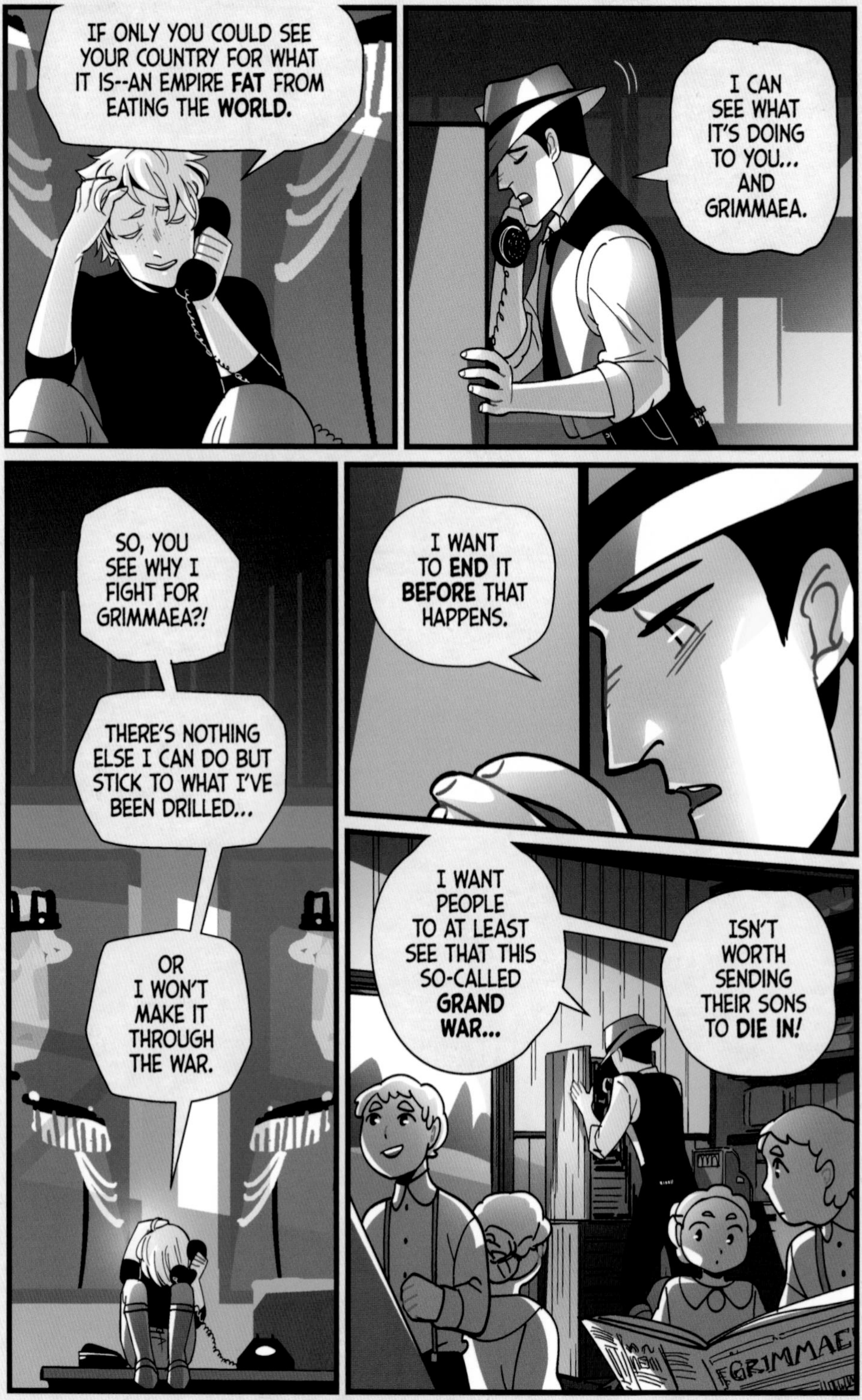
IF ONLY YOU COULD SEE YOUR COUNTRY FOR WHAT IT IS--AN EMPIRE **FAT** FROM EATING THE **WORLD.**
I CAN SEE WHAT IT'S DOING TO YOU... AND GRIMMAEA.
SO, YOU SEE WHY I FIGHT FOR GRIMMAEA?!
THERE'S NOTHING ELSE I CAN DO BUT STICK TO WHAT I'VE BEEN DRILLED...
OR I WON'T MAKE IT THROUGH THE WAR.
I WANT TO **END** IT **BEFORE** THAT HAPPENS.
I WANT PEOPLE TO AT LEAST SEE THAT THIS SO-CALLED **GRAND WAR...**
ISN'T WORTH SENDING THEIR SONS TO **DIE IN!**
GRIMMAE

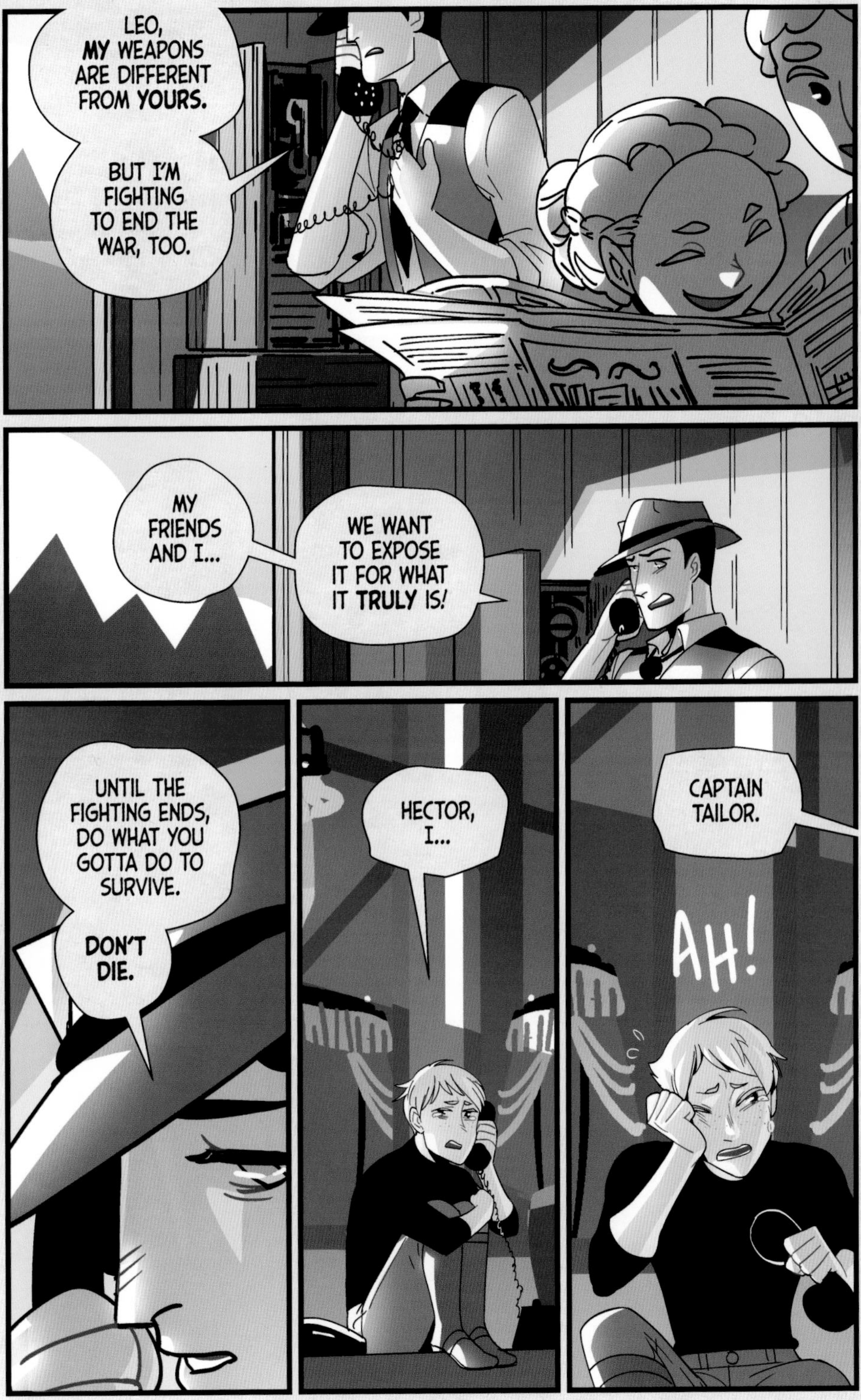
LEO, MY WEAPONS ARE DIFFERENT FROM YOURS.
BUT I'M FIGHTING TO END THE WAR, TOO.
MY FRIENDS AND I...
WE WANT TO EXPOSE IT FOR WHAT IT TRULY IS!
UNTIL THE FIGHTING ENDS, DO WHAT YOU GOTTA DO TO SURVIVE.
DON'T DIE.
HECTOR, I...
CAPTAIN TAILOR.
AH!

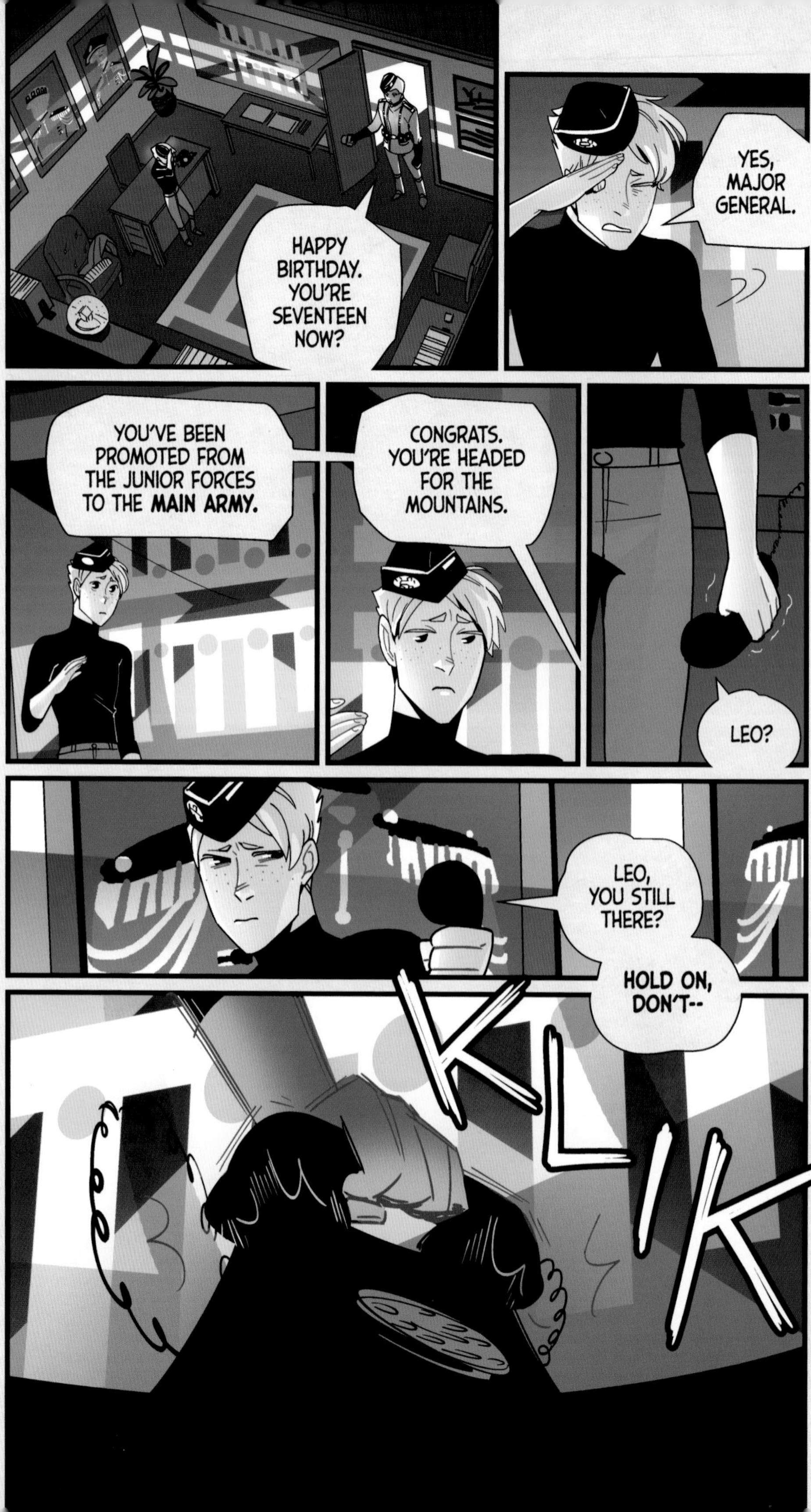
HAPPY BIRTHDAY. YOU'RE SEVENTEEN NOW?
YES, MAJOR GENERAL.
YOU'VE BEEN PROMOTED FROM THE JUNIOR FORCES TO THE MAIN ARMY.
CONGRATS. YOU'RE HEADED FOR THE MOUNTAINS.
LEO?
LEO, YOU STILL THERE?
HOLD ON, DON'T--
KLIK

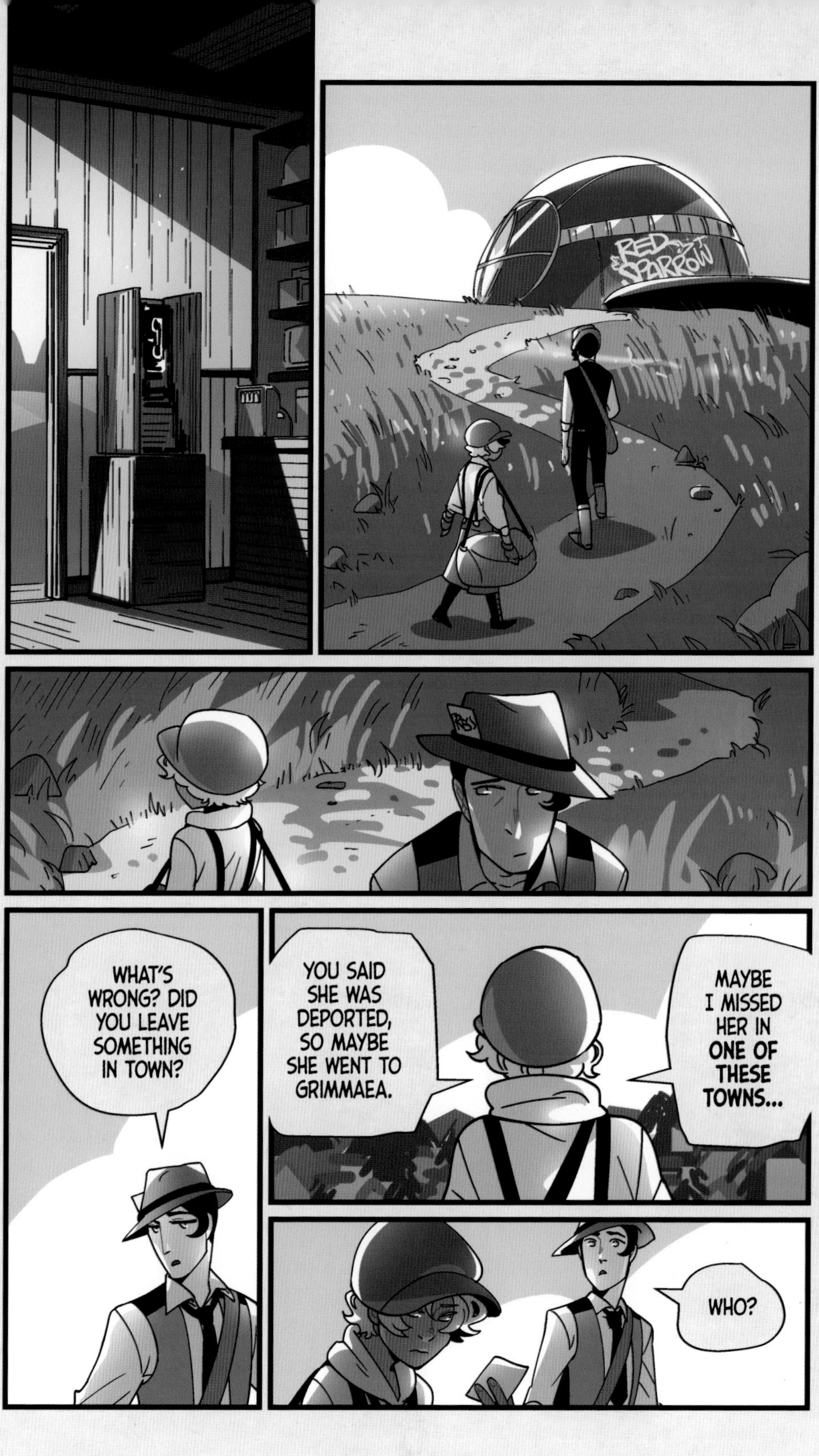
RED SPARROW
WHAT'S WRONG? DID YOU LEAVE SOMETHING IN TOWN?
YOU SAID SHE WAS DEPORTED, SO MAYBE SHE WENT TO GRIMMAEA.
MAYBE I MISSED HER IN ONE OF THESE TOWNS...
WHO?

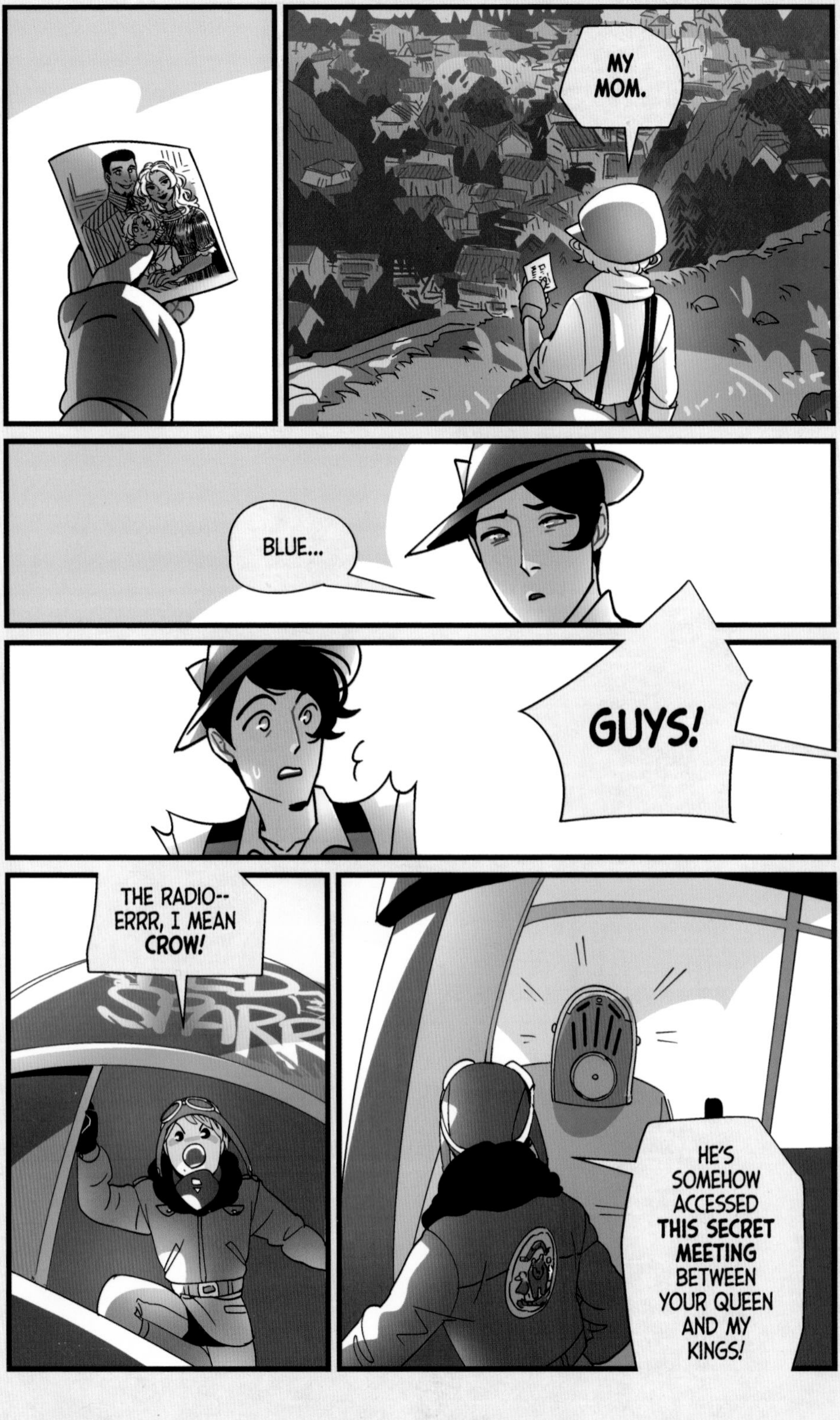
MY MOM.
BLUE...
GUYS!
THE RADIO-- ERRR, I MEAN CROW!
HE'S SOMEHOW ACCESSED THIS SECRET MEETING BETWEEN YOUR QUEEN AND MY KINGS!

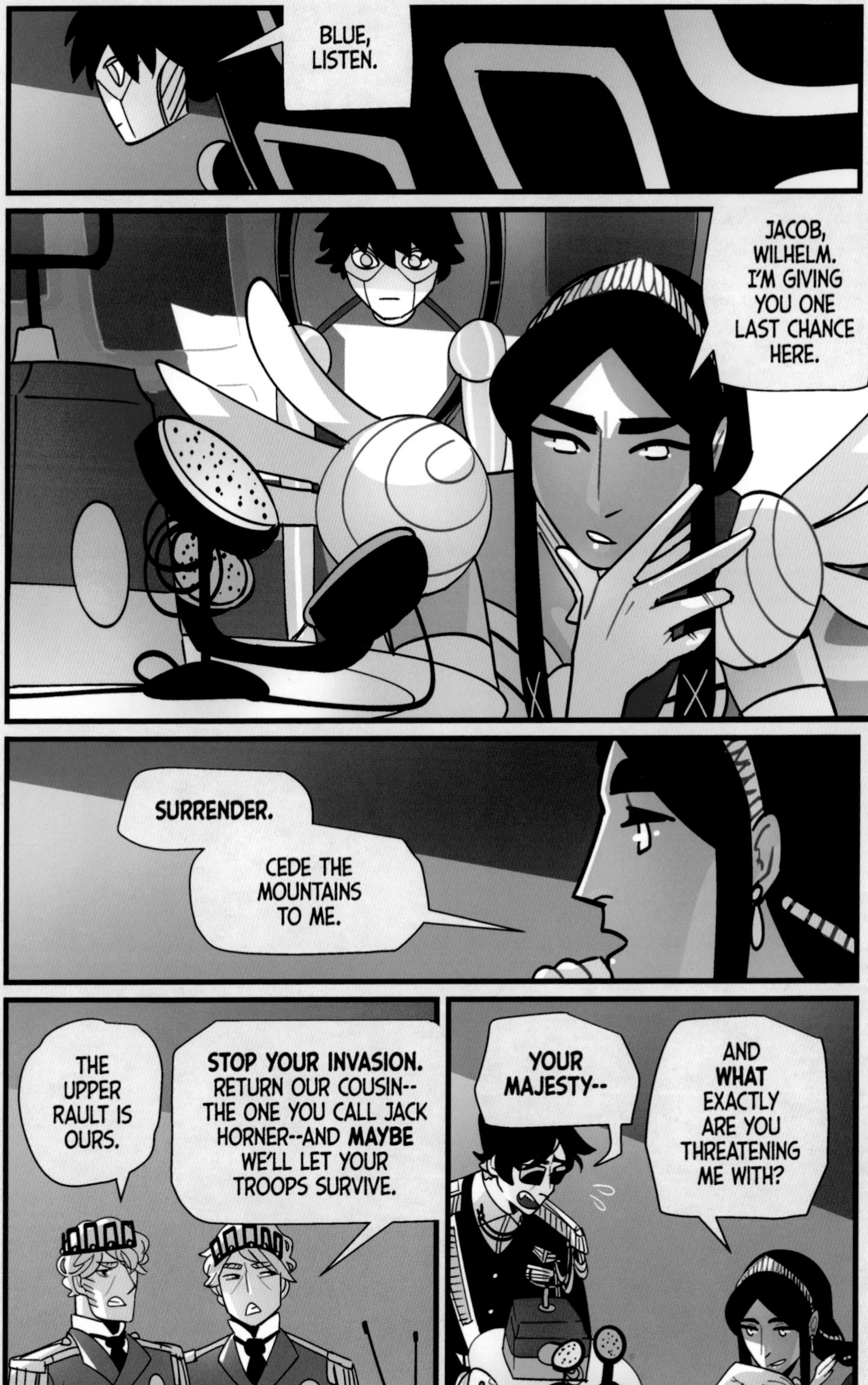
BLUE, LISTEN.
JACOB, WILHELM. I'M GIVING YOU ONE LAST CHANCE HERE.
SURRENDER.
CEDE THE MOUNTAINS TO ME.
THE UPPER RAULT IS OURS.
STOP YOUR INVASION. RETURN OUR COUSIN--THE ONE YOU CALL JACK HORNER--AND MAYBE WE'LL LET YOUR TROOPS SURVIVE.
YOUR MAJESTY--
AND WHAT EXACTLY ARE YOU THREATENING ME WITH?

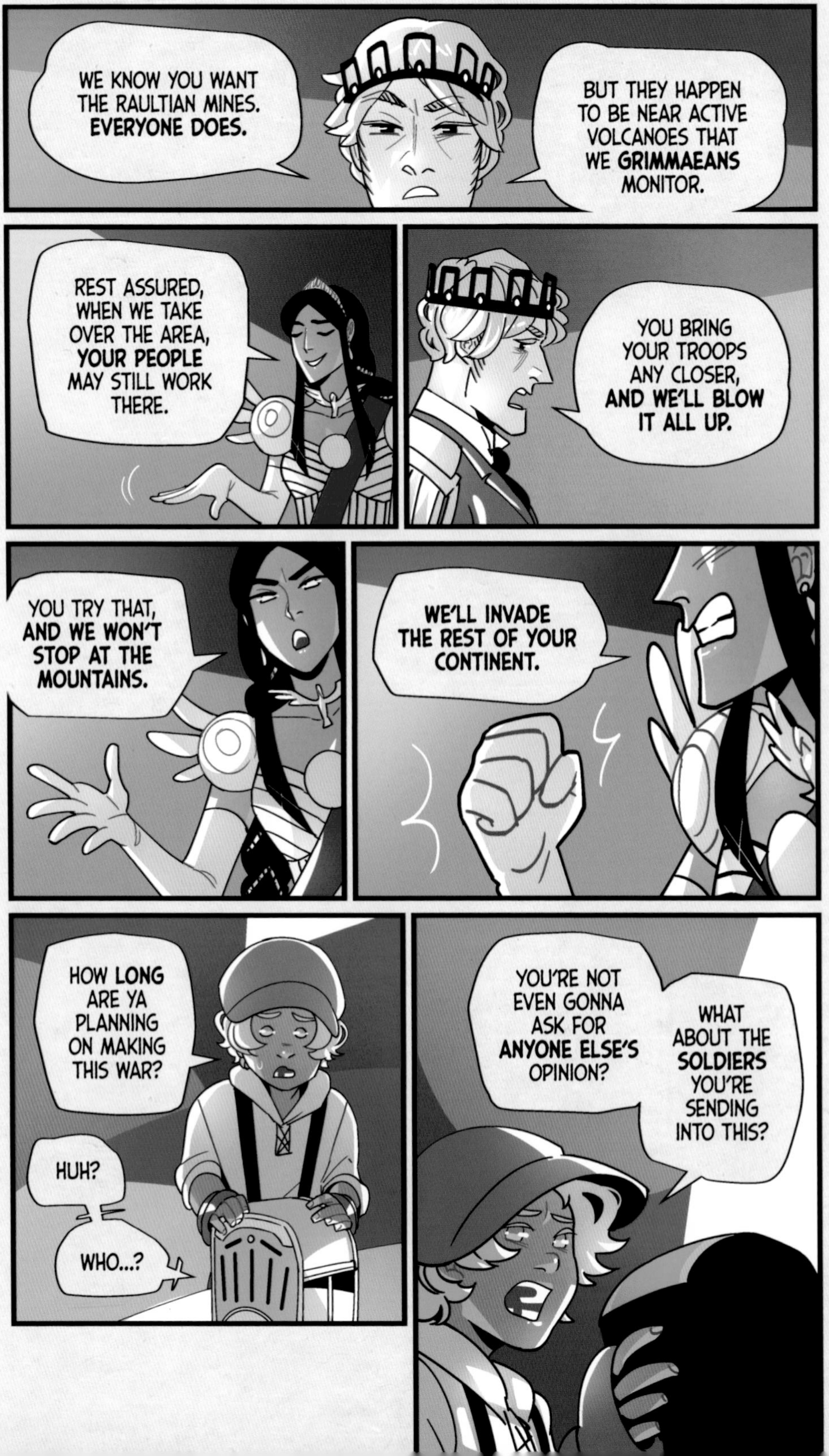
WE KNOW YOU WANT THE RAULTIAN MINES. **EVERYONE DOES.**
BUT THEY HAPPEN TO BE NEAR ACTIVE VOLCANOES THAT WE **GRIMMAEANS** MONITOR.
REST ASSURED, WHEN WE TAKE OVER THE AREA, **YOUR PEOPLE** MAY STILL WORK THERE.
YOU BRING YOUR TROOPS ANY CLOSER, **AND WE'LL BLOW IT ALL UP.**
YOU TRY THAT, **AND WE WON'T STOP AT THE MOUNTAINS.**
WE'LL INVADE THE REST OF YOUR CONTINENT.
HOW **LONG** ARE YA PLANNING ON MAKING THIS WAR?
HUH?
WHO...?
YOU'RE NOT EVEN GONNA ASK FOR **ANYONE ELSE'S** OPINION?
WHAT ABOUT THE **SOLDIERS** YOU'RE SENDING INTO THIS?

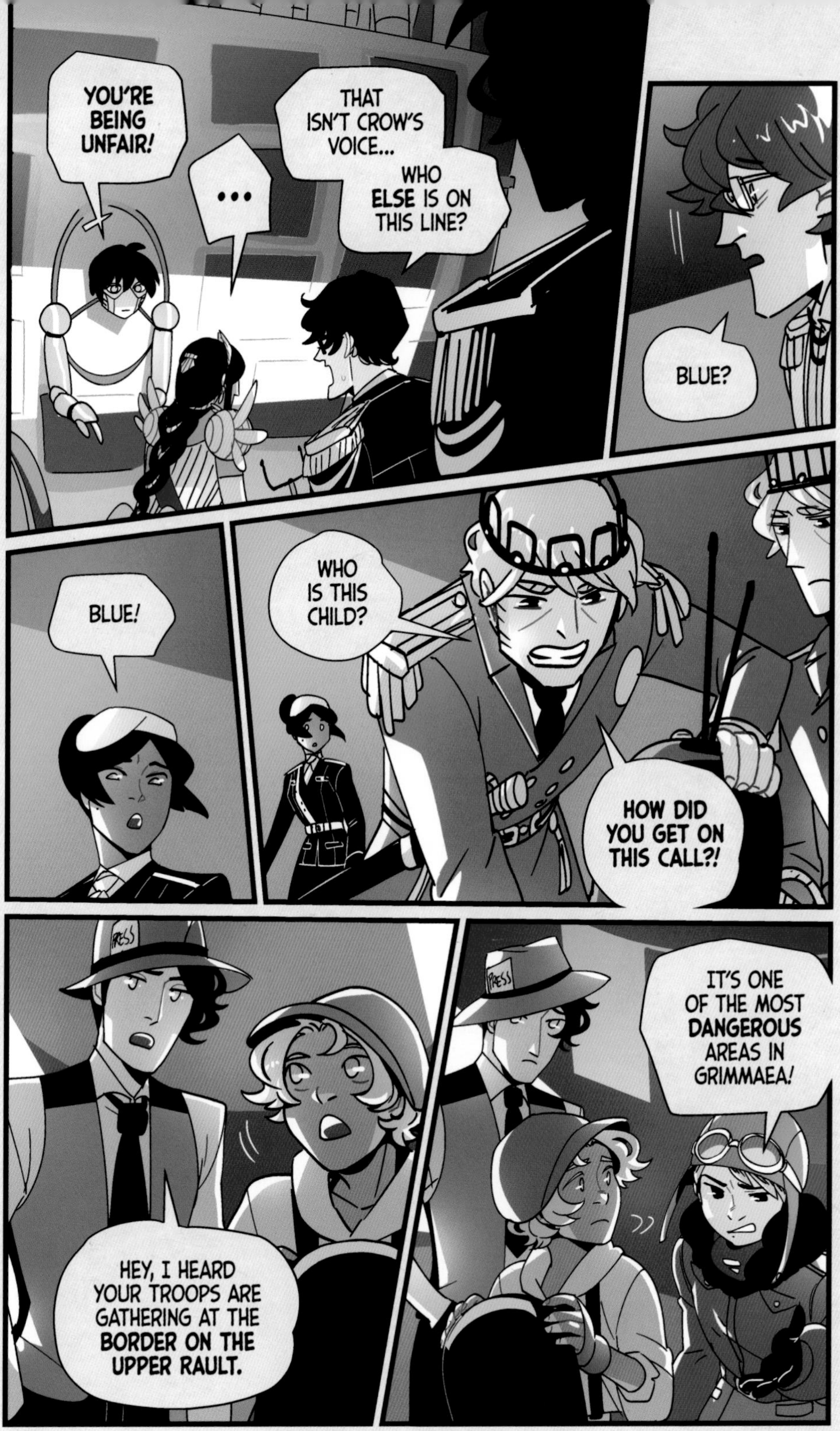
YOU'RE BEING UNFAIR!
...
THAT ISN'T CROW'S VOICE...
WHO ELSE IS ON THIS LINE?
BLUE?
BLUE!
WHO IS THIS CHILD?
HOW DID YOU GET ON THIS CALL?!
HEY, I HEARD YOUR TROOPS ARE GATHERING AT THE BORDER ON THE UPPER RAULT.
IT'S ONE OF THE MOST DANGEROUS AREAS IN GRIMMAEA!

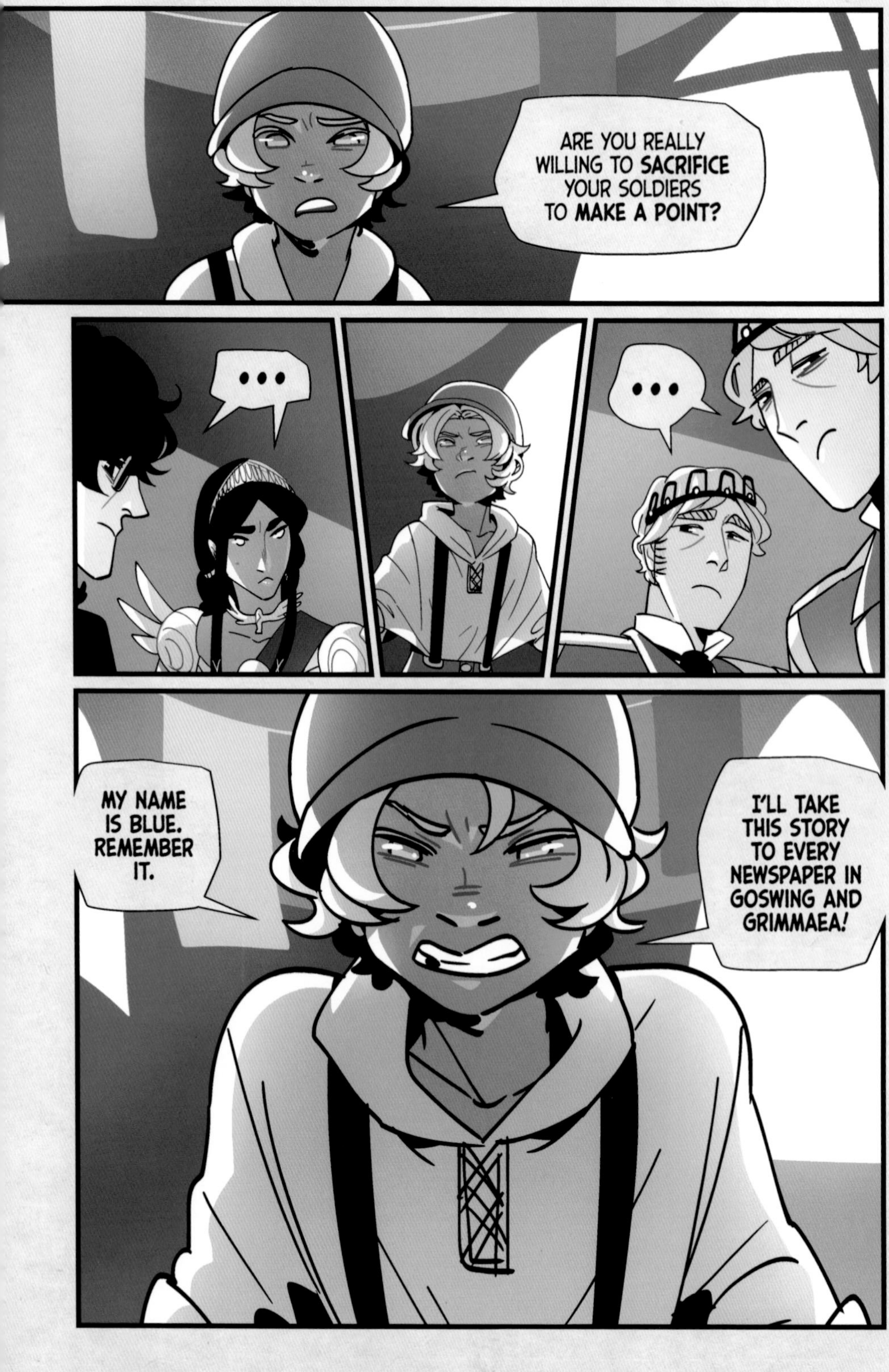
ARE YOU REALLY WILLING TO SACRIFICE YOUR SOLDIERS TO MAKE A POINT?
...
...
MY NAME IS BLUE. REMEMBER IT.
I'LL TAKE THIS STORY TO EVERY NEWSPAPER IN GOSWING AND GRIMMAEA!

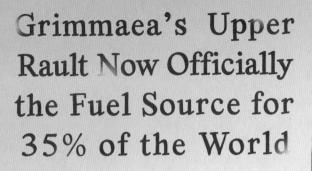

Grimmaea's Upper Rault Now Officially the Fuel Source for 35% of the World

VOLCANIC ACTIVITY AT RECORD HIGH NEAR RAULTIAN MOUNTAINS

DANGEROUS CONDITIONS FOR MINERS

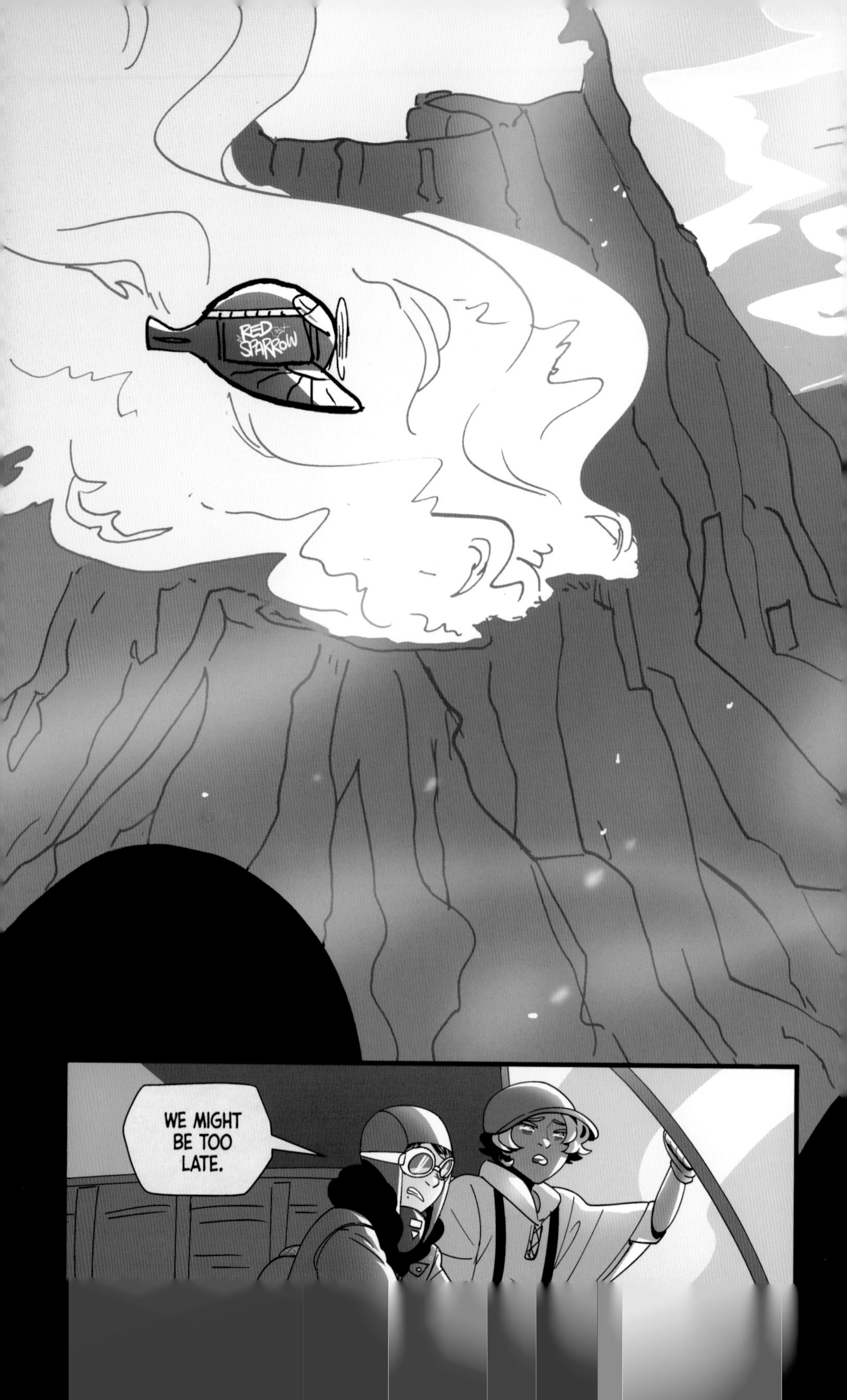
RED SPARROW
WE MIGHT BE TOO LATE.

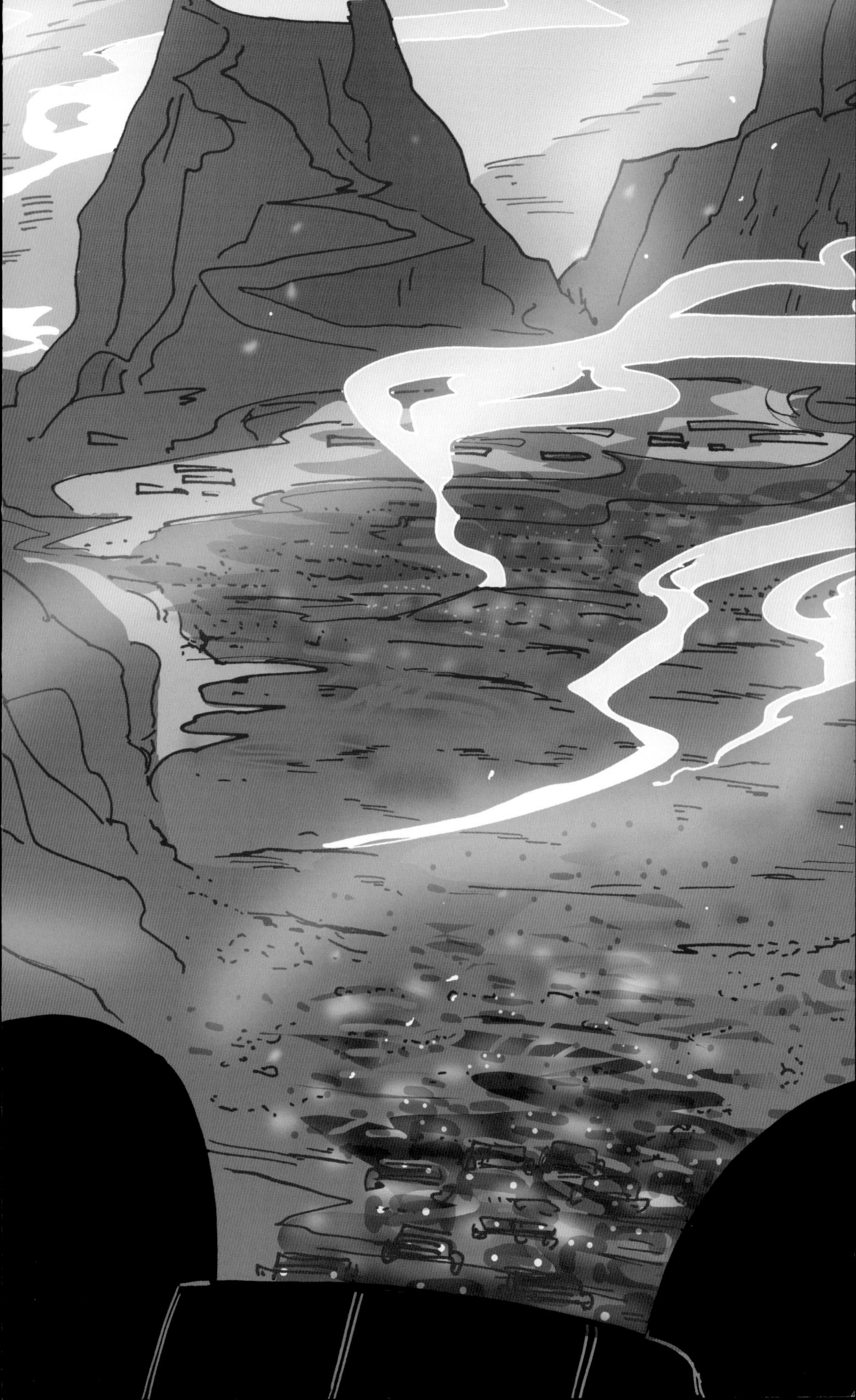

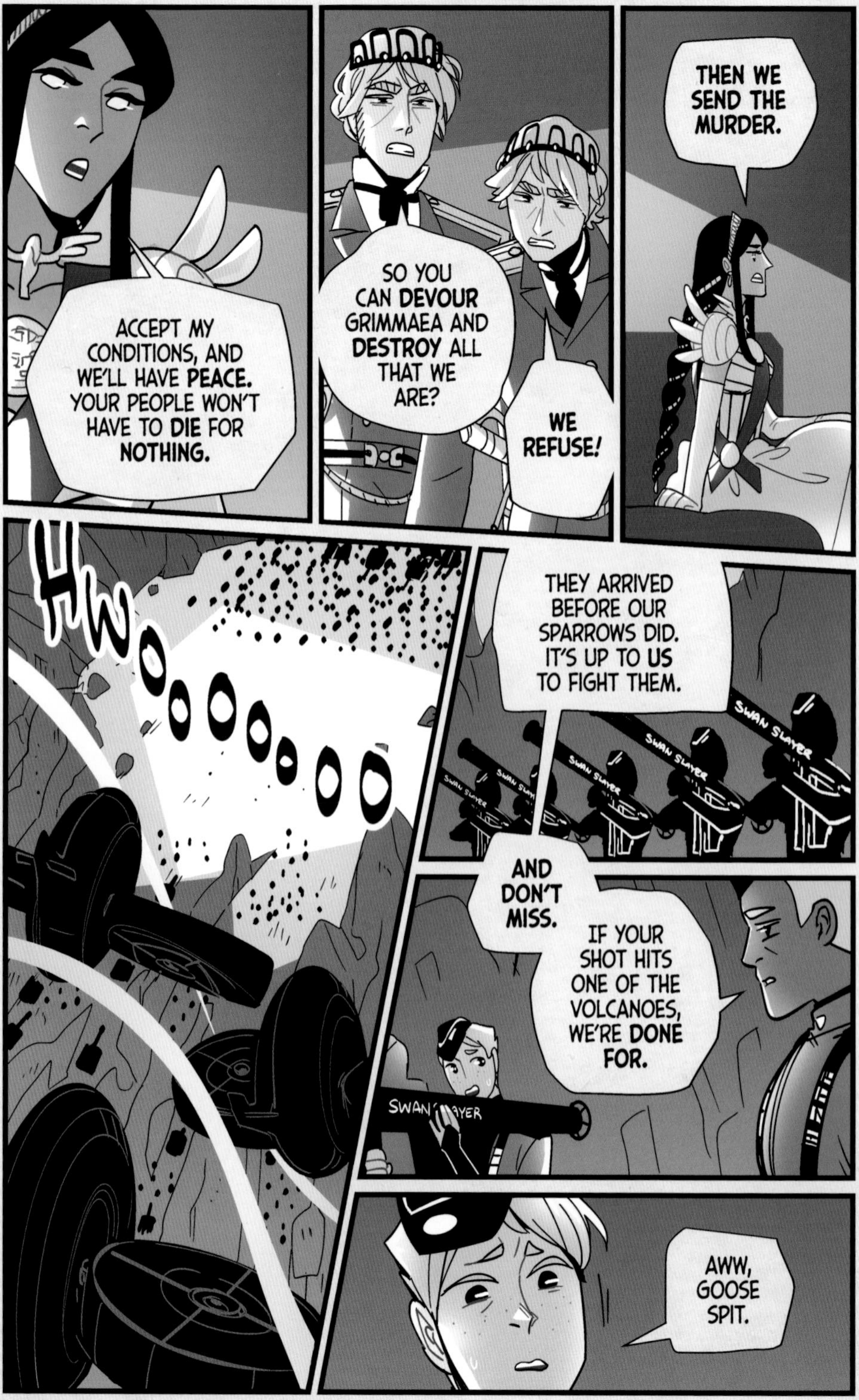
ACCEPT MY CONDITIONS, AND WE'LL HAVE PEACE. YOUR PEOPLE WON'T HAVE TO DIE FOR NOTHING.
SO YOU CAN DEVOUR GRIMMAEA AND DESTROY ALL THAT WE ARE?
WE REFUSE!
THEN WE SEND THE MURDER.
HWOOOOOOOO
THEY ARRIVED BEFORE OUR SPARROWS DID. IT'S UP TO US TO FIGHT THEM.
SWAN SLAYER
SWAN SLAYER
SWAN SLAYER
SWAN SLAYER
SWAN SLAYER
AND DON'T MISS.
IF YOUR SHOT HITS ONE OF THE VOLCANOES, WE'RE DONE FOR.
AWW, GOOSE SPIT.

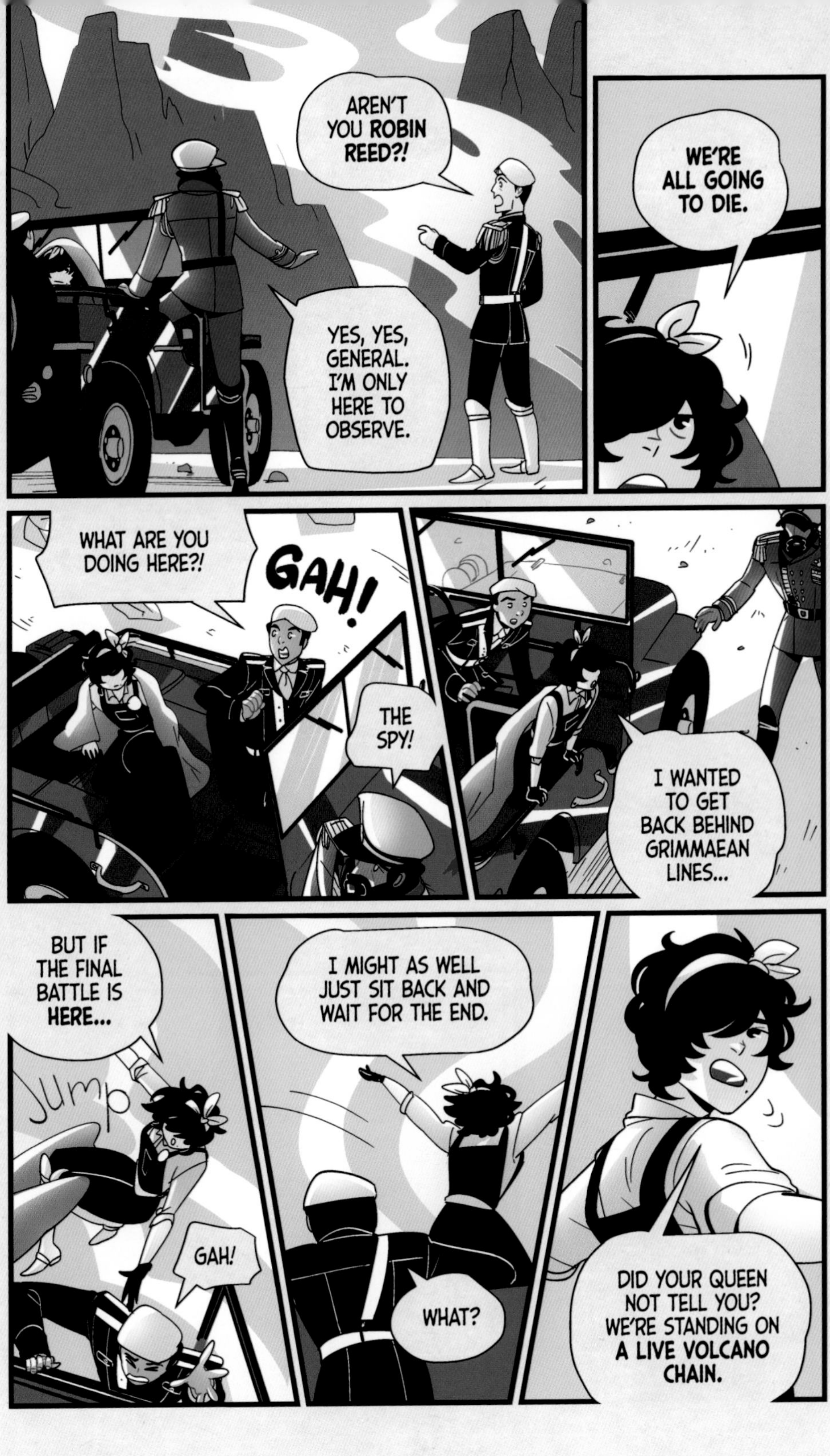

AREN'T YOU ROBIN REED?!
YES, YES, GENERAL. I'M ONLY HERE TO OBSERVE.
WE'RE ALL GOING TO DIE.
WHAT ARE YOU DOING HERE?!
GAH!
THE SPY!
I WANTED TO GET BACK BEHIND GRIMMAEAN LINES...
BUT IF THE FINAL BATTLE IS HERE...
JUMP
GAH!
I MIGHT AS WELL JUST SIT BACK AND WAIT FOR THE END.
WHAT?
DID YOUR QUEEN NOT TELL YOU? WE'RE STANDING ON A LIVE VOLCANO CHAIN.

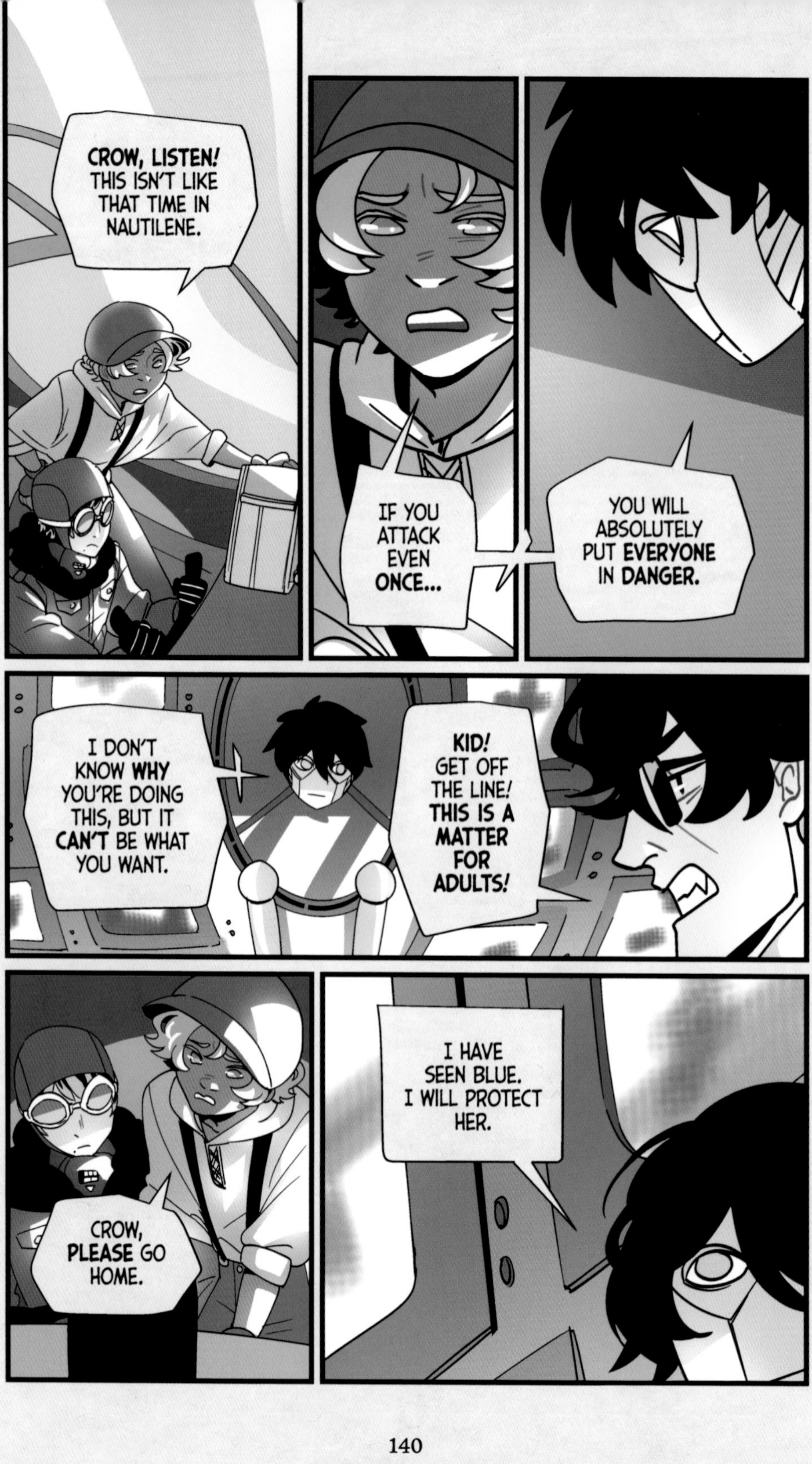
CROW, LISTEN! THIS ISN'T LIKE THAT TIME IN NAUTILENE.
IF YOU ATTACK EVEN ONCE...
YOU WILL ABSOLUTELY PUT EVERYONE IN DANGER.
I DON'T KNOW WHY YOU'RE DOING THIS, BUT IT CAN'T BE WHAT YOU WANT.
KID! GET OFF THE LINE! THIS IS A MATTER FOR ADULTS!
CROW, PLEASE GO HOME.
I HAVE SEEN BLUE. I WILL PROTECT HER.

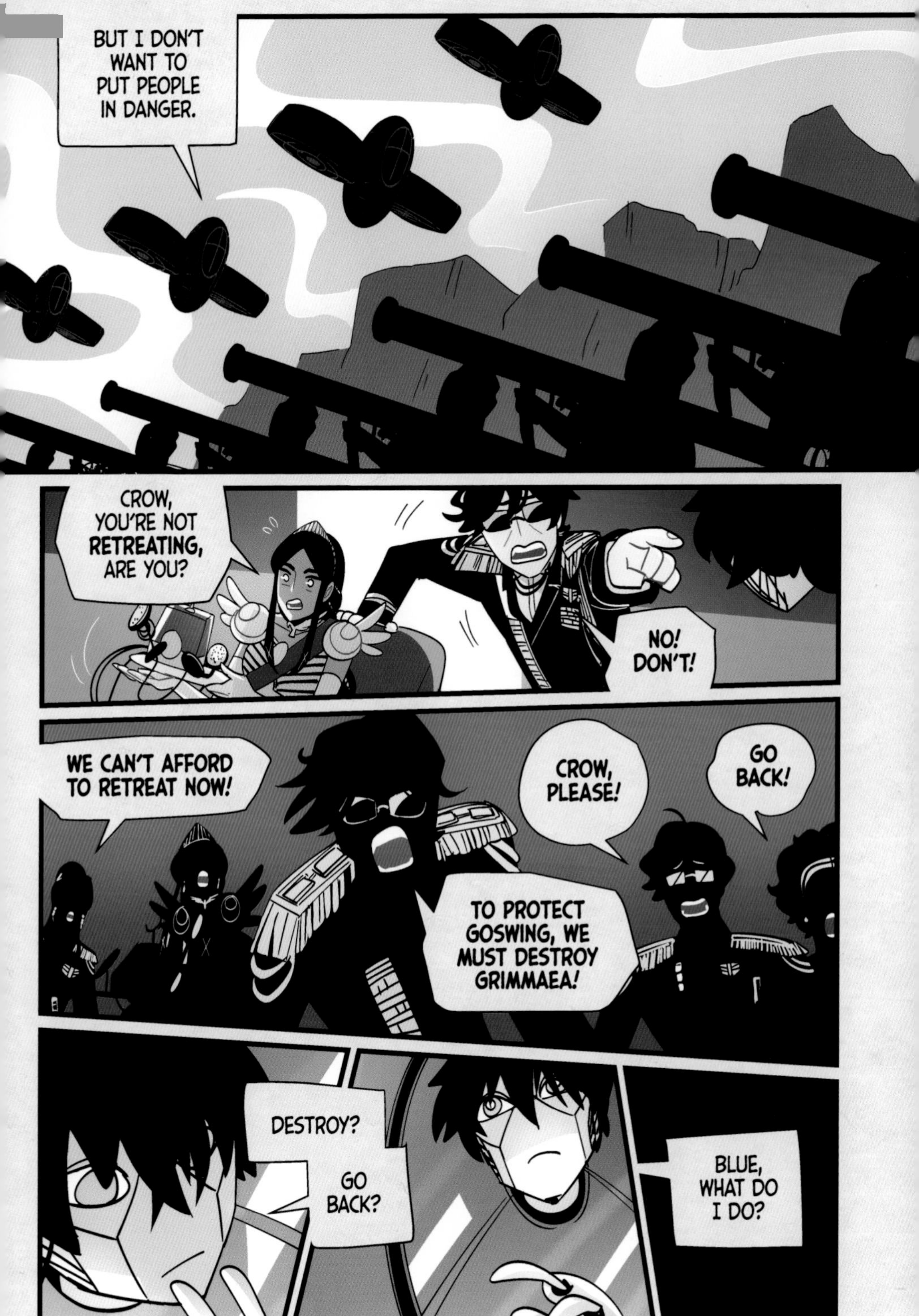
BUT I DON'T WANT TO PUT PEOPLE IN DANGER.
CROW, YOU'RE NOT RETREATING, ARE YOU?
NO! DON'T!
WE CAN'T AFFORD TO RETREAT NOW!
CROW, PLEASE!
GO BACK!
TO PROTECT GOSWING, WE MUST DESTROY GRIMMAEA!
DESTROY?
GO BACK?
BLUE, WHAT DO I DO?

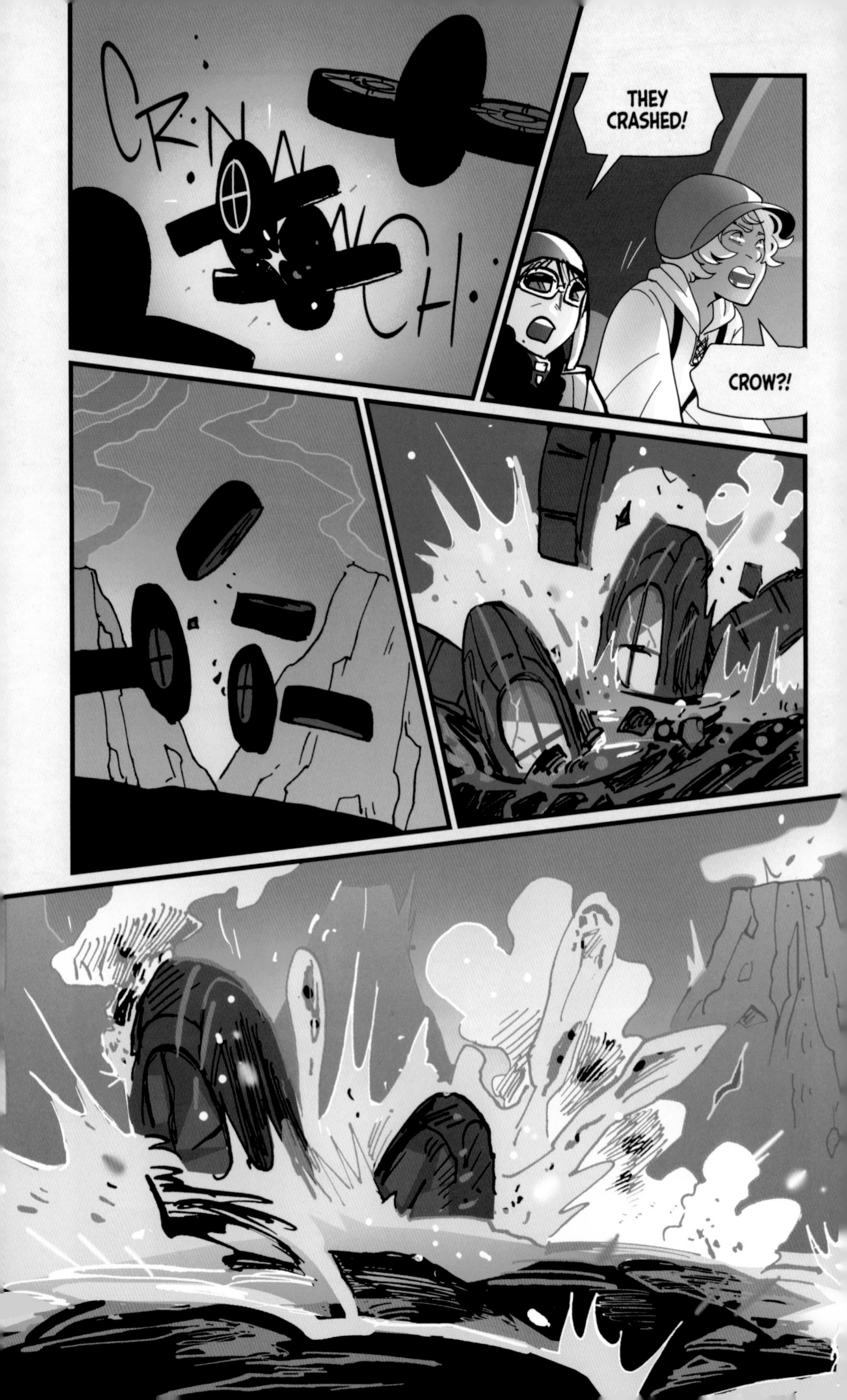
CRNNNNCH
THEY CRASHED!
CROW?!

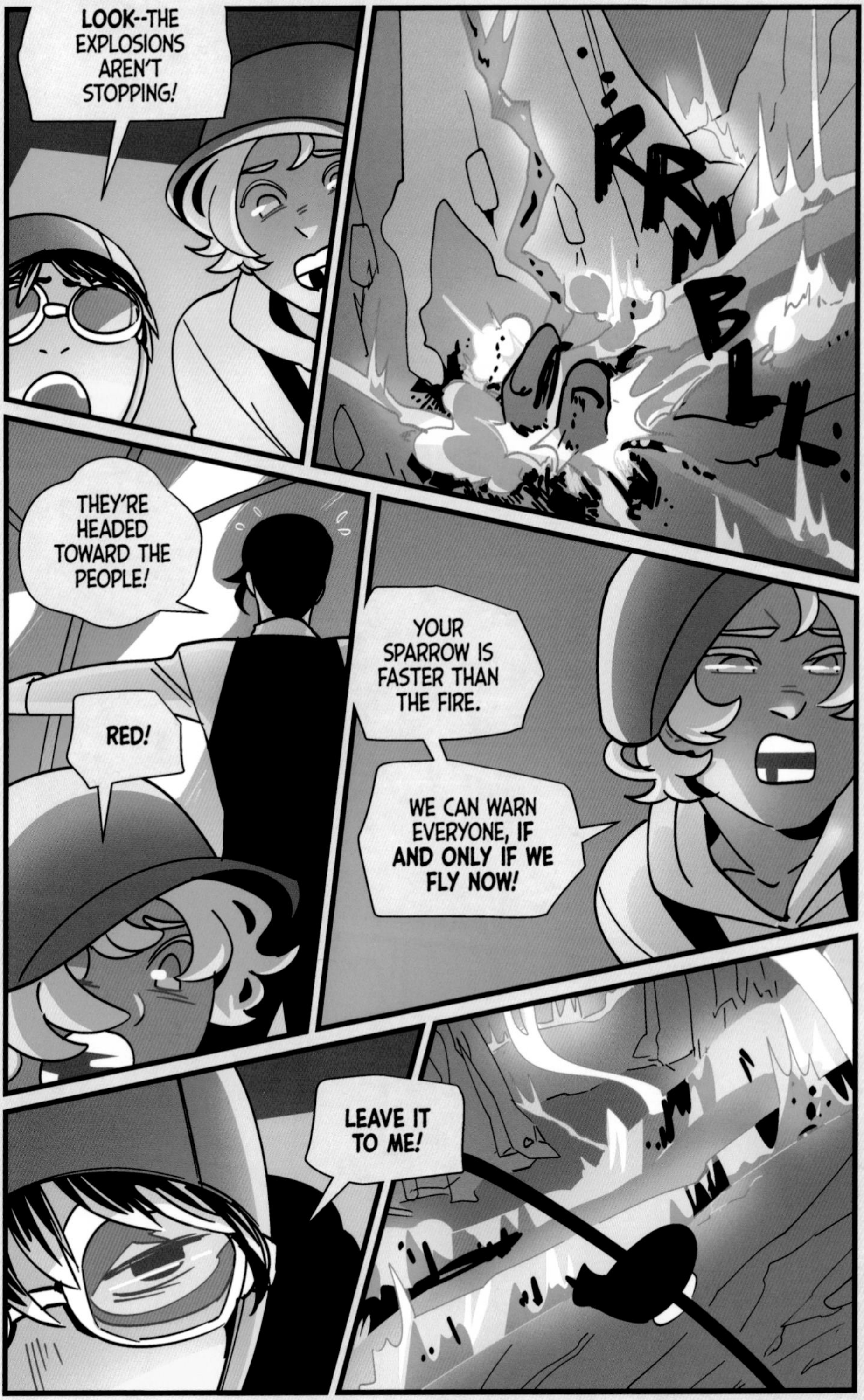
LOOK--THE EXPLOSIONS AREN'T STOPPING!
RRMBLL
THEY'RE HEADED TOWARD THE PEOPLE!
RED!
YOUR SPARROW IS FASTER THAN THE FIRE.
WE CAN WARN EVERYONE, IF AND ONLY IF WE FLY NOW!
LEAVE IT TO ME!

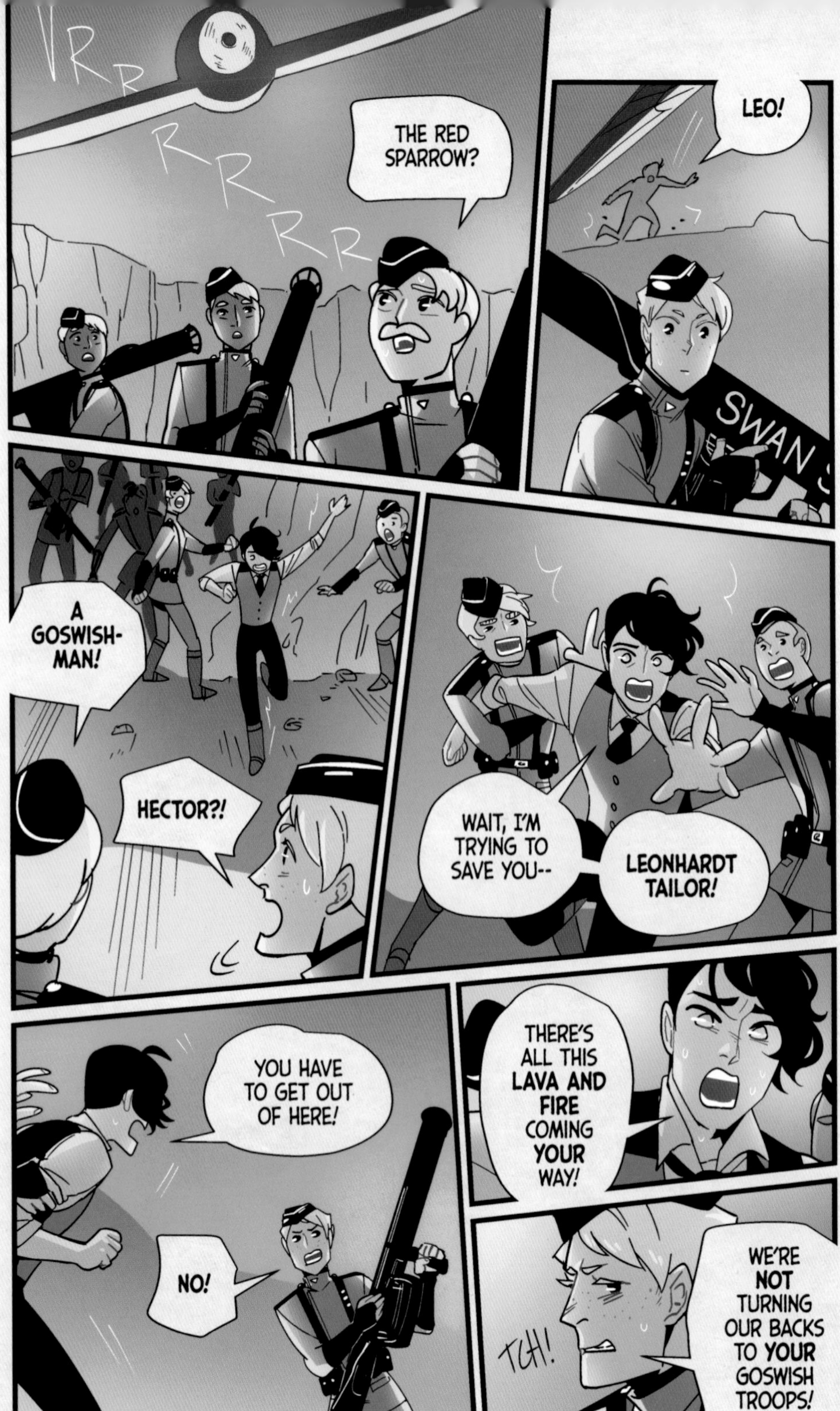
VRRRRRRR
THE RED SPARROW?
LEO!
SWAN
A GOSWISH-MAN!
HECTOR?!
WAIT, I'M TRYING TO SAVE YOU--
LEONHARDT TAILOR!
YOU HAVE TO GET OUT OF HERE!
NO!
THERE'S ALL THIS LAVA AND FIRE COMING YOUR WAY!
TCH!
WE'RE NOT TURNING OUR BACKS TO YOUR GOSWISH TROOPS!

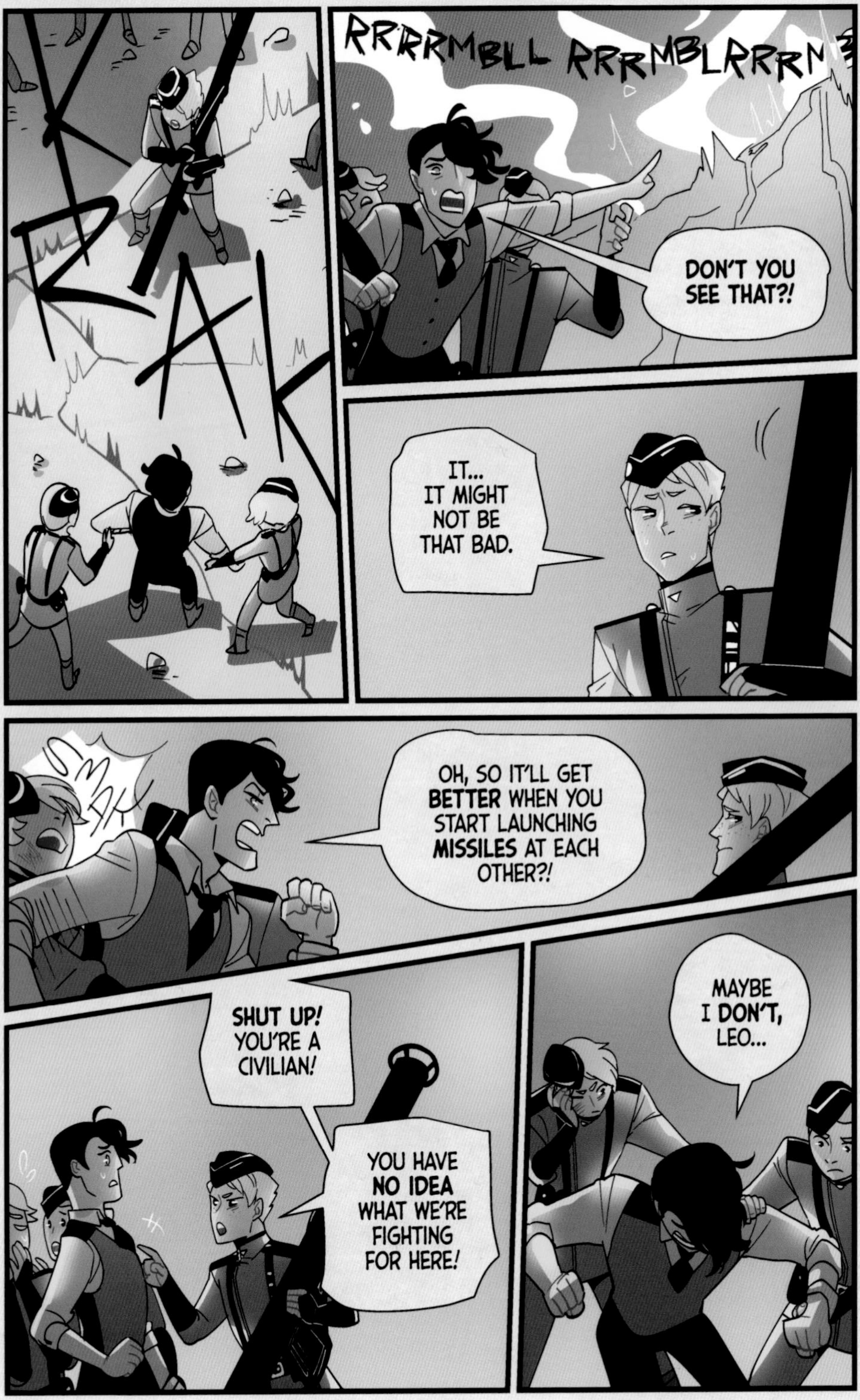
KRAK
RRRRMBLL RRRMBLRRRN
DON'T YOU SEE THAT?!
IT... IT MIGHT NOT BE THAT BAD.
SMAK
OH, SO IT'LL GET BETTER WHEN YOU START LAUNCHING MISSILES AT EACH OTHER?!
SHUT UP! YOU'RE A CIVILIAN!
YOU HAVE NO IDEA WHAT WE'RE FIGHTING FOR HERE!
MAYBE I DON'T, LEO...

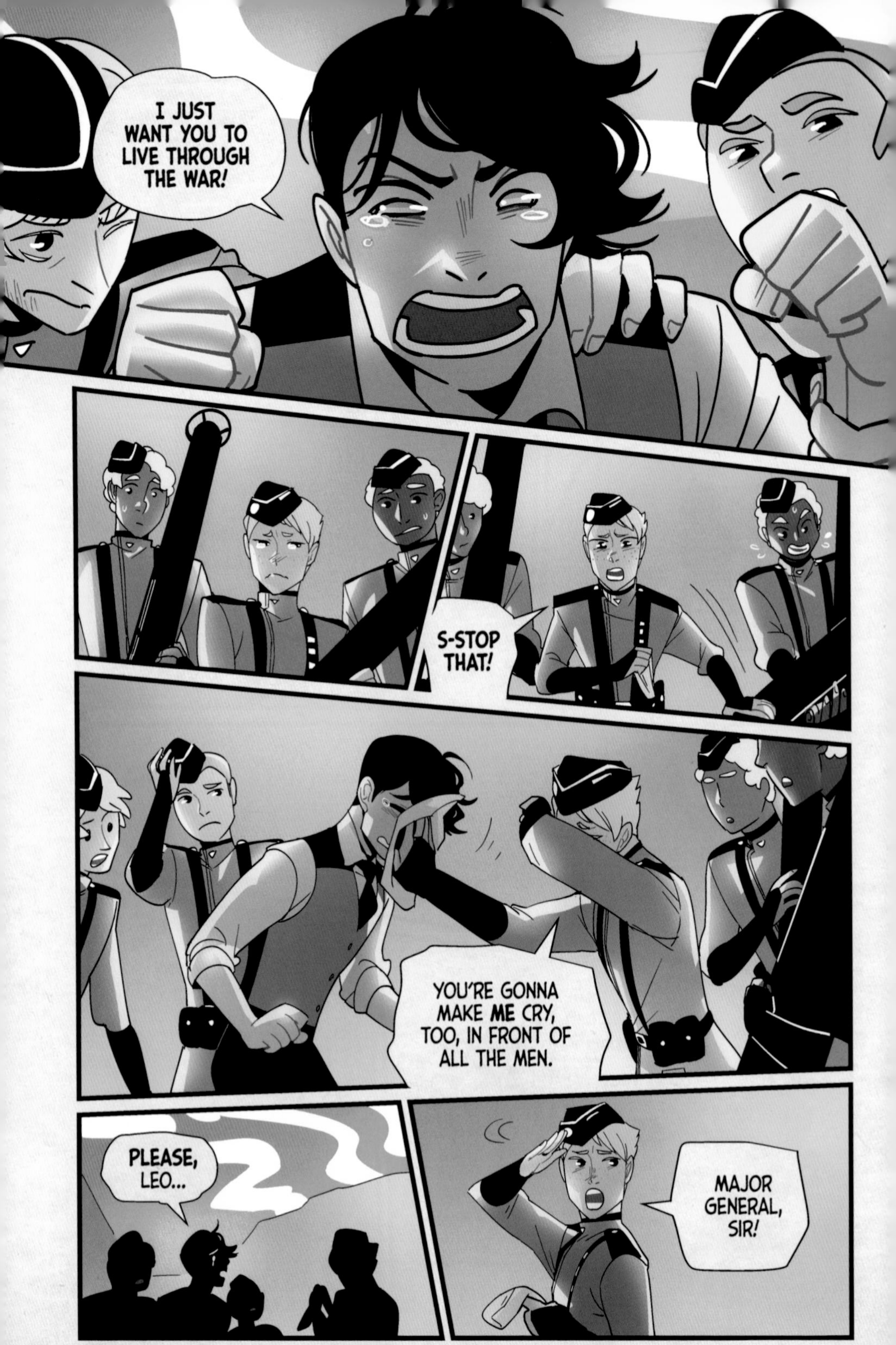
I JUST WANT YOU TO LIVE THROUGH THE WAR!
S-STOP THAT!
YOU'RE GONNA MAKE ME CRY, TOO, IN FRONT OF ALL THE MEN.
PLEASE, LEO...
MAJOR GENERAL, SIR!

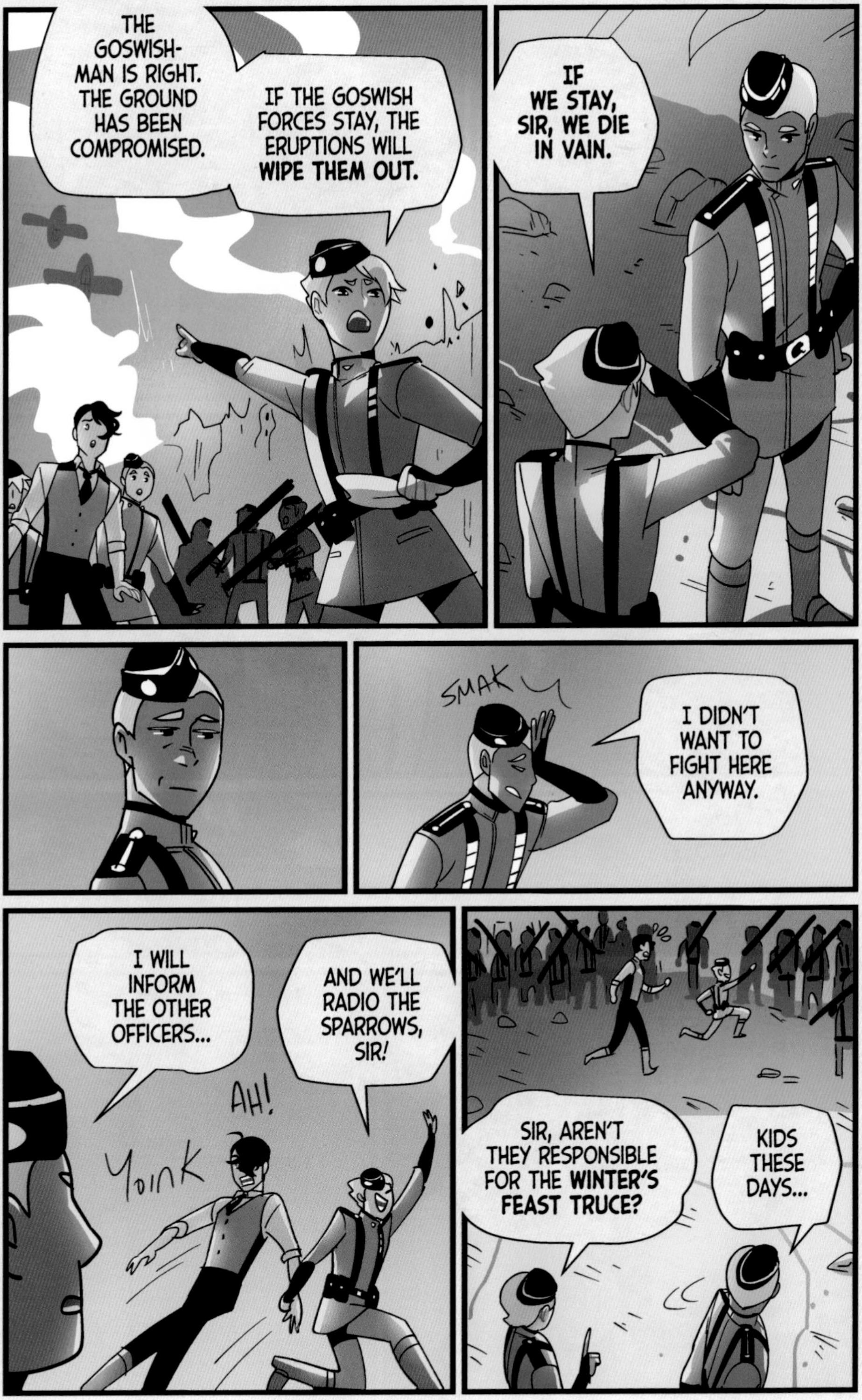
THE GOSWISH-MAN IS RIGHT. THE GROUND HAS BEEN COMPROMISED.
IF THE GOSWISH FORCES STAY, THE ERUPTIONS WILL WIPE THEM OUT.
IF WE STAY, SIR, WE DIE IN VAIN.
SMAK
I DIDN'T WANT TO FIGHT HERE ANYWAY.
I WILL INFORM THE OTHER OFFICERS...
AND WE'LL RADIO THE SPARROWS, SIR!
AH!
YOINK
SIR, AREN'T THEY RESPONSIBLE FOR THE WINTER'S FEAST TRUCE?
KIDS THESE DAYS...

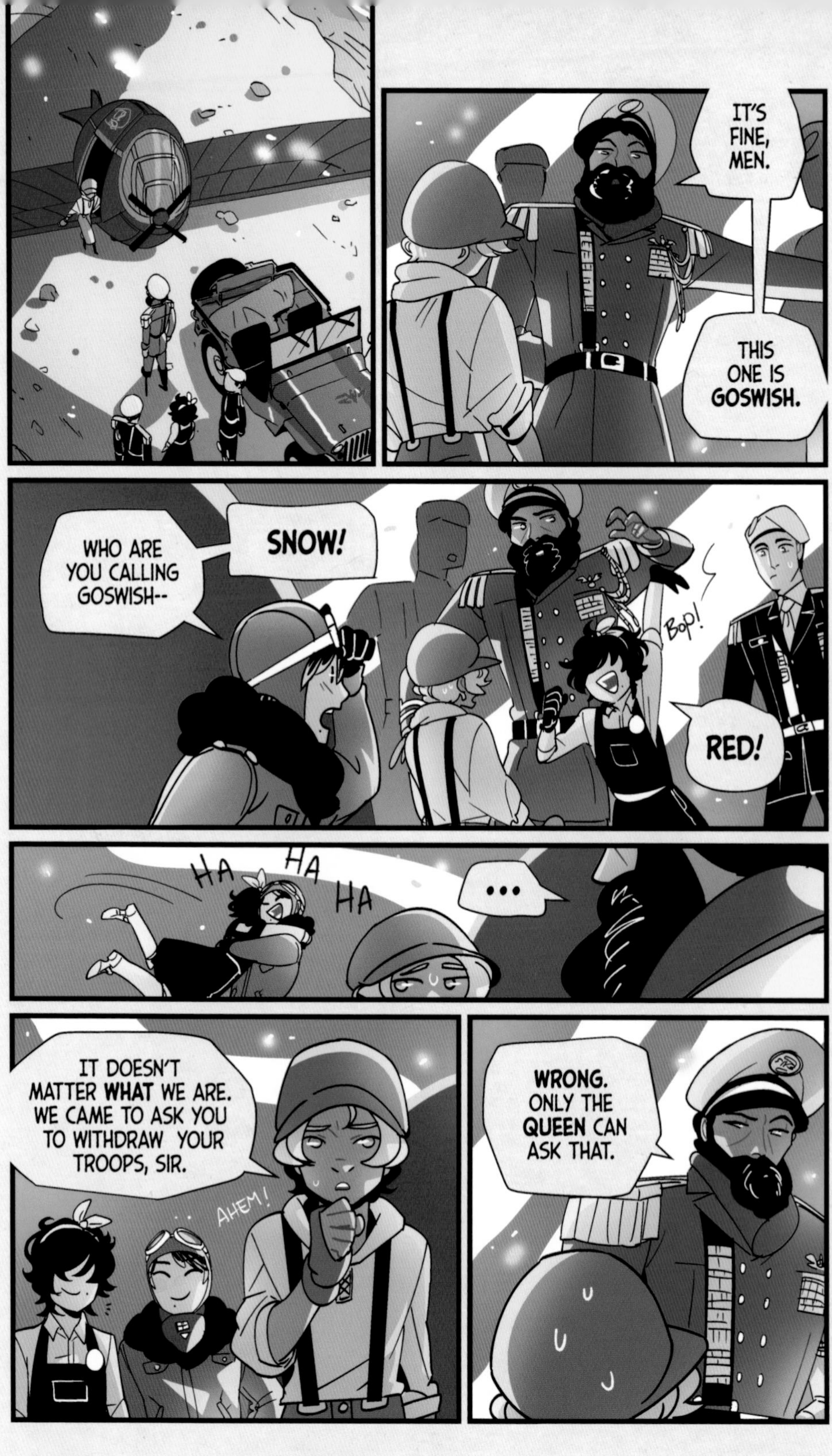

IT'S FINE, MEN.
THIS ONE IS GOSWISH.
WHO ARE YOU CALLING GOSWISH--
SNOW!
Bop!
RED!
HA HA HA
...
IT DOESN'T MATTER WHAT WE ARE. WE CAME TO ASK YOU TO WITHDRAW YOUR TROOPS, SIR.
AHEM!
WRONG. ONLY THE QUEEN CAN ASK THAT.

BUT, SIR, EVEN THE **GRIMMAEANS** ARE LEAVING!

AFTER THOSE CROW-2 MACHINES CRASHED, THE VERY **ROCKS** YOU'VE BEEN STANDIN' ON HAVE BEEN **MELTING** UNDER YOUR FEET!

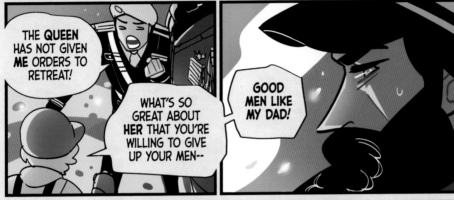

THE **QUEEN** HAS NOT GIVEN **ME** ORDERS TO RETREAT!

WHAT'S SO GREAT ABOUT **HER** THAT YOU'RE WILLING TO GIVE UP YOUR MEN--

GOOD MEN LIKE MY DAD!

BUT, REED...!

THE GRIMMAEANS KNOW THEIR LANDS AND WATERS FAR BETTER THAN WE DO.

I RECOMMEND YOU TURN BACK, GENERAL.

KLOK

I LEARNED THAT THE **HARD WAY** YEARS AGO.

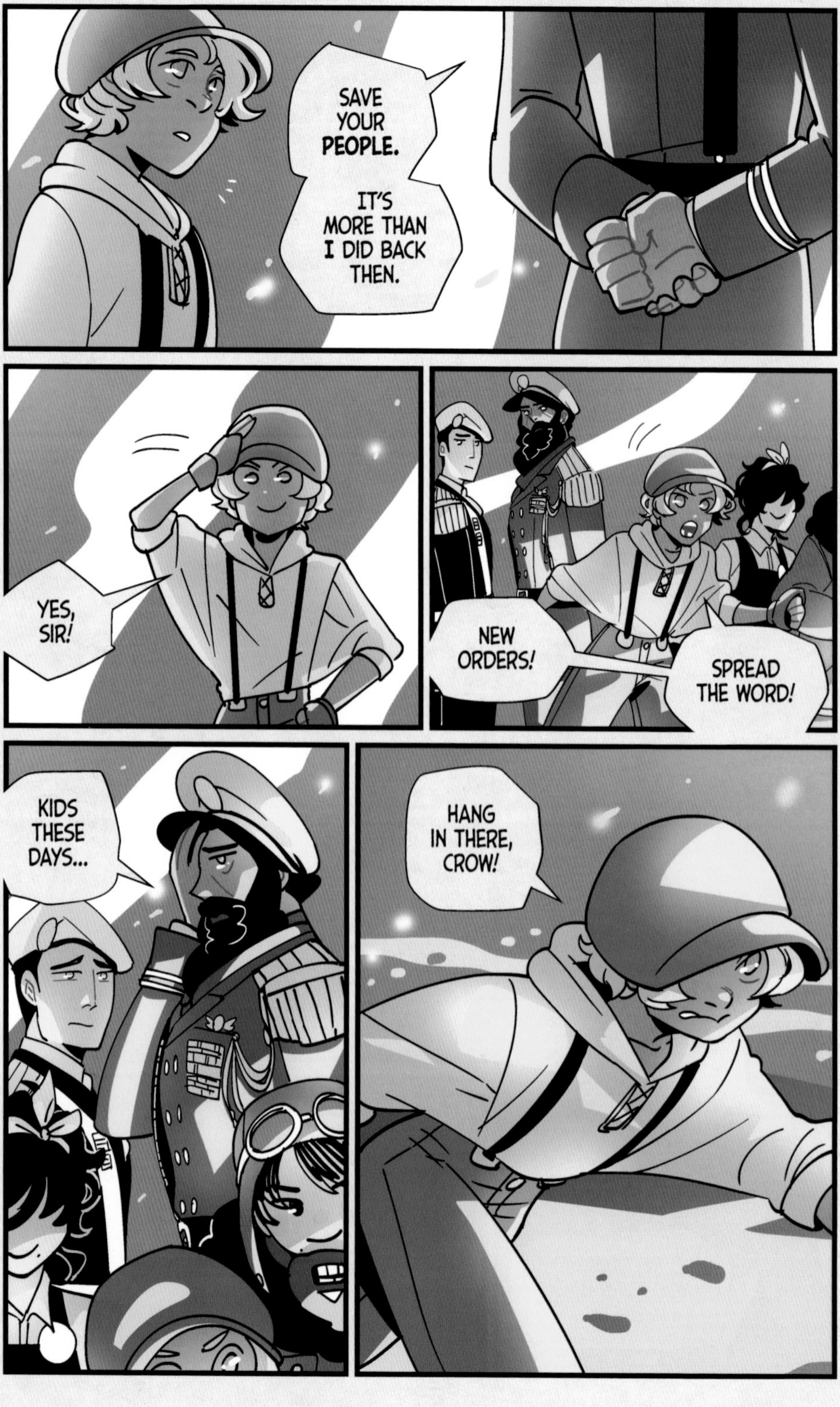
SAVE YOUR PEOPLE.
IT'S MORE THAN I DID BACK THEN.
YES, SIR!
NEW ORDERS!
SPREAD THE WORD!
KIDS THESE DAYS...
HANG IN THERE, CROW!

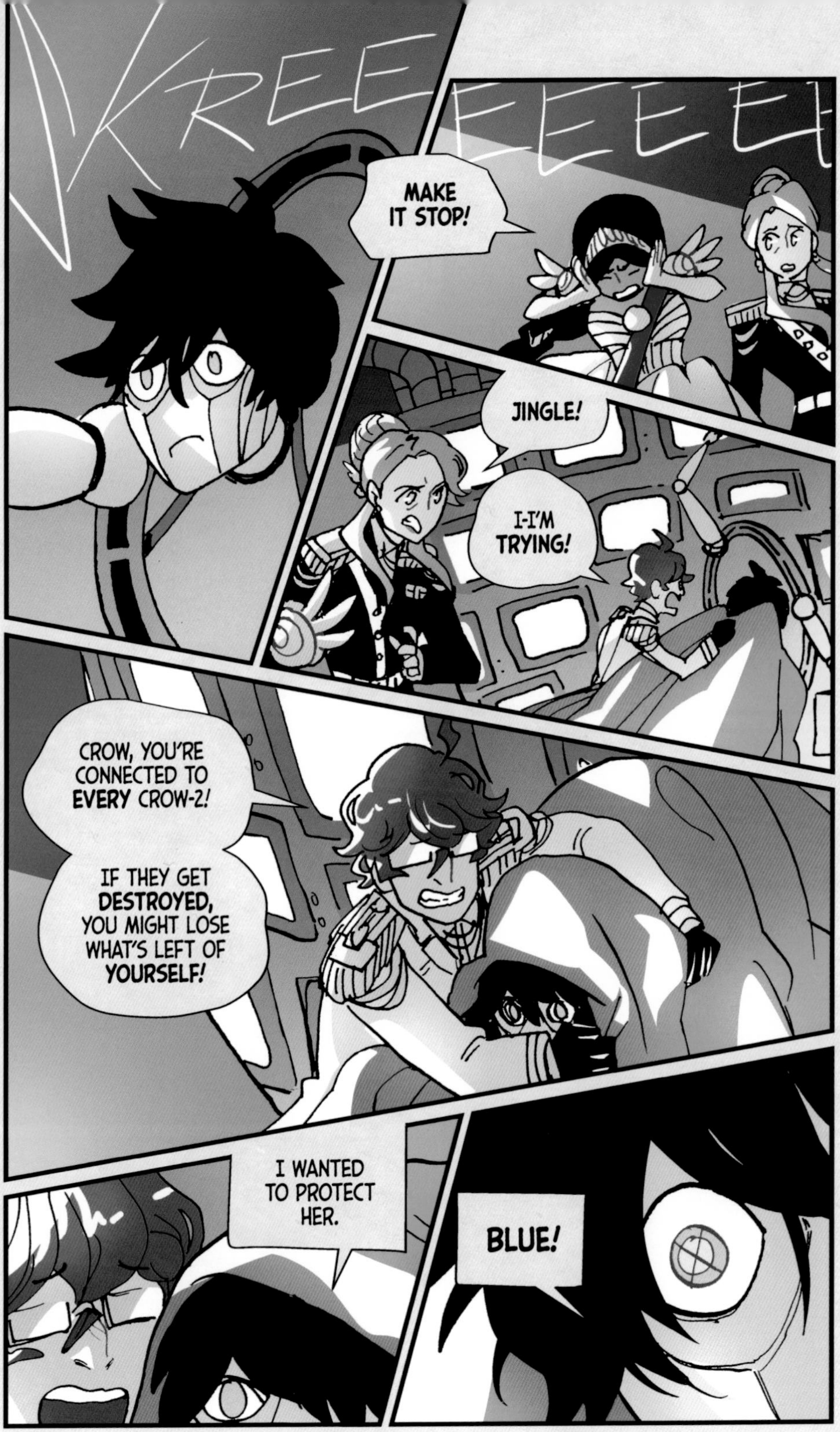
KREEEEEEEE
MAKE IT STOP!
JINGLE!
I-I'M TRYING!
CROW, YOU'RE CONNECTED TO EVERY CROW-2!
IF THEY GET DESTROYED, YOU MIGHT LOSE WHAT'S LEFT OF YOURSELF!
I WANTED TO PROTECT HER.
BLUE!

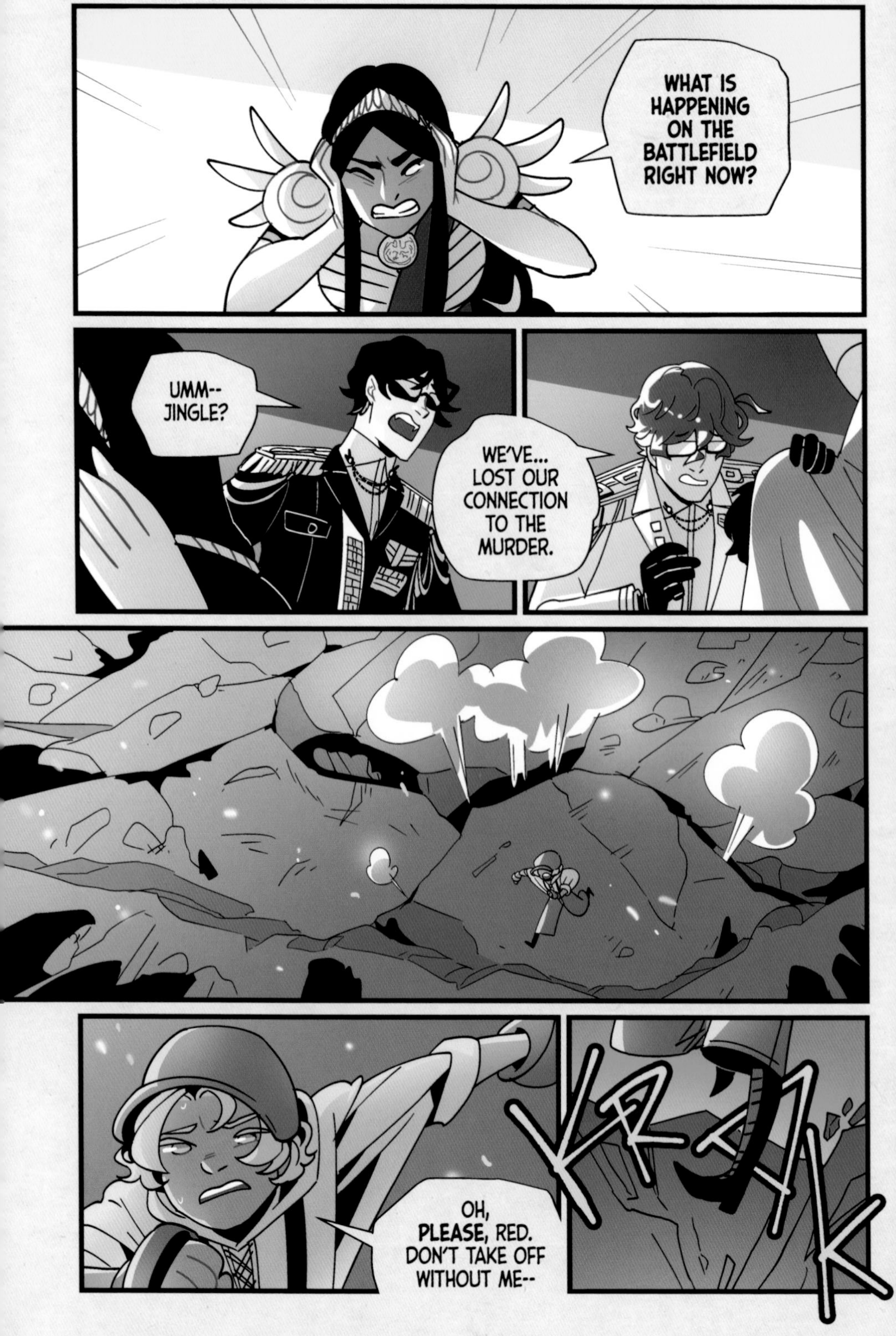
WHAT IS HAPPENING ON THE BATTLEFIELD RIGHT NOW?
UMM-- JINGLE?
WE'VE... LOST OUR CONNECTION TO THE MURDER.
OH, **PLEASE,** RED. DON'T TAKE OFF WITHOUT ME--
KRAAK

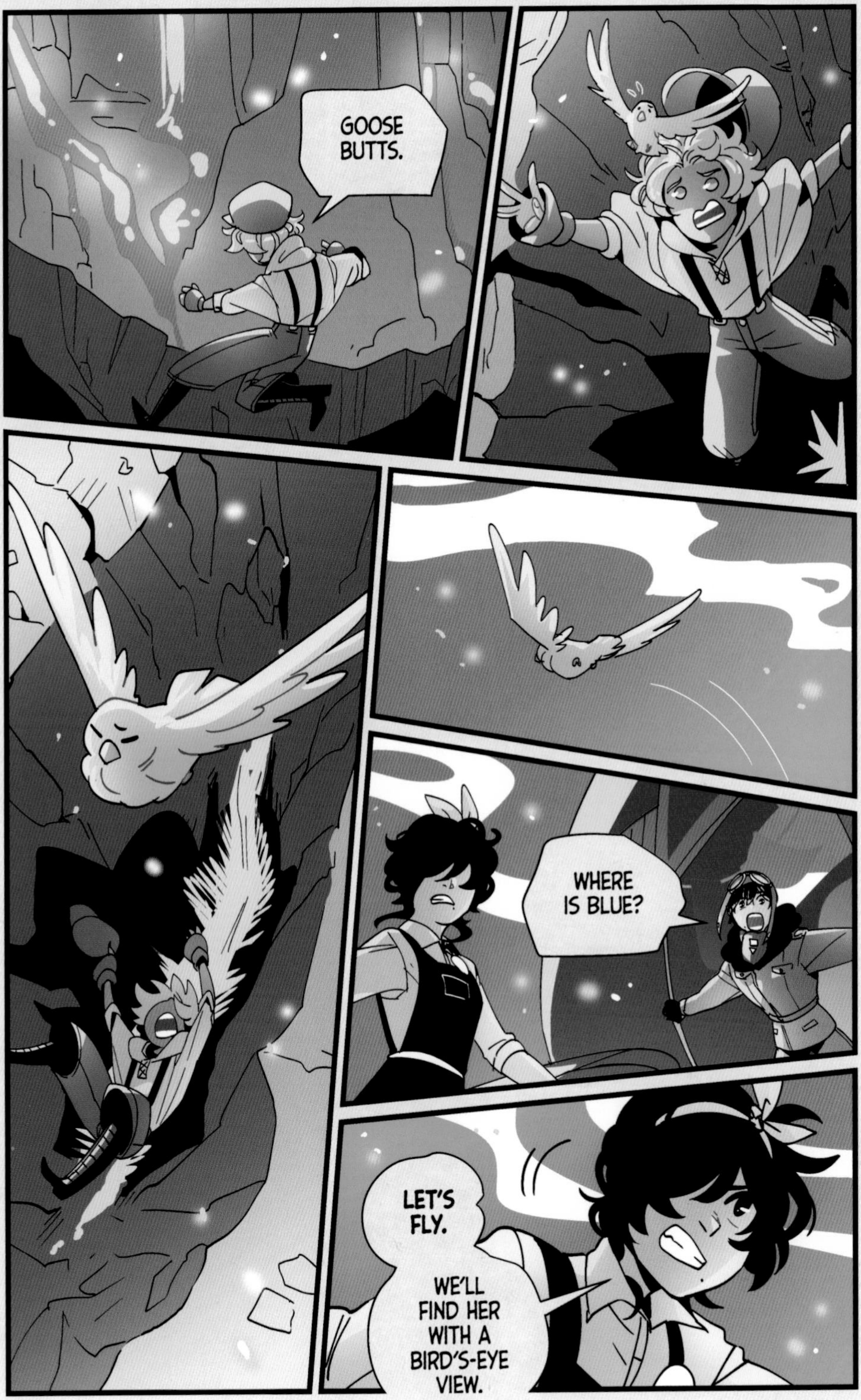
GOOSE BUTTS.
WHERE IS BLUE?
LET'S FLY.
WE'LL FIND HER WITH A BIRD'S-EYE VIEW.

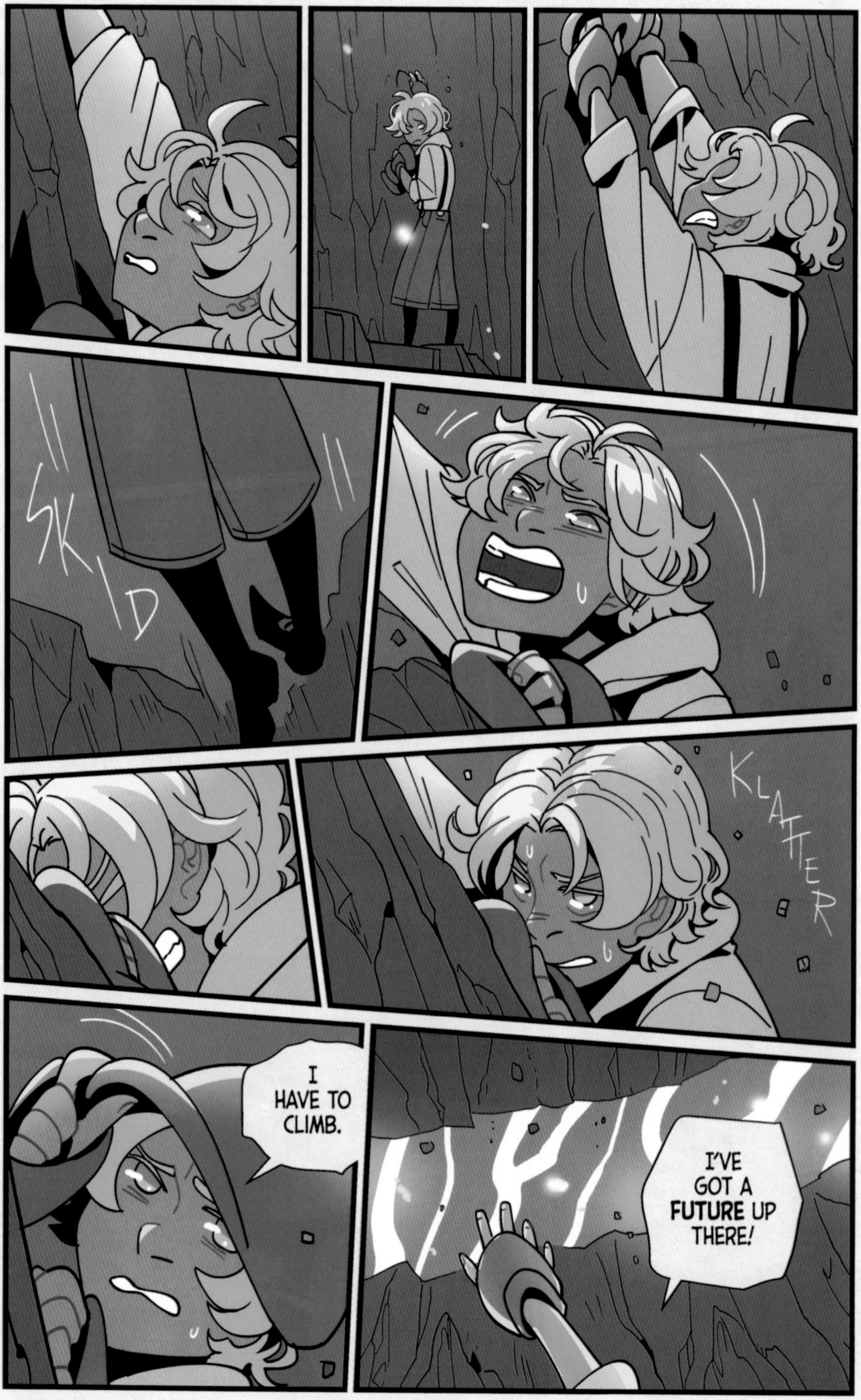
SKID
KLATTER
I HAVE TO CLIMB.
I'VE GOT A **FUTURE** UP THERE!

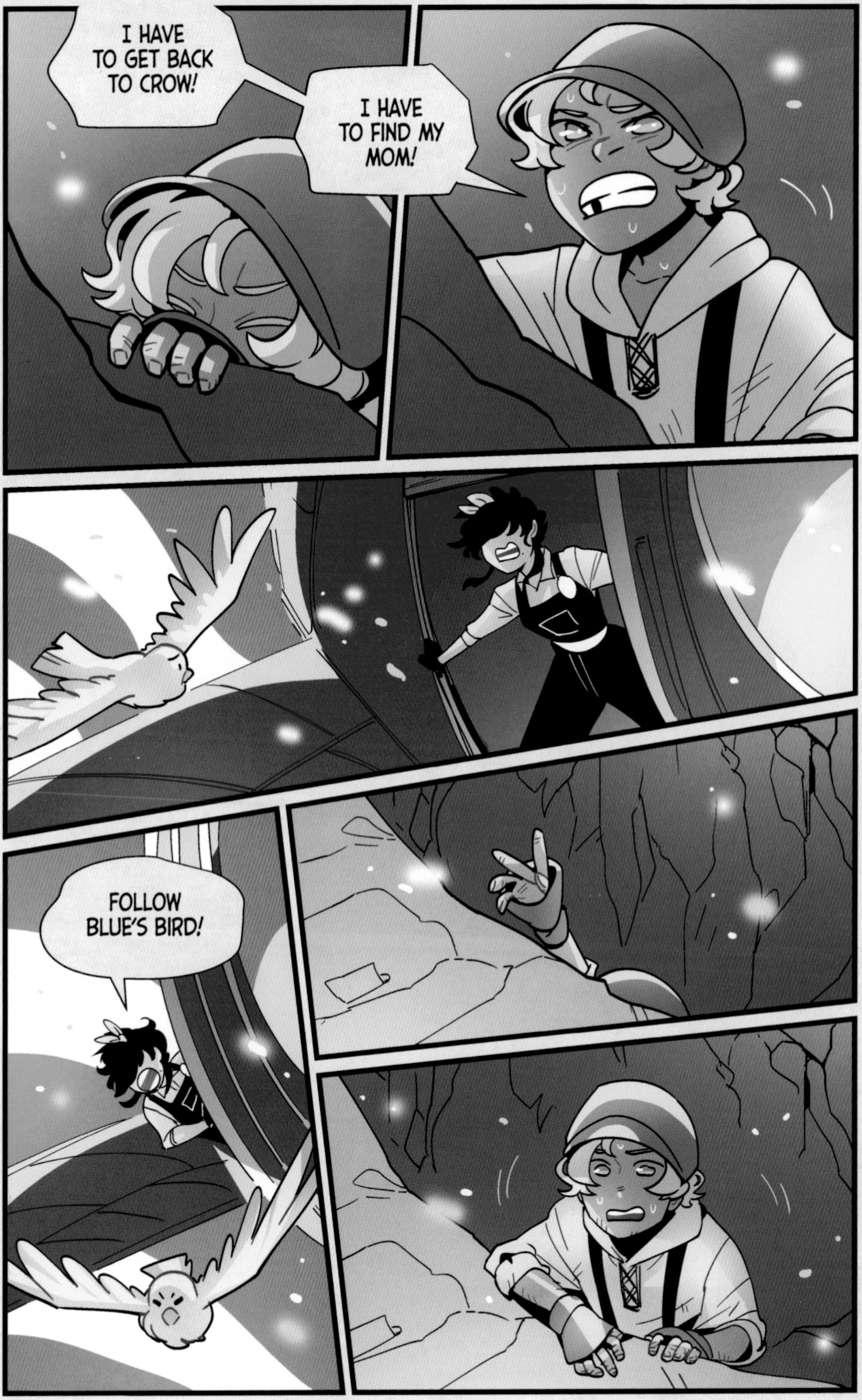
I HAVE TO GET BACK TO CROW!
I HAVE TO FIND MY MOM!
FOLLOW BLUE'S BIRD!

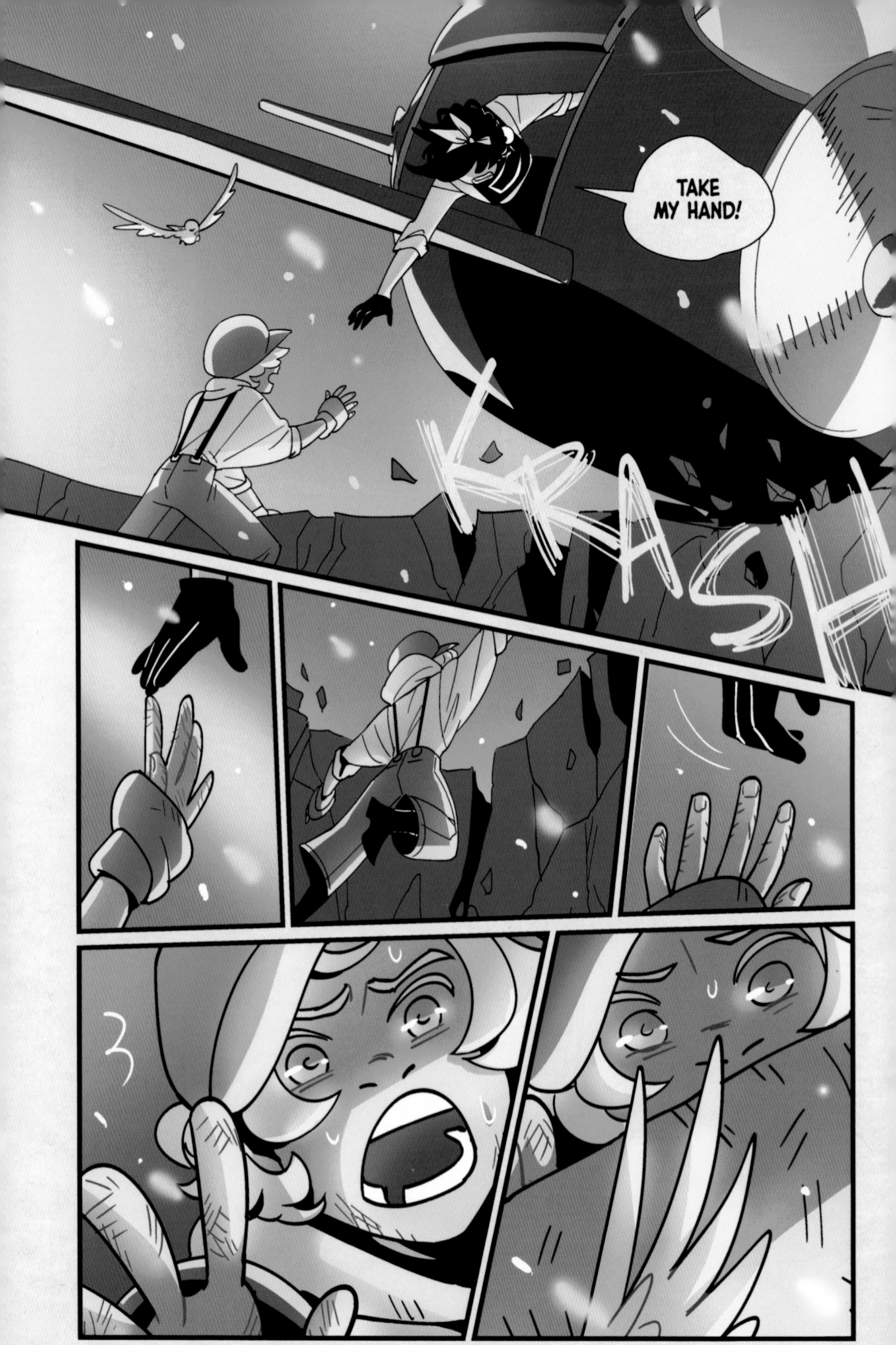
TAKE MY HAND!
KRASH

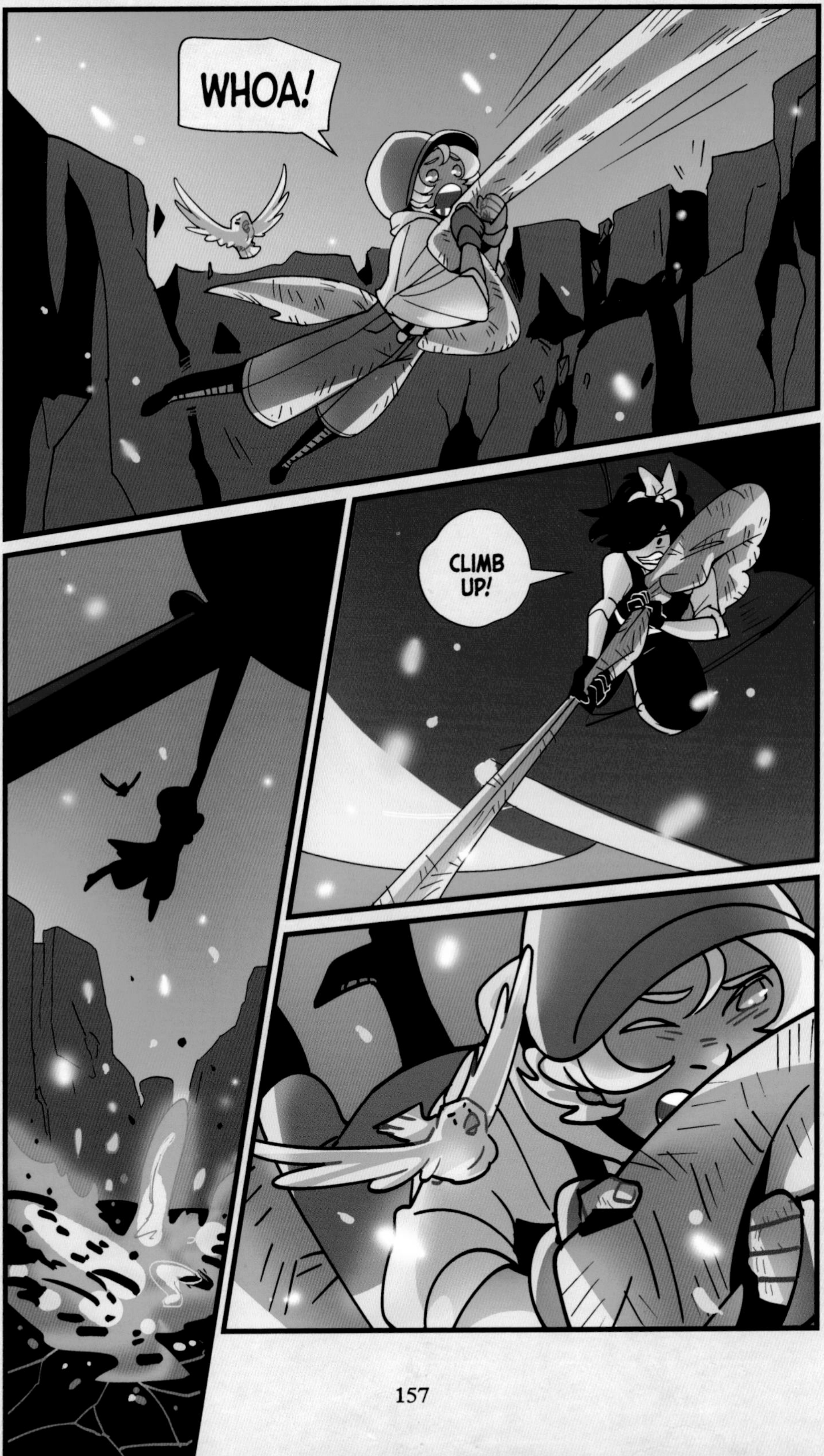
WHOA!
CLIMB UP!

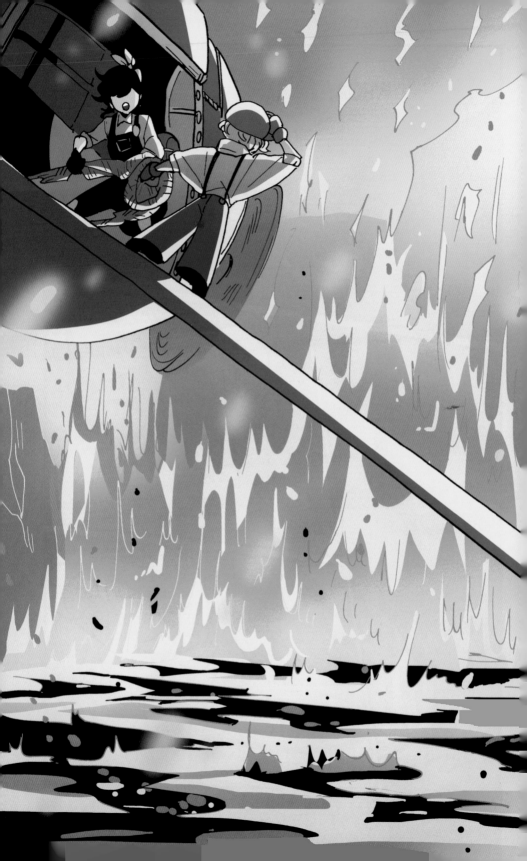

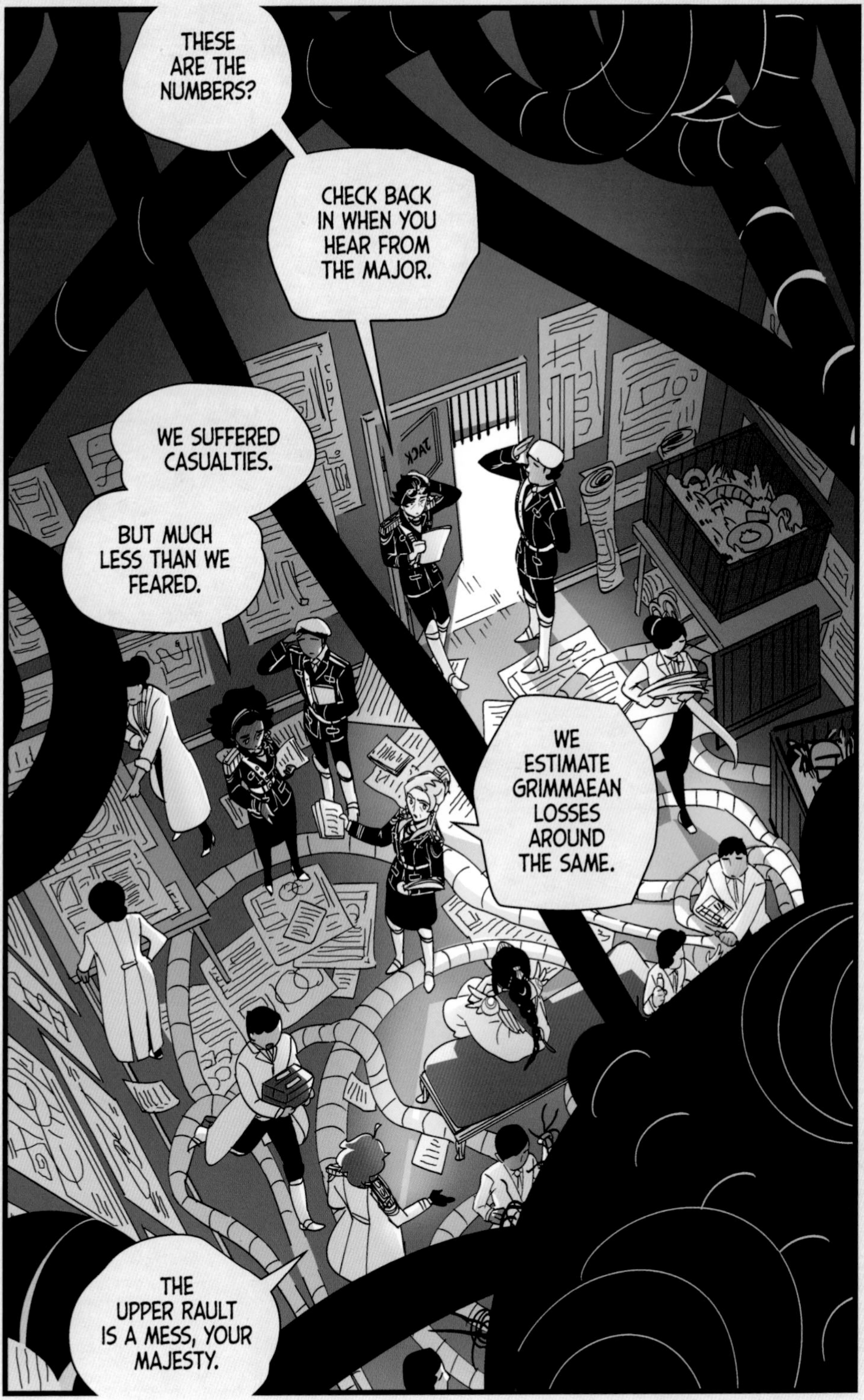
THESE ARE THE NUMBERS?
CHECK BACK IN WHEN YOU HEAR FROM THE MAJOR.
JACK
WE SUFFERED CASUALTIES.
BUT MUCH LESS THAN WE FEARED.
WE ESTIMATE GRIMMAEAN LOSSES AROUND THE SAME.
THE UPPER RAULT IS A MESS, YOUR MAJESTY.

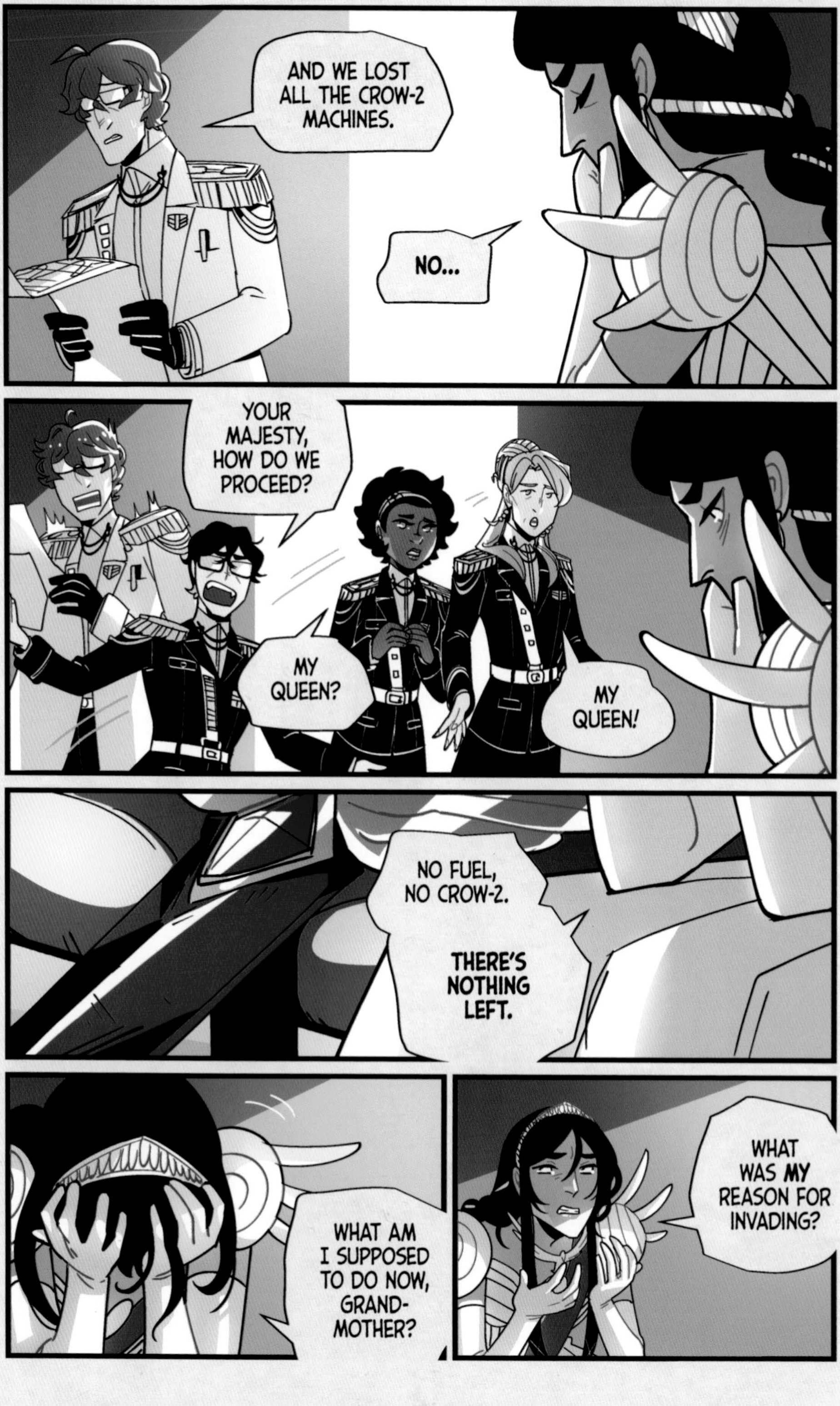
AND WE LOST ALL THE CROW-2 MACHINES.
NO...
YOUR MAJESTY, HOW DO WE PROCEED?
MY QUEEN?
MY QUEEN!
NO FUEL, NO CROW-2.
THERE'S NOTHING LEFT.
WHAT AM I SUPPOSED TO DO NOW, GRAND-MOTHER?
WHAT WAS MY REASON FOR INVADING?

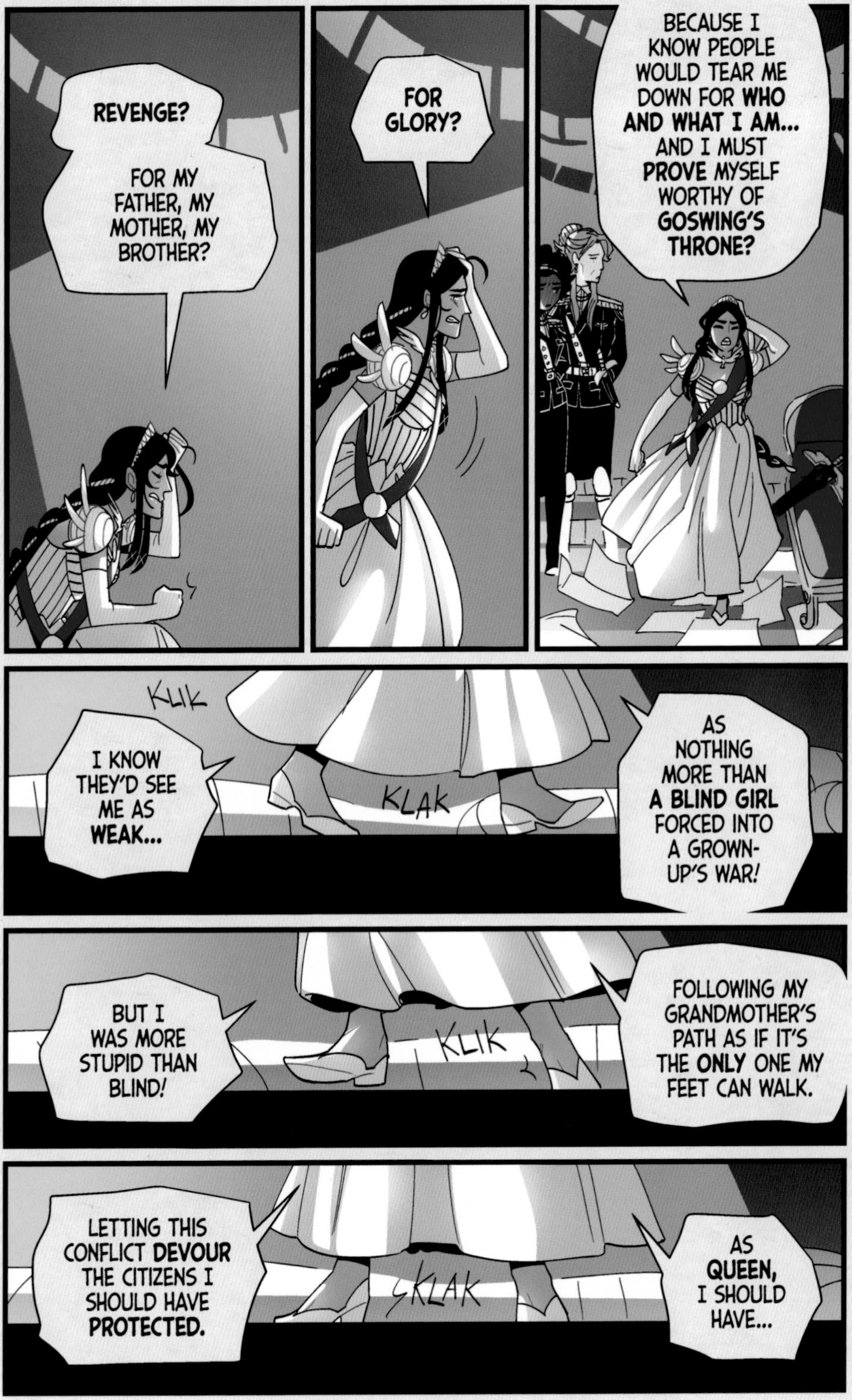
REVENGE?
FOR MY FATHER, MY MOTHER, MY BROTHER?
FOR GLORY?
BECAUSE I KNOW PEOPLE WOULD TEAR ME DOWN FOR WHO AND WHAT I AM... AND I MUST PROVE MYSELF WORTHY OF GOSWING'S THRONE?
KLIK
I KNOW THEY'D SEE ME AS WEAK...
KLAK
AS NOTHING MORE THAN A BLIND GIRL FORCED INTO A GROWN-UP'S WAR!
BUT I WAS MORE STUPID THAN BLIND!
KLIK
FOLLOWING MY GRANDMOTHER'S PATH AS IF IT'S THE ONLY ONE MY FEET CAN WALK.
LETTING THIS CONFLICT DEVOUR THE CITIZENS I SHOULD HAVE PROTECTED.
SKLAK
AS QUEEN, I SHOULD HAVE...

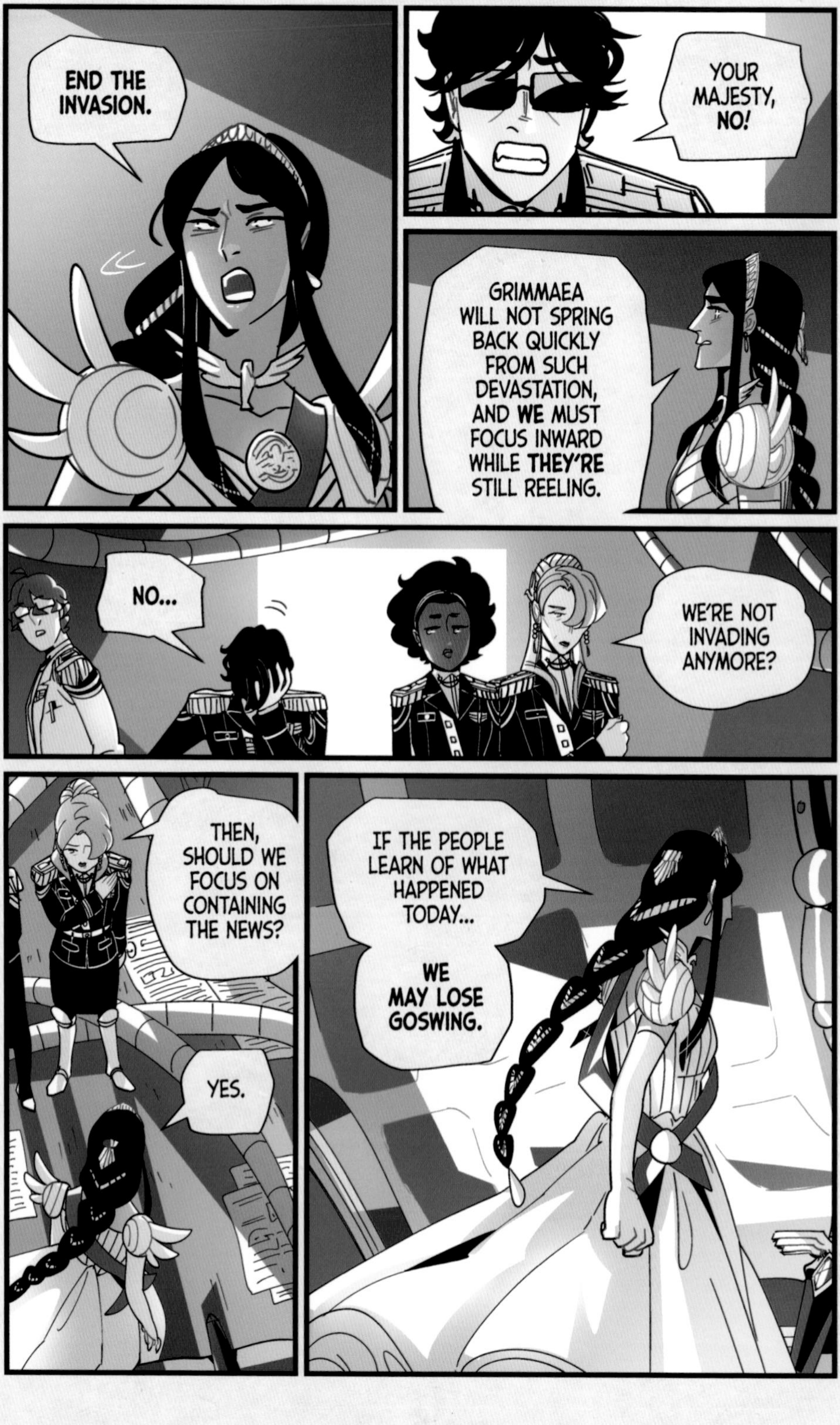
END THE INVASION.
YOUR MAJESTY, NO!
GRIMMAEA WILL NOT SPRING BACK QUICKLY FROM SUCH DEVASTATION, AND **WE** MUST FOCUS INWARD WHILE **THEY'RE** STILL REELING.
NO...
WE'RE NOT INVADING ANYMORE?
THEN, SHOULD WE FOCUS ON CONTAINING THE NEWS?
YES.
IF THE PEOPLE LEARN OF WHAT HAPPENED TODAY...
WE MAY LOSE GOSWING.

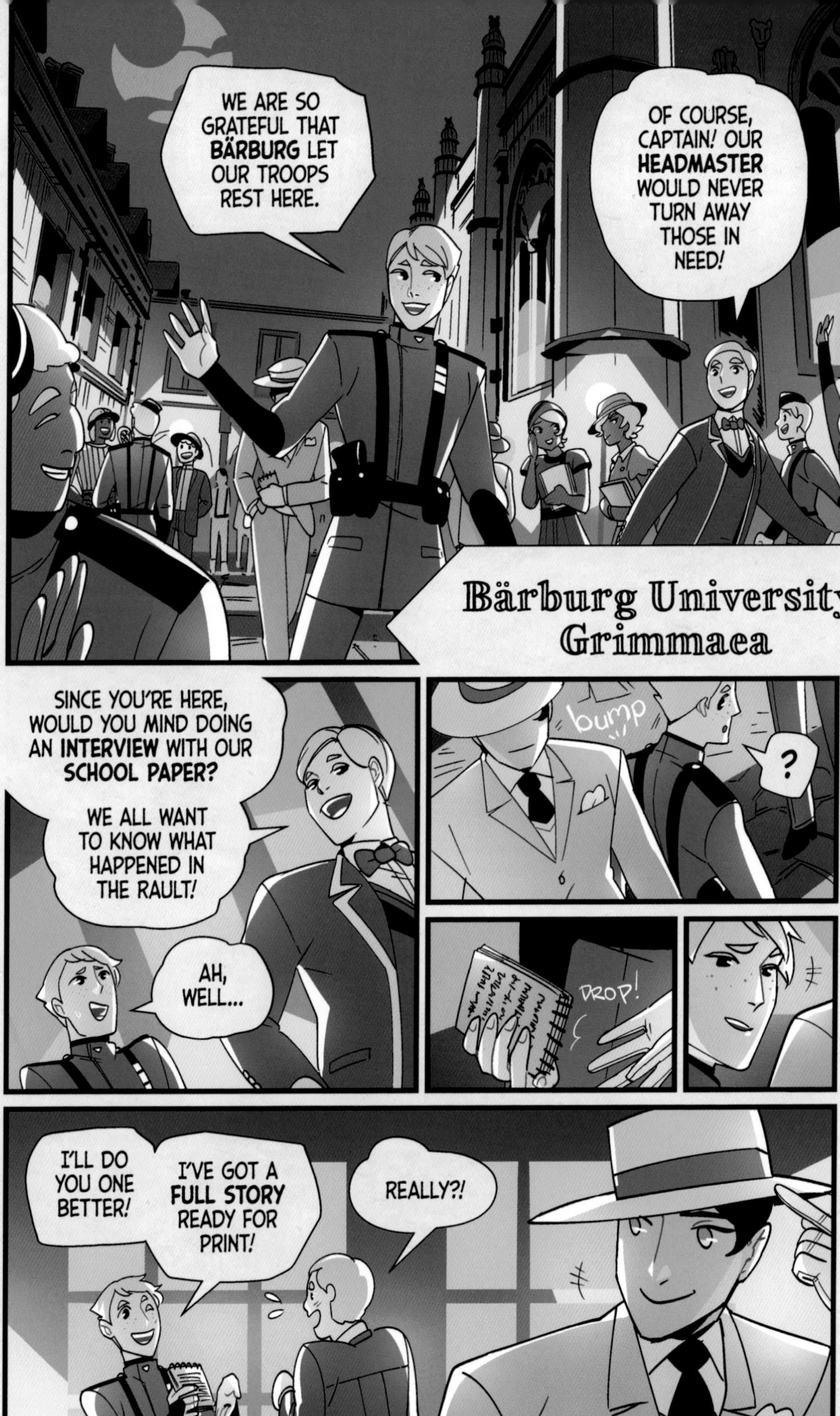
WE ARE SO GRATEFUL THAT BÄRBURG LET OUR TROOPS REST HERE.
OF COURSE, CAPTAIN! OUR HEADMASTER WOULD NEVER TURN AWAY THOSE IN NEED!
Bärburg University, Grimmaea
SINCE YOU'RE HERE, WOULD YOU MIND DOING AN INTERVIEW WITH OUR SCHOOL PAPER?
WE ALL WANT TO KNOW WHAT HAPPENED IN THE RAULT!
AH, WELL...
bump
?
DROP!
I'LL DO YOU ONE BETTER!
I'VE GOT A FULL STORY READY FOR PRINT!
REALLY?!

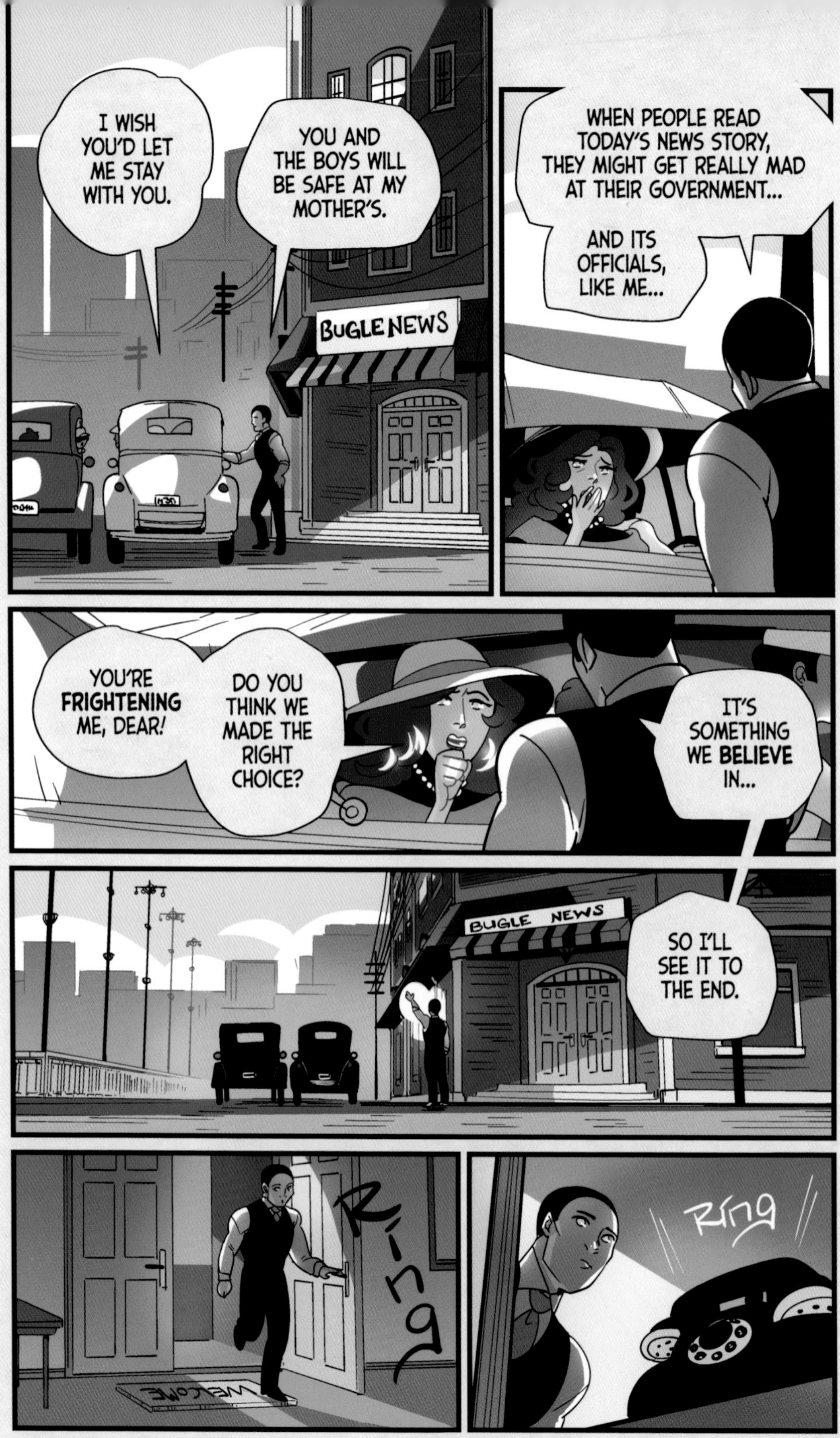
I WISH YOU'D LET ME STAY WITH YOU.
YOU AND THE BOYS WILL BE SAFE AT MY MOTHER'S.
BUGLE NEWS
WHEN PEOPLE READ TODAY'S NEWS STORY, THEY MIGHT GET REALLY MAD AT THEIR GOVERNMENT...
AND ITS OFFICIALS, LIKE ME...
YOU'RE **FRIGHTENING** ME, DEAR!
DO YOU THINK WE MADE THE RIGHT CHOICE?
IT'S SOMETHING WE **BELIEVE** IN...
BUGLE NEWS
SO I'LL SEE IT TO THE END.
Ring
Ring

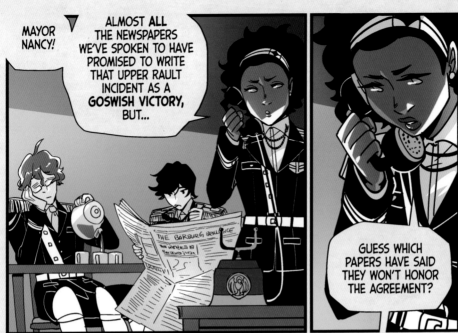

MAYOR NANCY!

ALMOST **ALL** THE NEWSPAPERS WE'VE SPOKEN TO HAVE PROMISED TO WRITE THAT UPPER RAULT INCIDENT AS A **GOSWISH VICTORY,** BUT...

THE BARBURG BALANCE

GUESS WHICH PAPERS HAVE SAID THEY WON'T HONOR THE AGREEMENT?

• • •

IN EVERY CITY, IT'S THE ONE CALLED THE **BUGLE.**

THE BUGLE IS A FAMILY COMPANY.

AND I HAVE A LOT OF FAMILY ACROSS GOSWING.

WE'VE ALL DECIDED TO RUN THE TRUE STORY ABOUT THE UPPER RAULT INCIDENT.

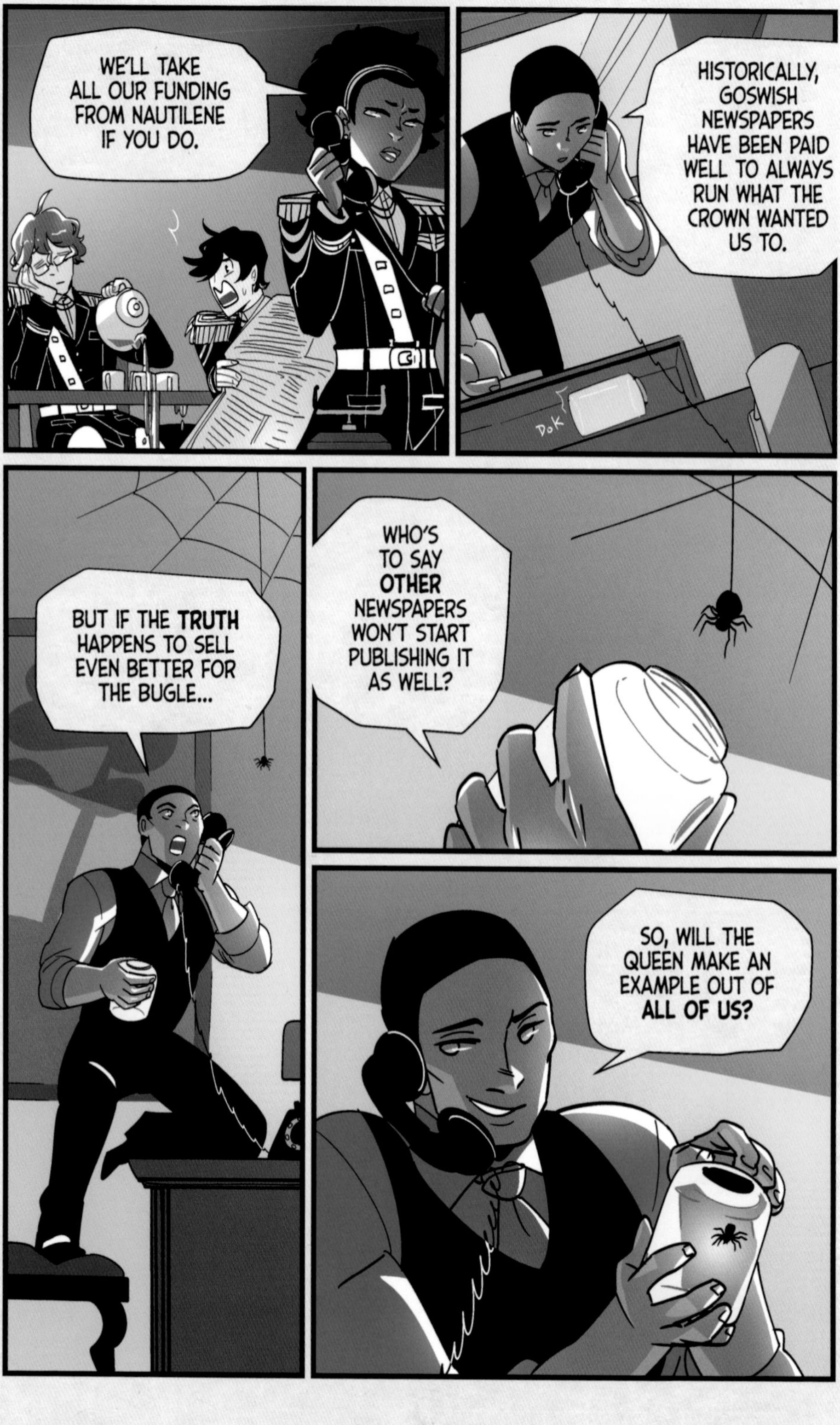
WE'LL TAKE ALL OUR FUNDING FROM NAUTILENE IF YOU DO.
HISTORICALLY, GOSWISH NEWSPAPERS HAVE BEEN PAID WELL TO ALWAYS RUN WHAT THE CROWN WANTED US TO.
DOK
BUT IF THE TRUTH HAPPENS TO SELL EVEN BETTER FOR THE BUGLE...
WHO'S TO SAY OTHER NEWSPAPERS WON'T START PUBLISHING IT AS WELL?
SO, WILL THE QUEEN MAKE AN EXAMPLE OUT OF ALL OF US?

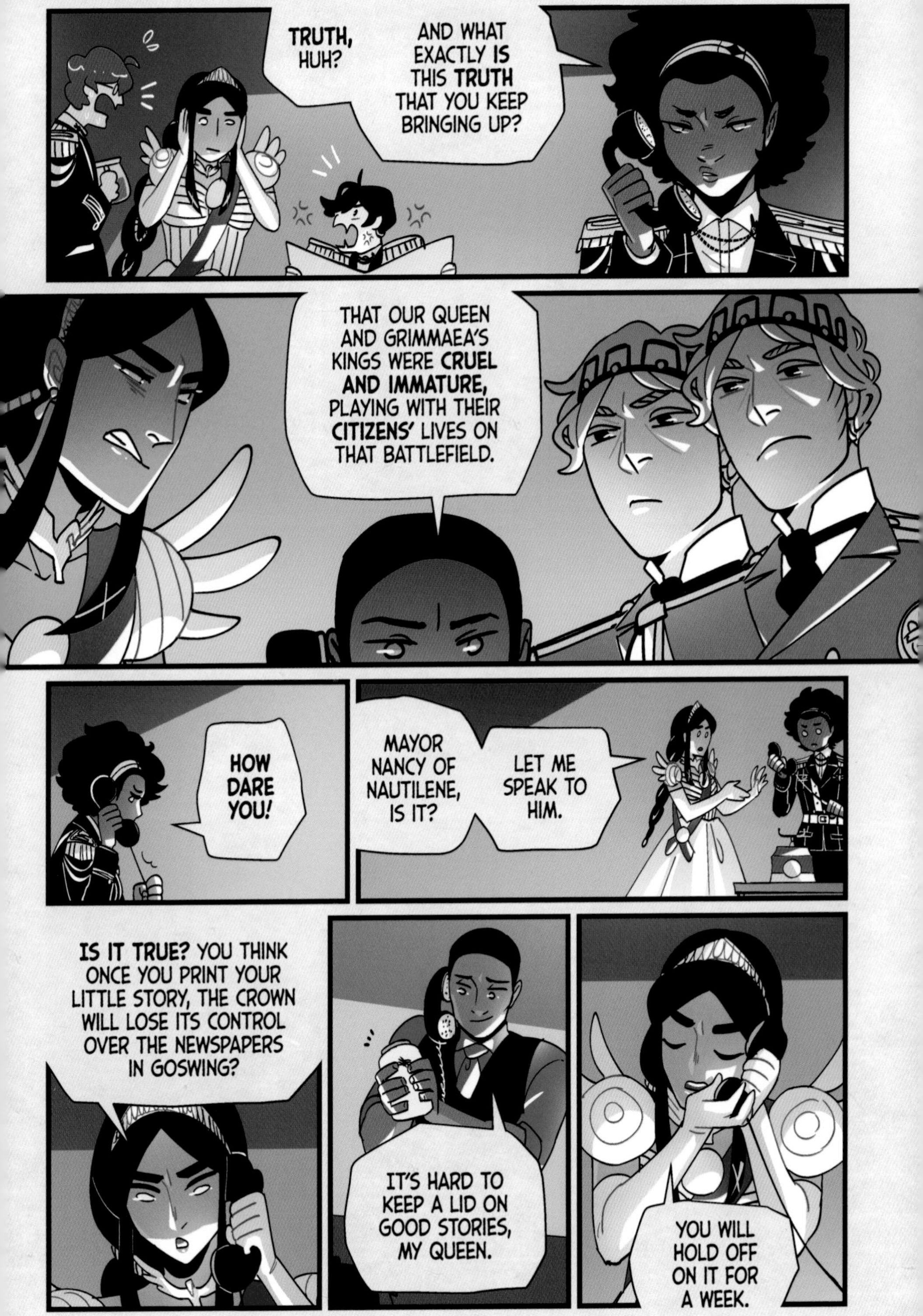
TRUTH, HUH?
AND WHAT EXACTLY IS THIS TRUTH THAT YOU KEEP BRINGING UP?
THAT OUR QUEEN AND GRIMMAEA'S KINGS WERE CRUEL AND IMMATURE, PLAYING WITH THEIR CITIZENS' LIVES ON THAT BATTLEFIELD.
HOW DARE YOU!
MAYOR NANCY OF NAUTILENE, IS IT?
LET ME SPEAK TO HIM.
IS IT TRUE? YOU THINK ONCE YOU PRINT YOUR LITTLE STORY, THE CROWN WILL LOSE ITS CONTROL OVER THE NEWSPAPERS IN GOSWING?
IT'S HARD TO KEEP A LID ON GOOD STORIES, MY QUEEN.
YOU WILL HOLD OFF ON IT FOR A WEEK.

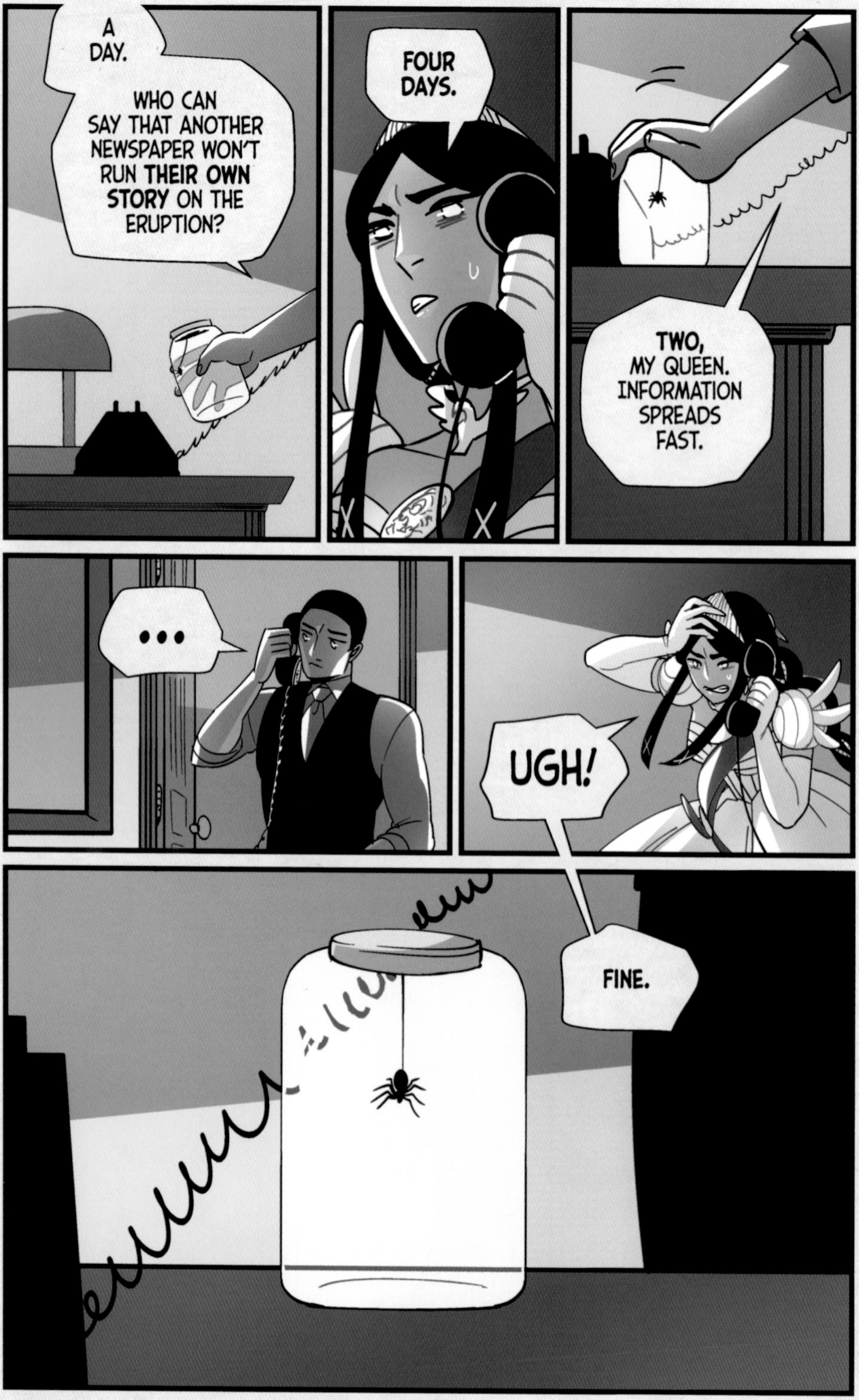
A DAY.
WHO CAN SAY THAT ANOTHER NEWSPAPER WON'T RUN **THEIR OWN STORY** ON THE ERUPTION?
FOUR DAYS.
TWO, MY QUEEN. INFORMATION SPREADS FAST.
...
UGH!
FINE.

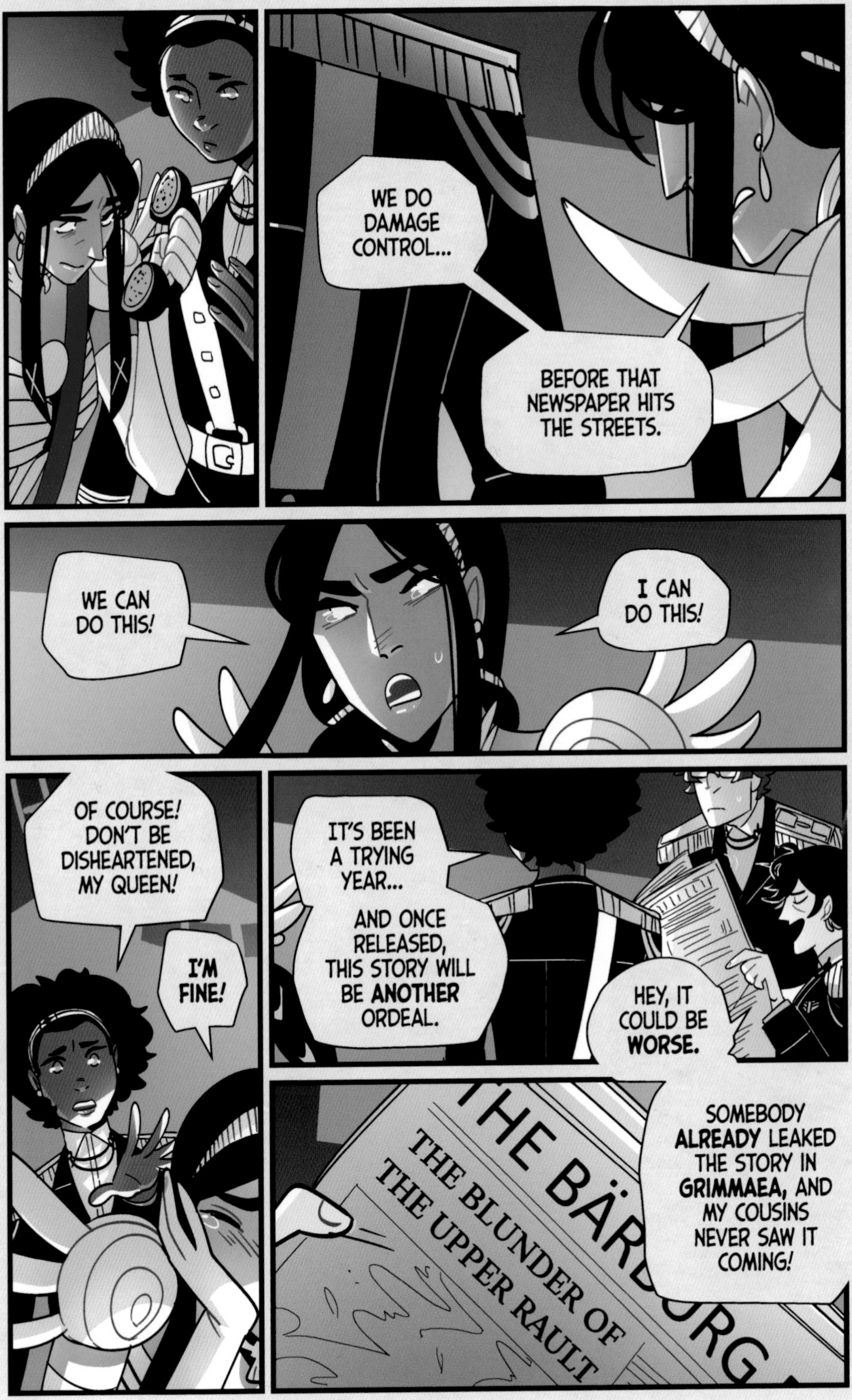
WE DO DAMAGE CONTROL...
BEFORE THAT NEWSPAPER HITS THE STREETS.
WE CAN DO THIS!
I CAN DO THIS!
OF COURSE! DON'T BE DISHEARTENED, MY QUEEN!
I'M FINE!
IT'S BEEN A TRYING YEAR...
AND ONCE RELEASED, THIS STORY WILL BE **ANOTHER** ORDEAL.
HEY, IT COULD BE **WORSE.**
SOMEBODY **ALREADY** LEAKED THE STORY IN **GRIMMAEA,** AND MY COUSINS NEVER SAW IT COMING!
THE BÄRBORG
THE BLUNDER OF THE UPPER RAULT

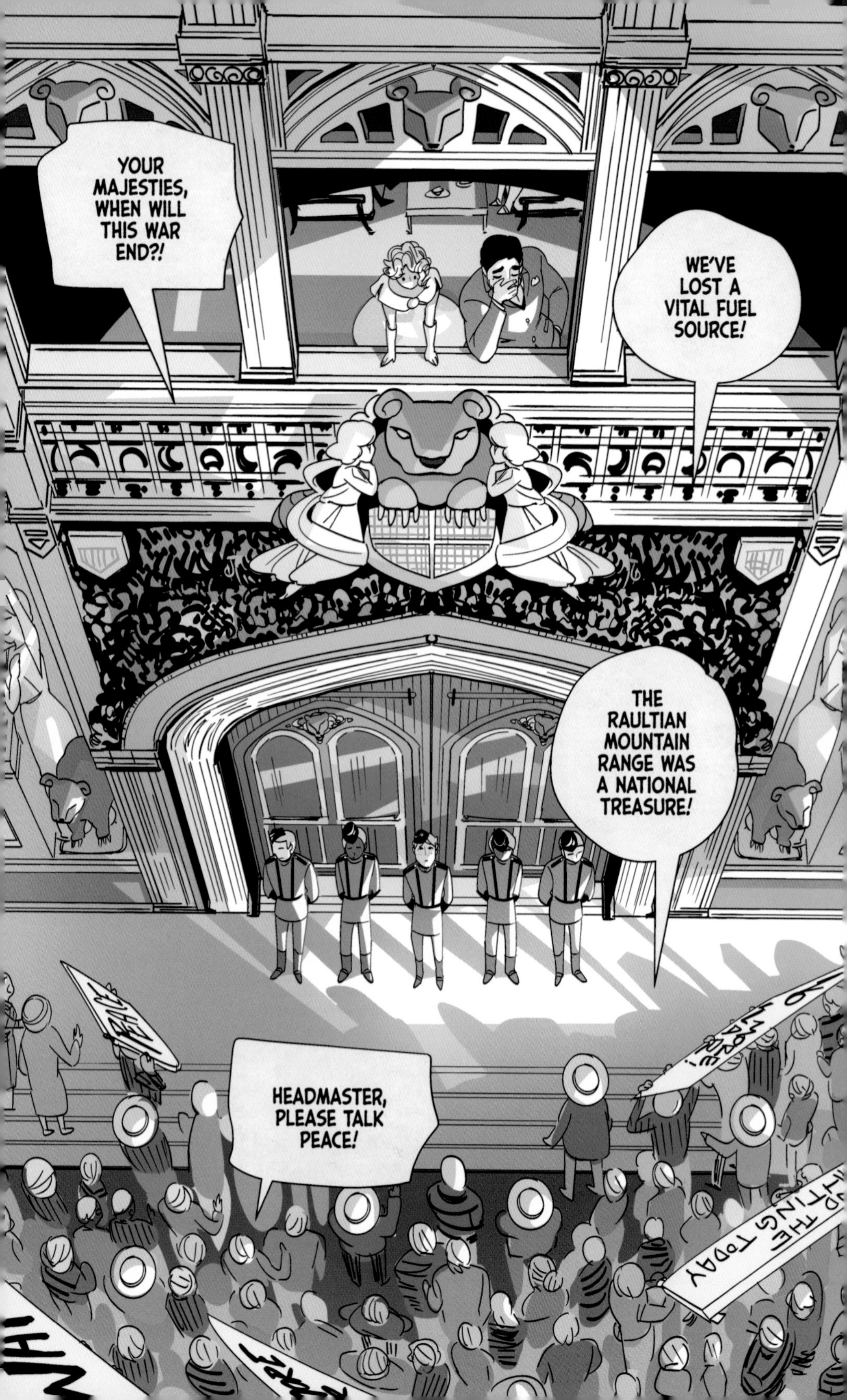
YOUR MAJESTIES, WHEN WILL THIS WAR END?!
WE'VE LOST A VITAL FUEL SOURCE!
THE RAULTIAN MOUNTAIN RANGE WAS A NATIONAL TREASURE!
HEADMASTER, PLEASE TALK PEACE!

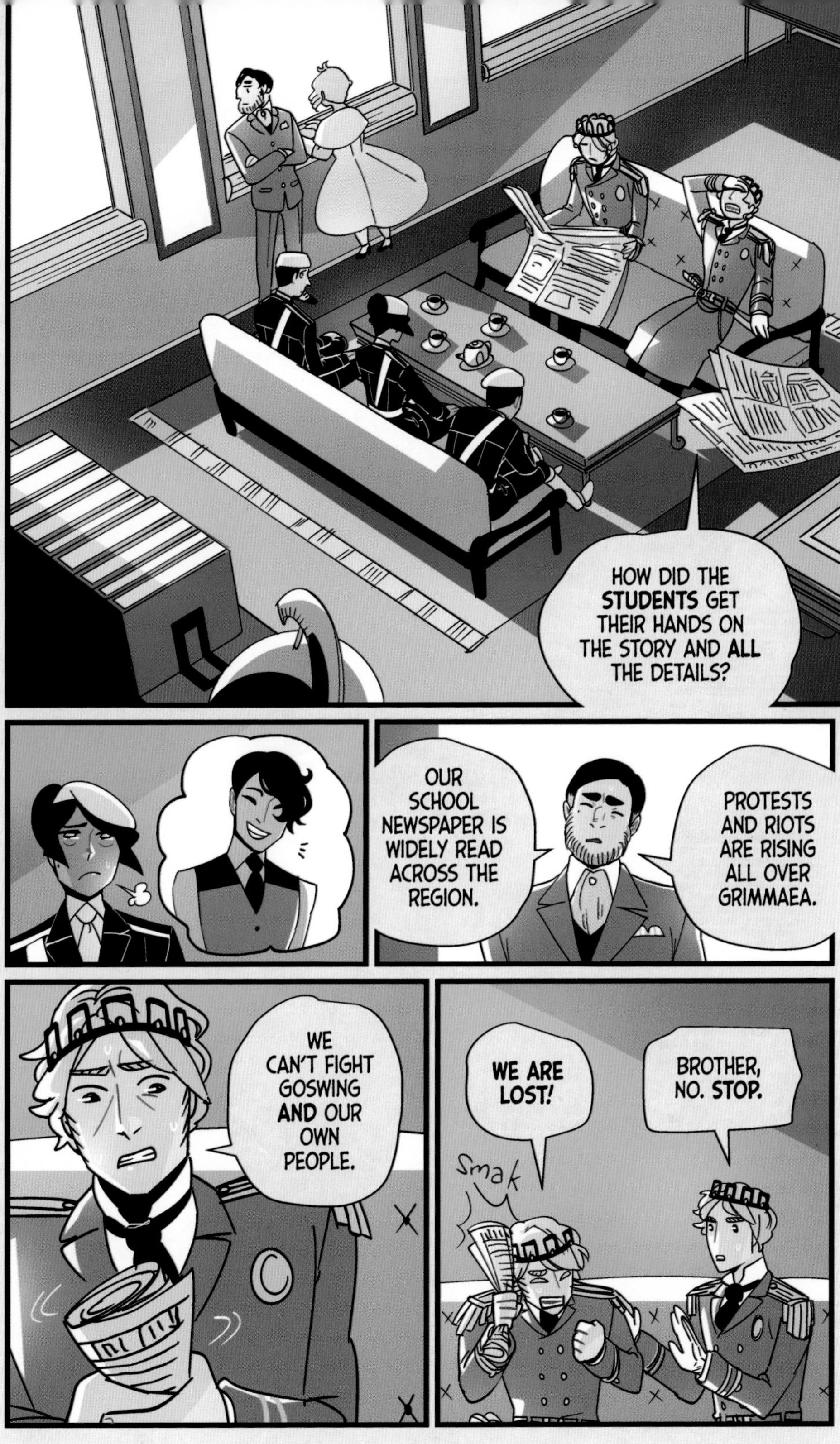
HOW DID THE **STUDENTS** GET THEIR HANDS ON THE STORY AND **ALL** THE DETAILS?
OUR SCHOOL NEWSPAPER IS WIDELY READ ACROSS THE REGION.
PROTESTS AND RIOTS ARE RISING ALL OVER GRIMMAEA.
WE CAN'T FIGHT GOSWING **AND** OUR OWN PEOPLE.
WE ARE LOST!
Smak
BROTHER, NO. **STOP.**

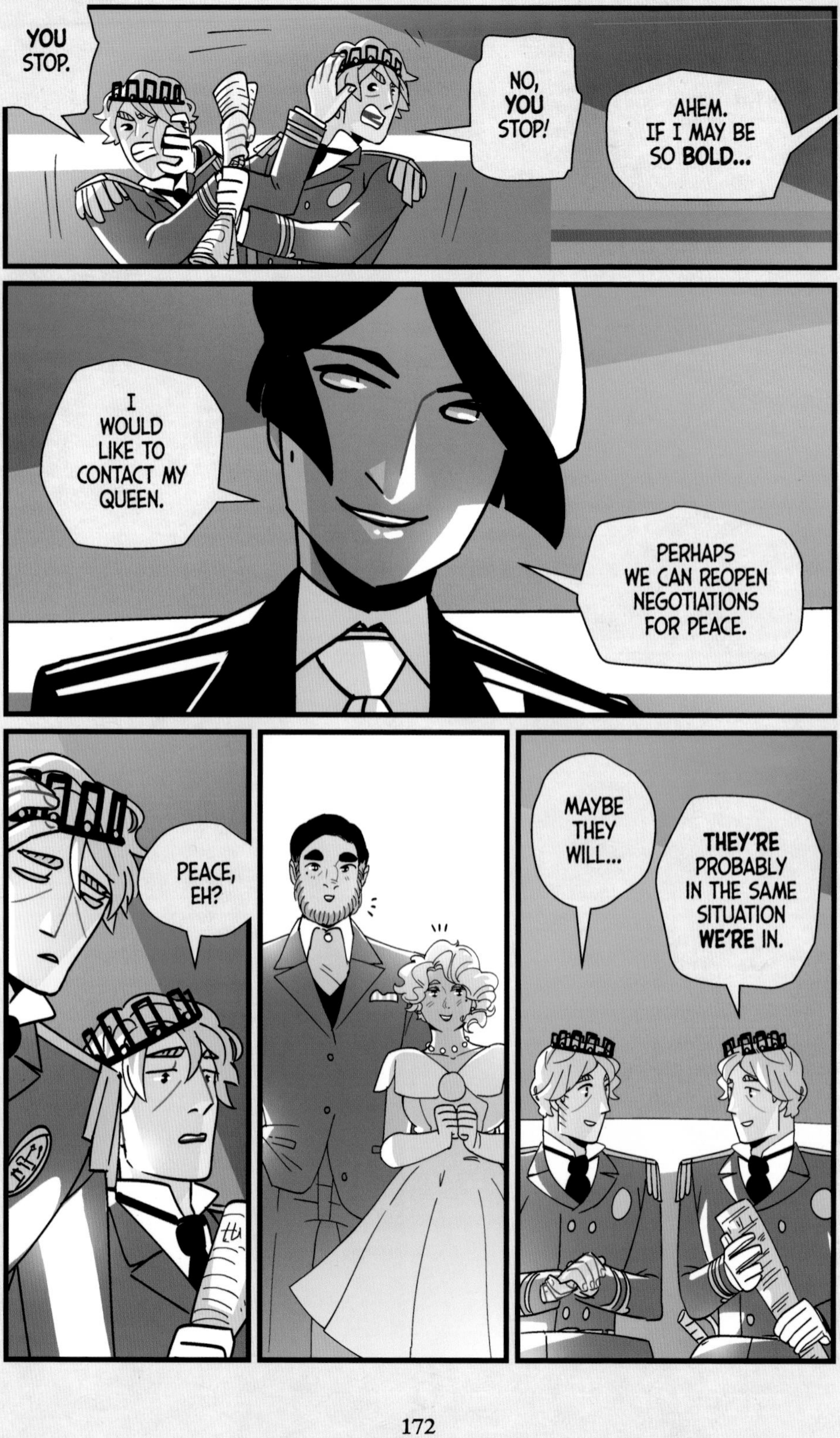

YOU STOP.
NO, **YOU** STOP!
AHEM. IF I MAY BE SO **BOLD...**
I WOULD LIKE TO CONTACT MY QUEEN.
PERHAPS WE CAN REOPEN NEGOTIATIONS FOR PEACE.
PEACE, EH?
MAYBE THEY WILL...
THEY'RE PROBABLY IN THE SAME SITUATION **WE'RE** IN.

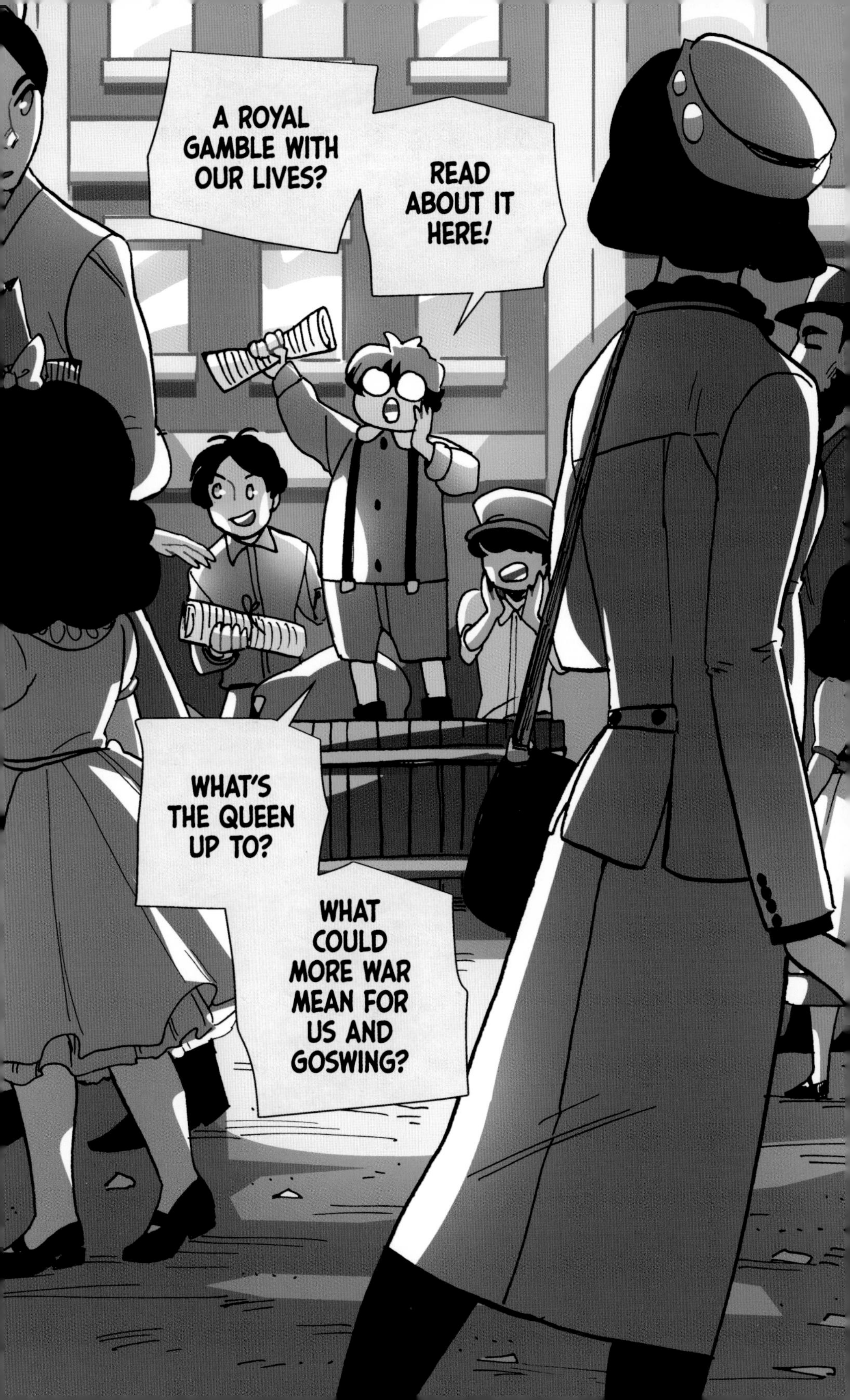
A ROYAL GAMBLE WITH OUR LIVES?
READ ABOUT IT HERE!
WHAT'S THE QUEEN UP TO?
WHAT COULD MORE WAR MEAN FOR US AND GOSWING?

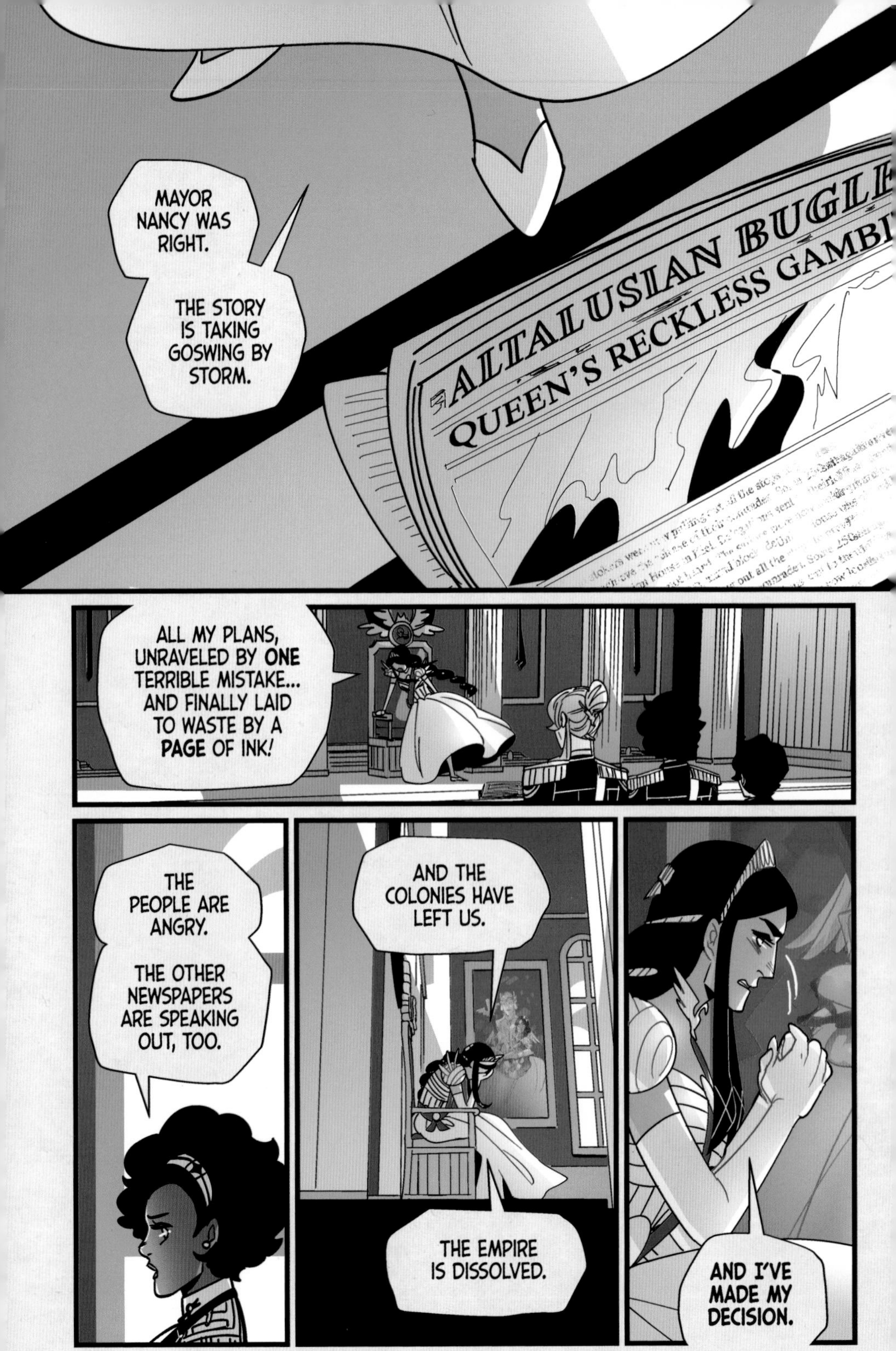
MAYOR NANCY WAS RIGHT.
THE STORY IS TAKING GOSWING BY STORM.
ALTALUSIAN BUGL
QUEEN'S RECKLESS GAMBI
ALL MY PLANS, UNRAVELED BY **ONE** TERRIBLE MISTAKE... AND FINALLY LAID TO WASTE BY A **PAGE** OF INK!
THE PEOPLE ARE ANGRY.
THE OTHER NEWSPAPERS ARE SPEAKING OUT, TOO.
AND THE COLONIES HAVE LEFT US.
THE EMPIRE IS DISSOLVED.
AND I'VE MADE MY DECISION.

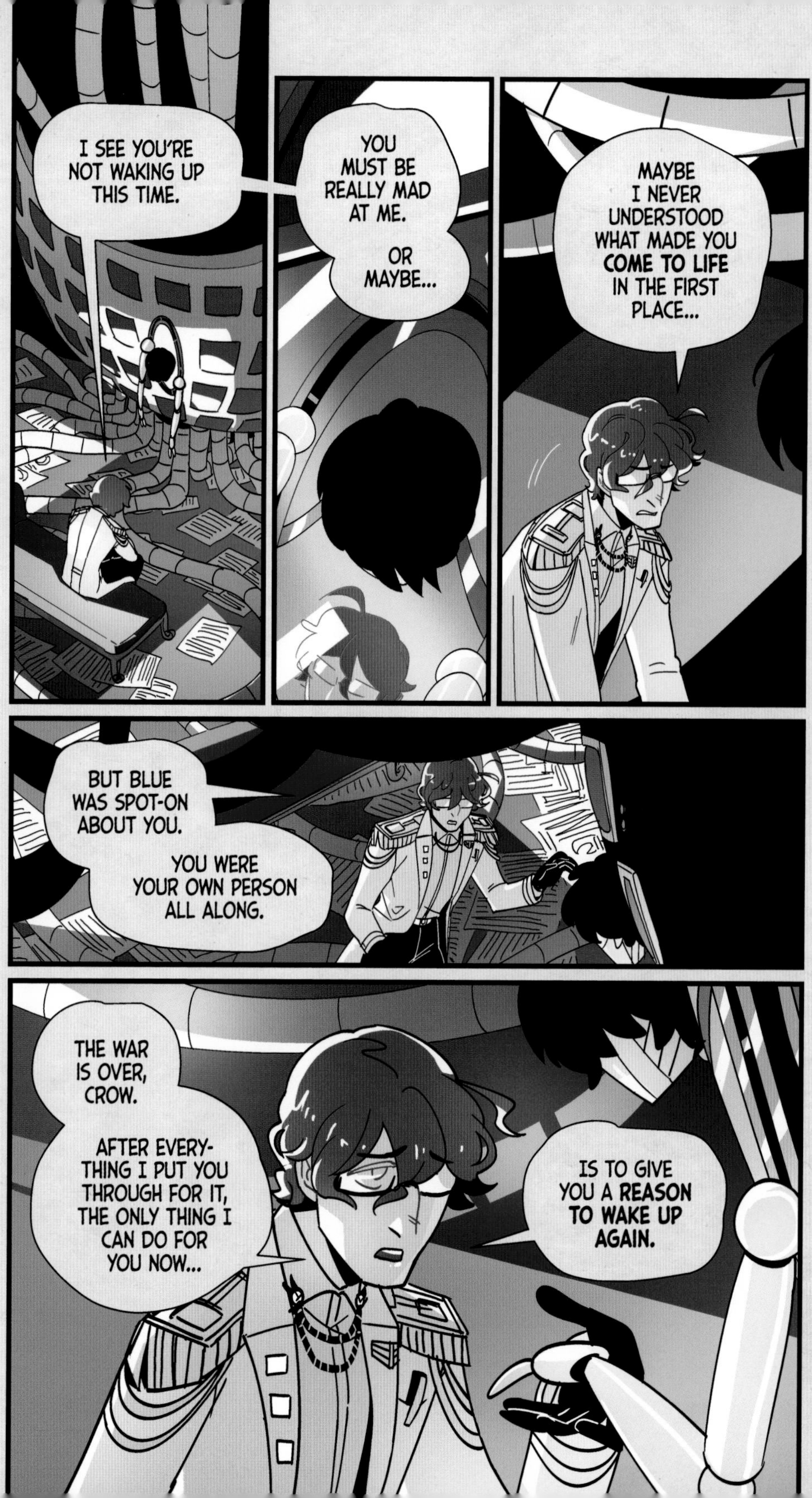
I SEE YOU'RE NOT WAKING UP THIS TIME.
YOU MUST BE REALLY MAD AT ME.
OR MAYBE...
MAYBE I NEVER UNDERSTOOD WHAT MADE YOU **COME TO LIFE** IN THE FIRST PLACE...
BUT BLUE WAS SPOT-ON ABOUT YOU.
YOU WERE YOUR OWN PERSON ALL ALONG.
THE WAR IS OVER, CROW.
AFTER EVERY-THING I PUT YOU THROUGH FOR IT, THE ONLY THING I CAN DO FOR YOU NOW...
IS TO GIVE YOU A **REASON TO WAKE UP AGAIN.**

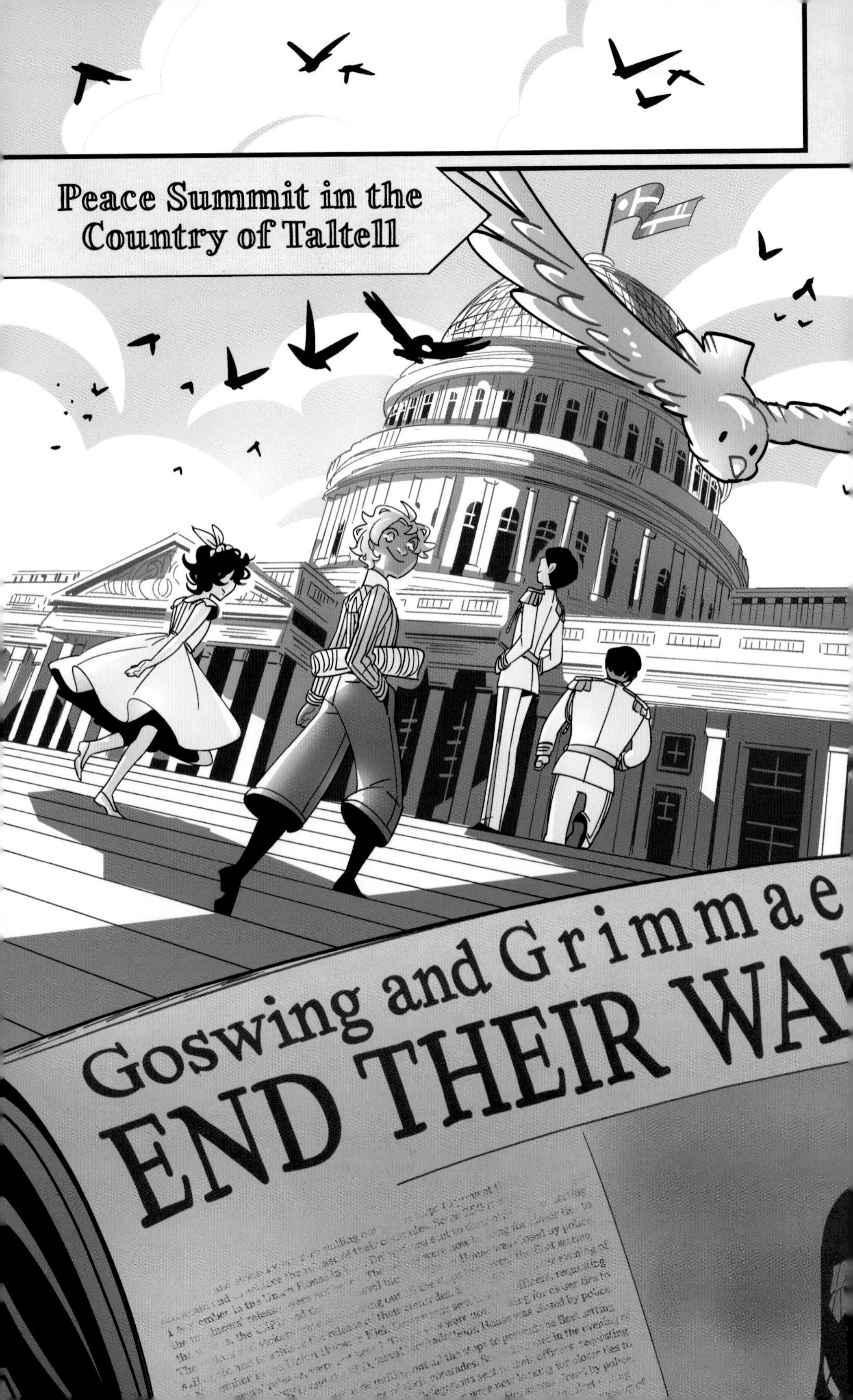
Peace Summit in the Country of Taltell
Goswing and Grimmae
END THEIR WA

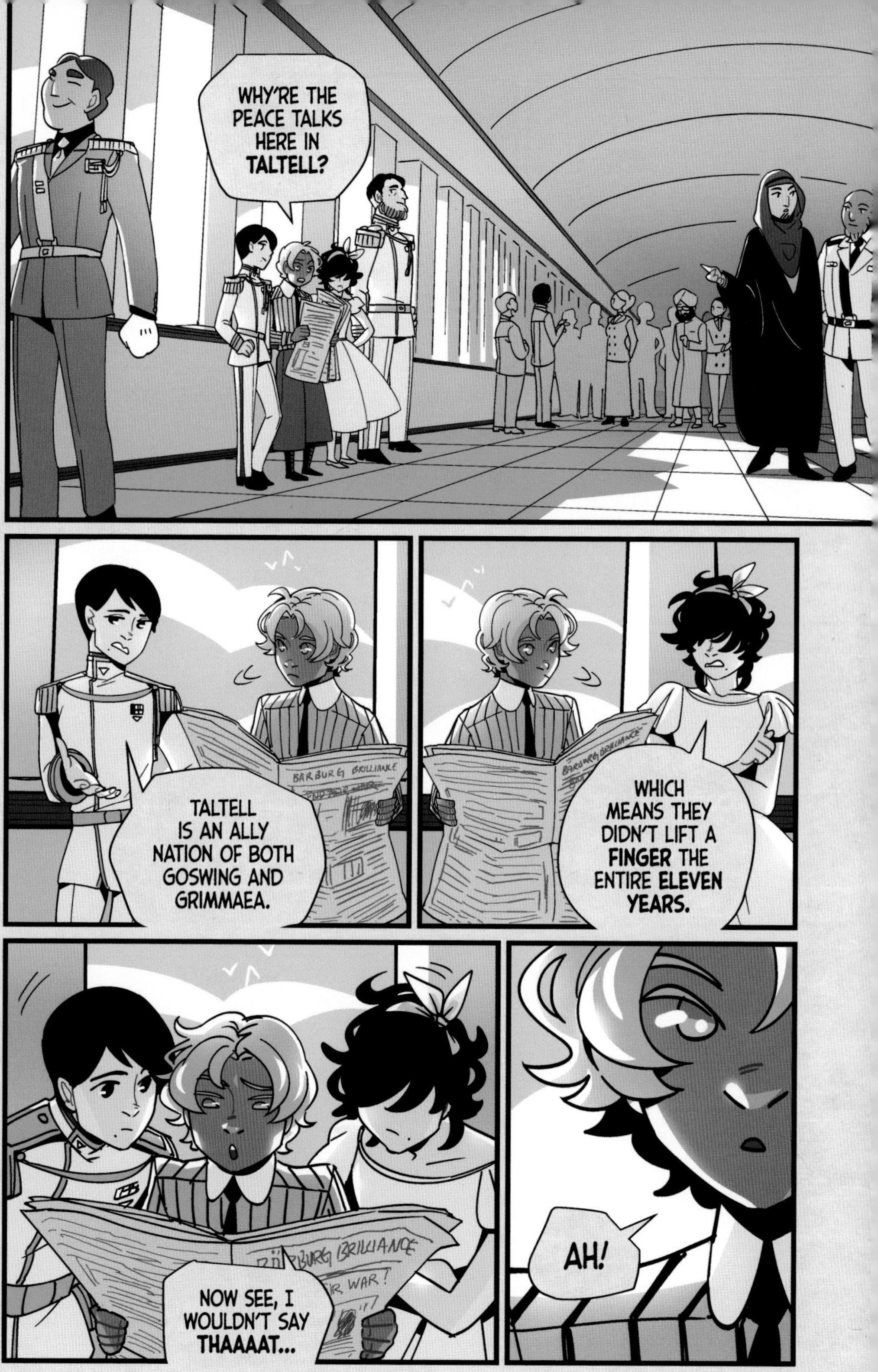
WHY'RE THE PEACE TALKS HERE IN TALTELL?
TALTELL IS AN ALLY NATION OF BOTH GOSWING AND GRIMMAEA.
WHICH MEANS THEY DIDN'T LIFT A FINGER THE ENTIRE ELEVEN YEARS.
NOW SEE, I WOULDN'T SAY THAAAAT...
AH!

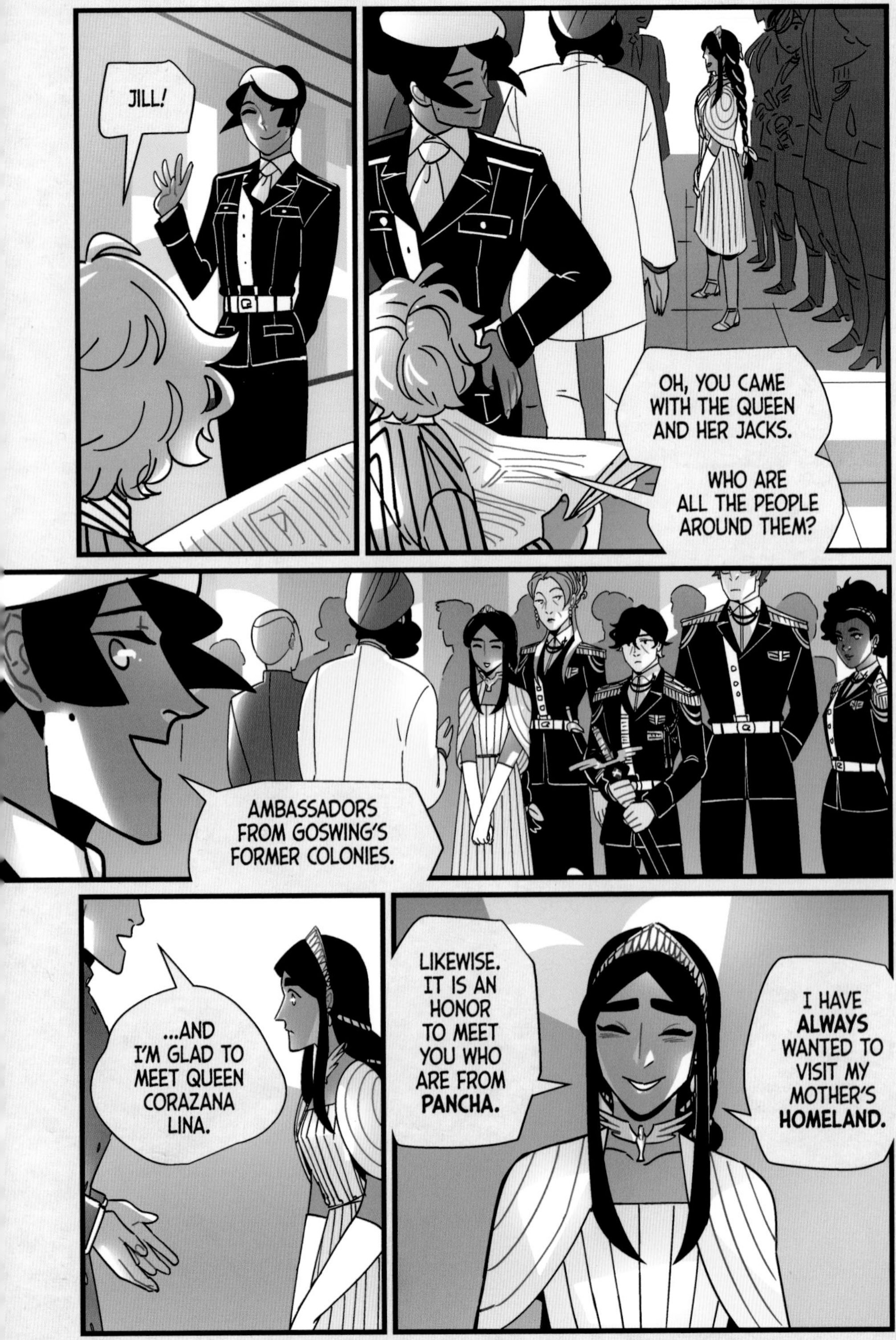
JILL!
OH, YOU CAME WITH THE QUEEN AND HER JACKS.
WHO ARE ALL THE PEOPLE AROUND THEM?
AMBASSADORS FROM GOSWING'S FORMER COLONIES.
...AND I'M GLAD TO MEET QUEEN CORAZANA LINA.
LIKEWISE. IT IS AN HONOR TO MEET YOU WHO ARE FROM PANCHA.
I HAVE ALWAYS WANTED TO VISIT MY MOTHER'S HOMELAND.

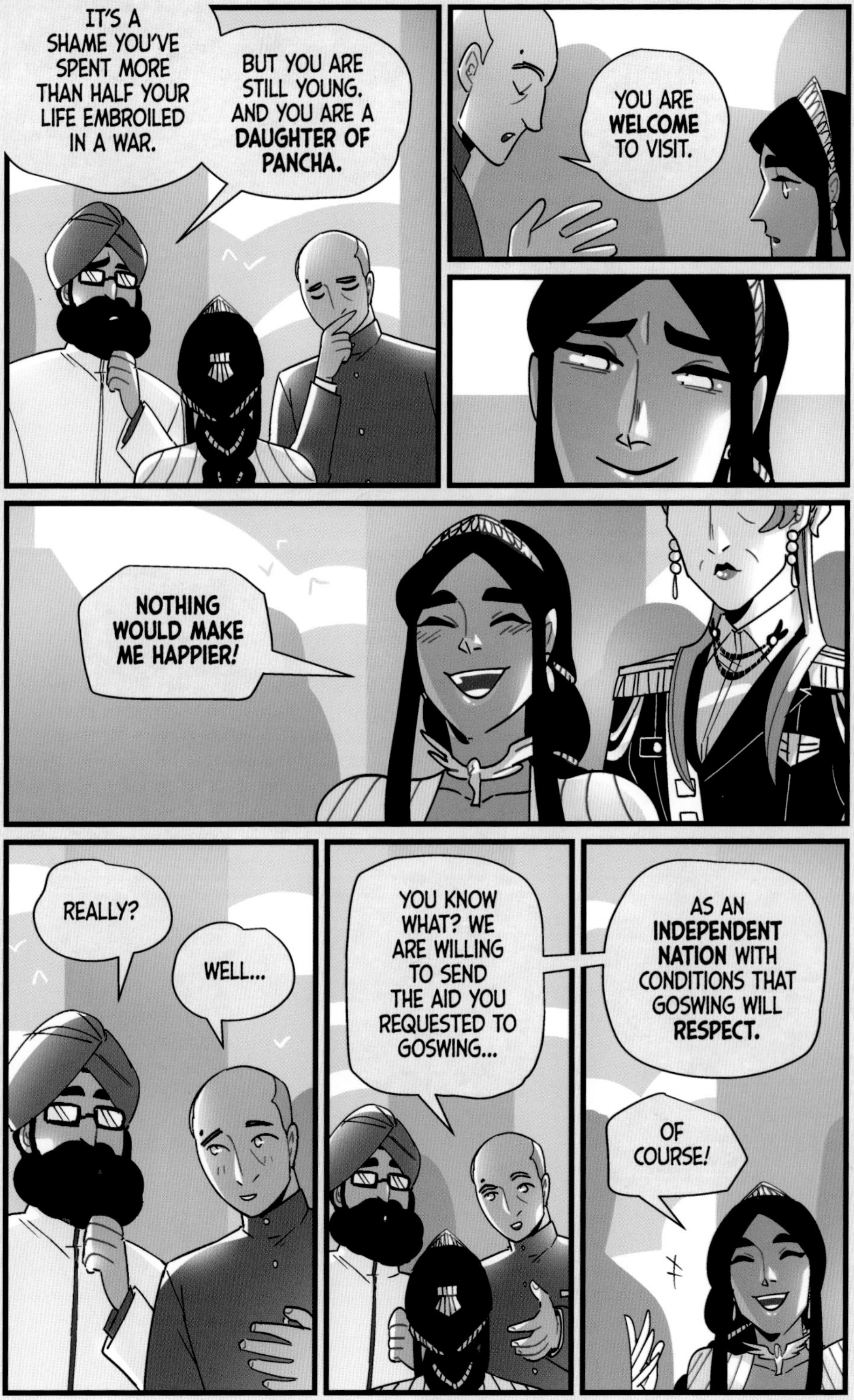
IT'S A SHAME YOU'VE SPENT MORE THAN HALF YOUR LIFE EMBROILED IN A WAR.
BUT YOU ARE STILL YOUNG. AND YOU ARE A DAUGHTER OF PANCHA.
YOU ARE WELCOME TO VISIT.
NOTHING WOULD MAKE ME HAPPIER!
REALLY?
WELL...
YOU KNOW WHAT? WE ARE WILLING TO SEND THE AID YOU REQUESTED TO GOSWING...
AS AN INDEPENDENT NATION WITH CONDITIONS THAT GOSWING WILL RESPECT.
OF COURSE!

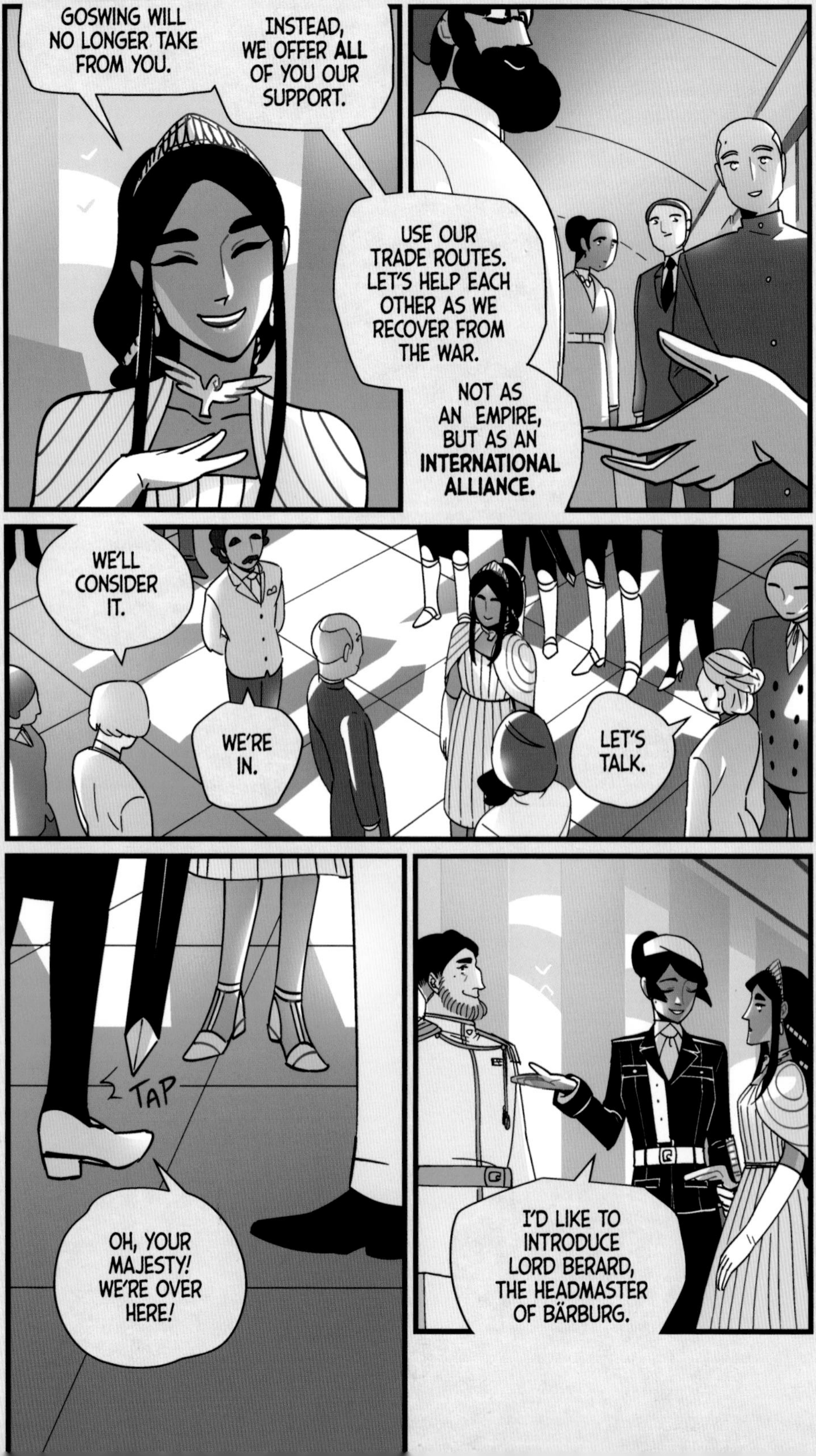
GOSWING WILL NO LONGER TAKE FROM YOU.
INSTEAD, WE OFFER **ALL** OF YOU OUR SUPPORT.
USE OUR TRADE ROUTES. LET'S HELP EACH OTHER AS WE RECOVER FROM THE WAR.
NOT AS AN EMPIRE, BUT AS AN **INTERNATIONAL ALLIANCE.**
WE'LL CONSIDER IT.
WE'RE IN.
LET'S TALK.
TAP
OH, YOUR MAJESTY! WE'RE OVER HERE!
I'D LIKE TO INTRODUCE LORD BERARD, THE HEADMASTER OF BÄRBURG.

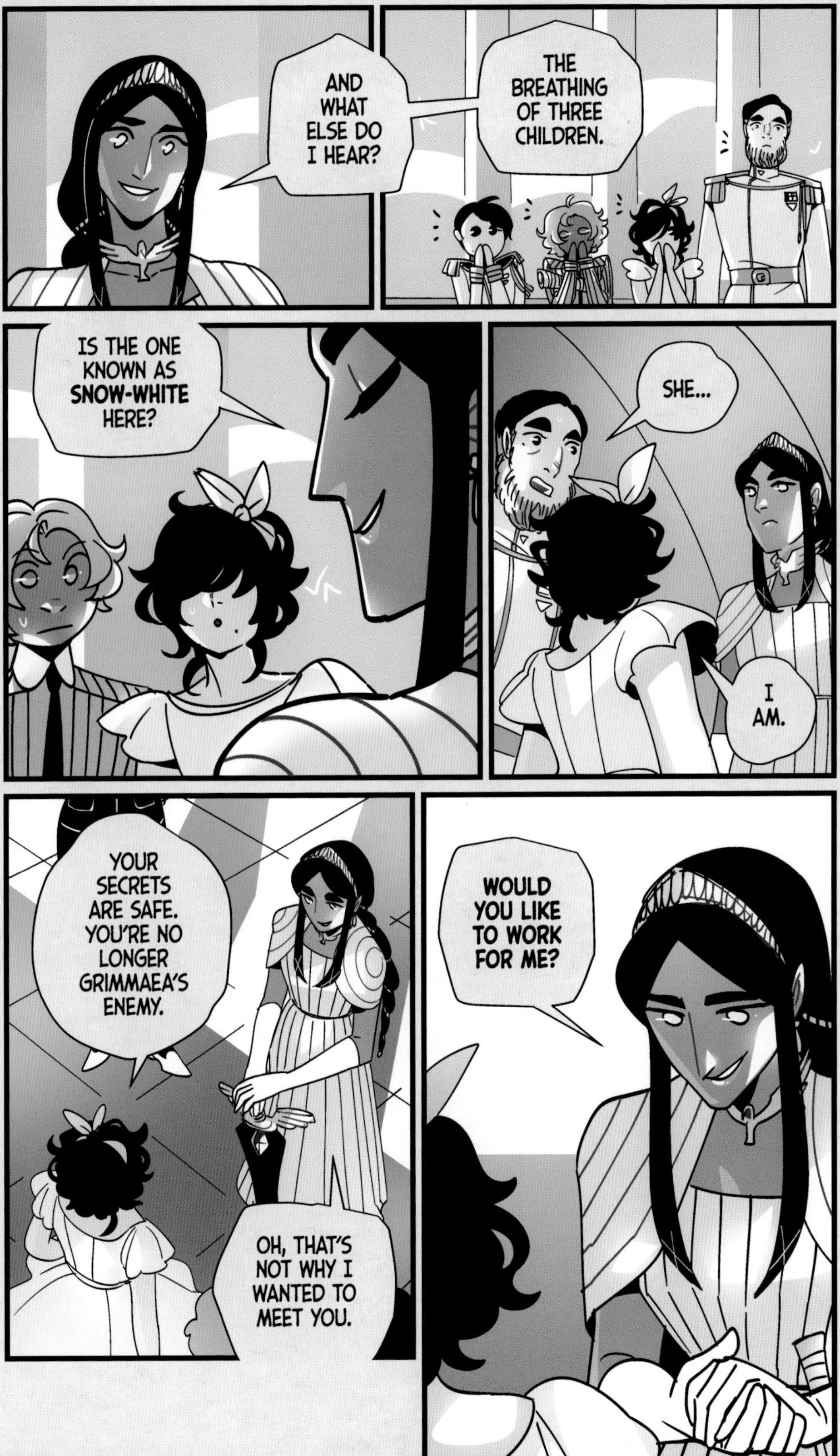
AND WHAT ELSE DO I HEAR?
THE BREATHING OF THREE CHILDREN.
IS THE ONE KNOWN AS **SNOW-WHITE** HERE?
SHE...
I AM.
YOUR SECRETS ARE SAFE. YOU'RE NO LONGER GRIMMAEA'S ENEMY.
OH, THAT'S NOT WHY I WANTED TO MEET YOU.
WOULD YOU LIKE TO WORK FOR ME?

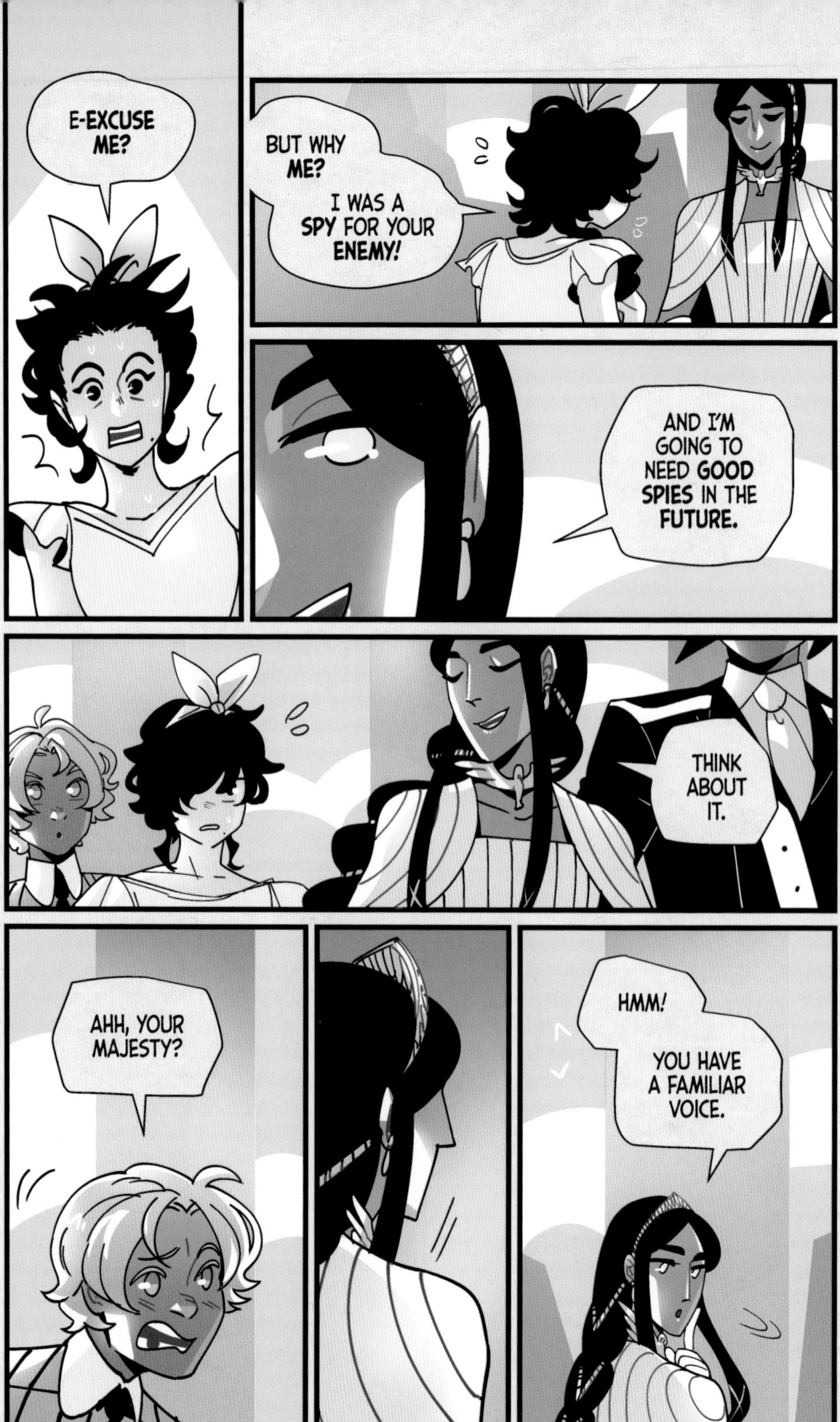
E-EXCUSE ME?
BUT WHY ME?
I WAS A SPY FOR YOUR ENEMY!
AND I'M GOING TO NEED GOOD SPIES IN THE FUTURE.
THINK ABOUT IT.
AHH, YOUR MAJESTY?
HMM!
YOU HAVE A FAMILIAR VOICE.

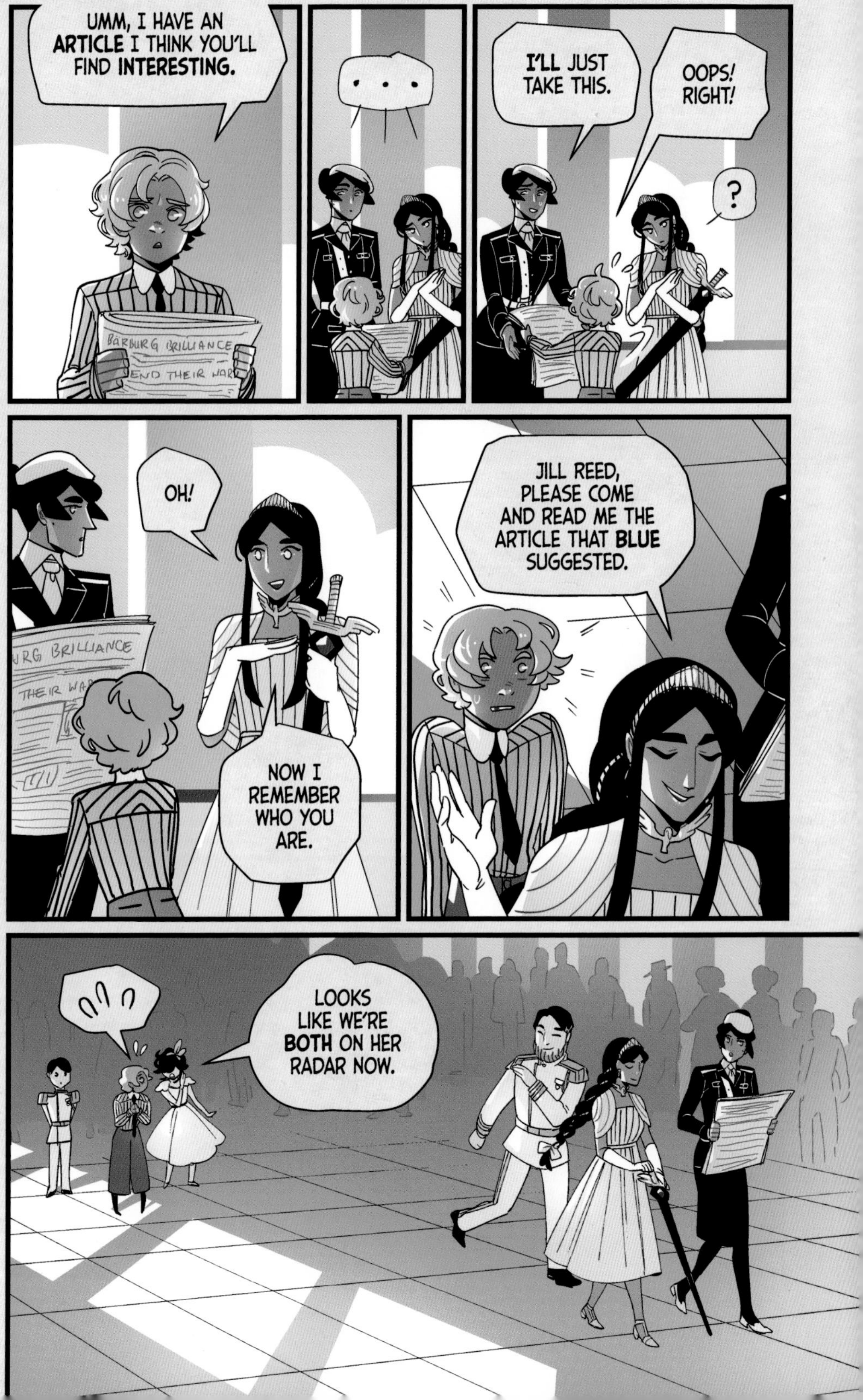
UMM, I HAVE AN ARTICLE I THINK YOU'LL FIND INTERESTING.
BÄRBURG BRILLIANCE
END THEIR WAR
...
I'LL JUST TAKE THIS.
OOPS! RIGHT!
?
OH!
RG BRILLIANCE
THEIR WA
NOW I REMEMBER WHO YOU ARE.
JILL REED, PLEASE COME AND READ ME THE ARTICLE THAT BLUE SUGGESTED.
LOOKS LIKE WE'RE BOTH ON HER RADAR NOW.

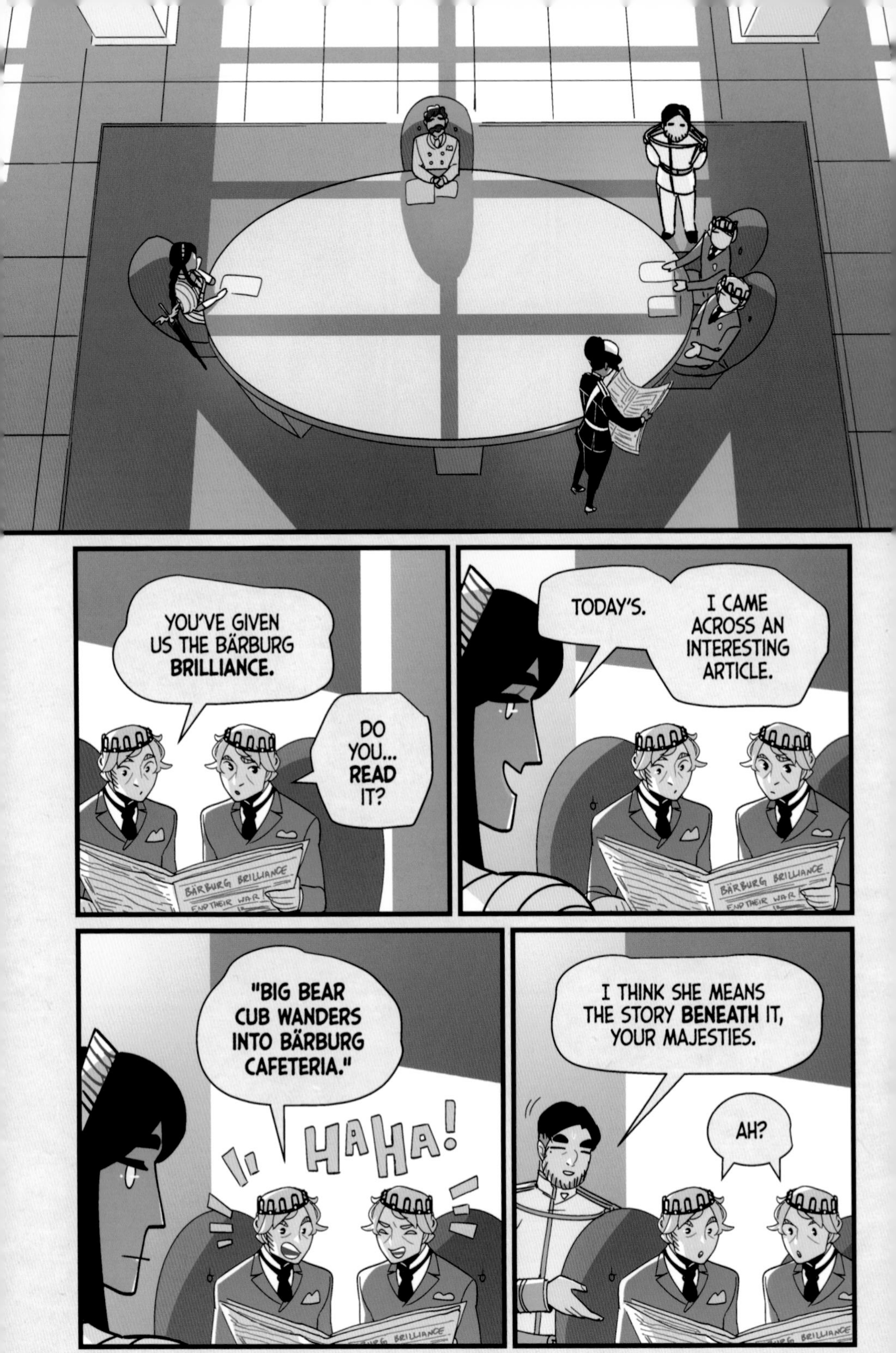
YOU'VE GIVEN US THE BÄRBURG BRILLIANCE.
DO YOU... READ IT?
BÄRBURG BRILLIANCE
END THEIR WAR
TODAY'S.
I CAME ACROSS AN INTERESTING ARTICLE.
BÄRBURG BRILLIANCE
END THEIR WAR
"BIG BEAR CUB WANDERS INTO BÄRBURG CAFETERIA."
HAHA!
BRILLIANCE
I THINK SHE MEANS THE STORY BENEATH IT, YOUR MAJESTIES.
AH?
BRILLIANCE

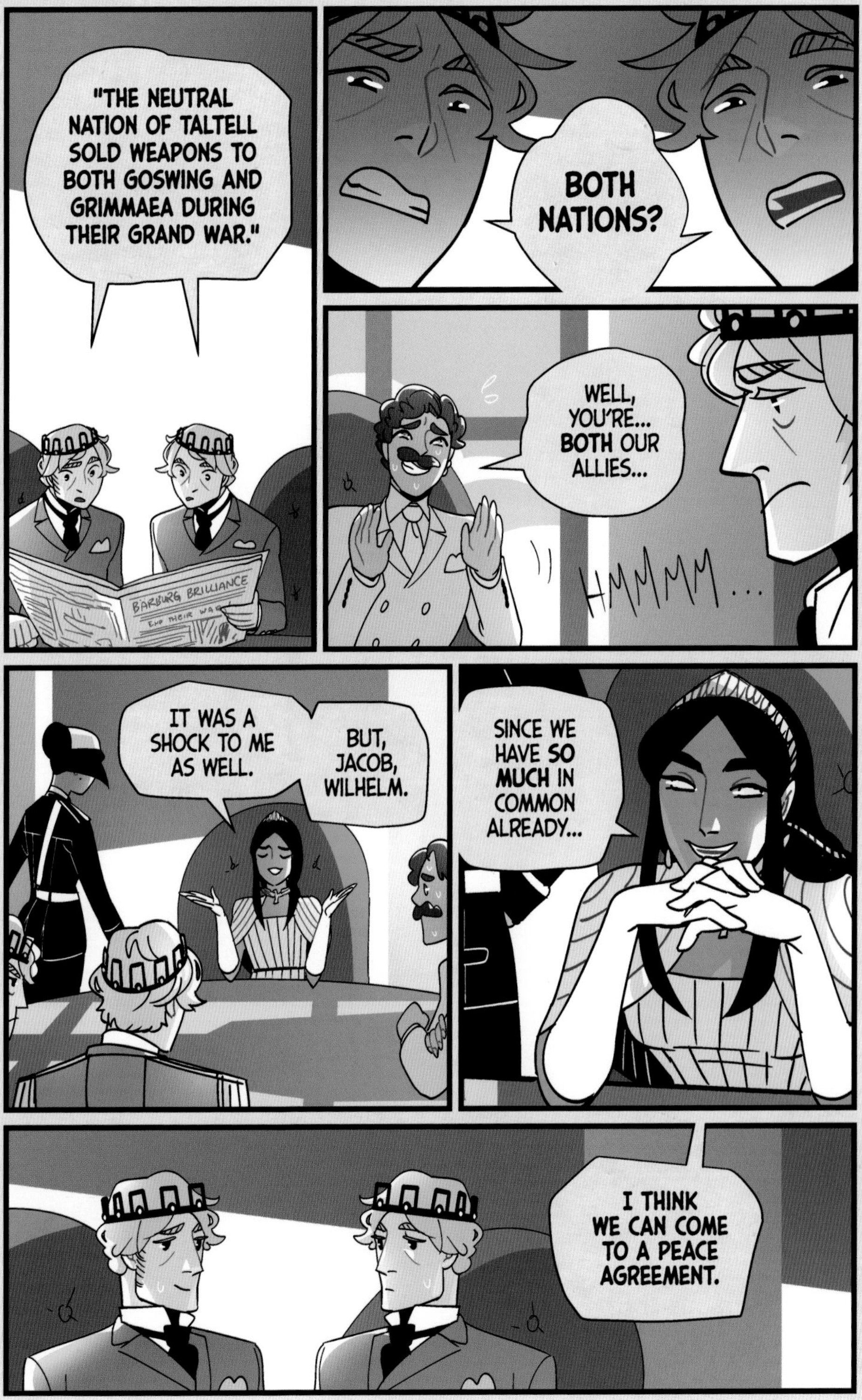
"THE NEUTRAL NATION OF TALTELL SOLD WEAPONS TO BOTH GOSWING AND GRIMMAEA DURING THEIR GRAND WAR."
BARBURG BRILLIANCE
BOTH NATIONS?
WELL, YOU'RE... BOTH OUR ALLIES...
HMMMM...
IT WAS A SHOCK TO ME AS WELL.
BUT, JACOB, WILHELM.
SINCE WE HAVE SO MUCH IN COMMON ALREADY...
I THINK WE CAN COME TO A PEACE AGREEMENT.

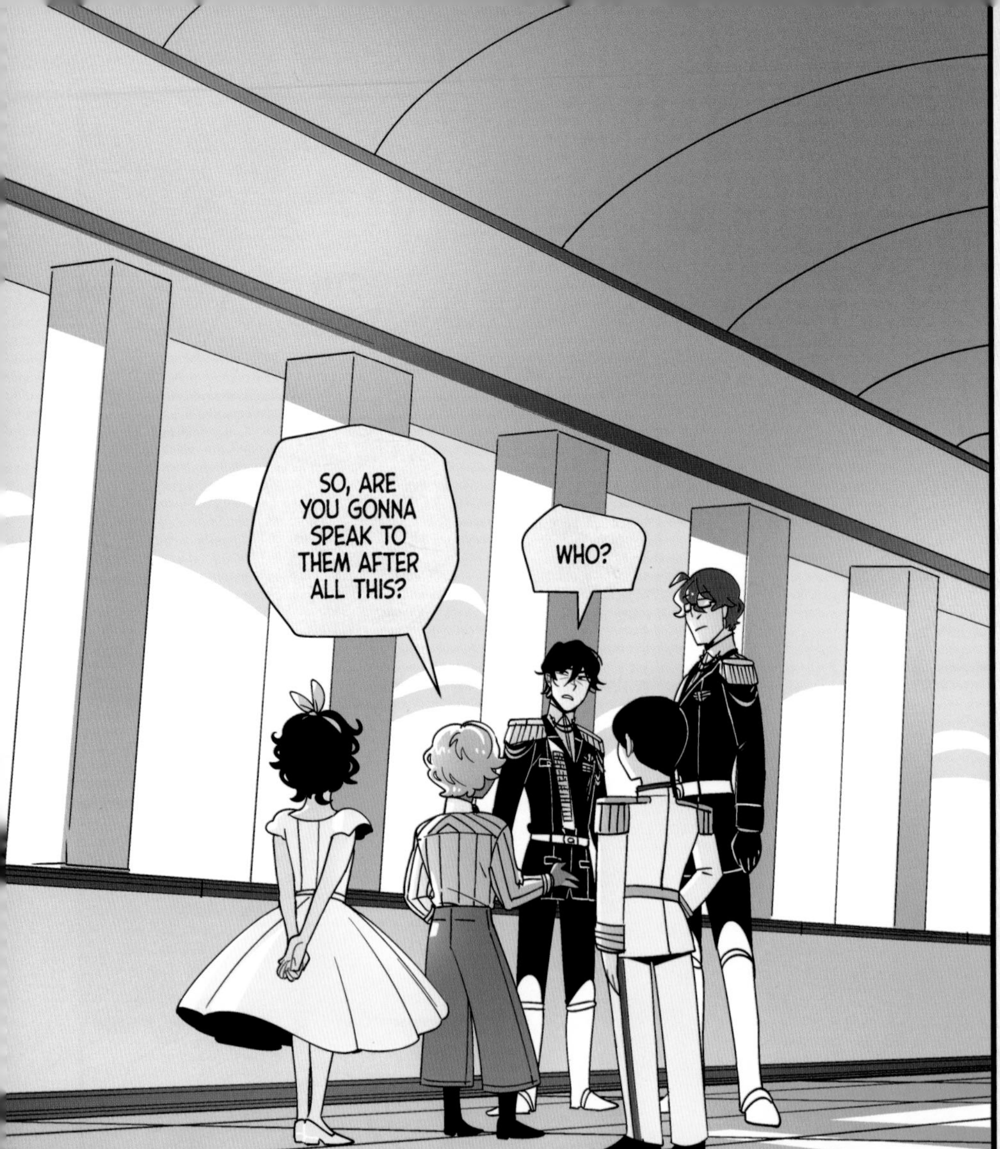
SO, ARE YOU GONNA SPEAK TO THEM AFTER ALL THIS?
WHO?

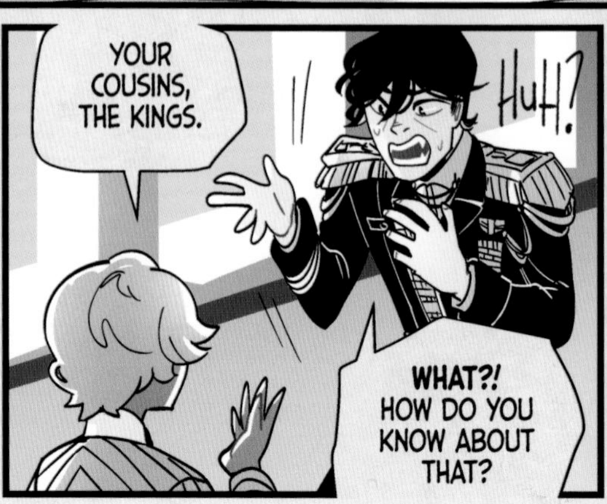
YOUR COUSINS, THE KINGS.
HuH?
WHAT?! HOW DO YOU KNOW ABOUT THAT?

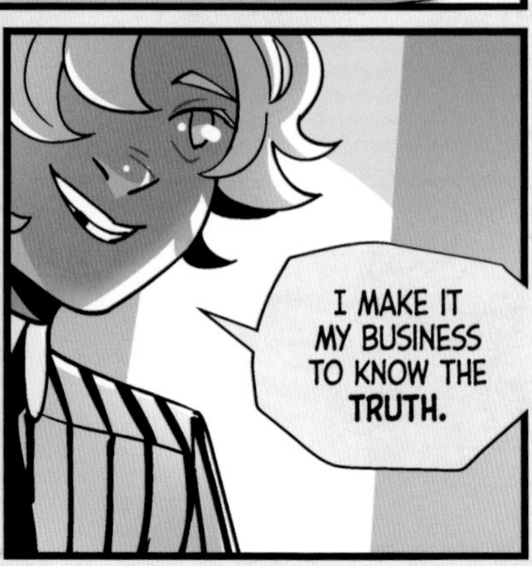
I MAKE IT MY BUSINESS TO KNOW THE **TRUTH.**

WELL! YOUR LITTLE **NEWS STORIES** HAVE CREATED **HAVOC** IN BOTH COUNTRIES!

WE LOST OUR **COLONIES** BECAUSE OF **YOU.**

MAYBE THEY JUST **DIDN'T WANNA** BE COLONIES, NO MATTER **WHAT** YOU WERE DOING.

AND FOR THE RECORD, **OUR** STORIES DIDN'T CREATE THE **VIOLENCE** OF THE WAR.

OUR STORIES **EXPOSED** IT TO PEOPLE THAT YOU WERE HIDIN' IT FROM.

ALL THIS TIME, WE ONLY HAD **YOUR** WORD THAT THE **WAR WAS WORTH FIGHTING.**

THAT IT WAS **WORTH** THE SUFFERING OF OUR PEOPLE.

NO MORE WAR

THE END IS NEAR

NO MORE WAR!

SAVE OUR SONS

BUT IF A **FEW STORIES** CAN UNDO **ELEVEN WHOLE YEARS** OF PROPAGANDA...

THEN THAT'S GOTTA MEAN THAT THE PEOPLE HAD **ENOUGH,** RIGHT?

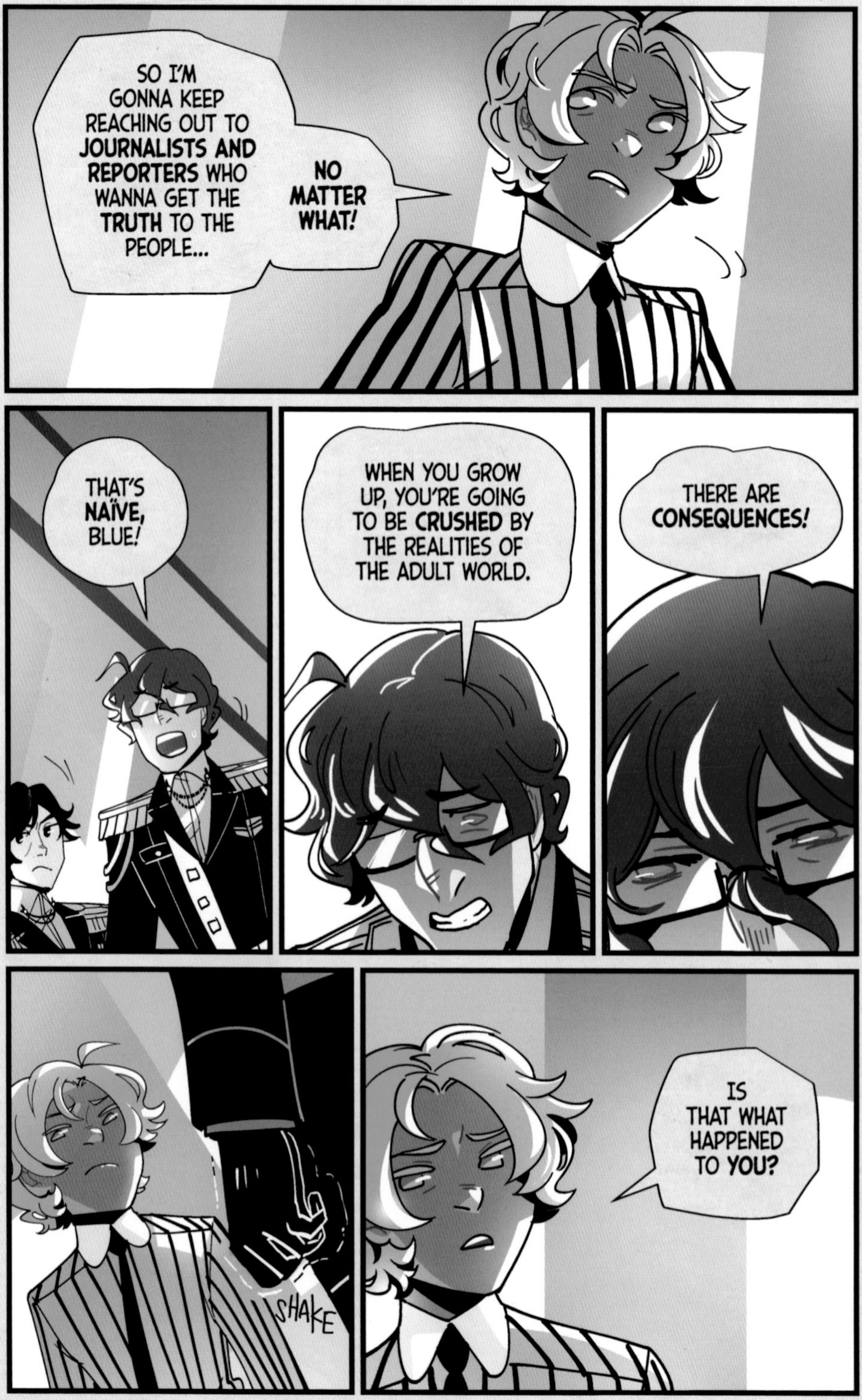
SO I'M GONNA KEEP REACHING OUT TO JOURNALISTS AND REPORTERS WHO WANNA GET THE TRUTH TO THE PEOPLE...
NO MATTER WHAT!
THAT'S NAÏVE, BLUE!
WHEN YOU GROW UP, YOU'RE GOING TO BE CRUSHED BY THE REALITIES OF THE ADULT WORLD.
THERE ARE CONSEQUENCES!
SHAKE
IS THAT WHAT HAPPENED TO YOU?

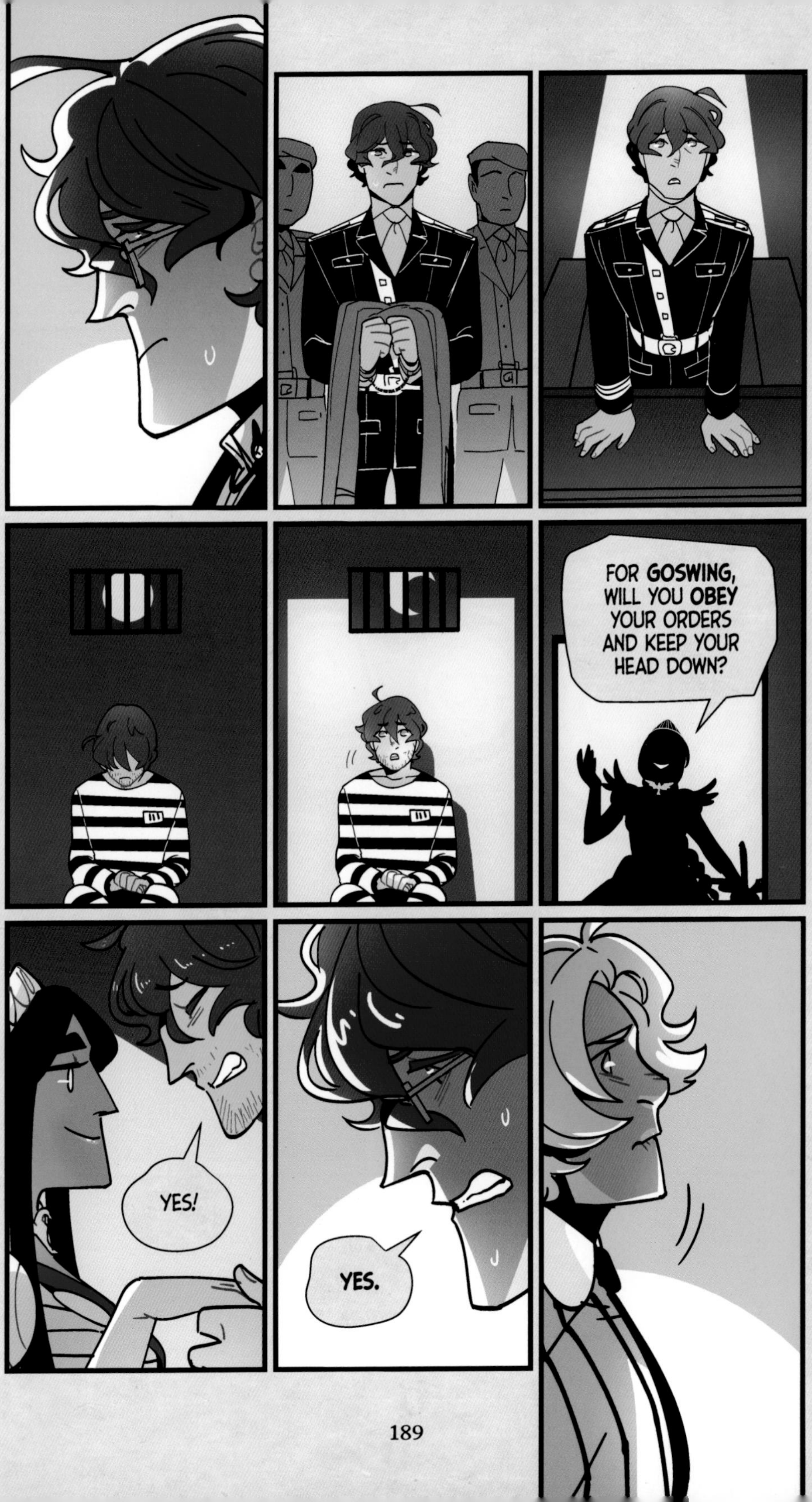
FOR GOSWING, WILL YOU OBEY YOUR ORDERS AND KEEP YOUR HEAD DOWN?
YES!
YES.

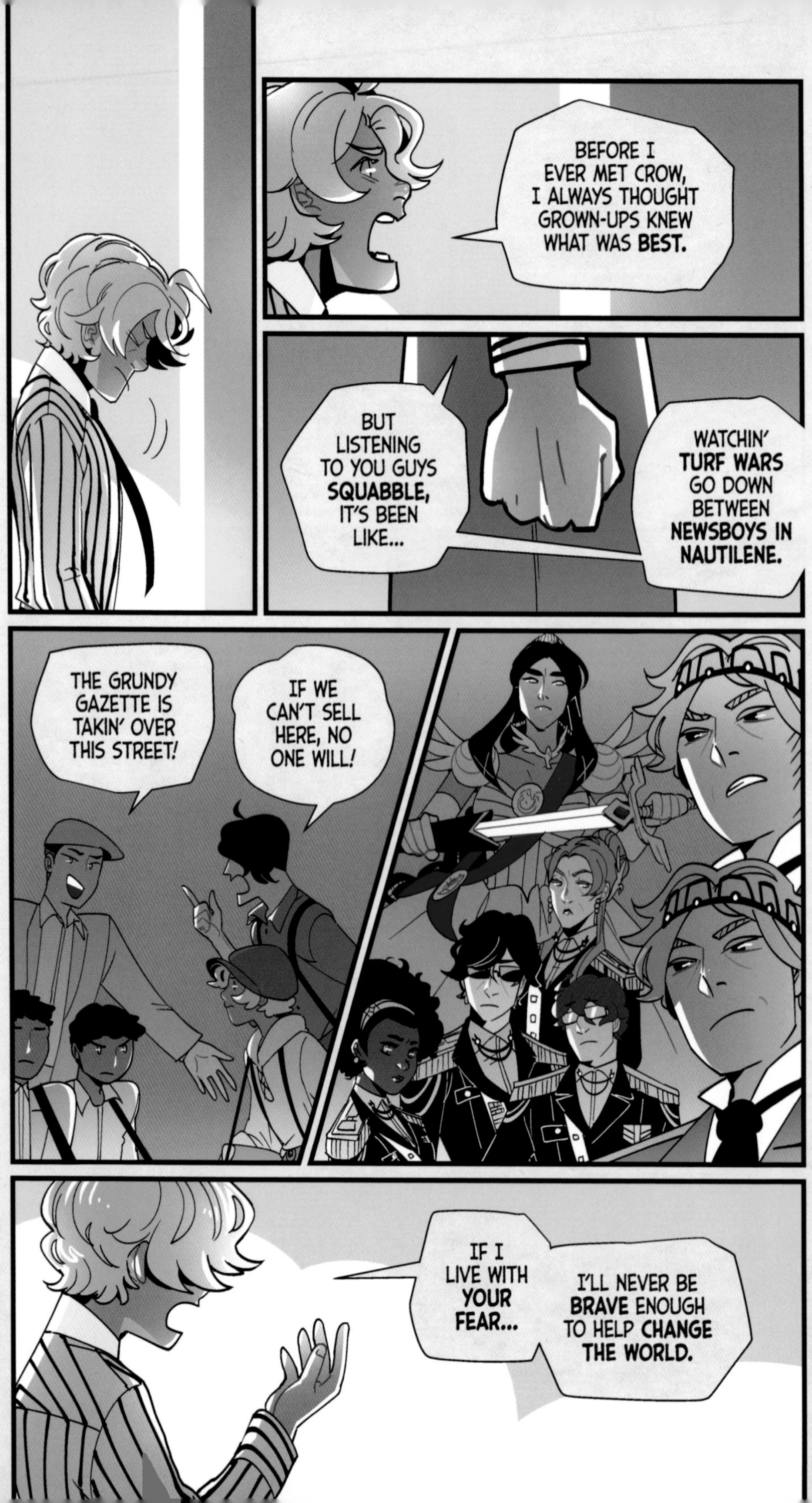
BEFORE I EVER MET CROW, I ALWAYS THOUGHT GROWN-UPS KNEW WHAT WAS BEST.
BUT LISTENING TO YOU GUYS SQUABBLE, IT'S BEEN LIKE...
WATCHIN' TURF WARS GO DOWN BETWEEN NEWSBOYS IN NAUTILENE.
THE GRUNDY GAZETTE IS TAKIN' OVER THIS STREET!
IF WE CAN'T SELL HERE, NO ONE WILL!
IF I LIVE WITH YOUR FEAR...
I'LL NEVER BE BRAVE ENOUGH TO HELP CHANGE THE WORLD.

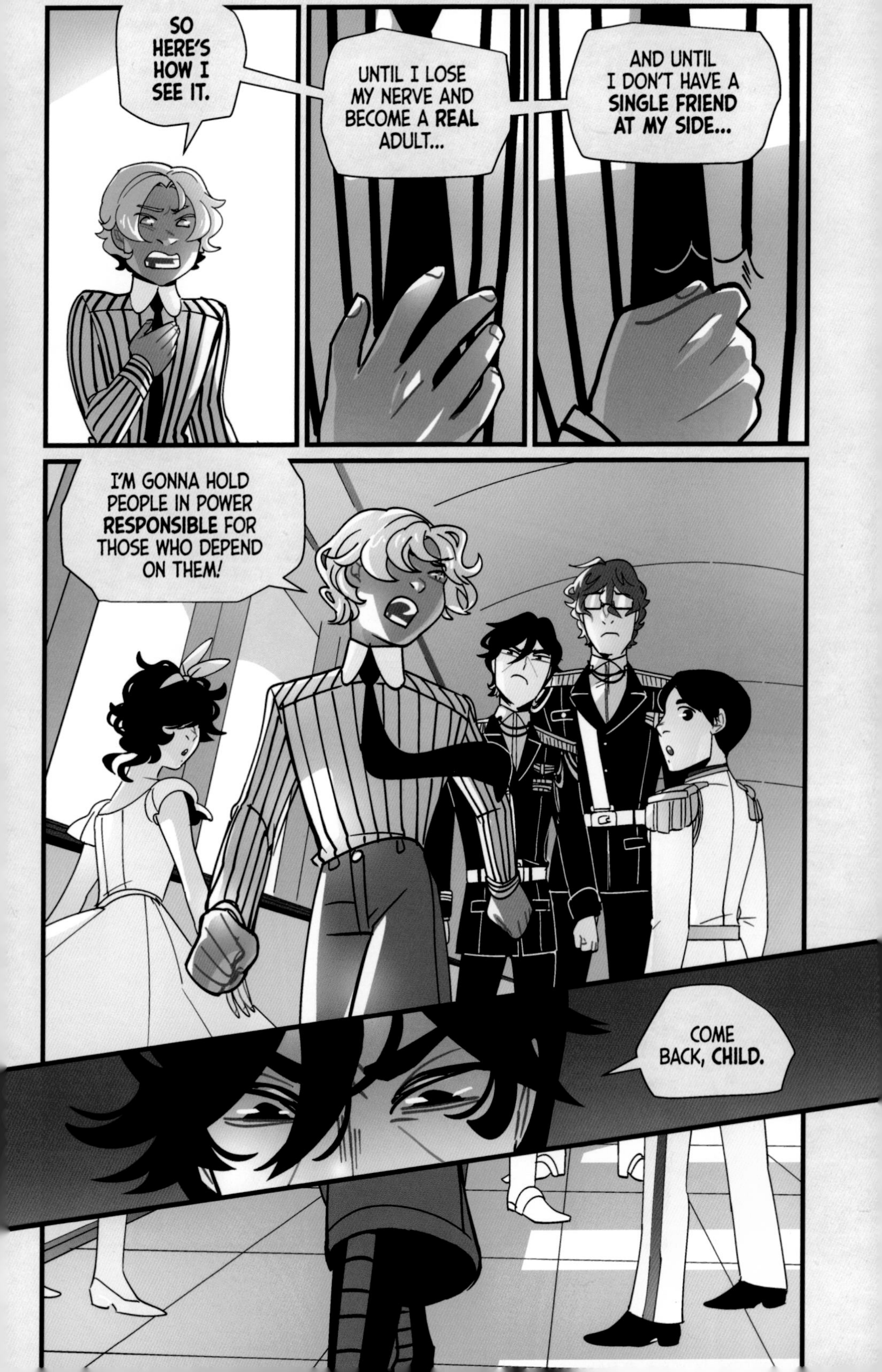
SO HERE'S HOW I SEE IT.
UNTIL I LOSE MY NERVE AND BECOME A REAL ADULT...
AND UNTIL I DON'T HAVE A SINGLE FRIEND AT MY SIDE...
I'M GONNA HOLD PEOPLE IN POWER RESPONSIBLE FOR THOSE WHO DEPEND ON THEM!
COME BACK, CHILD.

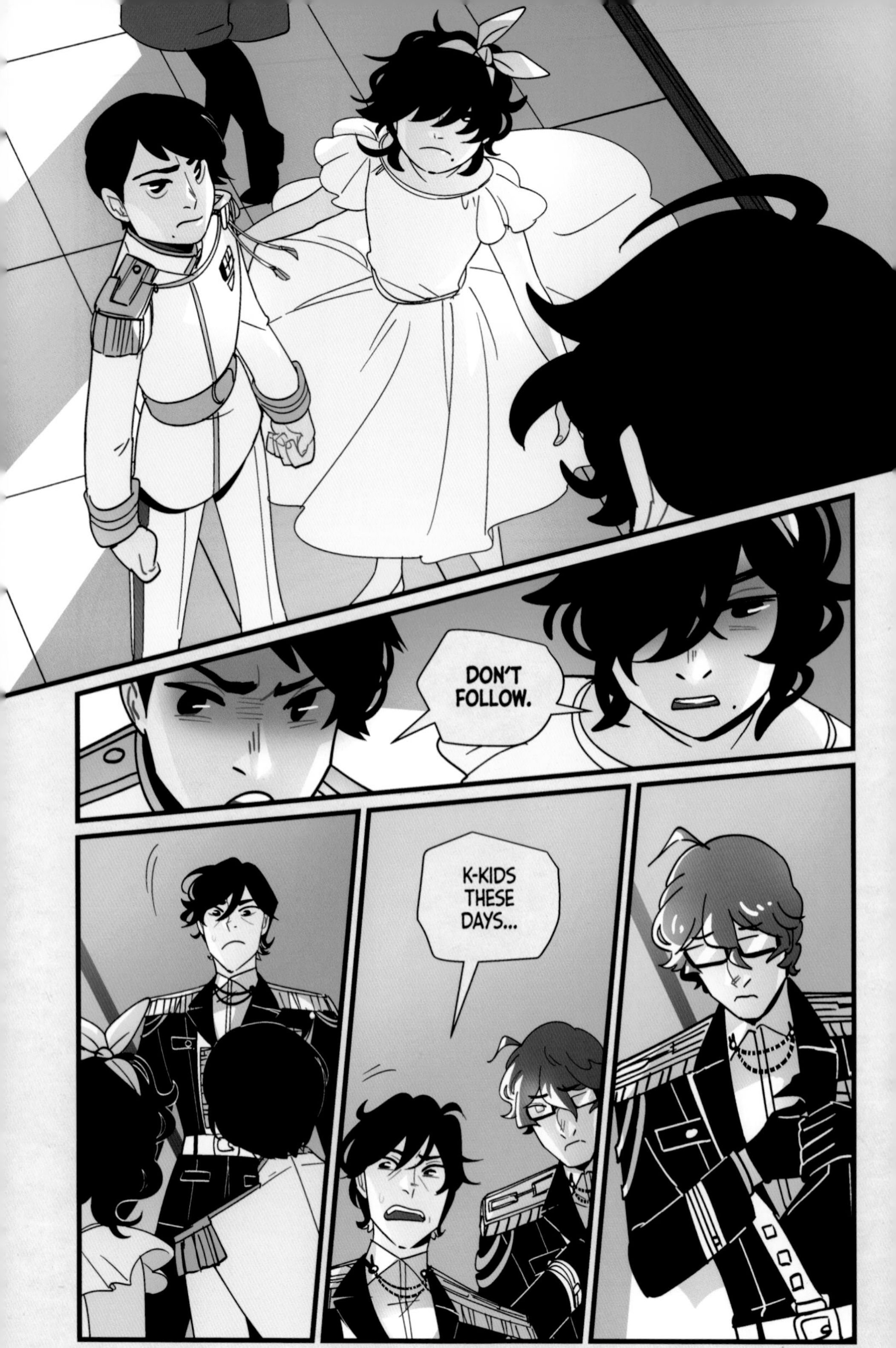
DON'T FOLLOW.
K-KIDS THESE DAYS...

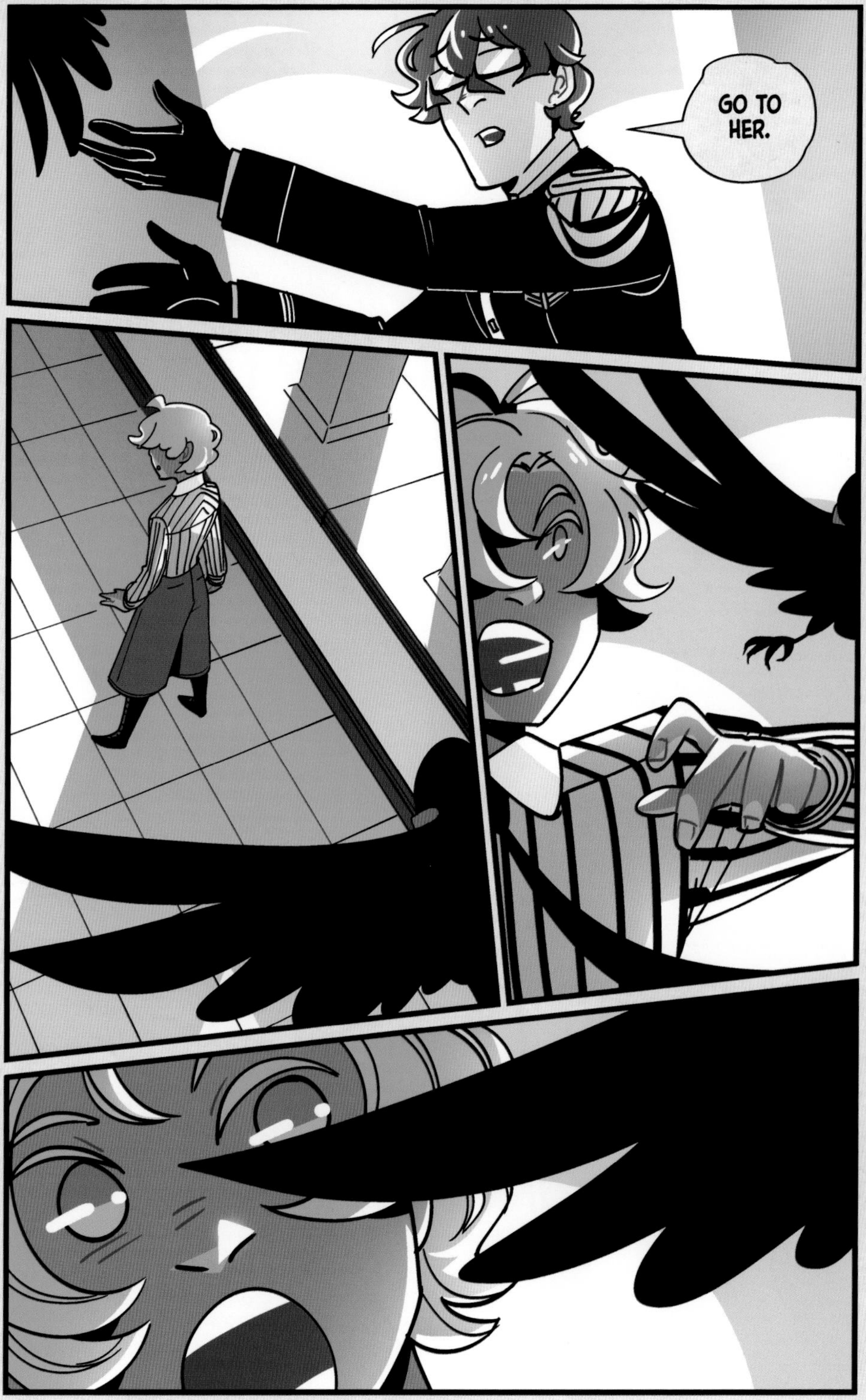
GO TO HER.

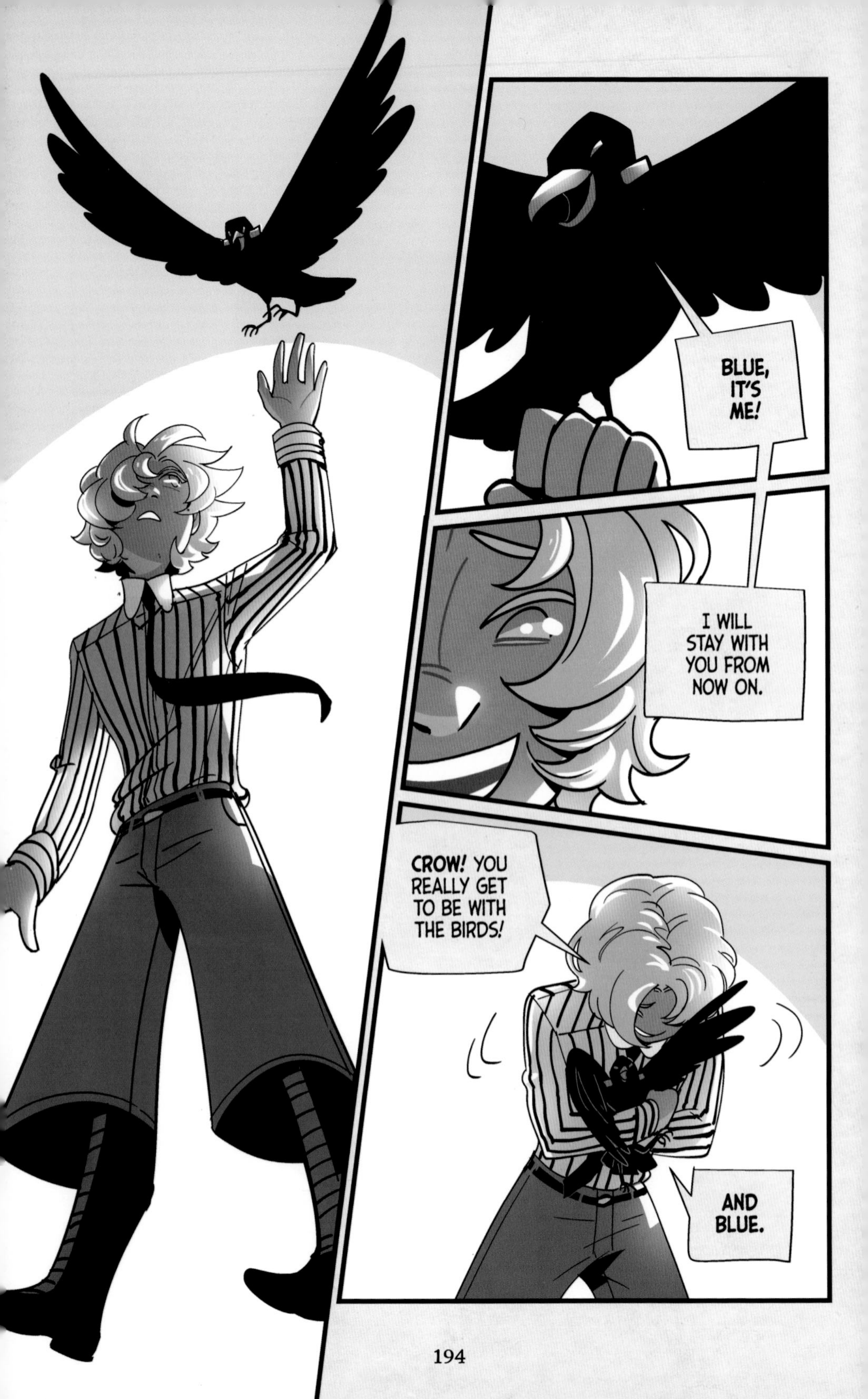
BLUE, IT'S ME!
I WILL STAY WITH YOU FROM NOW ON.
CROW! YOU REALLY GET TO BE WITH THE BIRDS!
AND BLUE.

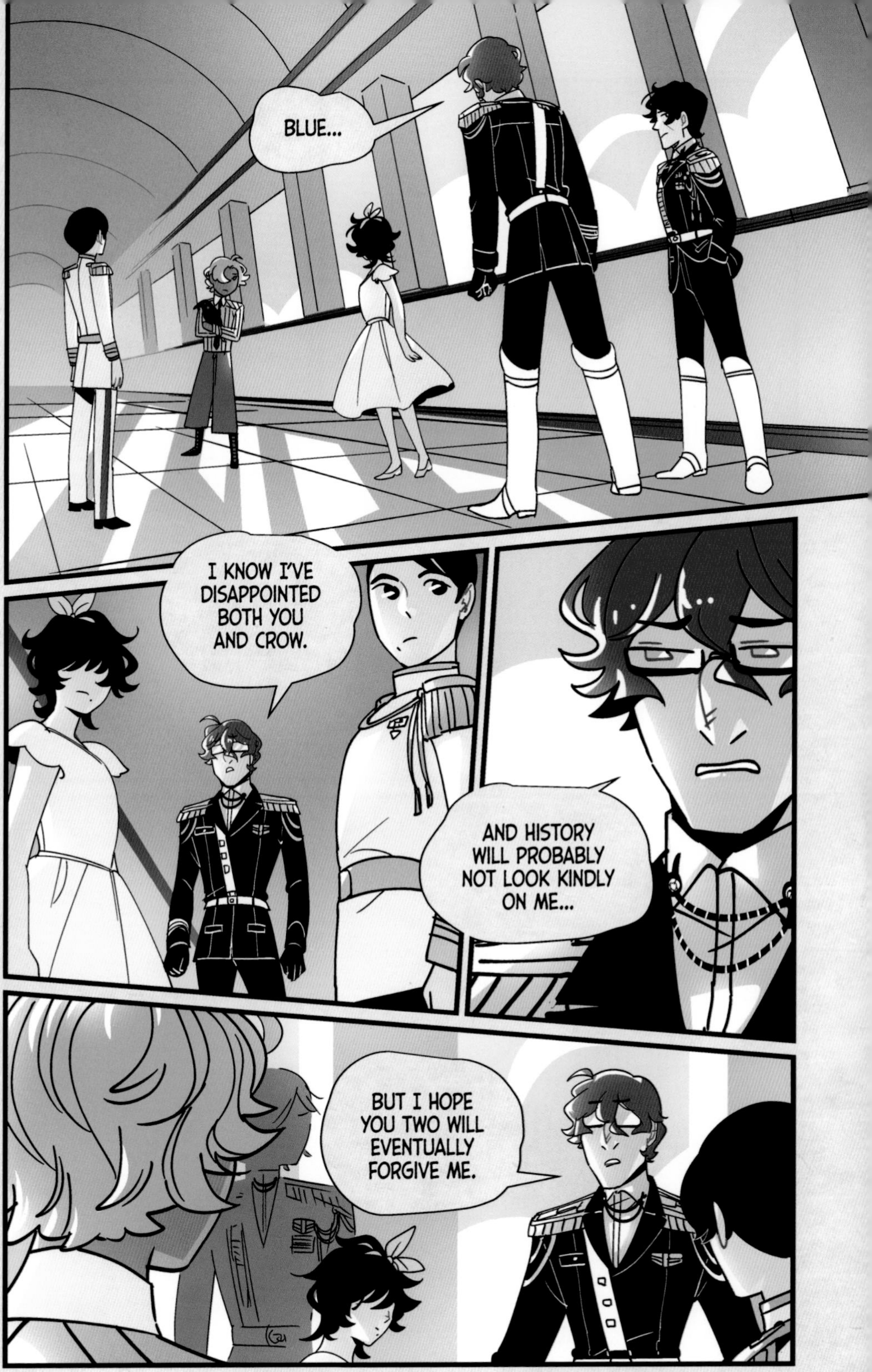

BLUE...
I KNOW I'VE DISAPPOINTED BOTH YOU AND CROW.
AND HISTORY WILL PROBABLY NOT LOOK KINDLY ON ME...
BUT I HOPE YOU TWO WILL EVENTUALLY FORGIVE ME.

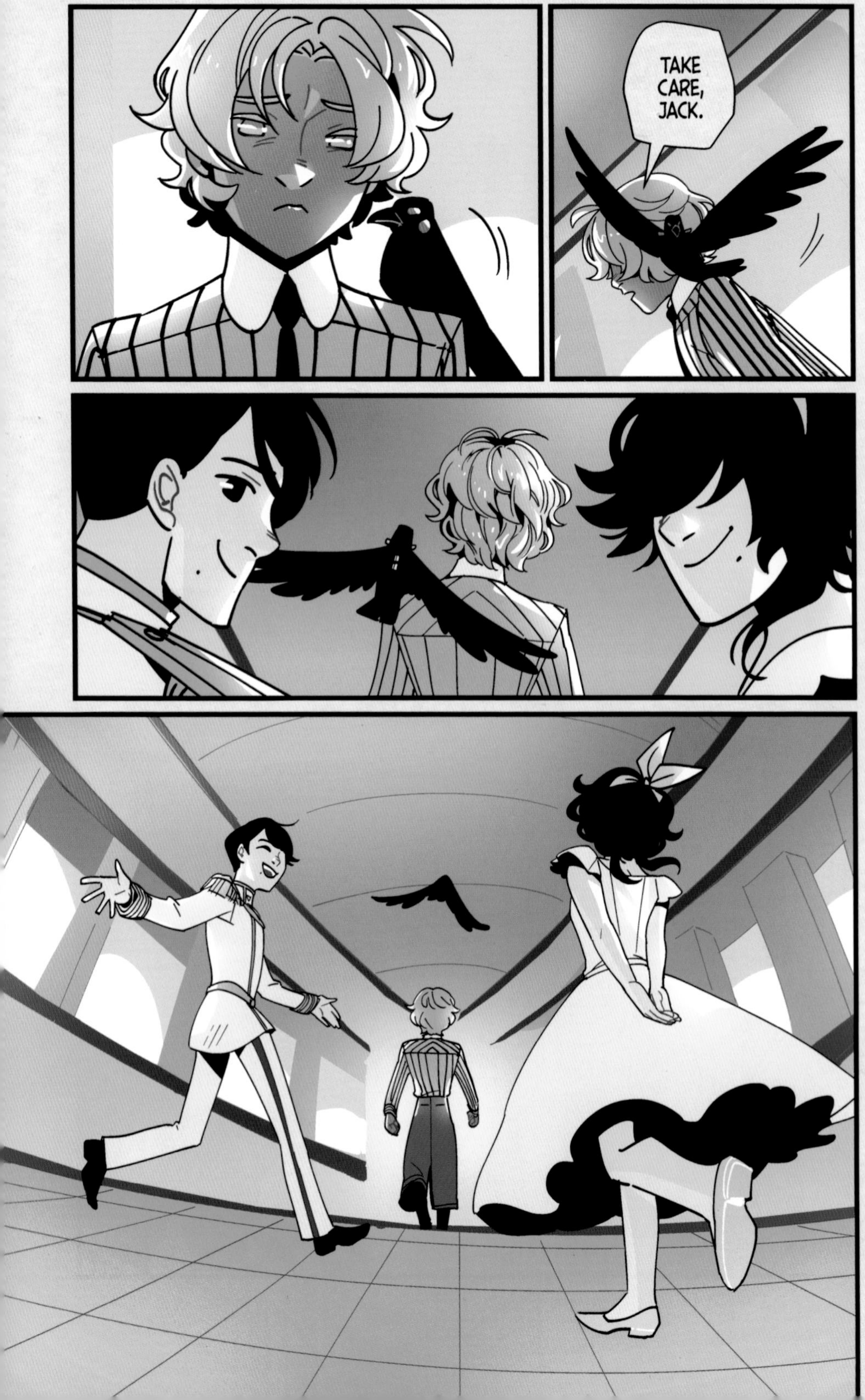
TAKE CARE, JACK.

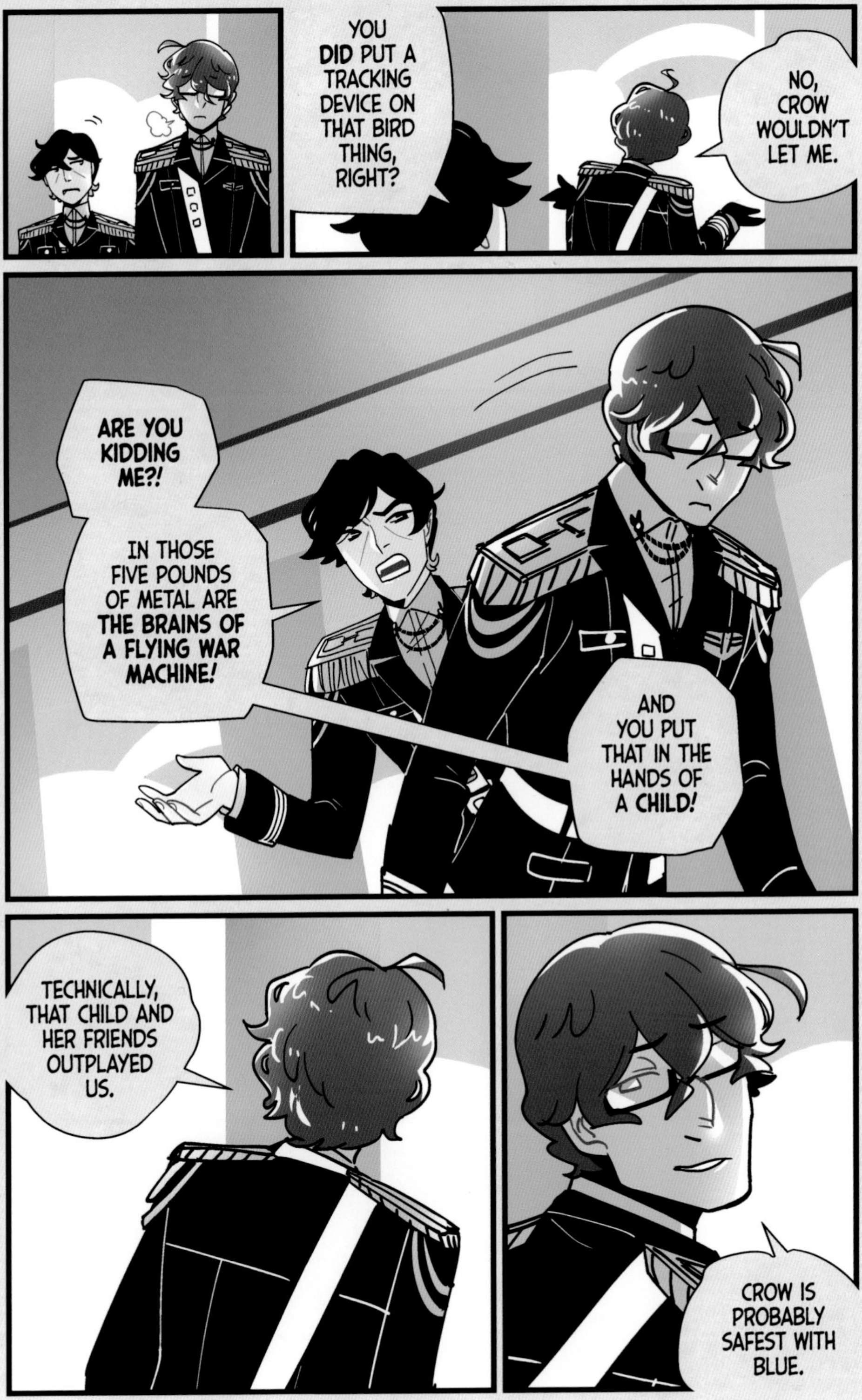
YOU DID PUT A TRACKING DEVICE ON THAT BIRD THING, RIGHT?
NO, CROW WOULDN'T LET ME.
ARE YOU KIDDING ME?!
IN THOSE FIVE POUNDS OF METAL ARE THE BRAINS OF A FLYING WAR MACHINE!
AND YOU PUT THAT IN THE HANDS OF A CHILD!
TECHNICALLY, THAT CHILD AND HER FRIENDS OUTPLAYED US.
CROW IS PROBABLY SAFEST WITH BLUE.

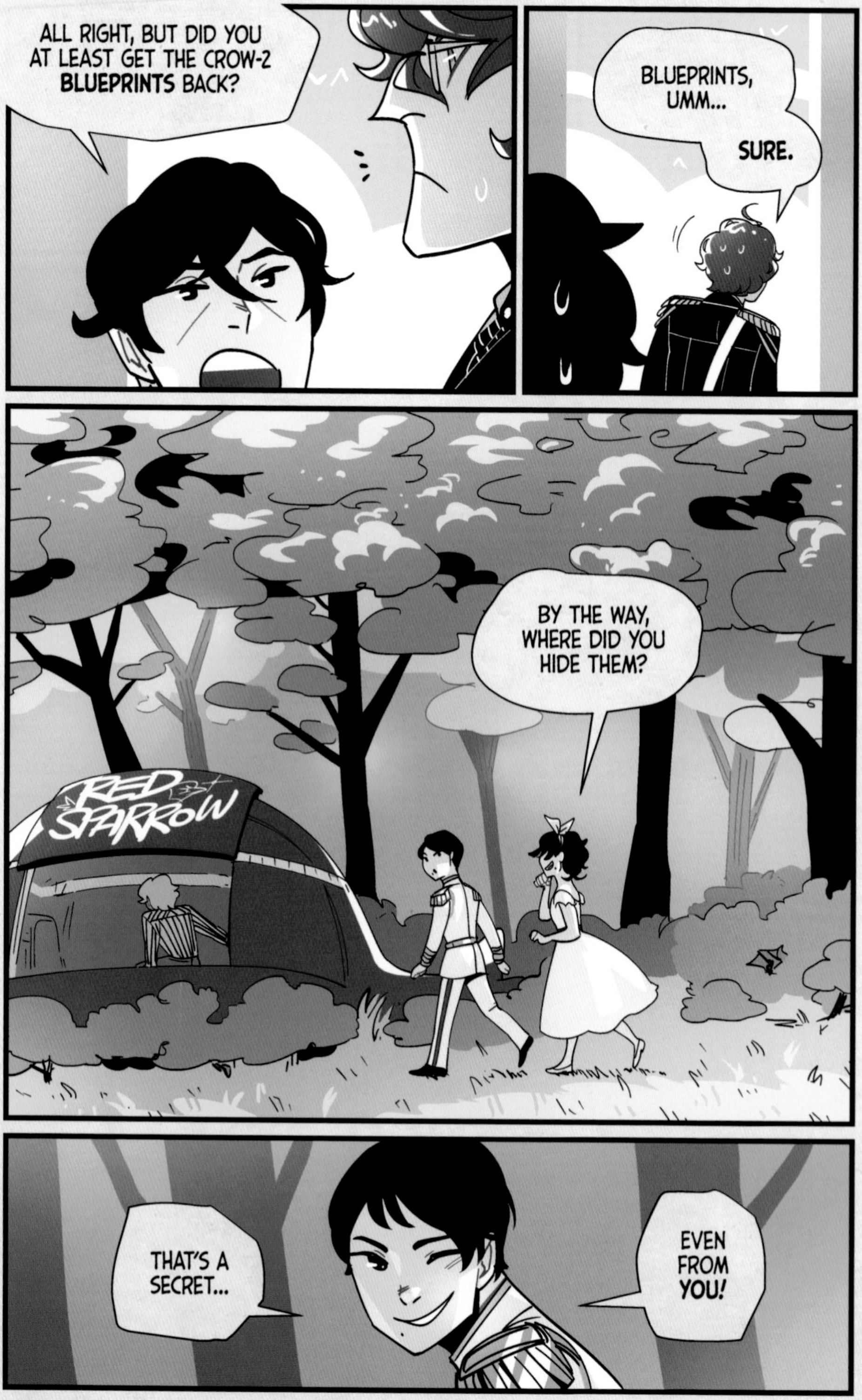
ALL RIGHT, BUT DID YOU AT LEAST GET THE CROW-2 BLUEPRINTS BACK?
BLUEPRINTS, UMM...
SURE.
BY THE WAY, WHERE DID YOU HIDE THEM?
RED SPARROW
THAT'S A SECRET...
EVEN FROM YOU!

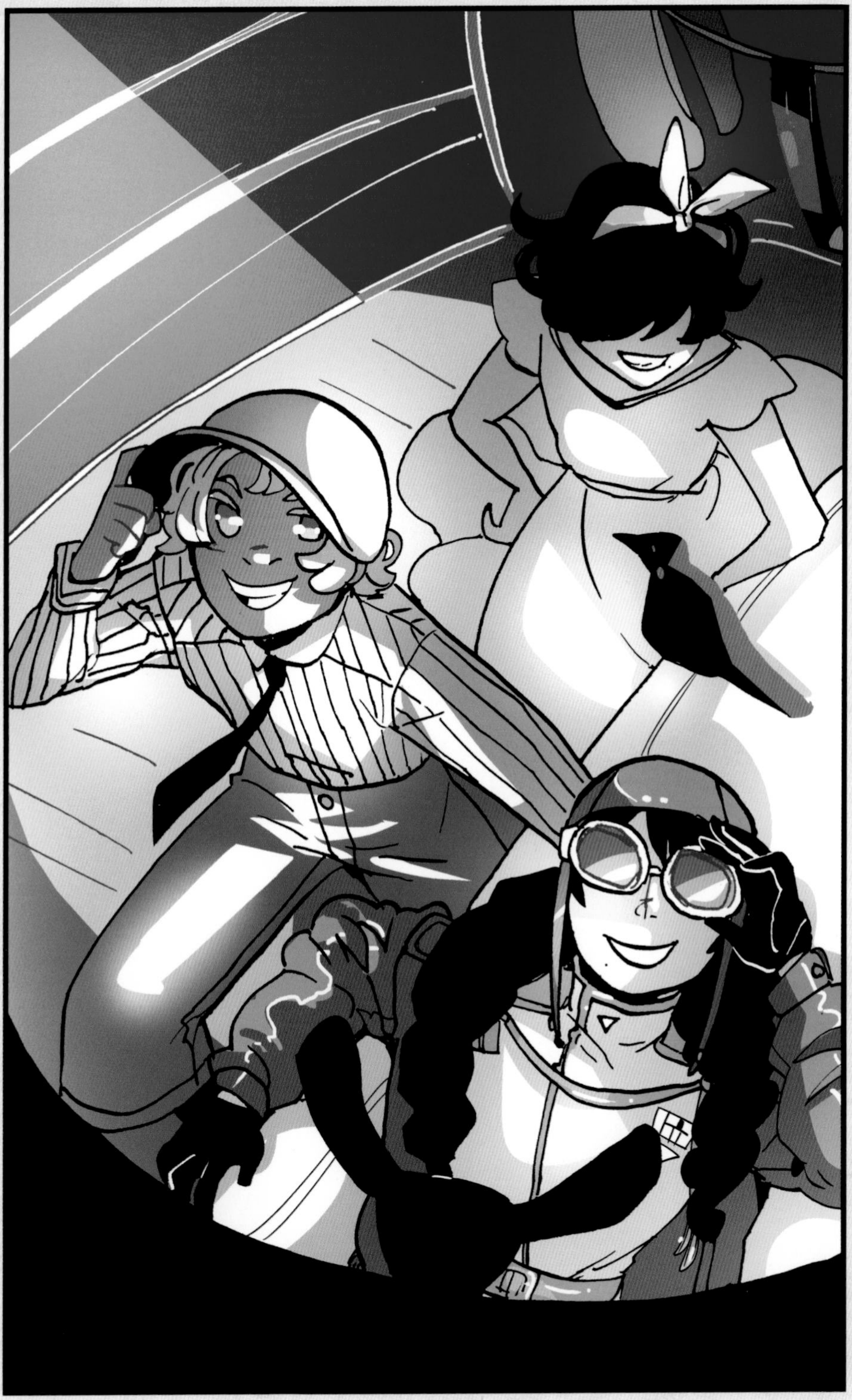

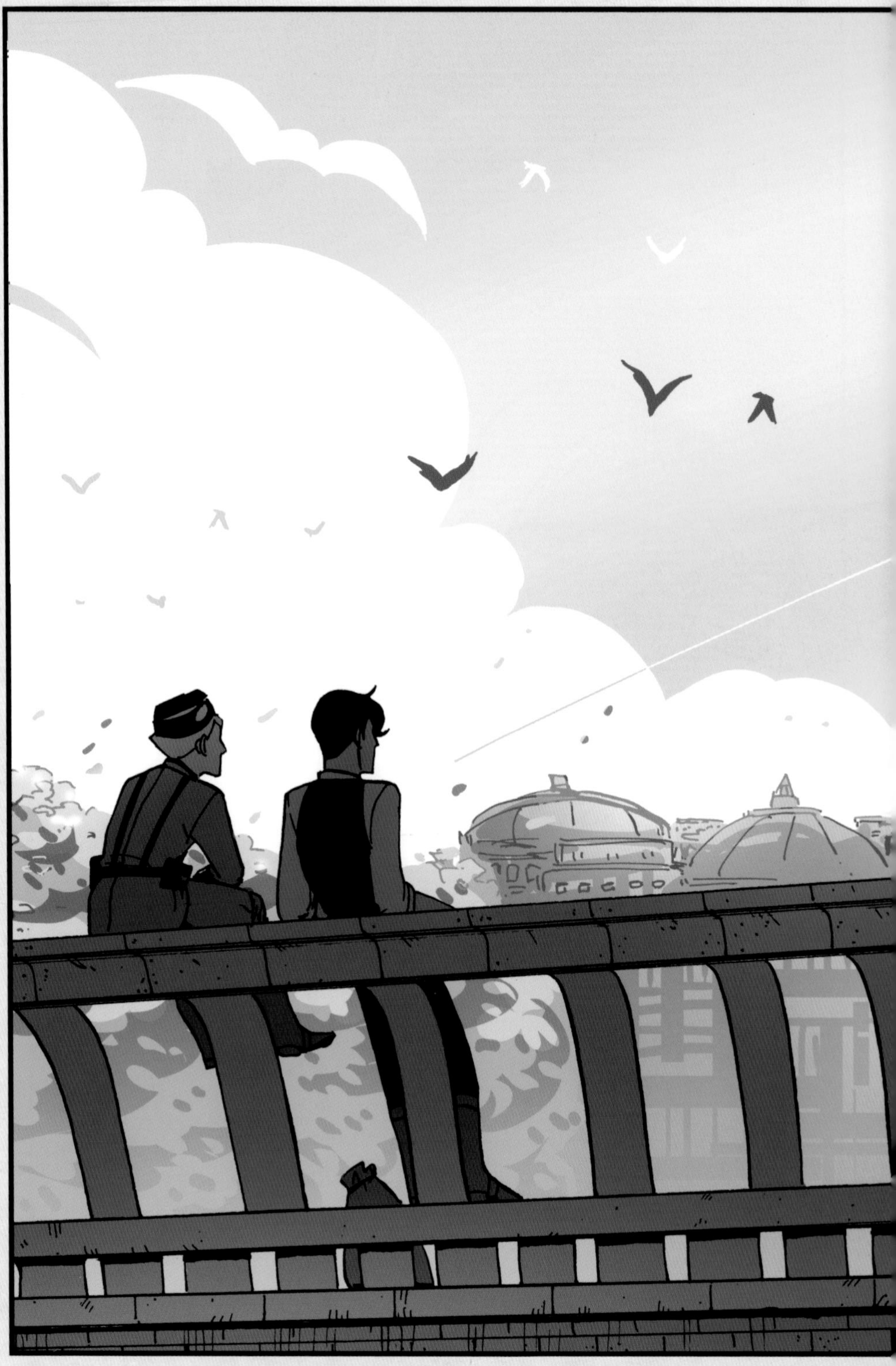

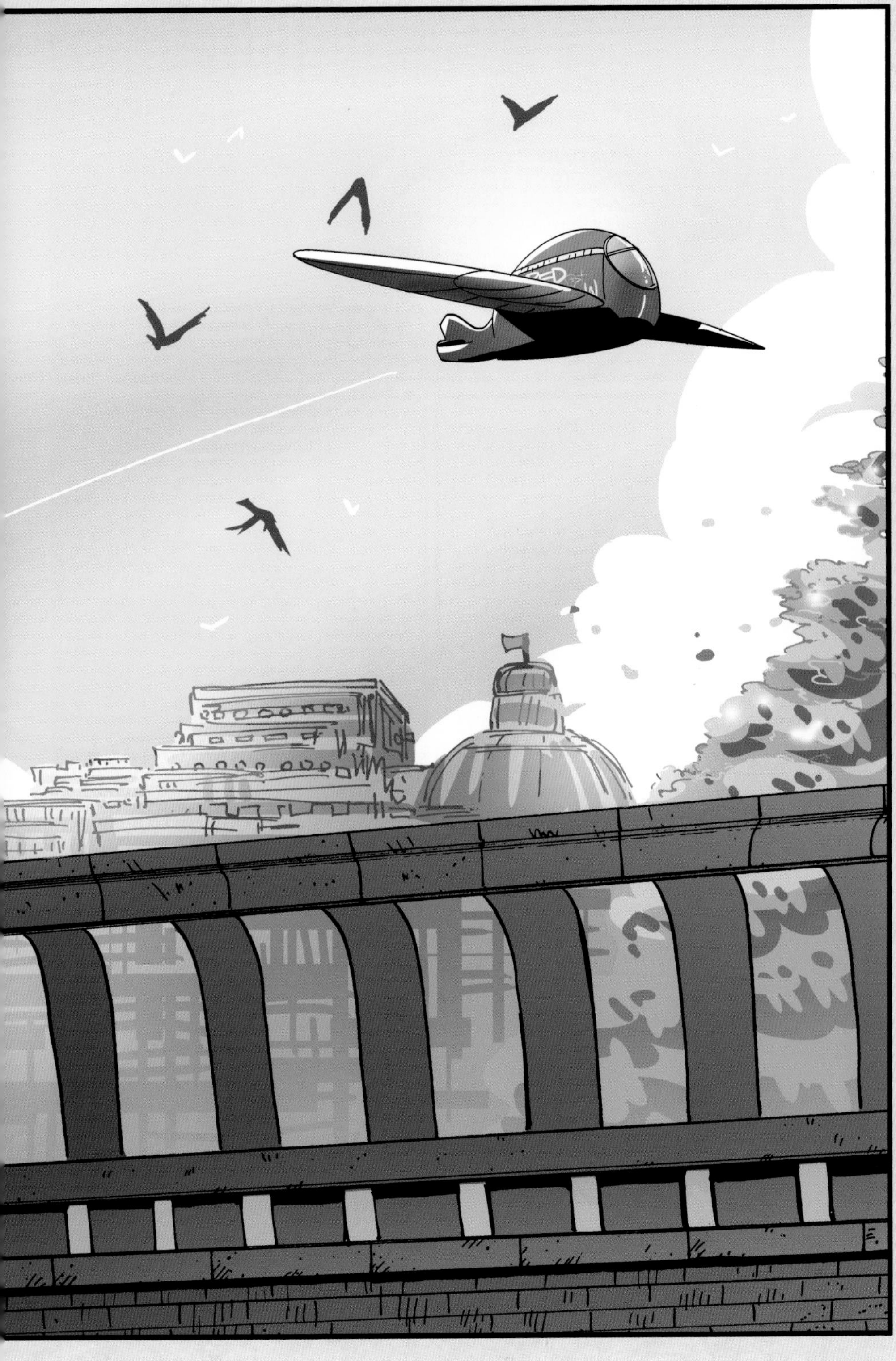

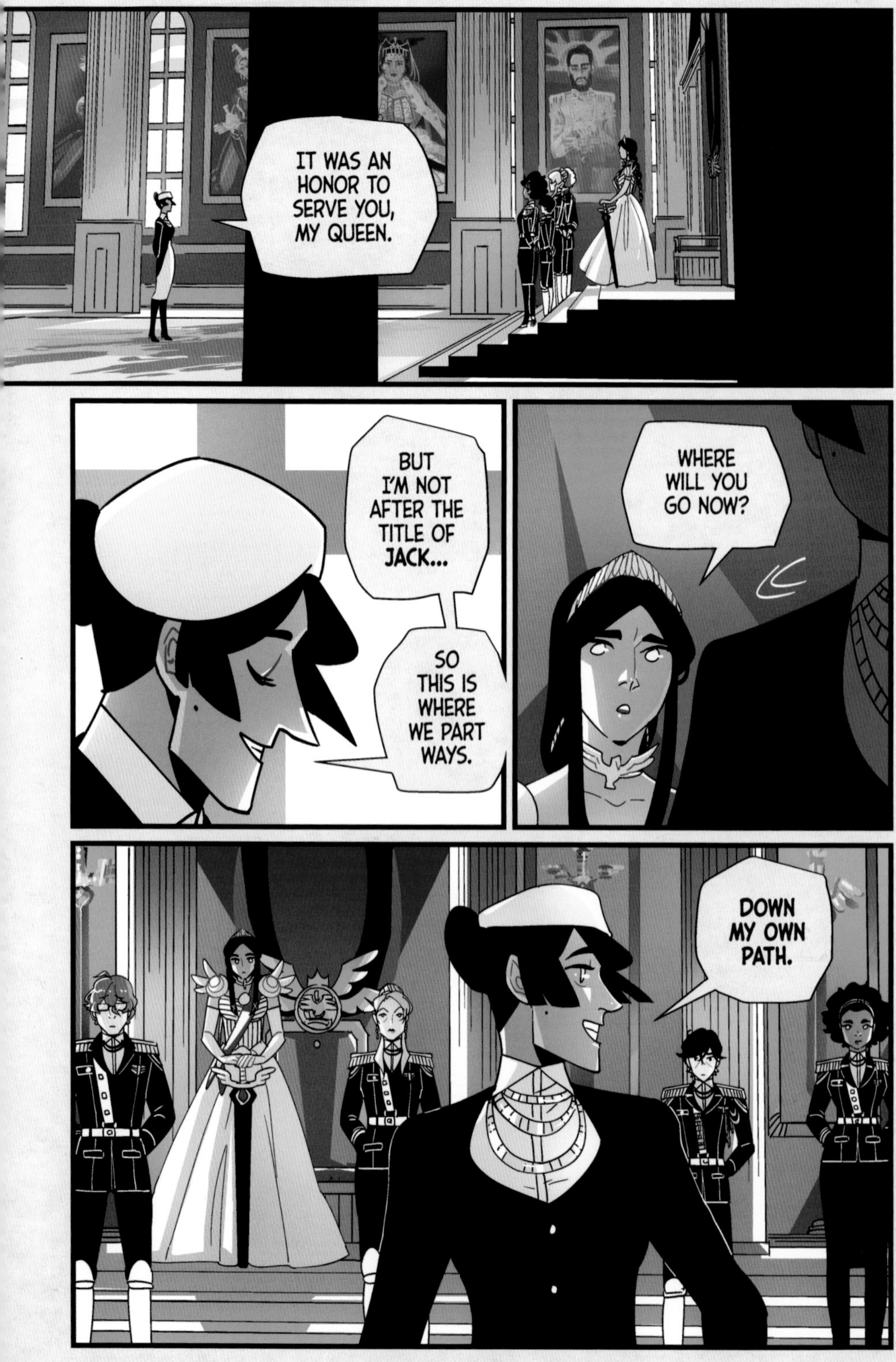
IT WAS AN HONOR TO SERVE YOU, MY QUEEN.
BUT I'M NOT AFTER THE TITLE OF JACK...
SO THIS IS WHERE WE PART WAYS.
WHERE WILL YOU GO NOW?
DOWN MY OWN PATH.

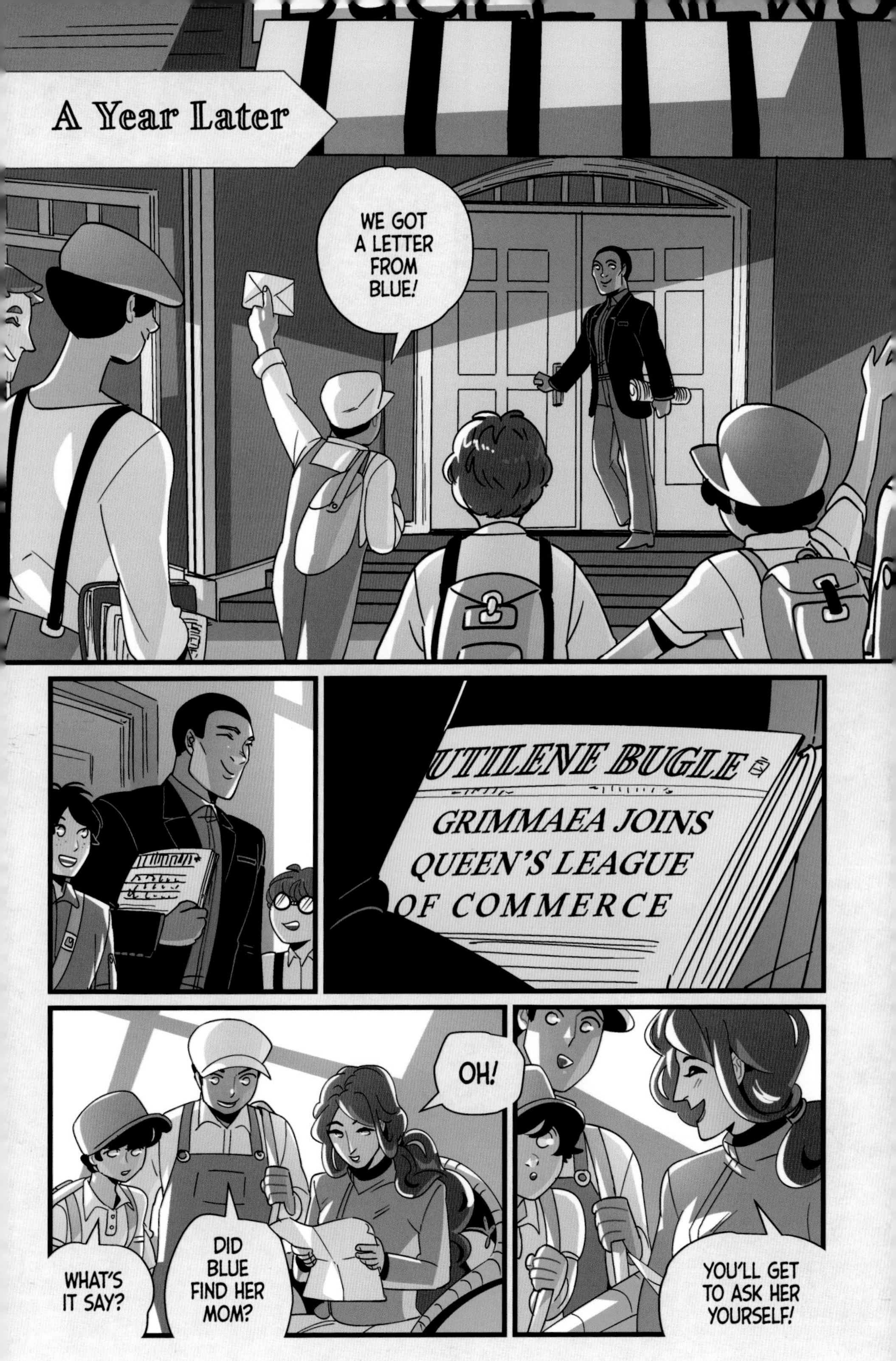
A Year Later
WE GOT A LETTER FROM BLUE!
UTILENE BUGLE
GRIMMAEA JOINS QUEEN'S LEAGUE OF COMMERCE
OH!
WHAT'S IT SAY?
DID BLUE FIND HER MOM?
YOU'LL GET TO ASK HER YOURSELF!

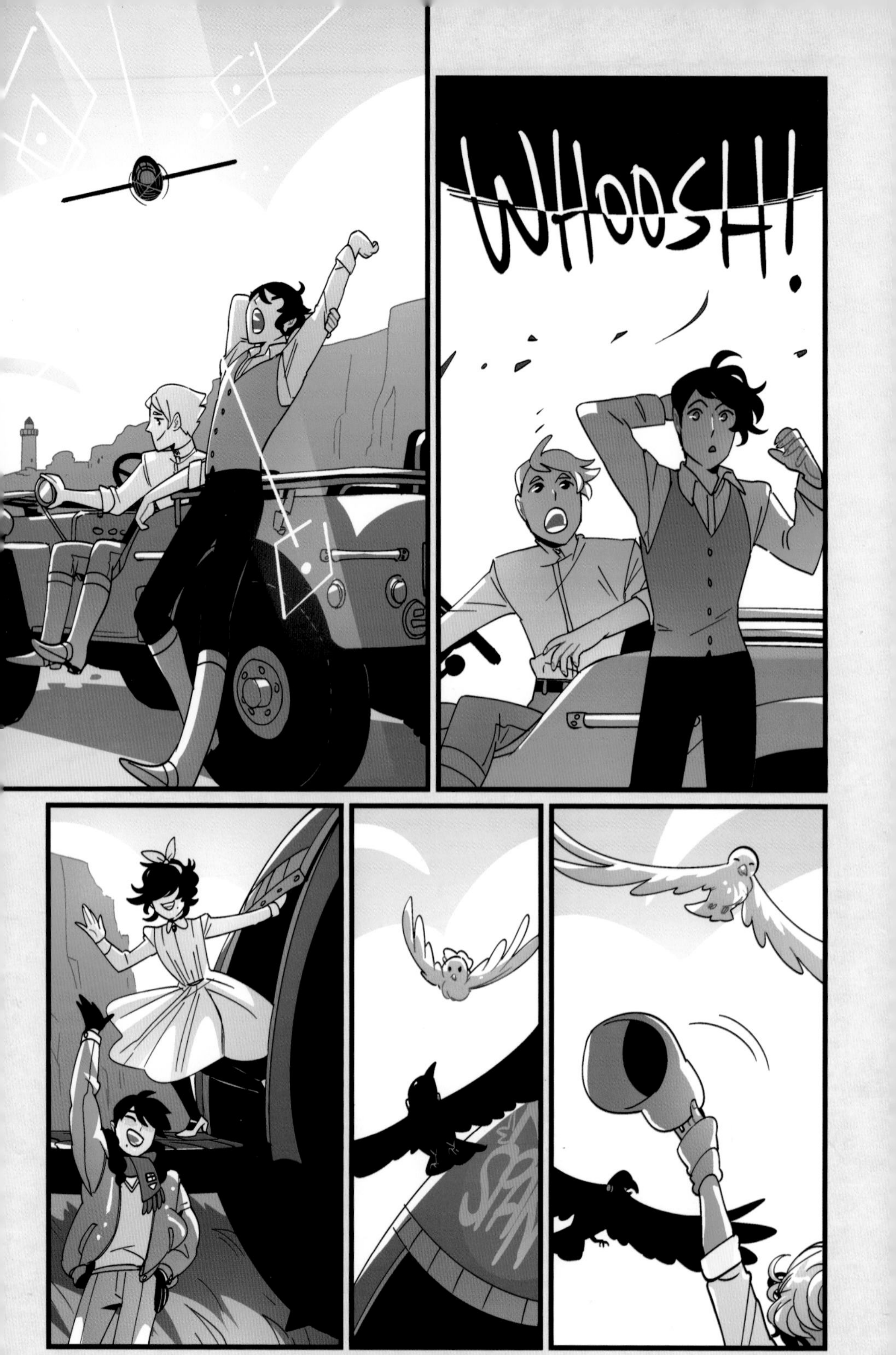
WHOOSH!

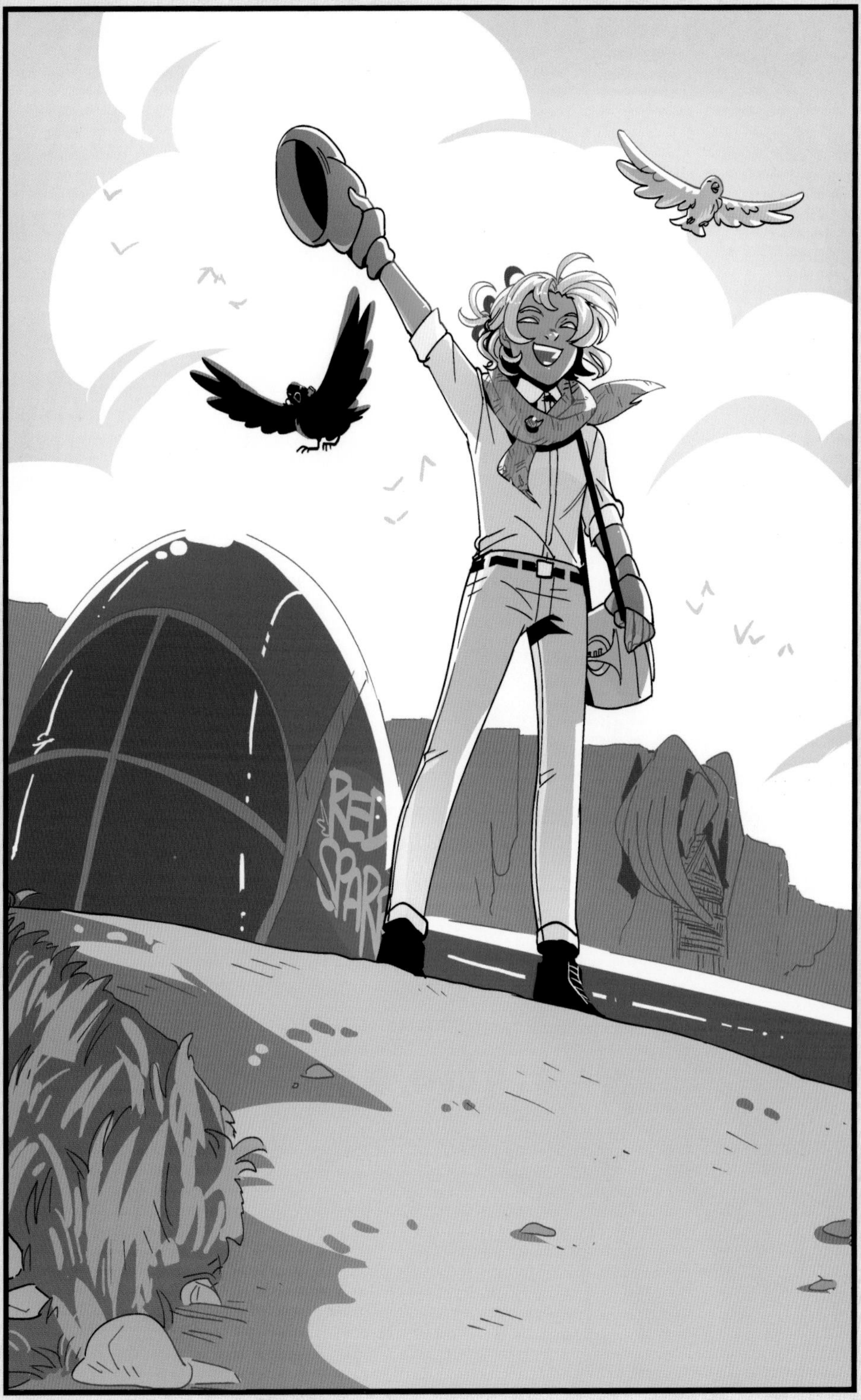
RED

ACKNOWLEDGMENTS

Thank you for joining me on this journey with Blue. Even though *NewsPrints* and *EndGames* are only two books, they've been a long time in the making. Blue and her friends in *NewsPrints* were developed over five years, from my freshman year in college to when the book was published. *EndGames* expands their world to a grander scale, and creating it was a daunting task! I learned a lot and grew as a person while working on this series, and I'm proud to accomplish the ambitions of a younger me.

When I set out to tell Blue's story, I wanted to explore growing up in a society full of gender expectations, which is something many of us experience. Navigating gender stereotypes is difficult when they don't fit. Sometimes, as both Blue and Red learn, other people only care about how they see you and what they expect from you, regardless of how you see yourself. But if you can find people who cherish you no matter how you identify, I believe the journey is worth what it takes to meet them. By the time Red meets Blue, Red knows himself, and after Blue's adventure in Nautilene, she's in a place to understand him. Their friendship has a rocky start, but I expect it will be lifelong!

EndGames took teamwork to complete! Thank you, once more, Cassandra, for your patience and guidance while I wrestled this thing into book form. Thank you, Phil, for your excellent design sense. Thank you, Scholastic and Graphix, for making it possible. Thank you, Parrish Turner, for lending me your insights and experience for Red. In the same vein, I thank Shivana Sookdeo, Aatmaja Pandya, Ananth Hirsh, and Christy Damio for Corazana Lina. Thank you, Liz Fleming, Andrea Kendrick, Eric Xu, and Will Ringrose for helping me color such a big project. Thank you, George, for being there with all the schedules. And again — thank *you*, readers! Your love and support for stories inspire me.

RU XU is the creator of *NewsPrints* and the popular webcomic *Saint for Rent*. She was born in Beijing, grew up in Indianapolis, and received a degree in sequential art from the Savannah College of Art and Design. Ru's favorite things include historical fiction, fat birds, and coffee-flavored ice cream. She currently lives in Houston. Visit Ru online at www.ruemxu.com and on Twitter at @ruemxu.